Unforgettable Novels of the West by Jack Ballas

GRANGER'S CLAIM: Colt Granger defends justice and his Montana claim against the murderous outlaws that are terrorizing settlers in the West—and have their own personal vendetta for Colt . . .

BANDIDO CABALLERO: Once a Confederate spy, Tom Fallon has found a new career stealing gold from the French and giving it to Mexican rebels. He's becoming a legend on both sides of the border as the mysterious gunslinger Bandido Caballero . . .

THE HARD LAND: Though Jess Sanford left Simon Bauman for dead, the man is still alive. And there's one thing more relentless than the law: a shamed son with all the wealth of the Bauman family behind him . . .

IRON HORSE WARRIOR: Hunting for his brother's killer, Chance Tenery takes a job on the Union Pacific Railroad and begins a long fight for his honor, his life, and the woman he comes to love . . .

ANGEL FIRE: When Kurt Buckner agrees to escort a woman to the Colorado Territory, he finds that hostile Indians are no danger—compared to the three men who want her dead . . .

POWDER RIVER: Case Gentry is no longer a Texas Ranger. But the night a two-bit gunhand rides up to his cabin, he has to bring back every instinct to survive . . .

GUN BOSS: Raised by an Apache tribe, Trace Gundy must call upon the fighting spirit he learned as a boy to avenge the loss of his beloved wife.

THE
RUGGED
TRAIL

JACK BALLAS

BERKLEY BOOKS, NEW YORK

THE RUGGED TRAIL

A Berkley Book / published by arrangement with
the author

PRINTING HISTORY
Berkley edition / May 1999

The Penguin Putnam Inc. World Wide Web site address is
http://www.penguinputnam.com

ISBN: 0-425-16855-7

BERKLEY®
Berkley Books are published by The Berkley Publishing Group,
a division of Penguin Putnam Inc.,
375 Hudson Street, New York, New York 10014.
BERKLEY and the "B" design are trademarks belonging to Penguin
Putnam Inc.

PRINTED IN THE UNITED STATES OF AMERICA

10 9 8 7 6 5 4 3 2 1

1

HAWKEN STANHOPE MCCLURE stood in the door of his stable, but the scents of fresh hay, feed, animal droppings, none of them penetrated the cold anger pushing at his brain. He faced two dangerous men and a woman even more dangerous.

They came to gloat over the loss of his possessions—and finally for his horses going on the auction block. They'd have to pay in blood, not with the ill-gotten gains they'd stolen during the war while, right or wrong, most Southern men and boys fought for their cause.

Willie Squires stood fingering the handle of his holstered handgun. "Hawk, we gonna bid on them horses, then we gonna take what the law says is ours. You gonna give it peaceably, or you gonna fight the three of us?"

"I answer to Hawk only to my friends. The name is Mr. McClure to white trash. Reckon that takes in you, your twin brother there, your other two brothers, wherever they are, and your sister yonder." He shifted his eyes to the woman. "And you, Miss Squires, when, and if, your brothers get up the guts to pull those handguns, you better leave your hands out from your sides. You touch that little gun in your reticule, you die. I'll kill you deader'n a gutted deer just as quick as I will them.''

She gasped, her lip curled in contempt. "You call *us* white trash? The shoe's on the other foot now. We own everything you had before the war—except them horses. We'll have them 'fore the sun sets tomorrow. Reckon that puts you down as bein' white trash now." She sputtered. "An'-an' you stand there and threaten to shoot me, a woman. Reckon you cain't even lay claim to being one o' them highfalutin' aristocrats you always run with. Course they's not many o' your kind left—is there?"

McClure twisted his lips in a bitter smile. "You just don't get it. Property's not what made me a gentleman, it's what's inside of me. It's still there, and it'll be there when I bury you an' that troop of cow-dung brothers of yours. Yes, I'll kill you, if you give me a reason. You try for that revolver you got stashed away—I have a reason."

He stared at her, his face stiff. He let a slight, cold smile crinkle the corners of his lips. "Try me."

Jim Squires, the taller of the twins, stepped forward. "The law says them horses gonna b'long to us. You're late in payin' your taxes. 'Sides you callin' us white trash is gonna get you deader'n hell, real sudden."

McClure hooked his thumb only an inch from the Colt .44 revolver stuck inside his belt. His mouth dry, stomach muscles tight, he couldn't give in to this trash. "The law says? Carpetbagger law says? Carpetbagger tax assessor says?" He shook his head. "When you pull those weapons, that's gonna decide who gets my horses."

The three stood there, fidgeted, obviously trying to make up their mind to make a fight of it. McClure could read every thought crossing their minds. They knew his reputation with a gun, but they wondered if three of them could beat him—two, if Yolanda stayed out of it. Abruptly, Willie, the shorter and meaner of the twins, jumped to the side, hand digging for his six-shooter. The tall Southerner palmed his .44, shot into Willie first, thumbed a shot into Jim's gut, thumbed another one into his chest, turned his Colt back to Willie, then shifted it to point at Yolanda, his thumb on the hammer. Both brothers lay in the dry manure of the stable.

Yolanda stood stiff as granite, stared at him, turned her eyes to her brothers, and again looked at him, her face a frozen mask of hatred. "Hawken McClure, remember, I have two more brothers, either of them better with a gun than you. You'd better leave Marengo County. The fact is you'd best leave Alabama and don't cross Choctaw County gettin' out. We're gonna trail you all the way to hell if we have to, but you're gonna pay for those two boys a-layin' there."

He squinted through the tendrils of gunsmoke weaving about them in the still air, and snorted, trying to clear his nose of the acrid smell. Then, never taking his eyes off her, he stooped at the side of each of the brothers, stripped them of their gunbelts, and guns, went through their pockets, took the money he found in them, and without counting stuffed it in his pockets. "Tellin' you fair, Miss Squires, y'all brought it to me. You took my land, my cattle, everything but my horses. I'm takin' back only a thin part of what's mine." He walked to her, took her reticule from her arm, dipped his hand into it, and removed a small revolver.

"Now you climb aboard that sorry piece of horseflesh you ride while I load what's left of your brothers on their horses. Then you head back to Choctaw County, get what's left of your family, start huntin' me, and you better hope to God while you're huntin' none o' you ever find me."

He dropped her handgun into his pocket. "But in case you have that in mind, and to make your task easier, I'll tell you I'm headin' for Texas, not to avoid you, but to stay outta the hands of what some call the law in these parts since the war."

He tipped his hat. "Be mighty proud to meet y'all out yonder." He slung her brothers across their saddles, tied hands and feet to cinch rings and handed the reins to her. His voice hardened. ''Now get on that nag, and get the hell outta here.''

While riding out, her eyes never left his, and if he'd ever seen pure downright hatred in a look, she gave him a full dose. She rode southwest toward Choctaw County.

When he lost her among the tall stately pines, he went to the cabin he'd built after he'd lost the plantation house to the carpetbaggers, went to the attic and rummaged around until he found two groundsheets, two blankets, and a packsaddle, all saved from his time in the Army of the Confederate States of America.

From the attic, he went below and collected a coffee-pot, frying pan, boiling pan, coffee, side of bacon, salt, flour, and other trail supplies. Then he packed two hundred rounds of .44 shells in his saddlebags. The .44's fit both his Colt and 1873 Winchester.

After packing his gear, he saddled his most prized possession, Black Knight, a big black gelding that measured seventeen hands at his shoulders. He called the horse Blacky.

Before shoving his Winchester into the saddle scabbard, he checked the loads, jacked one into the chamber, shoved another into the magazine, toed the stirrup, and sat there a moment, pondering whether to head for Mobile and catch a coastal vessel heading for Galveston, or ride up to Demopolis and ferry across the Tombigbee River.

If he went to Mobile, it might be a week before a ship left for Texas, and he'd still be within carpetbagger jurisdiction, and the harm carpetbaggers didn't do him, the Southern white trash scalawags would. He decided he'd be no better off there than facing the Linden sheriff. Too, he figured to sell his eight mares and two stallions to Ben Baty, about four miles north of Linden. He toed the stirrup and headed for Baty's plantation.

On the way, he skirted Linden, the county seat, crossed Chickasaw Bogue Creek, and reined his horse toward Baty's place.

Ben, a man about twenty years older than McClure's twenty-nine years, had been his friend since he was a toddler, and had taught Hawk the ways of a woodsman during his growing-up years. When he rode into the yard, Baty hailed him from the stable. "Hey, boy, what brings you up my way? And why the packhorse—you goin' somewhere?"

Hawk told him of the morning's happenings. "As the saying goes, Ben, and as so many of us have had reason to say since the war, I'm Gone to Texas—G.T.T. I came by to say good-bye, and to make you a deal if you think you can stay outta trouble on account of it."

"Let me worry 'bout the trouble, boy. What you got in mind?"

McClure cast him a grin, knowing it was bittersweet. "You been slavering over gettin' your hands on my horses for nigh onto ten years now. Well, I can't drive a mixed herd of mares and studs without more trouble than I can handle—so they're yours. I'll write you a bill of sale, it'll be legal 'cause the auction isn't till tomorrow afernoon, an' if you've got any spare cash—gold—layin' around, give me what you think they're worth—or whatever you can afford—or nothin', that is if you think you can keep the carpetbagger law off your tail."

Baty eyed him a moment. "Boy, many of my darkies stayed with me after the war, an' they can shoot as good as any man. Naw, I ain't worried 'bout the carpetbagger law. An' I'll tell you right now, I still got money buried from when I seen the Yankees were gonna overrun us. I'll give you a fair price. Come on in the house an' write me that bill of sale."

Sitting at Ben's desk, McClure looked up. "Ben, you better send some of your men down to my place right now, put a rope on those horses, and bring them to your stable. That Squires woman's mean to her bone marrow, and by tomorrow afternoon she'll be back with her brothers, an' the law. Hate to saddle you with trouble, but if you're willing to take it on . . ." He shrugged. "Well . . ."

Ben grinned. "Don't worry 'bout it, boy. It ain't nothin' I can't handle." He looked over McClure's shoulder. "Eight mares and two stallions. Reckon I know 'em all. Helped you break 'em." His grin widened. "For them ten horses I'd fight the Union all over again."

An hour later, McClure rode toward Demopolis, where he would catch the ferry across the Tombigbee. The next stream of any size he'd have to cross would be the Mississippi, but for now his problem was getting away from Marengo County without being arrested. Whoever came after him had bought themselves a peck of trouble: He'd made up his mind to fight.

Atop the eastern bank of the Mississippi, in Natchez, about one hundred eighty miles west of where McClure threaded his way through tall pines, Rebecca Brennan sat in a straight-back chair, her face stiff as old leather. Her nanny, Bessie Stowers, an old darky who'd helped raise her, pulled large handfuls of Becky's blue-black hair away from her head and scissored off each handful close to her head. "Lawd, child, every strand o' that beautiful hair I have to cut jest flat-out breaks my heart. Ain't there no other way we can do this?"

Tears flooded Rebecca's eyes. "Auntie, I've thought about this a long while. I can't come up with any other way. We've lost everything except the money Mama and Papa had the good sense to hide before the war. We're gonna take that money, and that golden stallion we've had hid out in the south pasture, head west, and build us a horse ranch." She blinked back the tears. "Or some sort o' ranch, or . . . or a new life of some kind." Her emotions now under control, she turned her head to the side and sniffed. "I smell woodsmoke. You cookin'?"

"Yes'm, little missy, like every other day, I'm fixin' yo' supper, but gettin' back to what we wuz talkin' 'bout, why you gotta make yo'self look like a boy? Me an' yo' Uncle Ned'll take care nobody bothers you." She smiled. " 'Sides that, with that shape, don't know as how we ever gonna get you strapped down to where them mama muscles don't show.''

Rebecca's face hardened still further. ''We got it to do, an' from now on, you and Uncle Ned must get used to calling me Reb. I hear those Texas cowboys don't take lightly to any man troubling a woman, but we're not gonna take the chance. There's always men and women everywhere who'll break the rules. Nope. I'll be a boy from here on out.''

Bessie, finished with Rebecca's hair, and turned her scissors to cutting down three sets of Ned's shirts and overalls to fit Rebecca. They had talked it over, so she cut them large enough that when sewed, they'd be loose enough to hide the un-boylike flare of Reb's hips and the swell of her breasts, but wouldn't bind tight enough to make her chest look like a boy's, because, she said binding them tight hurt, but Bessie had her way—she bound them tight.

Now ''Reb'' walked to the wagon, already loaded above the sideboards. She shook her head. ''We gotta throw away more of that stuff, Ned. We'll bog down in every creek, wear out the oxen, an' kill ourselves tryin' to get this wagon to wherever it is we settle.''

Ned shook his head. ''Ahh, little missy, we done throwed away jest 'bout all yo' nice things. You ain't gonna have nothin' left to make do with. One o' these days you gonna want to look like a woman agin. What you gonna do then?''

''Reckon we're gonna have to cross that bridge when we get to it. C'mon, let's get rid of all except what we absolutely have to have.'' She reached for another box, stopped, frowned, and said, ''Reckon I oughtta keep at least one complete change—keep one of my nicer dresses for when I feel safe becomin' a woman again.''

She helped Ned unpack, and repack, despite his protesting the entire time it just flat wasn't ladylike for her to be working like a darky. Finally, they reduced the load to the most basic clothing, bedding, cooking utensils, supplies, weapons and ammunition—and the money her folks had kept hidden from the Yankees and scala-wags.

Finished with the task, Reb looked at the pile of "nice" things she would have liked to bring along. A knot swelled her throat. In that pile, and several others up at the plantation house, was a way of life she only now realized was gone, dead, a thing of the past. With tears about to spill over her cheeks, she stood back, wiped her brow, and nodded. Then she forced a grin. "Know something, Ned, this is gonna be fun—I'm gonna make it so. Nobody's gonna pamper me, treat me like the daughter of a well-to-do planter—why heck, reckon I can shed all the womanly wiles and mannerisms expected of a young lady. Yep. It's gonna be fun." Despite her words, she swallowed hard.

Aunt Bessie, who walked up behind her, placed hands on her skinny hips, something she always did when she talked to Reb—and meant business. "Let me tell you somethin' right now, young'un. You ain't gonna shed all them things I spent a lifetime tryin' to teach you. Under them clothes, you still my baby girl, one yo' mama would be proud of if she wuz still with us, bless her soul."

Rebecca twisted to put her arms around the thin black woman. "Oh, auntie, I love you so much. I'll not make you ashamed of me," she grinned, "but can you picture a young boy riding sidesaddle?"

Bessie grumbled. "Humph! Reckon I gotta get used to some o' them things, but inside that wagon cover at night, you still gonna be a young lady, or I'll tan that pink little bottom o' yores."

Reb giggled, very un-boylike. "You've been threatening to do that ever since I was old enough to walk. Don't remember you ever carryin' out the threat."

Bessie grinned. "You ain't too old, missy. Don't push me."

Reb's glance swept the familiar surroundings—the plantation house, the carriage house, the stables, the cooking house, the smokehouse—and the knot again formed in her throat, and knowing she had one more chore to perform, the knot swelled even more.

"Well, let's eat supper, red-up the dishes, an' get the wagon rollin'. No need for us to tary here. We'll put a little distance behind us 'fore we make camp. Might as well get used to it." Her real reason for wanting to leave right then? She didn't know whether she could control her emotions much longer. She had to put all this behind her. Maybe if she couldn't see what she left, it would be easier. But when she'd done that last chore she'd set aside for herself, she wouldn't be able to see anything but a pile of ashes where all this had been.

When they made camp that night, only a couple of miles from where they started, a bright glow lingered above the trees, the only thing left of where her home had stood only hours before.

Far east of them Hawk McClure sat his horse above the Tombigbee River. He studied the ferry, the one man on it, and the wooded banks above and on each side of the trail leading to the large raft, for sign of men waiting there to ambush him. About to turn his eyes from the trees, he spotted movement, picked out one man squatted just off the near side of the trail, then found two more on the other side. All held rifles.

He got the dry mouth again. It happened every time he felt fear—and there was no better time for fear than now. Could he take on three armed men and win, maybe four if the ferry man got into it? He shrugged. He had it to do.

He thought on it a few moments, nodded, maybe it would work. He tied the gelding's reins to a sapling, looped the lead rope of the packhorse over the saddle horn, took one of the Squires brothers' revolvers he'd kept after the shooting, tucked it in his belt, pulled his Winchester from its scabbard, and slipped silently down the bank, using each sycamore tree trunk as cover while he again checked the whereabouts of the man he homed in on. Then the man made it easier, he struck a match to light a quirly. The match flare stood out like a beacon in the dark shadows.

McClure glanced at the sun's large, red half orb sinking behind the thick trees. He had less than an hour of light left to get the job done—if he got it done. He slipped to the next tree, then the next, until he stood only at arm's length behind the man he shadowed.

He allowed himself a grim smile. Ben Baty had taught him well. An Indian couldn't have made it this far with as little noise.

The carpetbagger, or scalawag deputy, depending on where he hailed from, Northern trash was no better than Southern trash, puffed on his cigarette, pulled a long red coal at its end, blew a cloud of smoke toward the trail, put both hands to his side, and pushed as though to get to his feet. At that moment, McClure pushed the muzzle of his .44 against the man's temple. "You make one peep, I'll blow your brains over a half acre of these trees."

The lawman eased himself back to the ground, held his head rigid. McClure pushed his revolver firm against the man's head while he studied him. Typical Southern white trash—tall, lean, unshaved, and dirty looking. "How many they send to capture me?"

"What you mean? We—I ain't been sent to capture nobody."

Hawk pushed the barrel hard against the man's head. "Don't lie to me, you sorry bastard, I'll let my thumb slip off the hammer right now an' find them myself."

The lean one tried to turn his head. McClure pushed harder. "All right, they's three o' us."

McClure ran that through his mind. If the man had said two, one, four, he wouldn't have believed him, but the words fit what he'd seen. "I'm gonna call to them to come across the trail. If they so much as motion toward their handguns—you're the first to get it."

He moved the muzzle of his Colt to the base of the man's skull. "You men across the trail there, stand, walk into the trail, an' keep your hands clear of your weapons.

I got a .44 stuck tight against your partner's skull. You gonna wear part of his brains if you make a move to make me nervous.''

"For hell sake, do like he said, *both o' you*." The lean man emphasized "both of you." A warning sounded in McClure's head. There were more than the two he'd spotted across the trail. Maybe others were on the side he stood on. He slammed his revolver against the man's head, slipped to the nearest tree behind him, and waited.

One of the men across yelled, "Ain't gonna work, McClure. Go ahead an' shoot 'im, then we'll arrest you for another murder. You ain't gonna git away. You gotta git over to that ferry across clear ground.''

Hawk, tempted to open fire, caught a shadow of movement to his left. He thumbed off a shot, moved to the next tree, and heard a crash in the brush, accompanied by a long, slow moan. He had no doubt he'd hit his target solid. Then he thought to run a bluff. They'd think the shot had been for the man he held his gun on, and that they had a chance with still another man on McClure's side of the trail.

They were in the brush and he couldn't pick them out with any certainty. He yelled, "Got the one over here. Y'all come on out." Two shots, sounding almost as one, clipped twigs over his head. He fired at the spots he figured the shots came from. No answer, no grunts, as of men hit. His bluff hadn't worked. "All right. I shot one o' your men over here. Knocked the other one in the head. If you got more men over here, I'll wait 'em out, otherwise y'all come on out, your hands empty. Leave your rifles there on the ground.''

The brush across the road parted and the two men stepped out into the middle of the road, hands held wide of their sides. McClure, trying to stay aware of all around him, kept most of his attention on the two in the trail. "Drop your gunbelts, then hold your hands high. You even look like you're gonna try for your handguns, I'll drop you.''

2

HAWK THUMBED OFF another shot toward where the wounded man lay. He moved to his right and stood by another old sycamore. The two in the road bent to grab their six-shooters. He thumbed two shots into the gravel at their feet. They stood as though jerked erect by a rope around their necks. "You want one in the gut, try that again." With those words, McClure slipped to another tree and waited.

Only a thin sliver of sun showed above the trees. He had to get rid of these men, and get on the ferry.

A glance at the boat showed the ferry man hunkered behind a barrel, waiting for the action to cease. Another low moan to Hawk's left marked the place where the man he'd shot fell. Revolver cocked, he slipped toward the sound.

Although it was dusk-dark under the trees, he spotted the darker bulk of the wounded man curled into a tight ball holding his stomach. Still not certain this was the last one sent to capture him, he continued to sweep the area with a searching glance. Finally satisfied, he moved to the side of the wounded man and picked up his six-gun. Then he unbuckled and pulled his belt from his body, felt around his waist for a hide-out, and stripped a money belt from him. He stood. "Where you hit?"

"Guts. Jest above my belt. For God's sake, help me."

McClure stared at the man, not feeling much of anything for now, but he knew the sight of the mortally wounded man would come back to him in the middle of the night—perhaps the middle of many nights.

Wisps of gunsmoke floated in delicate tendrils through the trees. He sniffed, trying to rid himself of the smell. It did no good. He glanced toward the trail. "You men out there, move to the side about ten feet and lie down. I'm comin' out." In only a moment he knelt at the side of the one closest to him, felt him for other weapons, found a long slim-bladed knife called an Arkansas Toothpick by many, then moved to the other and found the twin of the knife he'd taken from the first man.

He walked to where they'd dropped their guns and holsters, picked them up, and went to the edge of the trees where they'd waited for him. There, he found their rifles. He allowed himself a slight smile. They'd not have a chance to use them. He glanced at the two lying in the trail. "Go get your friend. Bury 'im, or get 'im to a doctor if he's still breathin'." His face feeling like stone, he added, "That one I hit on the head is alive. He'll have a headache for awhile."

He slung their gunbelts over his shoulder and, holding their rifles in his left hand, collected his horses, and walked toward the ferry, his right hand full of Colt .44.

The ferry operator stood, hands held shoulder high. "That ain't my fight, mister. I'll get you to the other side. That's where my cabin is anyway. This'll be my last trip 'fore sunup."

McClure studied the man—tall, skin tanned the color of old leather; he wore the remnants of a gray uniform. Hawk holstered his Colt. The man grinned. "Name's Jedediah Powers. What the hell they jump you for?"

Taking a chance the man was a Johnny Reb after seeing he still wore parts of the uniform, McClure said, "Carpetbaggers, an' scalawags, all white trash, figured

I owed 'em some taxes. Didn't think to pay 'em outta
my four dollars I got left. Shells for my .44 cost a lot
less." Although he carried a goodly sized poke from sale
of his horses, he'd only use it when he got where he
was going, and not even the Lord knew where that might
be.

Jed looked back at the trail beyond his boat landing.
"Figger they'll have second thoughts 'fore they come
after one who fought for the stars an' bars. Reckon
you're 'nother one o' our men what's headed for that
Texas country. Don't seem fair we gotta still be pun-
ished this long after the war."

"Jed, I figure the South's gonna pay for losin' the
war a lot longer'n you and I'll take up space on this
earth. Fairness has nothing to do with it. Politics is
what'll pull the strings, an' we'll pay, an' pay, an' pay."
He shook his head. "I figure to head west an' see if I
can't make a new life for myself." He waved his hand
to the east. "Neither I, nor most of my generation had
anything to do with building the plantations here, and I
reckon there's many a one of us who'd like to build
something of our own." He grinned. "Sure as hell
gonna try."

Jed steered the raft around a snag floating downstream, frowned, and looked at McClure. "You done
give me somethin' to think 'bout. I ain't got nothin' to
hold me here no more 'cept this here ferry. Think if I
can sell it you might see me out yonder in them western
lands."

McClure's grin widened. "Come on out. Hear tell
there's a whole bunch o' space out yonder lookin' for
people."

The raft bumped against the river's bank. Hawk led
his horses ashore, toed the stirrup, flicked his hand in a
wave, and headed down the narrow trail.

Darkness held him in its soft cloak, but the dirt road
would keep him tracking right, so he thought to ride a
couple or three miles before making camp.

●   ●   ●

About fifty miles southwest, in Choctaw County, Yolanda Squires pinned her two remaining brothers with a hard look, her ash blond hair contrasting blatantly with the black, oily sheen of her eyes. Her look caused them to squirm. "Gonna tell you boys somethin'—Hawk McClure's killed the twins. We're ridin' to hell if we have to, but we're gonna catch 'im an' make 'im pay. He ain't gonna die easy-like; he's gonna die slow an' hard like I hear them Indians out west make a man die. You got it?"

Bert and Tom stared at her. Bert, about five feet, eight inches tall and stocky, shuffled his feet. "What we gonna do with all that land an' stuff we done got since the war? We gonna leave it?"

Yolanda shook her head. "Nope, it'll be here for us when we get back." She moved her hands over her breasts, down her flat stomach, and on to the swell of her upper thighs. "You see, I've been mighty nice to the sheriff. He'll make sure it's still ours when we get back."

She looked from them to the saddled horses and two packhorses. "Now get them horses loaded with the stuff we'll need. I figger McClure won't go to Mobile, he'll go to Demopolis an' head west outta there. Reckon we oughtta catch 'im by the time we get to Vicksburg. If not there, we oughtta meet up with him at least by Shreve's Landing in Louisiana."

If their sister said it, that's the way it was—the brothers tied trail gear to the packhorses.

A day and a half after leaving the Tombigbee behind, McClure figured he should soon see the small town of Meridian. To avoid trouble with more scalawags, he skirted the edges of town and headed toward Jackson, where he again rode around the edges. Vicksburg and the Mississippi River would be his next problem.

There was no way to ride around Vicksburg; it sat on the bluffs overlooking the river. He shrugged mentally. If he came on trouble there, he'd meet it head-on.

Five days after leaving Marengo County, about two miles east of Vicksburg, a heavily loaded wagon blocked the trail a few yards ahead of him. Heavily loaded judging by the way the wheels cut into the damp soil.

An old darky walked at the head of the eight-ox team, and when McClure rode alongside, then to the head of the wagon, he noticed the darky leading the team was not alone. A young white boy maybe thirteen or fourteen years old sat on the wagon's seat next to a frail old negro woman. All three held rifles—and each rifle pointed at him.

McClure's eyes crinkled at the corners. He squelched the smile and tipped his hat. "Howdy, ya'll. If you don't shoot me, all I want to do is use part of this road to get me to the river crossing."

He faced the darky leading the oxen. "Uncle, I mean you no harm. Figure you an' your missus an' the young'un got enough trouble gettin' to wherever you're goin'." He kneed his gelding off the trail and rode ahead, aware the weapons of the three still pointed at him.

He shot a deer before reaching the river, then made camp outside of Vicksburg with a couple hours of daylight left. He put an entire back quarter of the deer on to cook, thinking it might keep better with the weather being hot and muggy. He poured himself a cup of coffee, and sat there staring into the fire, inhaling the mouthwatering aroma the food gave out. He tested the venison and found it not yet done.

He fidgeted. He couldn't get the old darkies and the young boy out of his mind. He wanted to see if they went on into Vicksburg, or intended to cross the river.

If they crossed into Louisiana, they had a long drive ahead of them. He'd come back this way after the war and found the ride from Monroe to Vicksburg the most boring and depressing one of his life. The flat fields— desolate, lying fallow—looked as though a plow hadn't turned their soil since before the war.

Too, there was something both brave and pitiful about

the boy and his companions. They must have lost all they had to the war and its aftermath, just as he had. He'd like to help—if they'd let him.

Along with those sentiments, an idea began to form. If those looking for him had sent a wire, they'd probably described the man they wanted as traveling alone. If the old negroes and the boy would let him join up with them, it might save him gun trouble on down the trail. A noise on the trail behind caused him to cock his head. He strained to listen.

The grinding of wagon wheels, the clank of trace chains, and the soft voice of the old darky urging on the oxen came to him. He stood. The wagon came abreast of his camp. "Hey, why don't you folks climb down and set a spell. Coffee's on. I got more venison here than I can eat. Haven't fixed any bread yet, but you're all welcome."

The old man looked at his two charges. The old woman nodded. "Why, we be much obliged, mistuh. Shore will save us a bunch o' fixin' this close to dark."

McClure went to stand by the boot and held his hands up to help the old woman down. Her look of surprise at this courtesy told him she was unaccustomed to consideration from those not of her color, or her family—her family being the old man and the white boy. She took his hand and lowered her feet to the ground.

He didn't hold his hands for the boy to climb down, but the youngster hesitated, looked at him as though expecting to be helped. Nah, it must be his imagination—a boy would jump down by himself.

The woman looked at him a moment, then said, "Ahm Bessie Stowers, this here's young Reb Brennan. We're all family now that the war's over, an' that worthless old man yonder's my husband, Ned."

McClure tipped his hat. "Nice to meet you folks. I'm Hawken McClure. Make yourself at home while Reb an' I help Ned unhitch an' stake the livestock out so they can feed." His glance went to the stallion. "Man! That's one beautiful horse." Then, a catch in his throat, he said,

"Till only a few days ago I had a couple of stud horses an' several mares with excellent bloodlines." He shrugged. "But I reckon till only recently we all had more than we're sittin' here with." He glanced at Reb. "C'mon, youngster, let's give Ned a hand."

The boy hesitated, looked at Bessie, and walked toward the team. Bessie busied herself making biscuits.

By the time they'd finished supper, Hawk figured they'd be good trail mates, if they agreed to let him ride with them. They carved out chores for themselves and got busy doing them. The boy didn't hold back on things he had to do either. McClure figured the youngster had had proper upbringing.

Supper finished, and the camp cleaned up, he knew by then who held the reins among the three, so he looked at Bessie. "It's late, an' unless y'all don't trust me, why don't you make camp right here?" He grinned. "Reckon there's plenty of room, so all you'll have to do is spread your blankets." His eyes crinkled at the corners, closing to slits. "Besides that, you'd have to hitch up your team again."

Bessie allowed his was a good idea. When they bedded down for the night, McClure thought it odd Reb slept in the wagon with Bessie, but he shrugged it off. Bessie seemed to keep the young'un under her wing like an old mother hen. He'd found out during supper that Ned and Bessie had belonged to Reb's parents, so he didn't wonder at the old woman being overly protective of the young son of her former masters; she'd probably had more to do with raising him than his parents.

The next morning, McClure made no effort to ride on ahead of his new acquaintances. When they boarded the ferry, one propelled by steam engines, a pair of scruffy-looking men about his owns age, both rail thin, boarded the boat at the same time. They could have been twins except one had flaming red hair.

Out of the corners of his eyes, Hawk studied them. He had no reason for distrust other than the fact he trusted no one in these lean years after the war, especially men whose only trail gear included a holstered six-shooter and rifles in saddle scabbards. He'd do well to be wary.

Too, they seemed overly interested in what the wagon held. They crowded close to its sides or to its back and made a pretense of looking elsewhere, but one of them always had his eyes fastened to the inside of the big Studebaker.

The boat docked and offloaded on the west side of the river, and the two men rode on ahead. McClure looked at Bessie. "Mrs. Stowers, I didn't like the looks of those men who crossed the river with us. They seemed more than a little concerned with what your wagon held. You and Reb get your rifles out and hold them across your knees. Gonna tell Ned to do the same." Without question they did as he recommended. He didn't consider their actions as a vote of trust. How could he—their weapons could kill him as easily as those of the two who rode ahead.

Although not invited, McClure stayed with the wagon, riding at its side, and as often as not he ranged ahead of them as much as a quarter of a mile searching the heavy weed growth at the side of the trail and the tall weeds covering the fields for sign of the two men who'd crossed the Mississippi with them.

Two days of this and the small family with the wagon seemed to put more and more trust in him. The fact was that Bessie looked to him for guidance on several occasions, mostly on things that needed doing when they were in camp, or setting up a guard at night.

The third night west of the Mississippi, Rebecca snuggled close to Bessie in the confines of the wagon. "Auntie, you s'pose Mr. McClure will stay with us till we get to Texas?"

"Don't know, chile, but I'm gonna tell you somethin' right now, I shore do feel a lot safer with him along. I got him figured for a Southern gentleman what's done had the same kind of treatment we had at the hands o'

all that white trash. Think he come from a family who
didn't have to make do. Think his folks had it all.''

Reb put her hand out to touch the old darky. ''Sounds
like you're beginning to think pretty highly of him,
Auntie.'' She pushed the blanket down and leaned
closer. ''You know what, he's about the most handsome
man I've ever seen, an' he seems so confident, like he
knows what to do about everything.''

Bessie chuckled. ''Sounds sorta like you want 'im to
know you ain't a little boy. Sounds like you want 'im
to look at you an' see you for a pretty lady.'' Her
chuckle deepened. ''Tell you right now, till we get
where we gonna stop for good, you gonna be a boy. He
ain't the only one we gonna have to trust.''

Rebecca pulled the covers back up to her chin and
whispered, ''You gonna ask him to join up with us, ride
on to Texas with us?''

''Missy, I been thinkin' 'bout that very thing. If it's
all right with you, I'll see what Ned thinks. Then we'll
ask 'im.''

''It's all right with me, Auntie. Good night, Auntie.
He's gonna have us up and movin' come daylight.''
With those words, she turned on her side and pretended
sleep, but her thoughts were on the tall man who'd come
into their lives.

She wondered about his background. What had his
home been like, his folks? Why did he seem so comfortable with the guns he carried? If she'd never seen
him before, and saw him without his guns, or his horse,
she'd know instinctively some part of him was missing.
One thing of which she was certain was that someday,
when she let him and the world know she was a woman,
he would be the most surprised man on earth.

He'd be surprised because she had no doubt but what
he accepted her as a young boy. He gave her chores like
a father would his son. The fact was, he'd set himself
up to teach her about living outdoors, how to make do
with what came to hand. In the short time they'd been
together he'd already taught her how to build a fire using

flint and steel, and he'd taught her a better way to sit her horse. He must have thought she didn't know anything for a boy her age. She'd have to be careful not to say or do anything to make him suspect she was a young lady of marrying age. What with her wanting him to know, that would be her hardest task.

The next day McClure again ranged out ahead of them, and came back to the wagon only in time for their nooning. He looked across the lip of his coffee cup at Bessie. "Auntie, you make about the best cup of coffee I reckon I ever tasted." He'd taken to calling her auntie because that's what Reb called her. "Figure I could get spoiled not having to drink my own brew."

Bessie pinned him with a look he'd learned she used only when she meant business. "Mistuh Hawk, if you'll do like we all done talked 'bout, you ain't gonna have to drink yore own. Fact is, you gonna set up to my table right often."

McClure smothered a smile. It sounded like she was driving up on what he'd intended to propose. "How you figure I'll be settin' up to your table very often?"

Bessie swept Rebecca and Ned with a glance, then looked back to him with a no-nonsense look, yet a hopeful one. "Mistuh Hawk, like I said, we done talked 'bout it, an' we'd be right proud if you'd travel with us like you been doin'. We feel a lot safer with you lookin' after us." She threw up her hands as though in horror. "Oh Lordy, I done made it sound like we want to be a burden on you. I don't mean it thataway a'tall. We figure to do our part. Fact is we want you to guard us, keep us safe."

McClure looked at the three of them, all sitting there expectantly, hopefully, awaiting his answer. He grinned. "Y'all know what?" His grin widened. "You saved me from having to beg you to take me on as a trail pardner." He nodded toward Reb. "Fact is, I'd sorta like to take on the job of teachin' young Reb there the things it'll take to make him a real frontiersman." He raised his eyebrows as though in apology. "Now, Reb, I didn't mean to infer you come up short on any of those things. It's just that I've lived a lot longer'n you, an' experienced more, so I figured to teach you some o' those things."

Reb looked solemnly at him. "Mr. McClure, I don't reckon I took your words as anything but well meaning. Yes, sir, know I got a lot to learn. I'd be happy to have you teach me."

Hawk stared into his cup a moment, then looked at the three of them. "Know it isn't the Southern way o' doin' things, but if y'all will drop the 'Mr. McClure,' and all the sirring, I reckon I'd be mighty pleased. Call me Hawk, that's what my friends call me." He stood. "I'm goin' out ahead again this afternoon, an' startin' tonight we're gonna take turns keepin' watch. Ned, Reb, an' I'll do the watchin'. You get a good night's sleep, Bessie."

She threw the dregs from her cup and stood facing him. "Gonna tell you somethin' right now, Mr. Hawk, y'all stand watch, I'm gonna do my share of it. I might be skinny, but I ain't no weaklin'. All right?"

A slight smile crinkled his lips. "Wouldn't have it any other way, Auntie. Reckon from here on, we share and share alike." He went to his horse, tightened the cinches, toed the stirrup, and rode out ahead of them.

Rebecca watched him ride down the trail, then realized she'd been holding her breath. "Whew! That's a load off my mind. With that man riding with us, I b'lieve we're gonna be as safe as with any ten other men."

Bessie clamped hands to hips and gave Rebecca that look she'd learned long ago meant she wanted no argument. "Young missy, I know you of a marryin' age, but I'm tellin' you now, don't you go to makin' cow eyes at that there man. You don't know nothin' 'bout 'im. Yes'm, he's big, strong, good-lookin', an' all that there hogwash. *But*, he might not come from a good family. He might have blood on his hands. He might be a footloose, fancy free kind o' man . . ."

"Oh, Auntie, I'm not about to make 'cow eyes' at him. He thinks I'm a boy. Gonna keep 'im thinkin' that, at least until he gets us where we're goin'. By then, I figure we'll know a lot more about him." She grinned. "Fact is, Auntie, I'm gonna make it my business to learn all I can about 'im."

Bessie's hard, don't-give-an-inch look softened. "Ah, missy, you know I'm jest thinkin' 'bout what's good for you. While you learnin' all 'bout 'im jest make gosh-danged sure he don't learn *all* 'bout you."

Rebecca folded her nanny in her arms and hugged tight. "Auntie, I love you so much. Don't worry, and I'm tellin' you if you don't want to give our secret away, you better get used to calling me Reb. It'll take only once your callin' me missy in front of him, and the cat'll be outta the bag."

"Yes'm, reckon it's jest hard to give up any part o' you." They climbed back to the wagon seat, and with Ned leading the team, they headed in the direction Mc-Clure had taken.

Hawk rode slowly, searching every inch of the weed-grown bar ditch on each side of the road. He had no doubt the two men from the ferry would be waiting for the wagon somewhere ahead, or if he appeared to have gone on ahead, they might wait until night to slip up on the camp and try to take the wagon. That stud horse of Reb's tied to the tailgate was enough incentive for road agents to attack, whether there was anything of value inside the wagon or not.

He tried to put himself into their shoes. Out here in the flatlands of the river's floodplains, with nothing but waist-high weeds to hide them, made for a bad place to attempt a surprise attack. But on ahead, four or five days' travel for the wagon, there were a few hills with mixed timber—oak, hickory, hackberry, interspersed with pine, growing to the edges of the trail. If he were a bandit, *that's* where he'd stage his holdup. But even with that thinking, he kept his eyes busy searching.

In the few short days since he'd met the old folks and the young'un, he'd come to care for them, and feel a responsibility toward them. Especially the boy. He thought to make a real boy out of him. Reb seemed sort of sissy, overprotected. He'd have to break him loose from Bessie's apron strings. But that might be a shame. The kid was such a nice, quiet youngster, maybe he should leave well enough alone. Oh well, he'd let time take care of what he'd do with the kid.

He'd not had a chance to study the tracks of the two men who rode ahead, too much traffic of the trail precluded identifying their horses' tracks. so he didn't know whether they'd turned off the trail toward one of the small towns. As a result, he studied the brush alongside with much more care.

True to his reckoning, about mid-afternoon of the fourth day, sparse timber began to show alongside the trail. Now he changed his method of looking for the two men. He didn't bother with the trees except for an occasional glance; instead, he rode the side of the road looking for horse tracks leaving the trail. He'd check the other side on his return to the wagon. He admitted to himself it was only a gut feeling the two men meant harm, but he'd learned to trust that feeling during the war.

It wasn't until the next day, after their nooning, that he spotted what he looked for. Tracks, two horses, left the road and slanted into the trees, which were much thicker now. He rode past the sign he'd picked up, not daring to track them into the woods. Any action of that nature would alert them that he suspected his party was in danger. He rode on another half mile or so and turned back, riding the opposite side of the road.

When he approached the spot where he'd seen their tracks, the hair on the back of his neck must have stood straight out. It made his neck tingle; his shoulder muscles tightened, and his mouth dried enough to cause him to feel like he could spit cotton: They might decide to shoot him, and then attack the wagon. When he was finally out of rifle range, his muscles relaxed. He figured they'd wait for the wagon to come abreast of their hiding place, or they might wait until night and slip up on the camp. He studied, thought hard for some way to keep those at the wagon safe from gunfire. Finally, he came up with a way. Whether it would do the trick or not— he shrugged mentally—he'd have to wait and see.

When he reached the wagon, they were only then beginning to enter the heavily wooded area. McClure stopped them in the middle of the trail. "Campsite's gonna be right here in the middle of the road. We'll build our fire out here too, clear of the trees, and if anyone wants to pass us, which isn't likely, it being nighttime, we'll move to the side."

Reb, in the husky voice Hawk attributed to the pre-voice-changing stage all young boys went through, asked, "You lookin' for trouble, Hawk?"

McClure thought to avoid getting the boy edgy and tell him no, but then decided they'd be better prepared if he told them the truth. "Got nothin' solid to go on, but figure we'll be better off if we're lookin' for it. We'll fix supper, eat two at a time while the other two stand watch, then the same situation for cleanin' up. By then it'll be dark."

While talking, he helped Ned with the livestock. "Soon's it's night dark, I want the three of you in the wagon—pull some of the supplies in front of you for a shield and keep your rifles trained outboard. I'll be gone awhile. When I return I'll hoot three times like an owl, then I'll wait a few seconds and do it again. If anyone approaches without givin' the signal, shoot to kill. Got it?"

"Yes, suh, Mr. Hawk, we got it." Bessie pulled her Winchester from the wagon, and a glance from her told Reb and Ned to do the same.

McClure looked at the three of them, a lump of pride swelling his throat. None of them showed fear. "One other thing. I've been tellin' you to let the hammer rest on empty." He shook his head. "Not this time. Fact is, anytime you're expecting trouble, have a shell in the chamber.'' He locked eyes with each of them. They each nodded.

While Bessie got supper started, he stripped the gear from his horse, rubbed him down, and tethered him on the grass at the side of the trail. He pulled his Winchester from its scabbard, and sat by the fire to check his weapons. Then he waited for Bessie to call them to supper.

Reb came over and sat at his side. ''Hawk, you be mighty careful out yonder, you hear?''

Surprised at the concern in the boy's voice, McClure smiled, put his arm around his shoulders, and squeezed, then tousled his hair. ''Boy, you gonna learn my name's Hawken Stanhope *Careful* McClure. Now, don't you worry. Y'all do as I said an' everything's gonna be all right. Okay?''

Reb nodded, then asked, ''Where'd you get a name like Hawken? Is it a family name?''

''Yep, it is. I had, maybe still have, a couple of uncles in St. Louis, Jake and Sam Hawken. They made some of the most famous rifles used in the early West. I'm named after the Hawken side of the family.''

Reb nodded. ''Figured as much.''

Finally finished eating and cleaning the camp area, McClure got them in the wagon and took care to see they had bedding and other things surrounding them, enough to shed a bullet. Then, satisfied he'd done all he could to keep them safe, he went into the woods at the side of the trail.

He wished he had a pair of moccasins like he'd seen some of the scouts wear during the war, but hell, he didn't have any, never had had, so he'd get along like always—but he used extra care in where he placed his feet.

Each step, he moved his foot down through the leaves until he felt solid ground beneath, then he'd pick up the other one and repeat the action. The men he wanted to find would probably sit by their fire until they figured their quarry had bedded down, then they'd make their move.

In the dark woods he tried to gauge where he'd seen their tracks leave the trail. He shook his head. He had no idea how to estimate the distance. His best bet would be to try and spot a flicker of firelight through the trees before he got too close.

After what seemed like hours of feeling ahead with his hands to keep low limbs from dragging across his face, and pushing his feet into the soft underfooting, he thought he saw light dancing against a tree's leaves maybe a hundred yards ahead. He tested the air, and failed to smell woodsmoke. Maybe he was yet too far away. He used extra care now, for where they might have tethered their horses remained a mystery, and he didn't want to startle the animals.

The hardwoods were his best friends. The slim, stately pines afforded almost no cover, where the thick, heavy trunks of the oaks and hickory stood as sentinels against discovery. The dank earth gave off a musty, mildewed scent, telling him of the moisture in and below the leafy carpet, which probably never dried. He didn't want to stretch out and crawl the rest of the way. He'd gotten this far on his feet.

Before moving from the shelter of one tree bole, he picked out the next one to give him cover; then he moved silently to it. Ben Baty had taught him well. Another fifty or so yards and their fire, dancing in grotesque shapes, came into view.

He stopped, searched the camp, and saw only the two men who'd been on the ferry with them. They'd tethered their horses on the other side of the fire, away from him. They talked, but their words were muffled. He moved closer.

Abruptly, both horses raised their heads, ears peaked, and looked directly toward him. He held his breath. If either of the two men he stalked were woodsmen, they'd take warning from their horses. His eyes went back to the two men. They sat there nursing a bottle, passing it

back and forth. McClure moved closer—close enough
to distinguish their words.

The one closest to him talked. "Hell, Bob, they
wasn't nothin' in that wagon worth havin', jest campin'
gear, beddin' an' stuff. Why for you wantta take that?"

Bob, the red-haired one, the one who sat on the opposite side of the fire, looked at his partner, disgust
showing in every line of his face. "Anse, you take a
good look at that there stud hoss? Why, hell, him alone's
worth more'n you an' me's gonna make in a year."

He took a drink from the bottle and passed it to his
friend. "Sides that, them ain't pore folks, they got
money with 'em, an' that big man who seems to be
takin' care o' them's bound to have a poke in a money
belt—or somewhere. We gonna make this little slow-
down in our trip worth a whole lot. You jest wait an'
see."

McClure thumbed the thong off the hammer of his
Colt, eased it from its holster, and stepped toward the
fire.

3

MCCLURE WORKED HIS right foot into the leafy carpet, pushed it deeper, then rested his weight on it. A twig snapped, sounded as loud as a gunshot to McClure's ears. Both men turned their eyes toward the noise.

McClure froze. Bob squinted into the darkness. "What was that? Sounded like somebody stepped on somethin'."

Anse's eyes looked as though he peered right at the spot where Hawk stood. "Nah, don't see nothin'. Probably one o' them small limbs fell outta a tree. They always doin' that once they get dry enough."

He switched his gaze from staring into the woods back to the redhead, and held the bottle toward him. "Here, take a slug o' this, it'll relax you some."

McClure waited until Bob tilted the bottle before he took another step, and now well within handgun range, he thumbed the Colt's hammer back. The ratcheting sound again drew the attention of the two.

"Reckon you were right, Bob. A twig did break, an' you're right again if you figure the noise you just heard was my .44 being cocked. Now sit like you are. Don't move or I might get nervous." He stepped into the circle of firelight. Anse sat closest to him. "Anse, re-e-eal slow-like, keeping your hands clear of your sides, roll over and spread-eagle on the ground."

He waited until the bandit did as he'd instructed, then turned his attention to the redhead. "Now it's your turn, Bob." Both of them prone, McClure stepped to the side of Anse, removed his six-gun from its holster, did the same with Bob, and stood back. "Now sit up and unbuckle your gunbelts."

When he'd collected the belts, he patted them down for knives and hide-outs, removed cash from their wallets, and found the money belts sewed inside their gunbelts empty. He stepped back from the fire. "Right cozy, me bein' able to call you by your first names." He picked up the bottle from which they'd been drinking. "Fact is I'm gonna have a drink o' your whiskey, then I'm gonna read to you from the book."

He took a large swig from the bottle, grimaced, and spit it into the fire, causing a great flare when the whiskey ignited. "Whew! How y'all drink that stuff?" He pinned them with a look he hoped would go right through them. "Tell you what I'm gonna do . . ." He stopped. "Either of you read an' write?"

Each shook his head. Hawk grinned. "All right, that makes it easier. Your X on the bill of sale I'm gonna write will make this deal legal. I'm gonna take your horses, guns, everything you have except bedding and saddles, then you can go on your way."

The grin slipped from his face and his voice hardened. "I could have—prob'ly should have—shot you two, and maybe sometime in the future I'll regret not doing so, but any way you look at it—you can go. Don't cross my trail again or I'll kill you." He bridled the two horses and led them from the circle of firelight.

He backed into the woods until trees stood between him and the bandits, then turned and headed for the wagon. When within about fifty yards, he gave the owl hoot as indicated, then led the bandits' horses to the tailgate. He tossed the road agents' weapons into the back of the large Studebaker, poured himself a cup of coffee, and sat by the fire.

Reb stared at him until he asked what was the matter. "Well, Hawk, you come into camp like you'd been for an after-supper stroll, draw a cup of coffee, and without a howdy-do sit by the fire to drink it. What you been doin'?"

He grinned. "Thought when I brought their gear an' horses in maybe that told the story. But I'll tell you. I read to them from the book an' sent them on their way. Didn't even have to shoot them."

"What're you gonna do with their horses?"

"Gonna do a little outlawin' myself. When we get to Monroe, I'm gonna sell 'em, gonna even give a bill of sale for them. They signed the one they gave me with two X's to make it legal."

Bessie, who'd been sitting there keeping her mouth shut, shook her head. "Lawdy mercy, I b'lieve we done fell in with a real badman." She looked at Reb. "Don't want you to never let that man teach you all them things he knows. You know, them things what you don't know *nothin'* 'bout."

Reb had to stifle a giggle, which she reminded herself would not have been very boylike. Bessie's words could have meant almost anything. She sipped her coffee, thinking how safe they were with this man they'd taken as their protector. She looked at him from under her hat brim. "Where you figure to end up, Hawk? Texas, New Mexico Territory, Colorado—where?"

He stared into the fire a moment, shook his head, and said, "Son, I just flat don't know. Think I'll ride till I see some land where there aren't people crowded too close, build me a cabin, an' see if I can't start a horse, or maybe a cow, ranch." He shook his head. "Nope, I haven't thought that far ahead. Y'all stay with me that far, we might even end up neighbors."

For some reason his words made Reb see a little sunshine in the black dark surrounding them. She didn't know why it should make a difference whether they were neighbors or not. She put it down to the fact she felt so safe with him around. Too, she'd made up her mind they'd stay with him as long as he let them. She had no idea how he'd be once they got to the western lands. She'd not had a chance to talk to him about his past, whether he knew anything about cattle, horses, farming, or what. But somehow she couldn't see him as a farmer. Not that there was anything wrong with a farmer, but he just flat didn't seem the type, whatever the *type* was.

When she and Bessie were inside the wagon, with blankets pulled up to their chins, Bessie turned to her. "Why for you reckon Mr. Hawk would take them men's horses? You reckon he wuz a outlaw back yonder wherever he come from?"

Rebbeca thought about Bessie's questions a moment before answering. "No, Auntie, I think he's had so much taken from him by folks of that ilk, he's made up his mind that whatever he can take from them he's justified in doing so. Especially if he has an indication they mean to take from him again—or those he cares about."

"You thinkin' in that pretty little head o' yores we'uns are folks he cares 'bout?"

Rebecca smiled into the darkness. "Oh, Auntie, I truly hope we are."

Sitting outside the firelight, rifle across his knees, McClure wondered the same thing. Why did he care what happened to the three people for whom he'd accepted responsibility? Yes, they were good cover for his identity with the law in these parts, but he could avoid whatever law he came up on. Finally, he figured his caring stemmed from having no one to call family since the war. These were good people, and if he'd ever had a little brother, he'd have liked to be able to teach him the lessons he'd learned the hard way. He'd teach Reb those things.

His mind now on Reb, he couldn't figure him out. In several ways, the boy was overly protected, but he never shirked a task, even seemed to try to take on an extra load to be sure he wasn't a burden on anyone. Hawk frowned. Hell, let Bessie hover over her chick as much as she wanted; he liked the kid the way he was—sensitive, yet when it came down to shouldering a man's responsibilities, the boy stood right there with the best.

He shifted his rifle to his other knee, thinking to have a pipe, then decided not to in the event there were curious eyes seeking to spot a sentry in the dark.

The next two days went without unusual incident, except for a sudden summer storm on the second day that did nothing toward cooling, only made the atmosphere close and humid, and the trail muddy and boggy.

Toward sundown, McClure led his party down the main street of Monroe. The town had grown since the last time he passed this way. It was obviously not like a lot of the towns farther west, towns in which, for whatever reason, the people pulled stakes and left for parts unknown, leaving the town to dry up and fall apart with time. This town had many brick buildings, a sign it intended to someday be a major hub of Louisiana business.

He led his party to the livery stable. An old man sat on a sawed-off tree stump in the shade outside the barn doors. He looked up at McClure, and spit a stream of tobacco juice to the side. "What can I do you for, son? Ain't got room for them oxen, all my stalls're full."

Before entering town, Hawk had talked with Bessie, and they'd decided to ride on to the other side of town before camping. They weren't far enough west for a hotel to accept negroes, and he, Ned, and Reb didn't really need to sleep indoors.

He looked at the old man. He talked to the man as though he had never seen the inside of a schoolhouse. "Got a couple o' horses I wantta sell. Ain't got 'nuff grain to feed 'em on the way, so we gonna have to let 'em go. I got a bill of sale from the last who owned 'em. I'll sign it."

The livery man looked at the horses. "Got no need

for more horses, an' them two don't look like much
anyway.''

McClure hid a grin. The horses he intended to sell
were far better than most. The old man had started the
dickering usually used in a horse trade, but Hawk knew
that game as well as any.

He gathered the reins in his hands and turned to leave.
''They're mighty fine horseflesh, an' you know it.'' He
shrugged. ''But hell, if you got no use fer 'em, reckon
we'll find a way to feed 'em.''

''Now, hold on there, young'un.'' The livery man
stood and looked at the geldings a little closer, then
looked at their teeth. ''Reckon I might be able to use
'em sometime in the future. Town's growin'.'' He
squinted at McClure, nodded, and said, ''Reckon, I
could give ye, oh, maybe thirty dollars fer the two of
'em.''

McClure led the horses away a few steps. ''No, figured on sixty each.'' He tipped his hat. ''Thanks anyway.'' The livery man again stopped him.

They haggled for over a half hour, and when McClure
walked away without the horses, he held a hundred dollars in his hand. He felt he'd made the best deal he
could, and he was certain the old man was satisfied.

The Ouachita River bordered Monroe on the west.
McClure studied it awhile and decided to cross before
making camp. If rain fell farther upstream and caused
the waters to rise, they could be trapped on the east side
for a while. He wasn't willing to chance it. Even though
he would have liked to eat in a cafe that night, he didn't
suggest it, knowing that if he tried to take the darkies
into a cafe he'd have a whole bunch of trouble. Bessie
was the one who suggested he take Reb in and set up
to a table proper-like.

McClure shook his head. ''Auntie, I wouldn't do you
an' uncle like that. We tied in together, an' that's the
way we gonna stay. We're family.'' He would've sworn
he saw tears glisten in the old woman's eyes.

''You're a good man, Mr. McClure, but me an' Ned

don't want to cut you an' young mis—uh, young Reb outta yore just deservin's.''

He smiled. ''Don't you ever worry 'bout it, Auntie. Like I said, we're family, an' if we can't all do it together, then we just flat aren't gonna do it.''

''Yes, suh.''

Behind McClure and his ''family,'' in Vicksburg, Yolanda Squires and her two brothers did sit up to a table that night, but Yolanda hardly tasted her food. She picked at it, thinking of the tall, green-eyed, black-haired man who'd killed her twin brothers.

The thought of him turned sour what little she ate. She took no comfort in the fact they'd ruined him financially. He was the only man she'd ever wanted. She had offered him everything she had, including her body—and he'd laughed at her.

The thought of that laugh, even now, made her feel like she would lose her supper. Damn him—conceited, holier-than-thou, uppity, spoiled son of a rich family. Well, she'd taken care of the rich family part. He now had less than the Squires family ever had. Yeah, he'd sold his horses to Ben Baty, but the sheriff told her he'd find some way to get them back.

She threw her fork into the middle of her almost full plate and looked at her brothers. ''When we meet up with Hawk McClure, don't give 'im a chance. I never figured he could take both the twins—but he did. He's good with that six-shooter. If it happens such that we can take him without killin' 'im first, that's the way I want it. I want to make 'im hurt.''

Tom slanted her a nasty grin. ''Why for you hate 'im so bad, sister? Thought back right after the war, you wuz kinda sweet on 'im. You offer 'im somethin' he told you he wouldn't have if it wuz wrapped up an' tied with a pretty pink bow?''

Blood surged to her head, and seeing through a red mist, she flicked her hand out and slapped him. She didn't care that all in the cafe turned to stare, the white marks of her fingers on Tom's cheek gave her a satisfied feeling, a feeling of power over her brothers. She wished she could extend that power to all men. Hard-eyed, she looked at the two. "Either of you ever say anything like that to me again—I'll kill you. Understand?" She stood. "We ain't usin' them rooms we rented for tonight. We're ridin'. Right now. Move it."

Tom and Bert stood, stared at her a moment, then turned toward the door. Neither would argue with her when she was like this.

An hour later, on the trail heading west toward Monroe, Bert pulled his horse down to a trot. "Sister, ain't gonna do us no good to kill these horses. We run 'em into the ground an' we'll never catch that bastard." He rubbed his hand across his two-day stubble of beard. " 'Sides that, we drag ourselves down to nothin' chasin' 'im night an' day, we ain't gonna be in no shape to face 'im. We better make camp soon."

Yolanda stared between her horse's ears. Bert was right. If she let herself be governed by temper they'd never catch McClure. She'd have to hold tight rein on her feelings. Her eyes lifted to look at her short brother, the meaner of the two.

Some of her anger drained, leaving a hard, cold knot in her chest. "You're right. We'll stop at the next place fit for campin'. It's gotta be a place we can water the horses."

Late afternoon of the second day after crossing the Mississippi, two men carrying saddles walked slowly down the trail ahead of the Squires. Yolanda had had them under her gaze for quite a spell. They'd walk awhile, put their saddle down, sit on them for a few minutes, then stand and walk again.

When she pulled abreast of the two, she pulled rein and slipped to the side of her saddle, studying them. After staring a moment, she asked, "What happened to yore hosses?"

"Tall, green-eyed jasper robbed us. Took ever'thin'

we had." The man who answered stood tall and reed-thin, with a headful of bright red hair.

Tom Squires looked at his sister, then back to the redhead. "He say what his name was?"

The man who'd hadn't spoken stared back at him a moment as though he'd gone crazy, then, his voice dripping sarcasm, he said, "Why shore, he in'roduced himself, an' I told 'im that redheaded jasper there wuz Bob Bridges, an' I wuz Anse Berglun." He shook his head. "You ever hear of a holdup man tellin' anybody what his name wuz?"

Yolanda interrupted. "Tell us more 'bout what the man looked like."

Bob Bridges scratched his head, stared at the ground a moment then nodded. "All right. He wuz tall, maybe six-one, coal black hair, eyes green as gourds, an' I reckon a woman'd say he wuz right good-lookin'. Why you wantta know?"

Just thinking of McClure angered her all over again. She felt blood rise to her face. "He robbed us too. Took eight mares an' a couple of prize stud hosses from us."

Anse shook his head. "Naw, must not of been the same man. This'n didn't have no horses with 'im, an' he wuz travelin' with a boy an' two darkies."

Bert nodded. "It wuz him, all right. He sold them horses what wuz rightfully ours, an' I reckon that's 'zactly what he's gonna do with yores. Don't make a damn who he wuz travelin' with."

Yolanda shifted her weight to sit straight in the saddle. "Oughtta be a wagon 'long this here road sooner or later. Catch a ride on it. Monroe ain't too far ahead, an' we gotta get goin', wantta get there 'fore dark." She nudged her horse into a walk, looked back at the two, and said she might see them down the trail a piece.

Upon reaching Monroe, Yolanda led her brothers directly to the livery. Still sitting her horse, she looked down at the old man running the stable. "You buy a couple o' horses in the last couple o' days?"

The man pinned her with a look that went right

through her. "All due respect, ma'am, I don't see as how my buyin' horses is any o' yore business. Why you askin'?"

Anger choked her. She swallowed a couple of times, then said, "If you'd describe the man who sold 'em to you, an' if he fits what I think he will, I'd like to see your bill of sale."

After studying her a few moments, the old man described Hawk in detail, stood, went to his office, and took a piece of paper from a table littered with everything from dirty coffee cups to hay straws. He held the paper out so she could read it. "Don't see as how it's any o' yore business, but here it is, signed by two gents with their X, an' Mr. McClure signed it that he wuz the one sold 'em to me. All legal."

Elation, yet with a great deal of caution, flooded Yolanda's chest. Elation because she was on the right trail, and caution because McClure had signed his right name, as though trying to lead them to him. As though he would pick the ground he wanted to fight on. "How long ago did he sell them to you?"

"Ohhh, reckon 'bout two days. He cain't be very far ahead travelin' like he is with them two darkies an' that sissy-lookin' boy."

She nodded. "Thanks. He's a old friend from back home. We'll catch 'im." She wheeled her horse, rode to the middle of town, and turned to Bert and Tom. "We'll stay here for the night. McClure travelin' with a wagon'll make it easy for us to catch 'im in a day of hard ridin'. Tom, we'll get a hotel room while you take the horses back to the livery, then we'll eat an' be on the road come sunup."

When Hawk got them up the next morning after camping alongside the Ouachita, he looked closely at his charges. They looked tired. "Tell you what we're gonna do, folks, we're gonna ride this day out, then we're gonna find us a nice stream, pull far enough off the road so no one will see us, an' rest up a couple of days. Give us a chance to wash clothes, and ourselves, an' just plain lay around awhile, then we'll push on for a few more days." He looked at them a few moments, letting a slight smile crease the corners of his lips. "Sound good to y'all?"

Reb pushed her hat back and scratched her head. "Sound good? Sounds like somethin' I hoped you'd do several days ago."

McClure wanted to give the Squires bunch a chance to get ahead of them. He'd noticed a lot of wagon tracks in the trail, so if, as he hoped, they'd about caught up with him, it would give them a chance to pass and lose his trail until he wanted them to catch him. At that time he'd lay out a few clues as to his whereabouts, and when the time came, he'd make sure the boy and two darkies were clear of the trouble he figured to take to the Squires family. They'd taken all of his possessions, but if things worked out for him, he was damned if they'd live to enjoy them.

About three o'clock, the sun still high in the heavens, McClure led his charges across a small stream, a stream probably fed by several of the myriad of springs often found in this country. He stopped, studied the shallow branch a few moments, and nodded. He motioned Ned to leave the road and head into the woods to his left. If the Squires followed closely, they'd probably not notice tracks leaving the left side of the trail.

He led them a good quarter of a mile south before he found the spot he wanted. He'd have liked to be able to find a jumble of boulders in which to make camp, but this country had few places like that, places like what he'd seen many of when in New Mexico Territory and Colorado.

"Y'all set up camp. I'm gonna scout around an' make certain we got this neck o' the woods all to ourselves. Soon's I make sure, each of you, one at a time, go to the stream and take a bath." He grinned. "These sponge baths we been takin' took the surface dirt off, but we all need a good scrubbin'."

Reb looked from McClure to Bessie, her face flushed.
She pulled her mouth to the side, shrugged, and went to
the wagon to get clean clothes. McClure read her look
as being hesitant to leave their company. "Don't worry,
son, I'll make real sure there's not a soul in the area
who could see you, or do you harm, an' we'll all stay
clear till after you're dressed."

He wondered why a boy Reb's age would be skittish
of people seeing him stripped down for a bath; surely
he'd been skinny-dipping with other boys. He shrugged.
Of course it was different being with boys his own age.
Yeah, that was probably it.

Before stripping his horse, he went into the thickly
wooded area, circled the campsite, went farther than he
thought it likely anyone would be, and returned.
"There's no one anywhere close-by. Go ahead and finish making camp. I'll strip my horse, an' help Ned put
the cattle to graze."

The next morning, thinking the Squires might be getting close, he wended his way through the trees to a
large oak at the side of the trail and slid down its trunk
until he sat with his back to it facing away from the
road. If horses, wagons, or even those afoot approached,
he could hear them. He'd wait until then to peer around
the large bole for a look-see.

Twice in the next hour the rattle of trace chains and
teamsters yelling at their teams caused him to look
around the tree. He gauged them as farmers coming from
a shopping trip to Monroe. In the next half hour five
mounted men rode by, all traveling singly. Fifteen more
minutes passed. He cocked his head to the side to listen
better. It sounded like several horses approached from
the east.

He slid on down the trunk, turned onto his stomach,
and peered around the bole. The lead rider came into
view from the curve in the trail. He'd know that person
anywhere, from any distance. Yolanda rode her sidesaddle like a queen, head held high—haughty—followed by her brothers.

Despite what he thought of her, she made a pretty picture. Yeah, she was a beautiful woman, with a body that quickly could bring a man's blood to a boil—but that face and body housed a mind and conscience as cold as a rattlesnake.

Every few moments, he broke his gaze from the group, then again locked his eyes on them. A steady look could be felt as strongly as a physical touch. They rode by him, only occasionally glancing at the trail. He reckoned they figured there were too many tracks ground into the trail to do them any good.

He watched until they disappeared around the next curve, put his hands down to push to his feet, then carefully lowered himself to the ground. Two riders rounded the curve to the east. He knew them both: Bob Bridges and Anse Berglund.

When they came abreast of him, he recognized their horses, the same ones he'd taken from them the other side of Monroe. They must have stolen them from the old liveryman—or convinced the law that McClure had taken them at gunpoint. If the first were true, Bridges and Berglund were branded as horse thieves, if the second were true, the law would be looking for *him*. In addition to being wanted in Alabama, they'd add more crimes to the list. Damn!

He stood and backtracked to the campsite. His three companions sat by the fire, drinking coffee—all clean. He grinned. "Reckon it's my turn now."

Reb looked at him, her face sober. "Yep, unless you think to stay downwind of us at a distance for the next few days." Hawk gave the boy a friendly punch on the shoulder. He winced. "Aw, now, youngster. Didn't mean to hurt you."

Reb smiled, then grimaced. "Didn't hurt. Reckon you just surprised me."

Hawk pulled clean clothes and razor from his saddlebags and headed toward the stream. He shook his head. He'd have to be more careful around the boy. He reckoned he didn't realize his own strength, but that thought did nothing to satisfy his wonderment at a thirteen- or fourteen-year-old boy not being hard-muscled.

While he washed himself and his clothes, he pondered his situation. He'd left the redhead and Anse with no money, nothing. The only way they could have gotten their horses back was for the crusty old liveryman to give them up, and McClure couldn't believe he'd do it without a fight—even if the law said he had to do so, and that wasn't likely unless the two outlaws had proof the horses belonged to them.

When he'd gone through their pockets, he'd not come on anything to indicate they had any kind of proof of ownership the law would recognize. He thought— hoped—he was in the clear.

He again focused on the Squires. The way they were riding, he figured they'd put about forty miles a day behind them. If he, Reb, and the two darkies rested two days, that'd put Yolanda and her brothers about eighty miles ahead of them. He nodded to himself, pleased with the thought, and satisfied he could keep track of them on into Texas. His description of Yolanda, as beautiful as she was, would make people able to tell him where the Squires had been.

The morning of the third day, Hawk had them back on the trail. He gauged their pace so as to put them in Ruston after dark. The fewer people who saw him the better, if the law had believed Anse and Red. He'd taken to calling Bob Bridges "Red," to keep his mind straight on them.

About ten o'clock of a moonless night five nights out of Monroe, McClure led his party down the main street of Ruston, and on through the town. He kept them moving until after midnight, when Reb protested. "Hawk, you figure to make us ride all night? We're gettin' mighty tired."

"Aw, son, reckon I figured to get us to a stream so's the animals could water. There we'd take time for a late breakfast and rest up a bit 'fore we got back on the trail." It was a flimsy excuse, but all he could think of at the time. Reb stared at him a moment, shrugged, and leaned back against the seat.

He began to wonder if letting the Squires get ahead of them was a good idea. Where he and his party made only fifteen or so miles a day with the wagon, the Squires would gain twenty-five miles a day on them, and he knew they'd soon realize he couldn't make as many miles as they could, so they'd most likely wait alongside the trail to ambush them. Now, that was a thought to worry about.

Hawk hadn't told Reb, Auntie, or Uncle anything about himself, and now he'd put them in jeopardy from his enemies. He couldn't—wouldn't—do that to them. He'd have to tell them and let them judge him as they would. And if they wanted him to ride on without them, then that's the way it had to be. But, he admitted to himself, he'd grown fond of the two darkies, and even that sissy boy had a strong hold on him. Yep, he'd get them the other side of Shreve's Landing, only a few hours away, sit them down, and lay it out for them. They'd have to cross the Red River before getting to the landing at Shreve.

Approaching the river, McClure kept eyeing a bank of dark clouds to the northwest, fact was he'd noticed weather building for the past day. If it rained much in that sector, the Red would probably be swollen and angry, not a situation to make him feel good about the crossing. Nope. He'd not take his party across if there was danger.

At the river, the ferry inched up to the shore about the time Ned pulled the wagon to load onto it. The ferry operator yelled to him. "Get that wagon aboard. River's risin' 'bout a foot a hour. Gonna make this my last trip—git 'er aboard."

4

MCCLURE STUDIED THE river a moment, then looked at the ferry operator. "How long's it take to cross?"

The man gave him a sour look. " 'Bout a half hour. Now hurry, git aboard."

Hawk frowned, calculated what another half foot of water would do to the margin of safety, then nodded to Ned. "Lead 'em on."

Their wagon, team, and a buckboard were the only vehicles on the ferry, along with the ferry operator and the buckboard driver.

About halfway across, the ferry man looked upstream, grabbed a long pole, held it out to McClure, then grabbed two more, one for Ned and one for the wagon driver. "Tree comin' down on us," he yelled. "Try to get those poles agin' the trunk, an' push like hell. Tree that size could capsize us."

McClure looked fearfully at his charges. Reb had grabbed another pole and held its end aimed at the tree's bole. Hawk added his to the three already pushing. The ferry man pulled his pole in, dropped it on the deck, grabbed the tiller, and turned the ferry's bow downstream. "Push that tree aft so's it'll miss us."

The pole the buckboard driver held broke in the middle. Then, as though he did this every day, he picked up the one the ferry operator had dropped and again pushed.

The boat's stern looked as though it arced toward the tree. The ferry man swung the tiller to bring the bow upstream, curving the stern away from the branched monster. The limbs at what had been the top of the tree raked the sides, then slipped free of the boat. "Okay, folks, stash them poles. I got 'er now. We're safe."

McClure put his arm across Reb's shoulder. "Good job, son. Your extra push mighta been what cleared us." Reb gave him a broad smile.

The boat operator peered into the gloom along the shore. "That there marshal's met every boat for the last week. Wonder who he's lookin' for."

McClure's gut tightened. He could be the one for whom the lawman looked. He glanced at the family he'd brought across Louisiana. He'd not had a chance to explain his background, and if the lawman looked for him, he might not have an opportunity to tell them his side of the story.

He eased his Colt in the holster, making certain he could get it out if he needed it, then pushed it back securely into the leather and pushed the thong over the hammer. The law out here might not be carpetbagger law, and he'd not add a killing to what the marshal might want him for.

The boat edged into the landing, bumped, came to a stop, and the ferry man jumped ashore and moored it to a tree stump. McClure stood close to Bessie. "Auntie, that marshal might be lookin' for me because of what I did back in Alabama. Don't y'all judge me too harshly. If I get a chance, I'll tell you about it." He stepped ashore.

A tall, weathered man, who looked to be in his early thirties, stepped toward McClure. "I reckon by the description I got over the wire you'll be Hawken McClure."

Although Hawk didn't feel like it, he smiled. "Yep,

and I reckon your reckon hit the nail on the head. What you want me for, Marshal?''

The marshal stood ready. He glanced at the six-shooter at McClure's side and gave Hawk a straight-on look. ''You figure to use that?''

McClure shook his head. ''If I figured that way, I wouldn't be standin' here talkin' ''

''Okay, them folks back in Alabama want you for three counts of murder, hoss stealin—eight mares an' two studs—an' robbin' two of the men you're accused of murderin'. That man you shot alongside the Tombigbee died 'fore they got 'im to the doctor.''

They stood close enough to Reb, Bessie, and Ned for them to hear every word. Bessie's eyes were wide, as though horrified, Ned shook his head as though not believing a word of it, and Reb stood with his head tilted back in stubborn disbelief.

McClure pinned the marshal with a hard look. ''You willin' to listen to my side o' the story, or you gonna send me back to them carpetbaggers?''

The marshal held out his hand. ''Since this looks to be a peaceful talk, I'm Bill McMillan.'' He pushed his hat back off his brow. ''An' we ain't sendin' you nowhere. We'll try you right here when the circuit judge gets here.''

McClure again glanced at the three with whom he'd traveled. ''McMillan, these people are ones I hooked up with just the other side o' Vicksburg. They haven't done any wrong. Give me a few moments to advise 'em on how to make the rest of their trip?''

He walked over to stand in front of the three. ''Sorry I didn't tell y'all why I was headed for Texas. Those charges the marshal enumerated are all true, 'cept the murder part. Every man I shot had a gun in his hand. The rest is true, dependin' how you look at the situation, and whether I was justified in what I did.

'' 'Nother thing, I tried to teach y'all how to take care o' yourselves on the trail. Do it my way, an' don't trust a soul. Always keep at least one o' you hid in the wagon with a Winchester pointed at whoever you meet.'' He nodded. ''Like I said, do it my way an' you'll get wherever you're goin' safely.'' He spun and went back to McMillan. ''All right, you got a lockup in this town, let's go. I'll tell you my side of the story when we get there.''

Reb stepped up alongside of him. ''Seems like we got a right to hear what he's got to say, Mr. McMillan. We trusted him—still do till what he says changes our minds.''

The marshal stared at Reb a moment. ''Son, I reckon what you say is only right. C'mon, let's all hear it.''

A surge of pride swelled McClure's throat. This young man might be sort of sissyfied, but he had the makings of a real man. But instead of listening to his story, they needed to be setting up camp. ''No, Reb. You go with your auntie and uncle. Help 'em set up camp an' start supper. I'll be all right.''

Bessie put in her two cents' worth. ''Ain't gonna do no such, Mistuh Hawk. You treated us mighty fine ever since you joined up with us. Seems fair we hear yore story too. Don't want to misjudge you. An' I'm gonna tell you straight, ain't a one o' us'uns 'bout to change our minds 'bout you no matter what you say.''

McClure and McMillan both guffawed. The marshal choked back his laughter and wiped tears from his eyes. ''Mr. McClure, sounds like you done made some mighty good friends.

''Tell you what we'll do. We'll stop by the cafe an' have 'em package up some supper, 'nuff for the five of us, then we'll sit in the hoosegow an' eat while you tell us what you did, an' why.''

Hawk looked at Bessie to see if she agreed. She nodded. They followed the lawman, with Ned leading the team of oxen. While they walked, McClure looked across his shoulder at McMillan, frowning. ''Marshal, a few minutes ago, you seemed to make up your mind to trust us, not just my friends, but me as well. Why?''

The lawman frowned. ''Good question, McClure.

Well, gonna tell you. I was a Texas ranger for might
nigh ten years, an' in all that time, dangerous time, I got
use to making quick decisions 'bout people, decisions
that could have cost me my life. I ain't been wrong yet.
Fact is, you're still wearin' your gun, an' you ain't made
a move toward it.'' He grinned. ''An to put the icing on
the cake, them people you seem to have taken responsibility for done give you all their trust. They've had
more time to figure you out than I have. 'Nother thing,
I figure if you wuz gonna run, or try to shoot me, you
had yore chance soon's you stepped off that ferryboat.''

A few minutes later, they gathered around the marshal's desk, spread the food out so they could all reach
what they wanted, and looked for McClure to begin.

He talked between bites. In telling his story, he left
out nothing. He didn't try to whitewash what he'd done,
but told it simply, the way it happened. Finished, he sat
back and swept them with a glance. ''I'm tellin' you
right now, I'd do the same thing again. That woman's
poison-mean, an' her brothers are no better. They're out
here ahead of us—lookin' for me. When I face 'em, I
figure to kill the three—well, not Yolanda. I'll have to
find a way to let her go.''

Very unladylike—or unboylike—Reb sat forward in
her chair. ''Damned if I'll let 'er go. She tries to shoot
you, I'll shoot her.''

McMillan and Hawk tried to choke back laughter, but
it didn't work—they laughed until tears flowed down
their cheeks. ''Tell you somethin', McClure, you got a
knack for makin' friends. That boy yonder ain't gonna
let you get killed.''

Reb sat looking at the table, her face red as a rosy
sunset. Then she looked up to stare each of them in the
eye for a moment. Then she faced McMillan. ''Gonna
tell you straight, Mr. Lawman, when I was only a little
g—uh, boy, Papa taught me to never be a fairweather
friend. He said when the goin' gets rough, that's when
your friends need you most. Reckon I took his words to
heart.''

Abruptly sober, McMillan stared at her a moment. "Son, you keep on thinkin' that way. An' I'll tell you what, when you get old enough, if you'd like I'll write you a letter to the Texas Ranger's Headquarters, tell 'em what a helluva ranger you'd make. When you grow to be a man, give it some thought."

With a smug smile, Reb nodded. "Yes, sir, when I grow to be a man, I'll surely do that." This time Bessie couldn't hold her laughter. Hawk and McMillan looked at her like she'd lost her mind. The marshal looked at McClure. "Didn't see nothin' funny 'bout that, did you?"

Hawk shook his head.

Bessie cut in, "Reckon it wasn't funny to y'all, but I done raised that boy from a tadpole. He just flat ain't cut out to be no lawman. If you knowed 'im like I do, you'd-a found it funny too."

McClure raised his eyebrows, wondering at Bessie's strange sense of humor, then shrugged and looked at McMillan. "Well, you've heard everything I did, right or wrong. Reckon now you can put me in one o' your cages till the circuit judge gets here. When you figure to see 'im?"

McMillan shoved his hat back and scratched his head. "Don't rightly know. It might be anywhere from a couple o' days to maybe a week."

He stared at the wall above their heads for a long minute, then looked at Hawk. "Tell you what I was thinkin'. I was tempted to turn you loose—tell you to run like hell to Texas an' keep on goin'." He shook his head. "But that wouldn't do you no good. The law would still want you. What I come up with is this: Stay here, get tried, and when the judge turns you loose, cain't nobody else try you for them things you're charged with. To try a man twice for the same crime is called double jeopardy. So when the judge turns you loose, you're free."

McClure stoked his pipe, frowning the whole time. "Yeah, McMillan, sounds pretty good, but that leaves the most important question—what happens if we got a jury made up of white trash? They'll send me to the state prison sure as hell.''

The marshal grimaced, then nodded. ''You're right. I know the judge pretty well. From him, I b'lieve you'll get justice, but the jury's gonna be the ones who might do you in.''

McClure stood. ''Tell you what, I'll not ask you to stick your neck out—an' I don't want to be runnin' the rest of my life. If the jury finds me guilty of any of those charges, reckon I'll deal with that when it happens.''

He looked at Bessie. ''Y'all go on ahead. If I get turned loose, I'll catch you.'' He shrugged. ''If not, you'll have time to go across country several times 'fore I could catch you.'' He unbuckled his gunbelt and handed it to McMillan, along with a slight smile. ''You better lock me up, or I might be tempted to head for Texas—that'll get you in trouble.''

The marshal accepted the gunbelt, shook his head, pulled open the door to the closest cell, and said over his shoulder, ''I'll do what I can to see you get a un-biased jury.''

Reb looked at him with a stubborn look. ''Tell you how it is, Hawk, we're not goin' anywhere till we know how you come outta this mess.''

McClure stared at the boy, wondering why he sounded so grown-up when the chips were down, but he had a stubborn set to his chin, so Hawk didn't argue with him. He shrugged and stepped into the cell.

Later that night, long after they'd cleaned up from supper, Bessie, Ned, and Rebecca sat by their fire. They'd gone over McClure's troubles time and time again. Finally, Rebecca took a swallow of coffee, then frowned. ''We haven't come up with anything to help Hawk, but I'll tell you one thing for sure, *we're gonna help him.* Legal or not, we're not leavin' that man here to fend for himself.''

Bessie studied Rebecca a long moment, then squared

her bony shoulders and said, "Child, you done growed up a heap in the last few hours. You talkin' like you got man feelin's for our friend, an' I'm gonna tell you somethin', if I ever got to give you to any man, *that's* the man I want it to be. He's a good man, a strawng man, a man what'd stand by you no matter what." She snapped her head in a nod. "Yes-siree-bob-tail, that's the man fo you."

Rebecca giggled. "Now, Auntie, sounds like you're trying to get rid of me. But to settle your thoughts, I'm not thinkin' 'bout him any way other than the best friend we ever had." She took another sip of her coffee. "I'm not sayin' that maybe after he finds out I'm a full-grown woman, an' I get to study the way he treats me, an' I admit to myself I'm old enough to think about him like you're suggesting—then, I might make up my mind about whether he's the one. But right now we've got the problem of how to help 'im. Let's get to bed an' sleep on it. We might come up with a way."

Even though it was late when she crawled between her covers, Rebecca lay awake thinking of their conversation and their problem. Finally, after coming up with one thing after another, and discarding each, one at a time, she nodded mentally. She'd do it the way she thought was the surest way to help Hawk, and she'd keep Bessie and Ned out of it. She didn't want them held responsible for something she'd done.

For perhaps the hundredth time since Bessie had unbound her breasts, she ran her hands down her body, took a deep breath, and wondered how long she'd have to act, and look, like a young boy. She again ran her hands over her breasts. It felt so good to be able to breathe in a normal fashion.

Her thoughts went to Hawk. She couldn't find it in her sense of justice to blame him for killing those men in Alabama. If she'd been a gun-handy man, she would have tried the same approach to solving her losses as had he.

She'd been shown trumped-up mortgage notes,

IOU's, and receipts for many items of property—land, buildings, the plantation house, livestock—and she'd had to sign them over to the same type of people who'd taken Hawk's property. With each piece of her inheritance lost she'd wished she could handle a gun. Yes. She would have taken the law into her own hands and been proud of it. Just as in Hawk's case, the law stood on the side of the white trash.

For the first time, she wondered what she, Auntie, and Uncle would do if Hawk were taken away from them. Already, he'd prevented them being relegated to utmost poverty by being robbed of the possessions they brought with them. She knew if they continued on this journey together, it would not be the last time he'd have to save their bacon. She came close to gasping loud enough to waken Bessie. All her thoughts had centered on Hawk helping them—now she had a chance to help him. Her solution as to how to do this firmed up. She'd do it her way.

The next day, Bessie fried chicken, baked biscuits, fixed a pot of greens, and lastly, cooked a deep pan peach pie. Rebecca watched as she removed the pie from the fire. "Auntie, what in this world did you cook so much for? We couldn't eat all that in three days."

Bessie snorted. "Done fixed 'nuff fo Mr. Hawk. You seen how that big man eats. Why, chile, they ain't gonna be a smidgeon o' these here victuals left when he gets through." She smiled a coy sort of smile. "I figgered we'uns gonna take him a basket o' hot tummy warmers."

Rebecca threw her arms around the old darkie. "Bless you, Auntie." She stood back and grinned. "Danged if I don't b'lieve that man's captured all three of our hearts."

"Wash yo mouth out, missy. I didn't teach you to use them words. Why, they almost cuss words. But I don't know who captured who. Seems to me like we done most o' the capturin'."

She got busy packing the supper she'd fixed for

Hawk. About through, she said, "Reckon we should oughtta take Mistuh Hawks supper to him first. We can come back an' eat after we know he's all right."

Rebecca looked at the package Bessie had prepared, nodded, and said, "You finish up with what you're doin'. I'm gonna get his razor an' stuff outta his saddle-bags. Much as he likes to stay clean and shaved, I reckon he needs his toilet articles pretty bad by now."

She went to the back of the wagon where they'd stowed McClure's gear, found the largest reticule she owned, and layed out the things she thought a man might need. Then she inspected the handguns he'd taken from the two who'd intended to rob them, and took the Colt .44—it had the newest look of those he'd collected— and dropped it to the bottom of her bag. Then as an afterthought, she took the soap out of the box Hawk had it in, took two handfuls of .44 cartridges, and dropped them into the soapbox. Last, she placed a complete change of clean clothing on top of the other things. She felt her face heat fiery-like when she handled his under-wear.

Bessie and Ned stood ready to leave for the jail when Rebecca walked around the end of the wagon. Her ret-icule obviously weighed more than would the small package of toilet articles.

"Lordy, chile, what you got in that there bag? Looks heavy enough to have a gun in it."

With the truth of Bessie's statement, Rebecca's face again felt like fire. "Auntie, when I got to packin' stuff for him—clean clothes, soap, his toilet articles—well, they weighed a ton."

Bessie looked at Ned. " Here now, you lazy thing, take that bundle from little missy an' carry it to the jail for her. Ned grasped the handles of the reticule, and when he lowered it to his side he cast a knowing look at Rebecca, a smile almost breaking through the crinkles at the corners of his mouth and eyes.

He nodded. "Yes'm, figure it's only right a growed-up man should carry somethin' a thirteen-yeah-old boy cain't carry.'' He scratched his head. "Gonna tell you though, a boy, or man, carryin' what's s'posed to be a woman's bag's gonna look awful danged funny.'' They exchanged packages. Bessie took the reticule.

When they walked through the jail door, Reb went to the marshal sitting at his desk. "Mr. McMillan, we brought you an' Hawk some supper. While you show Auntie where to lay it out, I'll take him back some clothes and toilet articles we brought, if that's all right with you.''

The lawman nodded. "Go ahead. I'll help Bessie an' Ned set up my desk sortta like we had it the other night.''

Careful to handle the large handbag as though it were light, Reb slipped the handles from Bessie's fingers and headed to the cell area.

"Brought you some stuff I thought you could make do with, Hawk. Your shavin' stuff, clothes, you know, things you gonna need till the judge gets here.'' Reb pushed the reticule through the bars to him.

As soon as he hefted it, he looked at Reb, frowning. "Reb, if this's what I think it is, take it outta here. I'm not lookin' to shoot the marshal.''

Reb's chin poked out, his jaws knotted. "Gonna tell you somethin', Hawk. Mr. McMillan and the judge might be good men. It's those who'll be on that jury you gotta be able to get by. Keep it. Stashe it inside your shirt. You might need it.''

McClure studied the boy a moment. He knew Reb was right, but he didn't want to involve him. "Not gonna get you in trouble, son.'' He held the handbag toward Reb.

Reb stepped back out of reach. "Listen to me, Hawk. No one can say I brought you that stuff. I'm gonna have two horses, saddled, with rifles and scabbards, along with a packhorse. I'll have your saddlebags too. I noticed that was where you kept most o' your spare cartridges.

"I'll be at the edge of town. If the jury goes against

you, we'll ride like Satan was after us. Can't any horse in this or any other town catch the two I'll have. If the decision is in your favor, we'll simply ride out like we owned the county."

Reb stepped toward the door. "I'm gonna send Auntie and Uncle on their way in the morning, tell 'em we'll meet them in Nacogdoches, if we don't catch 'em 'fore then." Reb pinned Hawk with a look that would brook no argument. "Now I'm tellin' you, Hawken McClure, use that .44 if you have to. We'll worry 'bout the consequences once we're in Texas. Hear tell they understand that sort o' thing better'n most, so use that Colt."

Reb spun, pulled the door open, and disappeared into McMillan's office, closing the door behind him. McClure stared at the closed door a moment. For a boy so young, that one thought like a full-grown man. Hawk wondered why that was, then marked it down to having been raised by adult-thinking people, never having been around boys his own age. Yeah, that must be it, and for now, he was glad the boy was on his side. But regardless of what happened, he wanted to keep him and the two darkies clear of his troubles.

While thinking about Reb, McClure pushed his hand into the reticule. His fingers closed on the handle of the Colt. He stuffed it inside his shirt, then carefully placed his clothing and toilet articles at the foot of his bunk. He found himself wishing for more than the six cartridges the six-shooter held, until he felt the weight of his soap box. He grinned and emptied its contents into his pockets. That boy thought of everything.

The door to the marshal's office opened. "You 'bout ready to eat, McClure? Yore friends done brought you a real barn-burnin', rompin' stompin supper what'll stick to yore ribs all night. Come on out an' set."

When they'd finished eating, and the three men's pipes filled the room with smoke, McClure studied each person in the room. There was no way he would jeopardize any of them. If he had to, he'd shoot every man of the jury. He'd try to avoid shooting the judge—if he kept his hands clear of a gun—but he'd be damned if he'd aim a six-shooter at McMillan, he was too decent a man.

He stood. "Reckon it's time I got back in my cell an' let you folks get to the wagon 'fore black dark. First, though, I need to talk to the boy a minute." He smiled at them. "Grown man to a growin' boy advice sort o' talk." He indicated he wanted Reb in the cell block with him. "Only take a minute, folks."

When the door closed behind Reb, Hawk took him by the shoulder. "Son, you gonna be out yonder holdin' the horses. If you hear gunfire, wait long enough for me to get to you—oh, maybe two, three minutes—no more. If I'm not there by then, take the horses and get gone— fast. You understand? There's no point in you gettin' caught up in my troubles, troubles that'd brand you an outlaw."

Reb stared at him, not answering. He gripped the boy's shoulder hard enough to make him wince. "Do it my way, son. Don't want you danglin' from the end of a hangman's rope." Then the fact he'd caused Reb to wince sank into his thinking. He dropped his hand like it'd touched live coals. "Aw, I'm sorry if I was too rough, Reb. Reckon it just means so much to me that you stay clear of trouble I've caused." He smiled. "Forgive me?"

Reb nodded and turned toward the door. Hawk would have sworn the boy's eyes misted, almost as though he was on the verge of crying. Then he said, "We'll do it your way, Hawk, but only to keep you from worryin' 'bout us." Reb opened the door and left. McClure held his big, work-hardened hands in front of him and stared at them. He sometimes forgot his own strength. He'd have to be more careful with the boy from here on. Hell, that boy was almost like a son to him.

Reb came to see McClure for the next three days, and brought him and the marshal food from the cafe. The boy told McMillan the darkies were getting old and needed their rest, so they didn't come with her.

Ned and Bessie had a good start toward Nacogdoches, although Bessie had raised hell when Rebecca told her she was staying behind—alone. But they left.

While they ate their evening meal, the lawman said the judge had arrived in town that afternoon and would hold the trial the next day. And for at least the tenth time, McMillan tried to convince McClure to get himself a lawyer. Hawk shook his head. "Marshal, I'm gonna tell it to the jury just like it happened. If they're the right kind of people, they'll believe me, an' will let me go." He leaned forward in his chair. "You see, I'm not claimin' I didn't kill those men. Hell, I admit it. I shot them to keep them from killin' me. Self-defense is a good defense if I have a fair jury." He shrugged. "If I don't, then they'll find me guilty of murder."

"I sure hope you're playin' your cards right, Hawk. Ain't nothin' I can do for you."

McClure nodded. "I know that. There's two witnesses. One's the sister of the first two men I shot, the other is the ferry operator there at the Tombigbee River. One would lie against me; the other would verify my story, at least the part of it he saw."

"Why don't we wait till we can bring the witness from the ferry?" McMillan pinned a hopeful look on McClure.

Hawk shook his head. "Won't work. It all comes down to what kind o' jury I have."

"Yeah, reckon it all hangs on whether they are the kind o' people we got in Texas, you know, them what believes in self-defense." The lawman shrugged. "We'll find out tomorrow."

When the marshal escorted McClure from the jail the next morning, a bank of clouds darkened the northwest. McMillan flipped a thumb toward them. "Reckon we're gonna get rain 'fore dark."

McClure, his stomach churning, glanced toward the dark clouds, and hoped if he had to run the rain would be heavy enough to wash out any tracks he and Reb might lay down. He'd worried throughout the night about getting Reb mixed up in his troubles, but he knew the boy would not listen to any other way. Too, if he had to shoot his way out of the courtroom, he worried for fear of hitting innocent bystanders. His neck and shoulder muscles tightened.

The prosecutor stood in the middle of a group of men questioning them. McMillan walked up to them. "Whatcha doin', lawyer?"

The man, tall, thin, pale—and arrogant—glanced at the marshal as though looking at cow dung. "That is no concern of yours, marshal. But I'm in the process of selecting a jury."

McMillan shook his head. "No, sir, you ain't. The accused, or his attorney, has a right to play a part in this, an' he ain't got no lawyer, so I reckon he's gonna select some o' them too."

The lawyer stared at the marshal. "What's your interest in this, McMillan?"

The lawman stared back. "My interest is the same as yours should be—justice. You don't seem to give a damn 'bout that though, do you?"

The prosecutor went squinty-eyed. "What you mean by that, Mr. Lawman?"

McMillan returned his look. "What I mean is that you don't give a damn about justice for nobody. You'd hang an innocent man as fast as you would a guilty one if it got you even one vote in the coming election."

"I take that as a personal affront, McMillan. I demand an apology."

The marshal gave him a cold smile. "I meant it as a personal affront, an' you stand 'bout as much chance o' gettin' a apology outta me as a one-legged man has of winnin' a butt-kickin' contest." He looked over his shoulder at McClure. "C'm'ere, Mr. McClure. You gonna help select yore jury."

McClure studied the potential jurors. Most were white trash but, his stomach feeling as if a bucket of worms wriggled around in it, he settled on one criterion. If the man fought for the Confederacy, he figured he would understand his actions. He let them know he was an ex–Johnny Reb, and he let them know that the men who died back there in Alabama intended to kill him, had even set up an ambush to do so. Then he asked them one question: "Were you a Confederate soldier?" If the response was yes, he chose them. He chose six, as did the prosecutor.

As soon as the jury was seated, the judge called the court to order and read the charges.

The prosecutor spent two hours pounding on the jury about the heinous crimes, three of them murder, committed by McClure.

Hawk watched the jury while the lawyer lambasted him. As he had anticipated when picking his share of those who would judge him, they looked bored, and in fact rolled their eyes skyward at times to show their contempt, while those the prosecutor had picked ooohed, aaahed, and shook their heads in disbelief that a human being could cold-bloodedly take a life.

When McClure stood to defend himself, his first words admitted killing the three. "If I hadn't shot them, they would have killed me. They all had weapons in hand when I pulled my handgun." He eyed every man in the jury box, then the people in the crowded courtroom. "There's not a man here—if he *is* a man—who wouldn't have done the same. I'll tell you what happened."

With every muscle in his body tight as a bowstring, he told what had happened, and while he talked, he tried to read the way the jury was responding to his words. When he finished, he knew he'd done a bad job—but he'd told the truth. Now the waiting began.

5

WHILE MCCLURE TALKED to the jury, Rebecca stood at the edge of town, holding the bridles of two horses and the packhorse's lead rope. Every passing minute rubbed her nerves until she thought she'd go crazy, and with each moment she said a silent prayer for the gentle but dangerous man who'd befriended the only family she knew.

Woodsmoke from cooking fires drifted from the town, a scent she'd always liked, but this time she hardly noticed it. People passing down the rough, well-trodden road never failed to cast her a questioning look, then glance at the two thoroughbred horses with her.

She glanced behind, wishing there were woods there, but all her eyes found were cleared fields. Her nerves frayed more by the minute. Then she thought of the weapons she'd removed from the back of the wagon before sending Bessie and Ned on their way. She'd put four handguns in Hawk's saddlebags. She'd pulled one of them, a Colt .44, from the bags and stuffed it inside her shirt. The weapon weighed a ton to her thinking, but if she had to, she'd handle it.

She'd no more than gotten the handgun stashed inside

her shirt, when a big, bearded, mean-looking man kneed his horse off the road toward her.

"What you doin' with them two fine animals, boy?"

"Don't see as that's any o' your business, mister."

The man's face stiffened, his lips thinned, and his eyes turned reddish. "You got a mighty smart mouth, boy. Think I'll take you down a notch, then we gonna take them horses to the sheriff an' find out if'n it's my business."

Rebecca slipped her hand inside her shirt and pulled the .44 out where he could see it. She pointed it at him and eared back the hammer. "Mister, you ain't takin' me down a notch, an' you ain't takin' me to the sheriff. My pa'll be along after a while, then we gonna see who gets taken down a notch." She used grammar like she thought a young, uneducated boy might.

The Colt weighed heavy in her small hand, causing it to tremble. "Now you, easy-like, turn that horse so's your back's to me, an' don't try to turn where you can look at me or you ain't gonna be able to turn nowhere. You unnerstan'?"

The man stared at the six-shooter, then turned his eyes to Rebecca. "Put that gun down, boy. You liable to fire it—hurt somebody."

"You do like I said mister; turn around. I figure on firing it, an' I figure on you bein' the one what gets hurt 'less'n you do like I say—right now." Rebecca knew she had the hard part done. Cocking the Colt had been even harder than she thought, but now she wondered if she could hit the man if he forced her to fire.

The bully's eyes widened, apparently thinking a scared thirteen-year-old would pull the trigger quicker than a grown man. He neck-reined his horse to put his back to her.

"Now, you just sit there like that, mister. I'll tell you when to leave." She bent her knees, sank to sit on the ground, and rested the heavy Colt on her legs. She wanted to tell the bully to ride on, but feared he would ride to the law and tell him what had happened. That would mess up her and Hawk's plan of escape. She sat there, wondering how things were going with the trial, worried sick Hawk would have to shoot his way out of the courtroom, and wondered if he'd actually fire, with his fear of hitting an innocent person. He was a dangerous man—but not a mean one. Every few seconds she cast a glance toward town, hoping to see her friend walking toward her.

McClure stated his case, straightforward and simple, as he'd done in McMillan's office, but he worried that he wasn't convincing the jury.

In his rebuttal, the prosecutor hammered on the cold-blooded murders committed by the accused. And he brought out the fact that they had only McClure's word the men drew weapons against him and he only protected himself.

In his closing stement, McClure again eyed every man on the jury, then in a quiet voice said, "I want you to give each of us a good hard look. Decide whether you trust that slick willy shyster," he pointed at the prosecutor, "or do you trust me to tell the truth?"

The judge charged the jury, told them to search their conscience before making their decision, told them he would allow a simple majority to decide McClure's fate and sent them from the courtroom.

Then the wait began, a wait that seemed days long. McClure decided that whatever the verdict, he'd walk, or run, to the edge of town, collect Reb and the horses, and light out for Texas. Although reluctant to use a gun to get away, he selected the shyster as his first target; then he'd take out the jurors—the ones he figured as white trash.

Based on who'd selected each man to serve, Hawk thought there might be a hung jury. Even then he figured to run.

Finally, the twelve men filed back to their seats. The judge asked if they'd reached a decision. The foreman stood. "Yes, suh, Judge, we done decided. It's right here on this sheet o' paper.'' Making a great show of again looking at the paper, he handed the bailiff the sheet he held in his hands. The judge read it, frowned, handed it back to the bailiff, and instructed the foreman to read it.

The foreman again tried to show the importance of his actions. He carefully unfolded the paper, looked at McClure, then with what McClure thought was a smirk, or perhaps a look of congratulations, he looked at the prosecutor. "We done found, by a eight-to-four vote, Mr. McClure there's *guilty*."

The courtroom erupted in a brawl. Those for a hanging attacked those for an acquittal. McClure pulled the .44 Reb had slipped to him from his shirt, slugged the two deputies assigned to take him back to his cell, sprinted toward the bunch who had exhibited their sentiments for an acquittal, held the handgun so those closest to him could see he was armed, but had no intention of firing into the mixed crowd. Then he pushed and slugged his way toward McMillan standing in the door holding Hawk's gun and gunbelt.

The marshal held the gunbelt toward McClure. "Good meeting you, Hawk. Take these and get outta town fast." He yelled to make himself heard.

McClure made a show of jerking his gunbelt from the marshal. He didn't want the lawman taking blame for his getting away. Then, close enough to be heard by only McMillan, he said, "Gonna take a punch at you. Fall when I swing."

He swung. The marshal fell backward. McClure pushed through the crowd, some of them helping him, others trying to drag him to the boardwalk.

Breaking clear of the crowd, he ran a zigzag course toward the edge of town amid a volley of gunshots, some close enough to tug at his shirt. He strapped on his gun and holster while he ran.

Not far ahead of him Reb sat on the ground holding a gun on a bearded man. Reb apparently saw him as soon as he saw the boy. Reb stood, yelled at the man to get gone, and pulled the horses toward Hawk. "How'd it go?"

Grinning, McClure grabbed the reins and toed the stirrup. "Guilty, an' there're a whole bunch o' people back yonder mad enough to spit fire. Let's get gone. They wanted to see a hangin', an' I cheated 'em outta it, along with McMillan's help." He told Reb this while riding hell-bent-for-election away from Shreve's Landing.

They kept the horses at a dead run. About ten men, by McClure's best guess, rode behind, firing wildly in his general direction. He put his horse and himself between the angry crowd and Reb. He wouldn't be responsible for the boy getting a slug meant for him. After about twenty minutes most of those chasing him peeled off, reined in, and left the chase. McClure glanced over his shoulder several times, until finally he decided they were no longer pursued. He reined his horse to a walk. "Slow your horse. They've quit chasin' us." He grinned, couldn't stop. "Son, wish I could tell you you're lookin' at a free man, that no other court can try me for those charges again, but that just flat isn't true. Maybe Texas believes in self-defense more than some o' those Louisianans. Let's head for Nacogdoches an' find the rest of our family."

About a hundred miles west of Shreve's Landing, when McClure and Reb rode toward Nacogdoches, Yolanda and her brothers rode into Tyler. Bert looked across his shoulder at his sister. "Tellin' you right now, Yolanda, we done rode too far. McClure's gonna take them folks to San 'Tone. We done lost 'em."

She sneered. "You believe that if you want, but we gonna check out Dallas an' Foat Worth first, then we gonna head to San 'Tone. Right now you goin' in that saloon, get a bottle o' whiskey, an' bring it to the hotel." She pushed her hat to the back of her head, wiped sweat, and settled her hat back on her head. "We gonna have a couple o' drinks, find a place to eat supper, get a good night's sleep, then head for Dallas in the mornin'."

Bert shrugged, reined in to the hitchrack, threw his leg across his horse's rump, and went to the saloon. Yolanda led Tom toward the hotel.

She asked the clerk how far to Dallas. " 'Bout eighty miles, ma'am. 'Bout a day-an'-a-half ride—one day if you ride them hosses into the ground."

She nodded her thanks, signed for two rooms, and she and Tom lugged their bedrolls to their rooms. Then she went to her brothers' room to await Bert and the bottle.

She looked at Tom. "We'll make it less'n a day an' a half. Know it seems like they gonna get too far ahead of us, but that wagon's slowin' 'em down." She nodded. "Yep, we're ahead of them for now, but when they catch up, an' we find what trail they might take, we'll jest wait 'long side the trail and take 'em on then. That boy an' them two nigras gonna be easy to handle. McClure might be a little harder."

Tom grinned, and brushed the handle of his handgun with the tips of his fingers. "You ain't seen me use a six-shooter, sister. I can handle two like him."

She cast him a disdainful look. "That kind o' thinkin'll get you a long time dead. That man is both fast and accurate. I want all three of us to be pointin' a gun at him. I want him—want 'im bad."

Tom slanted her a nasty grin. "How you mean that, sister? Know you been wantin' 'im ever since he come back from the war." His grin widened. "B'lieve yore kind o' wantin's done changed some since then. Right?"

She slapped him, hard enough to cause him to sit on the bed that was at the back of his knees. His eyes spit hate at her. "Yolanda, you gonna do that once too often—then I'm gonna blow yore brains all over Texas. You hear what I'm sayin'?"

Their looks clashed, both of them filled with poison. Bert walked through the door holding a bottle. He looked from one to the other of them. "Little fight?" He held out the bottle. "This'll smooth things over. Let's have drink."

Yolanda looked at Tom a long moment. "You ever

try what you jest said, you better be standin' behind me.''

Tom nodded and held out a glass for Bert to fill. "No, sister. I'll be standin' where I can look at yore face. I want to watch every bit o' pain you show.''

Yolanda took her drink and sat on the edge of the bed. For now, she needed her brothers, both of them if she figured to kill McClure. After they took care of Hawk, she'd shed them—dead or alive. She didn't really care that McClure had killed the twins; her reasons for wanting him dead were personal.

Inwardly, she smiled. What her brothers didn't know was that all the property they'd acquired since the war was in her name. She'd use them as long as she needed them—then?

After supper they went to their rooms and turned in. They had a long ride ahead on the morrow. Yolanda lay awake long into the night. Her thoughts centered on McClure. Her every thought brought poisonous bile to her throat. She'd offered him so much. With her, and the property she'd taken from him, he could have gone back to being a gentleman. His laugh still rang in her ears. Damn him. She'd see him suffer the pangs of hell until she put him out of his misery.

Below Henderson, Texas, still a full half a day from Nacogdoches, McClure reined his horse off the trail into a heavy stand of second-growth pine. "We'll camp for tonight and probably get to Nacogdoches for our noonin' tomorrow.''

Rebecca had mixed feelings about spending the night alone with Hawk. She trusted him to be a gentleman, but didn't know how to treat the private things for which she'd need time. Fear she'd give away the fact she was a grown woman, of marrying age, sat heavy in her thoughts. She hung back a little.

Hawk twisted in the saddle. Then as though having read her mind, he said, "Come on, son, I'm not gonna intrude on your privacy, gonna treat you just like I would if Bessie were here.''

"Aw, Hawk, I wasn't worried 'bout that. It's . . . it's just that I've never been around grown-up men before. Know you're gonna treat me like you've been treatin' me.''

After finding a spot among tall stately pines, not timbered out, or burned, they made camp, fixed supper, and sat to eat. Rebecca felt Hawk's eyes studying her. She slanted him a glance. "What's the matter, I do somethin' wrong?''

He shook his head. "No. Just tryin' to figure you out, young fellow. You look like a boy, most of the time act like a boy, but at other times you talk, sound, an' think like a grown-up.'' He chuckled. "Reckon my thinkin' comes from never having been around a youngster your age.'' He frowned. "Then too, reckon you bein' with grown-ups most o' your life, never havin' a chance to play an' act like most boys, has made you think like an adult.''

The more he talked, the more Rebecca slunk down against her saddle. He was coming too close to figuring out that she wasn't what she pretended to be. She put her cup to her lips, covering much of her face. Then, looking at him straight-on, she said, "Reckon you've got it figured, Hawk. My folks always treated me like I was the same age as them. Seemed they expected me to think like them, seemed they expected me to think things out for myself. Reckon with them treatin' me like that I got to thinkin' I could ponder on somethin' awhile, an' come up with an answer good as anybody.'' She took a swallow of her coffee. "Tell me 'bout yourself, your family, about the war, how you were raised.''

McClure smiled, a bittersweet smile to her thinking, packed his pipe, poured them each another cup of coffee, then stared into the fire. "Tell you, son, a lot o' those things are hard to talk 'bout even now this long after the war, but you, and Bessie and Ned, have a right to know 'bout me, so I'll tell you.'' He picked a twig from the fire and put it to his pipe, then talked through a great cloud of smoke. "We had a nice plantation, not as large as most, but as large as Papa thought to handle efficiently.

"Papa wouldn't stand for me bein' raised like some o' those spoiled boys from other families. He put me out in the fields with our nigras, and worked me just as hard as any." He smiled. "Didn't take much pushin' on his part. As a matter of pride I did the pushin', tried to work hard as any man there, an' reckon I did my part— as much as my size an' age let me.

"Then I went off to the war. Didn't really know what it was all about, but finally figured slavery had very little to do with it. The states figured it was their right to govern themselves, an' the politicians in Washington didn't see it that way." He sighed. "Not arguin' who was right or wrong, but many good men, a lot o' them boys not much older'n you, died miserable, cold, bodies-torn-apart deaths. Then while I was in northern Virginia, still fightin' the war, Mama and Papa died, two months apart. I couldn't bear the thought of goin' home and not findin' them there, and everything I'd ever known changed. Too, the only friends I ever had, nigra boys, they were all gone.

"I went west, joined the Army of the United States, fought with them, scouted for them, then got up enough nerve to come home, see what had happened to my world."

His jaws tight, he stared at her, his face hard. "I've already told you a few of the changes I found there. Everything taken, or sold for taxes." He took a swallow of coffee. "And you already know why I'm on the run."

He tossed the dregs from his cup and spread his blanket. "Reckon if you'd been a few years older, your life would've been much the same as mine. You're lucky, son. I wouldn't wish that war on anyone, North or South.

He pulled his boots off, crawled between his blankets, and looked at Rebecca. "Take only your boots off. We might have to move fast during the night." He grinned.

"Don't worry, son, we'll get a bath when we get to Nacogdoches."

Rebecca realized he'd talked about himself as much as he was of a mind to. She spread her blankets across the fire from him, slipped between them, but was a long time going to sleep. She thought of the things Hawk had told her. One thing was settled for sure: Hawk came from a "good" family. Not that she cared a whit from what or who he sprang; he was a good man, a man any would be proud to call friend. But now she would be able to satisfy Bessie's worries about his family. She giggled to herself. To hear Bessie talk, one would think she came from a long line of royalty. She glanced across the fire and saw Hawk breathing deeply as in sleep. She breathed in a great breath of pine-scented air, turned on her side, and soon slept.

The next day they reached the outskirts of Nacogdoches. Established about 1690, it was one of the oldest towns in the country.

They didn't have to look for the two darkies. At the north edge of town, the wagon sat alongside the trail. Bessie and Ned sat on the wagon seat, their eyes trained to the north.

Hawk reined in alongside, grinning. "Y'all figure we'd gotten lost?"

Bessie shook her head. "No, suh, Mr. Hawk, we reckoned with the young mistuh draggin' you back it'd take a while." She smiled. "We sho is glad to see y'all, though."

Ned squirmed on the seat beside her. "What we'uns really worried 'bout wuz, how'd that judge treat you?"

McClure pinned them with a look that in itself said it all. "I'm runnin'. Know how you darkies must of felt when Mr. Lincoln set you free. I hoped to feel the same way, but that jury didn't see it like I told it." He shrugged. "Reckon to their thinkin' a man shouldn't defend himself—or his property."

Ned shook his head. "Now, don't that beat all.

Course, that trash on the jury prob'ly ain't nevuh had nothing to defend.''

''Talkin' 'bout bein' free, it wuzn't like we wuz evuh whipped or nothin' like that when we b'longed to Mistuh Brennan,'' Bessie said. ''Aftuh gittin' freed, it wuz jest knowin' we could go an' do whatever we had a notion to do.'' She grinned. ''Sho is a good feelin', ain't it?''

McClure smiled. ''Tell you right now, I almost have that feelin'. We're in Texas, an' they have a much different outlook on a man takin' care o' what's his.'' He glanced around the spot they'd parked the big Studebaker. ''Tell you what, we'll drive the wagon to the livery, and get hotel rooms for the night. Figure Reb's got saddle sores on his behind by now.'' He glanced at Reb, only to see his face a bright red. ''Aw now, boy, didn't mean to embarrass you. Know Auntie's seen your little ole naked behind when you were a baby.''

If possible, Reb's face flamed even brighter. ''Yeah, Hawk, reckon a room, an'a good bath, will do us all good.''

The wagon taken care of, and his ''family'' in their rooms, McClure decided to go to the saloon, have a drink, and see if he could get information as to whether the Squires bunch had been through town. Before leaving the hotel, he told them he'd meet them in the dining room at six for supper.

In the saloon, he stood next to a young man about his own age. He noticed when the man told him his name, Bill Longley, that he looked for some kind of reaction. When McClure introduced himself without acknowledging having ever heard of the gunfighter, Longley apparently relaxed.

They talked awhile, and McClure found out the gunfighter had been in town several days and hadn't seen anything of the Squires bunch. ''Yeah, I'd of knowed if they been through town, but ain't seen nothin' of 'em. You huntin' them—or they huntin' you?''

McClure grinned. ''Reckon some o' both. They want

me dead, but I'm gonna make damned certain we meet when I want us to, and where I want us to. I want them as bad as they want me, but facin' three, maybe two, of 'em, I need an edge.''

Longley nodded. ''Good thinkin'. 'Bout the way I'd do it.''

After another drink, the gunfighter bid Hawk good night and left. The bartender slid along the bar to face McClure. ''You know who you were talkin' to?''

Hawk nodded. ''Yeah, I've heard of Longley for quite a spell now.''

''Weren't you nervous? I hear he'll shoot a man just for the hell of it.''

McClure shook his head. ''Nope. Not nervous. Didn't figure to give him reason to draw down on me, an' if he had,'' he shrugged, ''reckon we'd of seen who was the best.''

The bartender shook his head. ''Well now, mister, I'm here to tell you I get nervous jest havin' him drinkin' in this saloon. Wish he'd take his business somewhere else.''

''Why, hell, bartender, feelin' that way you oughtta move outta Texas. Reckon there're a lot o' men here would take offense at the drop of a hat.'' McClure finished his drink and left.

He walked along the street wondering where he would ultimately end up. After the war, he'd come west, hating to go home and see his ravaged South, knowing it would never again be as he'd known it.

In the West he'd fought Indians, mostly Apache and Comanche. For two years before he left to head home, he'd had reason to use all the skills Ben Baty had taught him. As an Army scout he'd had need for those skills.

He'd seen a lot, and learned a lot. That northern New Mexico and southwestern Colorado country was beautiful. He wanted to see more of it.

But how responsible was he for the boy and the two Negroes? Did they have anything to help them get a start in this raw new land, other than the wagon and stallion?

He couldn't get them out in the middle of nowhere in the south Texas desert and leave them. Besides, that boy needed a man Hawk's age to take him in tow, teach him about being a man, teach him how to live with little to make do with. He nodded to himself. Yeah, the boy had the makings of a man, had a strong streak of iron in him, and was as loyal as any man, but he needed to develop his body, get some muscle—why, hell, the lad's shoulders were soft as a woman's. McClure pondered that problem awhile, shook his head, and decided he didn't know the answers. He turned toward the hotel.

After a bath, supper, and a good night's sleep, Hawk felt like a new man when he walked into the dining room the next morning. His "family" had already drunk coffee, waiting for their meal. He pulled out his chair to sit, looked toward the door when it swung open, only to see Longley walk in, stop, and stare at the two darkies sitting with Reb. McClure had heard that the gunman had nothing but hate for Negroes—all Negroes. He thumbed the thong off the hammer of his Colt.

Longley's eyes never left Bessie and Ned. "What you nigras doin' heah, settin' with white folks?"

McClure stepped forward. "Let me tell you how it is, Longley. That boy yonder wuz orphaned by the Yankees at the end o' the war. Those two nigras, who raised the boy from a wet, stinkin' little tadpole, stepped in an' figured to finish the job. They been takin' care of him ever since. To my thinkin' they deserve to be treated like white folks."

Longley, obviously tense, ready to draw and kill the two darkies, looked at McClure. "What's yore stake in this, McClure?"

Hawk shook his head, locked eyes with the gunman, and said, "Not a damned thing other than the fact I figure to show 'em the way to the New Mexico Territory." His voice softened. "An' I'll tell you somethin' else, Longley, I figure to get there with all three of 'em, alive, an' well."

Longley held his eyes on Hawk's. "You know who I am an' you ain't even a little nervous, McClure?"

"Yeah, I know who you are, but I'll tell you how it is. In the last few years I been through the fires o' hell, an' I've never seen a man I'm afraid of. You might shoot me—but I'm not afraid of you."

The gunfighter stared at McClure another moment, then nodded. "Figured you for that sort o' man when I met you." He glanced at Bessie and Ned. "I'll find me another cafe to eat in. Ain't gonna eat with no nigras, but I hope you get them folks to wherever you're goin' safely." He smiled, winked, and walked out.

Not until the door closed behind the gunfighter did McClure take a deep breath. Save for the whim of the killer, the room would now be shrouded in gunsmoke. At least two bodies would lie on the floor dead—maybe more, three if the gunfighter had shot him first. Hawk knew himself to be good with both rifle and handgun, but he doubted he could stack up with Longley. His stomach quieted. He shrugged his shirtsleeves out of his wet armpits, pulled his chair out, and sat with his friends.

Bessie and Ned stared at him, their mouths slightly open. Reb looked a question at him. "Was that man gonna shoot you, Auntie, and Uncle?"

" 'Fraid so, son. That man, as you call 'im, is one of the most cold-blooded killers in the West. He's been known to shoot darkies just to see if the gun he was thinkin' 'bout buyin' shot straight."

Reb studied him a long moment. "You were gonna shoot it out with him to protect us? You didn't seem at all afraid."

Suddenly tired, Hawk smiled. "To answer your question, Reb, yep, I figured to shoot it out with him." His smile widened to a grin. "As to being scared, what things seem, and what they are, are two different things. I'll tell you this, I don't usually sweat like a winded horse in the cool of the mornin' like I'm doin' right this minute." He shrugged. "But you gonna find out someday, a man does what he's gotta do—or he ain't much man.''

Very un-boylike, Reb, little above a whisper, said, "Hawk McClure, to my way of thinkin', you fit into bein' *much man* in anybody's world." His face turned bright red as soon as he said it.

Hawk let a slight smile break the corners of his lips. "Thank you, youngster. I take those words as one of the best compliments I've had." Puzzled, he added, "Sometimes you sound, and think, almost grown-up." He shrugged. "Course we've already talked 'bout that."

Bessie cut in before Reb had a chance to say anything. "Lordy day, you right, Mr. Hawk. I used to tell her— uh, his mama, 'That boy ain't never gonna have a chance to be a real little boy less'n y'all stop treatin' him like he's done growed up.' Didn't do much good though, they jest kept on a treatin' him growed, tellin' 'im he wuz their 'little man.' " She slapped her thigh. "Goodness gracious, you shoulda seed that there little wet, squallin' thing throw back his shoulders and tell me he wuz a big boy."

They all chuckled, except Reb, who sat there red-faced, looking at Bessie as though he'd been betrayed. He turned to McClure. "Hawk, you gonna take us to where we can build a home and settle down?"

He nodded. "Way I got it figured, son, that's exactly what I'm gonna do."

Their breakfast came and they continued talking while eating. McClure frowned into his coffee cup, then looked at Reb. "Son, I gave what you asked me a lot o' thought before I came to the conclusion I just told you. I figure y'all won't make it unless you have some-one along who knows what to do in many of the situations we're gonna face out yonder." He smiled. "Course if y'all don't want me along, I'll leave whenever you say. 'Nother thing, the law might have a lot to say 'bout whether I continue on with y'all."

"Oh no, Hawk, accordin' to what you've said before, you still need to teach me how to be a man." Reb swept

Ned and Bessie with a glance. "I vote we need to make Hawk welcome as long as he'll stay with us." Reb grimaced. "Course we don't want him to feel we've become a burden, so we're gonna have to make sure we all do our part in helpin' 'im, an' makin' 'im welcome."

Bessie clapped her hands on her skinny hips. "Mr. Hawk, reckon if'n you'll stay with us till you git tired o' havin' us around we'd be sorely beholden to you."

McClure chuckled. "Well, reckon we've settled that. I'll stay with you till we're sure you're settled and secure in the knowledge you can make it on your own. Okay?"

He got a resounding "Okay," tinged with more relief than he would have thought, from each of them.

"All right. We've had a chance to rest overnight, so reckon we better get goin'." He stood. "Figure to head for San 'Tone when we leave here. Those three huntin' me must have gone to Dallas. That'll add miles to their trip before comin' onto our trail. Let's get goin'."

Six weeks later, after passing through several settlements, including Lufkin and Bryan, in all of which McClure checked to see if the Squires had come that way, he led them into the square in front of the Alamo. He waved his hand to encompass all around him. "Folks, this's San 'Tone. Know y'all think we've put some hard miles behind us. Know you think we been in Texas forever, but we've still got more miles ahead o' us than we've put behind, an' let me tell you now: If you think for one minute you've seen hard travelin', wait'll you see that west Texas country." He wiped sweat from his brow. "Glad we had 'bout five hundred miles to get you used to the trail, an' to harden you up a little. You gonna need it." He cast Reb a glance. "Son, you're beginnin' to harden up. Seems like your shoulders're beginnin' to take on a little muscle. Grippin' 'em last night, they seemed more firm. Glad to see it."

At his words, Bessie's head snapped to the side to look a question at Reb, like, 'What was McClure doing touching her little girl?' Reb blushed.

That night in their room, Bessie pinned Rebecca with a no-nonsense look. "Little missy, what you lettin' that man touch you for? He ain't got no right to lay a hand on you."

Rebecca gave Auntie as good a look as she received. "Gonna tell you, Auntie." She'd taken to using phrases much like Hawk. "That man, as you call him, thinks he's dealing with a boy. I've noticed about once a week he grips my shoulder and squeezes." She unbuttoned her shirt while she talked. "At first I wondered why he did it. Now I realize he's checking to see if he's makin' a man of me, getting my muscles to harden." She took the tight bindings from her breasts, breathed deeply, and massaged circulation back into her tortured flesh.

Bessie's smile widened to turn into a grin. "Lordy day, missy, if he could see you now, reckon he'd know they ain't no way he's gonna turn you into a man."

The thought caused heat to flood Rebecca's face. Continuing to massage her sides and back, she slanted Bessie a look. "Tell you, if he was seein' me right now, I'd just flat sink right through this floor." She cupped her breasts in both hands and grinned. "You know what? I do believe these muscles *are* getting more firm."

Bessie frowned. "He evah check them to see if they gittin' hard, I'm gonna unload that there twelve-gauge shotgun into 'im."

Rebecca giggled. "Oh, Auntie, even with thinkin' me to be a boy, he's the perfect gentleman. Why, when he sinks his ax into a stick of firewood and hits a knot, the strongest thing I've heard 'im say is an occasional 'Damn.'" She nodded. "Yep, you don't have a worry there, Hawk's a pure-dee Southern gentleman."

In his room two doors down the hall, Hawk worried. What was wrong with the boy? Was he sick? He'd grown to have a strong affection for Reb. He'd always wished for a little brother—or a son—whom he could become a friend with and lead into manhood, but if Reb was sick, McClure figured he'd have to lighten up on the chores he'd have him perform. Each time he touched the boy's shoulder, and failed to find his young muscles taking on a ropy feeling, Hawk's worry became deeper.

He'd not had strong enough reason thus far to question Reb's health—but he resolved right there in the dark of his room to lighten up on the load, and to keep his hands to himself. If something was wrong with the boy, he didn't want to know. He'd just give Reb work he thought he could handle, but tasks that would challenge his strength, and maybe slowly build him up.

The next morning, he told Bessie he'd take Reb and Uncle with him. They'd been through rain, mud, and dust. The wagon needed to be made ready for the long trek across the desert, and he wanted them to see what he did to it other than grease the wheels.

He wanted to buy a spare axle and a couple of water barrels. He explained to them all why he wanted the man and the boy to see what he demanded of the water barrels he'd purchase. "They gotta already be filled with water so the staves are swelled to each other. Not even a drop of water can leak from them. We gonna be in country where every drop o' water is more precious than gold. Fact is, I've known miners who would've traded every ounce o' dust they'd panned in months for one swallow of water."

He pushed his hat to the back of his head and mopped his brow. "What I've told you should be enough said 'bout water, but I'm gonna tell you more. There'll be days, perhaps weeks, when you'll think your body's gonna rot if you don't get a bath. It won't rot, an' you aren't gonna use any of our water from the barrels for anything but drinkin', cookin', and the animals havin' a swallow of it now and again.

"You're gonna do without a bath till we cross a creek, or sump, or whatever holds water—then, we first fill the barrels, and after that we make certain the animals get a good drink, then, if there's water left, we bathe, an' use it for whatever other purpose we think we need it. Y'all got it?"

Reb frowned. "Hawk, is there no other way to get where we're goin'?"

McClure shook his head. "Son, if there is, I don't know the route. Far to the north, there might be. I've not been in the Lakota or Blackfeet country, and those Indians can be every bit as savage as the Comanche and Apache we might have to face.

"And the country?" He shook his head. "From what I hear from those who have been there, the land's as brutal as this country we have to cross, the weather's just as hot in the summer, an' the winters are like none of us has ever seen—cold enough to freeze spit from a short man 'fore it hits the ground. They tell spit'll bounce like a marble when it hits the frozen ground."

Bessie listened through Hawk's entire talk, then said, "Why we gonna go 'cross this heah bad land down heah? From what I heah, they's some mighty fine country down southeast of us—good farm or ranch land."

McClure pulled his pipe from his pocket and stoked it. He nodded. "Auntie, it's every bit as good as you've heard, but that land's all settled." He shook his head. "Another reason is all the counties around that country are still under carpetbagger law. Don't b'lieve y'all want that. You said you wanted a fresh start, a chance to get cheap land, land without heavy taxes being heaped on you, land where bein' a Southerner won't draw the anger of most." He shrugged. "The country I'm takin' you to is like that. But—if you want, I'll take you to the southeast and let you make up your own mind."

Reb cut in. "Where do you intend to settle, Hawk?"

He squinted at the dusty street, then looked the boy in the eye. "Well, young'un, I'll get y'all to where you're satisfied is your kind o' country, then I'm headin' to southwest Colorado. See if I can set myself up to ranch.

"Too, there's a new town there, Durango they're callin' it since it moved 'bout two miles south. Was Animas City before. Be a town to visit when we want to see some new faces, hear some news, an' you, Bessie, bein' a lady, you can hear all the latest gossip. It'll be a place to go to break the monotony an' lonesomeness of ranchin'." He grinned. "There I go, talkin' like y'all gonna stay with me right on cross-country."

Reb looked from Bessie to Ned. "You heard the man. Let's make up our mind which we want—freedom, an' good ranch land, or good ranchland without freedom."

Ned, for the first time, spoke his piece. "Tellin' y'all, Bessie an' me done been married fawty-two years, but y'all decide to take that country where we gotta kowtow to lawmen what ain't zactly lookin' out foah us, then I'm goin' with Mistuh Hawk without you. With lawmen like that, we ain't gonna have no freedom."

Bessie studied her husband for the longest moment, then nodded—and grinned. "Reckon Ned, as worthless a nigra as he is, ain't leavin' heah 'thout me." The grin slipped from her face. "Yes suh, Mr. Hawk, we done lived without freedom for most o' our lives. I ain't willin' to give it up 'cept for one reason, and that reason is—if my little . . . uh, boy wants to settle here in the southeast Texas country, reckon then I'd jest flat have to stay."

Reb smiled. "Don't reckon you gonna get an argument outta me. Fact is, I don't think Hawk's finished with makin' a man outta me. I got a lot o' changin' to do—in more ways than one."

Bessie and Ned's laughter brought tears to their eyes. McClure looked at them, frowned, and shook his head. Damned if the whole bunch didn't have the strangest sense of humor he'd ever seen. He'd have to study on it and see if maybe it was *him* that had no sense of humor.

JEDEDIAH POWERS COUNTED the money along with the man across the table. When each banknote fell to the table, he wondered if he'd done the right thing in selling his ferry business. When he'd counted twelve hundred dollars, they shook hands to close the deal. He sighed. Too late to back out now.

He walked to his horse, thinking of the man who'd given him the idea about heading west. Hawken Mc-Clure hadn't impressed him as being a man who made dumb decisions, besides, ten, twenty years from now, what would he have other than the ferry and scrounging for a living? Too, they might build a bridge across the river; that'd damn sure put him out of business.

He shrugged, feeling as though a weight lifted from his shoulders. He'd made the decision, right or wrong. He didn't owe anyone a dime, and was free to do as he pleased. He gathered the lead rope of his packhorse in his hands, toed the stirrup, and headed west.

Two weeks later he rode into Shreve's Landing wondering where McClure might have headed. On a hunch, he stopped by the marshal's office. As each of them sat with a cup of coffee and puffed his pipe, Marshal Mc-

Millan studied the man before him. "You say you run the ferry there at Demopolis, an' watched the gunfight 'tween McClure and them deputies?"

Jed grinned. "Yep, reckon you could say I seen most of it, what time I wan't hunkered down behind somethin' to keep from catchin' stray lead. Why?"

"What kind o' people you figure them lawmen were? Did they give McClure a chance to hand over his firearms?"

Feeling like a man of means since he sold his business, Jed eyed McMillan. "Tell you straight, Marshal, them men were pure-dee white trash, an' nope, they didn't figure to give 'im a chance to do nothin' but die. They wuz set up to bushwhack 'im, but he wuz smarter'n them. Even then, he give 'em a chance to drop their guns. He wuz a right decent man to my way of figurin' it."

McMillan's insides were smiling. He'd been right about the tall Southerner. He took a swallow of his coffee and nodded. "Way I had 'im figured too. He told me he wuz gonna head for Dallas, but that was before the trial. Figure in case he had to run he wanted to lay a false trail for me." He grinned. "You want my thinkin', I'd say he went to San 'Tone. You figure to join up with 'im?"

Powers tapped his fingernails against his cup, wondering if that was the reason he'd searched out McClure's route. Finally, he nodded. "Yep, jest now made that deeecision. Reckon I could do a lot worse'n partner up with a gent like him." He shook his head. "Course he don't know I got that in mind. Reckon I'll have to wait an' see how he figures things."

McMillan told him McClure traveled with two darkies and a boy. "Seemed to hold them three folks in high regard. And I'm gonna tell you, them three woulda done anything for Hawk." He grinned. "Fact is, the boy didn't know I knew, but he slipped McClure a handgun before the trial. I figured if he had to shoot his way outta that courtroom I'd do like you done over there on the

Tombigbee—hunker down behind somethin' an' wait
for the shootin' to stop. Fact is, reckon I done what I
could to get in the way o' folks shootin' at him, wantin'
to hang 'im when he run after the jury found 'im
guilty.'' He frowned, shook his head, and pinned Powers
with a look that would go right through a man. ''Gonna
tell you, they'll be some in Texas what'll want to try
'im again an' string 'im up. You tie in with him, an'
you might find yourself in a bunch o' trouble.''

Powers chuckled. ''Reckon it might be worth a bunch
o' trouble to partner up with a man like him.'' He told
McMillan McClure was a right good man, left the marshal's office, and headed for San Antonio.

After finding no one in Dallas or Fort Worth who remembered seeing anyone of McClure's description, Yolanda and her brothers, turned their eyes toward San
Antonio.

They rode into the old Spanish Mission town two days
after McClure led his party out of town. They followed
their regular routine. While Tom and his sister got rooms
at the hotel, Bert went to the saloon for a bottle of whiskey.

They sat in Yolanda's room drinking, and as usual
Yolanda laid out her plans. ''First, we gonna find out if
they're here, or been here, then we gonna find out which
direction they went, then we gonna let 'em get slam the
other side o' nowhere, and then we're gonna end this
thing an' go home, go home an' live like white folks.''

Bert looked at his sister a moment. ''We better stock
up on supplies. Don't know how long it's gonna take to
catch 'em—or to set up the place to ambush 'em.''

She pinned him with a hard look. ''You figurin' to
take over runnin' this show, little brother? If you ain't,
I'll tell you what we gonna do, an' it don't include
loadin' ourselves down with a bunch o' stuff to haul
around.''

Bert didn't respond, but his eyes went flat and deadly.
Yolanda thought if it came down to having to kill them

after she got through with what she planned for McClure, she'd take out Bert first. Tom was putty in her hands—to a point.

She knocked back the rest of her drink, poured another, and put her legs on the bed. "We'll go eat, then I want the two o' you to hit the saloons, find out if McClure's in town, an' if he ain't, how long's he been gone an' which direction."

"Hell, sister, I figure he's gone on west. That's where he's been goin' ever since he left Alabama." Tom looked pleased that he'd contributed something. Too, Yolanda didn't seem to like Bert saying anything.

She tipped her glass, swallowed, and shook her head. "There's a whole lot of good land south and southeast of here. It ever enter your thick skull he mighta gone down there?"

"Might of. I ain't given it much thought."

To her thinking, Tom looked like a whipped pup, but then he always looked like somebody had just kicked him in the tail. She twisted her mouth into a grimace. "You ain't never given *nothin'* much thought, Tom. You might try thinkin' someday if it don't hurt your head too much." She swung her legs off the bed. "Now, I'll tell you what we gonna do. When we find where we're likely to find McClure, we gonna rest up here two, maybe three days, then we're gonna go get 'im."

The next afternoon, toward sundown, Jedediah hitched his horse in front of the building next door to the Alamo; the sign over the door said it was the "Minger Hotel." He had twisted to go in when he stopped and studied three people about to walk into the general mercantile store across the square. Two men—one short and blocky, the other medium height and skinny—walked with one of the most beautiful but haughty women he'd seen.

After they disappeared into the store, Powers stood there, his brow puckered. What was it McClure had told him about two men and a beautiful woman? He nodded.

Yeah, they fit McClure's description of the ones hunting him. Jed decided to find a way to talk to one, or both, of the men. He left his horses hitched, pulled his Winchester from the saddle boot, and walked toward the store.

Inside, as soon as his eyes adjusted to the dimly lighted room, he spotted the three, and worked his way around the stacked goods to where the pretty lady stood fingering some cloth. She looked at him. "You work here?"

"No, ma'am, come from over east of here a few hundred miles." He grinned. "Headed for Californy, see if they left any o' that gold in the ground for me to find."

Her chin tilted, and she looked down her nose at him. "Didn't ask where you were goin'. Want somebody to wait on me." She turned her back to him.

One of the men with her, the skinny one, sidled to Jed's side. "Been here long?"

Jed shook his head. "Jest rode in. Ain't even had a drink yet." He held out his hand. "Name's Jedediah Powers."

The skinny man shook hands, and said, "Name's Tom Squires, that short, stumpy man yonder's my brother, an' the woman what walked away's my sister, Yolanda. She ain't very friendly."

Powers went quiet inside. These were the three hunting McClure. He'd have to be careful not to let on he was from Alabama. He nodded. "Yeah, noticed she wasn't friendly, but most ladies ain't 'less'n they know you." Then, fishing for information, he asked, "You folks from around heah?"

Tom shook his head. "Naw, we come from Alabama." He grinned. "Don't even know where we're goin' from here. Jest got in yestiddy."

Powers thought a moment, then decided to say no more—but to keep close watch on the three, and when they left, to follow them. He was certain they'd do all the checking necessary to determine which direction McClure and his party had gone.

He cast a glance at Yolanda. She sure fit McClure's description right down to a nubbin, and to his thinking, she was more deadly than a rattlesnake. He tipped his hat, bought a pound of tobacco, and left.

Jed walked around the square, passed the Texas Ranger headquarters for that part of the state, then stopped and retraced his steps. When he walked into the Rangers office, a young man, about twenty-five, asked, "What can I do for you, suh? Ranger Temple here."

Powers smiled. "Don't need nothin, Sergeant. Jest stopped in to say I met one o' your members over at Shreve's Landing, man by the name of McMillan. He said if I had a chance, for me to stop by an' tell y'all howdy for him. Me an' my friend, Hawken McClure, taken a likin' to him."

Ranger Temple studied Powers a moment, his face sober. "McClure stopped in to see me three or four days ago. Told me all about the shootin' over in Alabama, the trial in Shreves—an' that he had no witnesses to verify his story except a man runnin' a ferry across the Tombigbee—an' it was too late to get him for the trial. Are you that ferry man?"

Powers grinned. "You hit that nail dead center on the head, Ranger. I seen it all, an' 'cordin' to McMillan, Hawk told it fair an' square the way it happened. He told it like I seen it."

Temple nodded. "Way I had 'im figured. He won't get no trouble outta the Rangers if I have anything to say 'bout it. If you see 'im, you might tell 'im that."

Powers looked at the ranger a moment. "That's the news I wuz hopin' fer. McClure's a right decent man. Don't figger he's one to cross, but treat 'im right, an' he'll do to ride the river with." He tipped his hat, nodded, and left.

About the time Powers left the Rangers office, Yolanda led her brothers from the store. "Y'all hang out in the saloons, find out if anybody's seen McClure, then come back to the hotel." She pinned Tom with a no-nonsense look. "Tom, I'm tellin' you, don't drink so

much you get to lettin' yore tongue wag at both ends.
Don't need to let nobody know what we're doin'. Got
it?''

"Yeah, sister, I ain't gonna let on to nothin'.''

She turned her steps toward a ladies ready-to-wear
shop.

Two days later, Bert talked with a man who said Mc-
Clure told him he and his party were headed for El Paso,
and they'd been gone from San Antonio four or five
days. Bert left him, went to Yolanda's room, and told
her what he'd found out.

She stood, looked at her bedroll, decided it would take
only a few minutes to get ready for the trail, then turned
back to Bert. "Find Tom before the fool lets the world
know what we're about. Tell 'im we leave in the mornin' bright an' early." Before he could open the door, she
said, "Don't want no extra gear. We gonna travel fast
an' get it over with."

"Yolanda, the man what told me where they headed
also said it's a long, dry ride out west o' here. You
reckon we better take on some extra canteens?''

She stared at him a moment. "What the hell did I jest
tell you, brother? Seems I said we wuz gonna travel
fast—no extra gear. Them words wuzn't jest so's I could
hear myself talk. Go find Tom."

McClure sat on the edge of Buckhorn Draw, stared to
its bottom, saw a narrow trickle of water, and reined his
horse back toward the wagon.

He'd been as concerned with finding water as he had
feared seeing Comanche. Twice since leaving the wagon
that morning, he'd crossed pony tracks. Studying them,
he'd seen tracks of one pony with a toed-in left rear
hoof. That horse had been in both sets of tracks. He
thought the small band, about five riders, had gone on,
and they'd not have to worry about them.

When he rode to the wagon, his throat swelled. Reb's
white complexion had burned and peeled, burned and

peeled. Didn't seem the boy's skin would ever tan and harden like an outdoorsman. A glance at the two darkies showed that, even though their skin didn't show the sun's ravages, the heat and dryness had sucked the vitality from their faces. Hawk took advantage of every opportunity to encourage them.

"We gonna camp by a stream tonight, folks. Looked like enough water to clean our bodies a bit, let the horses get their fill, an' have enough left over to wash clothes." He stepped from the saddle, went to the water barrels, and tapped on each. "We've done right well with savin' water, but before we do anything, we'll fill the barrels. Don't know where the next water'll be."

He studied Reb's face a moment. "Son, don't reckon you're ever gonna take on a tan, so keep that big floppy hat pulled down so's to shade your face. I've seen men in the army with compexions like yours," he shook his head, "they never took on a tan either."

A slight smile pushed its way through the grime and tiredness covering Reb's face. "Does that mean you're not gonna be able to make a man outta me, Hawk?"

"Why heck no, youngster. Way I figure it, you're just about as good a man right now as I've ever seen." His gaze dropped to Reb's hands. He shook his head. "Shoulda got you a smaller handgun though. That .44 is just flat too big an' heavy for a boy to handle." He thought a moment, then nodded. "Reckon we can take care o' that when we get to Fort Stockton." He toed the stirrup. "We better hightail it if we're gonna make that stream 'fore black dark."

Before allowing them to build a fire that night, McClure scouted up-and downstream along Buckhorn Draw, then went to the top and made sure no Comanche were in the area. Even then they had a small, smokeless fire—enough to cook supper and boil coffee—and when all was ready he doused the fire with sand.

Sitting there in the dark, they talked in hushed tones. Bessie took a swallow of her coffee, then swept their shadowy forms with a glance. "Y'all know what, we

ain't seen a pine tree, no big oaks, nothin' I'd call a sho
'nuff tree in 'bout two, maybe three weeks.''

Hawk chuckled. ''Folks, we're a long way from anything we Southerners would call a tree, but I promise
you, we'll get to some o' the prettiest country you ever
did see. It's got pines, aspen, oaks, cottonwoods,
spruce—why heck, just 'bout any kind o' tree it'd take
to make a land beautiful.'' They fell silent for a long
moment, then McClure added, ''Want to caution you
though, it's not gonna look like the country we left. You
gonna think God got angry and tilted most o' that country up on end. It's got mountains like you've never before seen.''

''Lordy day, Mr. Hawk, I ain't never seen no mountains of no kind befoe.''

Reb sat forward, probably to see them better. ''Hawk,
this land we're travelin' across, nothin' but stuff you've
told us is mesquite, scrub oak, yucca, Spanish dagger,
prickly pear, every known kind of cactus, an' alkali
soil—is there anything out here for a cow or horse to
eat that'll keep 'em alive?''

He nodded. ''Sure is. Someday I reckon we'll be
seein' cattle all across this land—when the Comanche
decide to leave us alone. Fact is, cattle'll eat those mesquite beans an' get fat on 'em.''

Ned chuckled. ''Sho do hope you ain't gonna decide
to set up to ranch here in this country. Don't b'lieve I
could stand a whole summer like we done seen.''

McClure stood. ''No, Uncle, don't worry your head
'bout that. We're goin' to Colorado. Now reckon we
better get some sleep. Tomorrow's gonna be another
hard day.''

The next morning, before heading out, they filled the
water barrels, bathed, and washed clothes. When Reb
came back to the wagon, McClure noticed the boy's
hair—wet, stringy, and falling almost to his shoulders.
''Boy, when we get to Fort Stockton, reckon you gonna
have to get a haircut.''

Reb shook his head. ''Nope, I figure to let it grow

long like I hear Wild Bill Hickok wears his."

Hawk smiled. "You might change your mind with a few more days of this heat," he shrugged, "but don't worry 'bout it, I've seen many a boy out this way who figured it the way you do." He almost let himself reach out and grip the boy's shoulder to see if it had hardened any since he'd last touched him. But he drew back as though from a hot stove. He still couldn't imagine why the boy wouldn't harden up, but one thing was for damned sure—he didn't want to find out. Who knew how sick the boy might be? Nope, he didn't want to know.

Rebecca noticed the way he quickly drew his hand back after reaching toward her. In the last couple of weeks she'd become aware that he stayed away from her and never touched her. Was he beginning to suspect she was a woman? Had she said something to hurt his feelings? Although reluctant to admit it to herself, she missed his big strong hand gripping her shoulder. She wished they could go back to his testing her "manly strength." She sighed and climbed to the wagon seat; she'd ride the stallion later in the day.

Every time Hawk returned from riding out ahead of them to scout, he'd relieve Ned at leading the team, letting the old darkie climb to the wagon seat and rest. The more Rebecca observed the thoughtful, kindly things the big Alabamian did to lighten their load, the higher rose her opinion of him. She'd never known a man so tender, and fought herself from wishing she could find out if he would be as tender and caring toward her—if he knew she was a woman.

She'd been told many times how pretty she was, but she wondered if the grimy, ill-kept person McClure thought was a boy would ever be pretty again—and would she be pretty in his eyes?

She took her rifle in hand and placed it across her knees as Hawk insisted she and Bessie do while riding.

Mid-afternoon, a wagon going in the opposite direction came alongside. A man drove, and a washed-out, sun-weathered woman sat alongside of him while two towheaded boys peeked over their shoulder. "Where you folks headin'?" the man asked.

"Colorado," Bessie answered. "Is it very far ahead?"

"Far? Why, I hope to smile. That country's a whole lot farther'n we ever been. We goin' back where they's real folks 'sides Injuns an' outlaws. Them towns west o' us, what few they is, is rough, scorched, an' ain't fit fer no human bein's. I'm ready to smell pine trees, fresh mowed hay, wisteria, magnolias—any kind o' flowers. I wuz you, I'd turn that there vehicle round an' git back where you come from."

Forgetting her role as a young boy, Rebecca shook her head. "Nope, we set out for that mountain country, an' that's where we're goin'."

The man raised his hand in farewell. "Then good luck to you, youngster. Hope you make it." They drove on.

About a mile ahead of them, McClure climbed from his horse, knelt at the side of pony tracks, ran his fingers around the edges, and stood. He didn't hope to be able to guess at how long ago they'd been made, but tried it anyway, having no better way to gauge the riders' whereabouts. The tracks were of five horses, and the fact they were shod made no difference. The Comanche stole horses from each side of the border, from Mexican and whites. They were as likely to ride horses with shoes as those without. He reined Blacky back toward the wagon.

He didn't want to yell for fear of his voice carrying in the stillness, so he waited until he was within talking distance then said, "Ned, get in the wagon with Bessie and Reb. All o' you pull stuff in front of you, jack a shell into the chamber of your rifles, and stay still. I'll lead the team."

He slipped from the saddle and tied his horse to the tailgate, alongside Reb's stallion. "Reb, you keep watch out the back in case those redskin devils try to take the horses." He stared into the boy's eyes. "Don't need to tell you, son, shoot at their chest. Don't waste a shot tryin' to hit their head." He twisted to look at Bessie and Ned. "Same goes for you. Got it?"

They each nodded, then Bessie spoke up. "Mr. Hawk, we all a-layin' here in the wagon gonna get some kind o' pertection that way. What you gonna do standin' right out there so's they can see you?"

Feeling no humor, McClure let his mouth crinkle at the corners. "Well, Bessie, I figure to get in between the two lead oxen 'fore the shootin' starts—if there is shooting. Reckon that'll give me some protection."

Reb looked him in the eye. "Hawk McClure, now you be downright careful out there where God an' everybody can see you."

He nodded. "Figure to, son. Been shot a couple o' times. It isn't anything I relish experiencing again." He walked to the head of the team, took the lead rope in hand, and stepped toward the west.

Hair at the nape of his neck tingled as though trying to stand on end. His back muscles knotted and pained between his shoulder blades. His stomach churned. At any moment a bullet or an arrow might tear through his body. Then the sound of pony hooves, muffled by alkali dust, penetrated his consciousness. With a shell in the chamber of his Winchester, he slipped between the two lead oxen. The sounds came from his right. He gave that direction most of his attention.

Five Comanche warriors broke through the chaparral, all with heavy leather leggings, headbands, and bare upper bodies. Three carried rifles; the other two held bows with nocked arrows. They rode into the middle of the trail, apparently having seen only one person. McClure stopped the team, pulled back the hammer of his rifle, and pointed it toward them.

Sweat ran from every pore in his body. He had no chance to get more than two of the Indians if they looked for a fight, and the nonchalant but wary way they held their weapons said they not only looked for a fight—but an easy one.

The lead rider stared at him a moment. "We not hurt. You give horses."

Anger overrode McClure's fear. "Like hell. You move toward those horses, there'll be cuttin' off of fingers an' wailin' an' cryin' in your lodges tonight."

Their leader stared at him through flat, black eyes. "We take if you not give."

To hell with putting off what can't be avoided. Mc-Clure moved his rifle barrel to center on the leader's chest, squeezed the trigger, jacked a shell into the chamber, and knocked the second rider from his pony's back. While that warrior fell from his horse, a third clutched his chest and fell. Bessie and Ned had joined the fight. The last two headed for the tailgate. Hawk swung his rifle to cover them, but not soon enough. The body of the wagon stood between.

Reb! The boy covered the rear of the wagon alone. McClure's gut rolled and tightened against his fear. He broke and ran for the wagon's rear. Two shots sounded, almost as one. "Lord, please don't let the boy be hurt." His words slipped out between stiff, dry lips.

He'd not reached the middle of the Studebaker when two Comanche warriors came into view—both on the ground. He rounded the tailgate and looked into Reb's eyes. The boy stood there, rifle smoking. The acrid stench of cordite bridged the space between them. His eyes wide, face pale, Reb swallowed twice, straightened his shoulders, and, to all appearances calm, jacked another shell into the chamber. "You save me more'n these two, Hawk?"

His eyes swept the boy from head to foot. "You all right, boy?" Reb nodded and looked at the downed Indians, then ran to the side of the trail, retched, and threw up. Still bent over, he looked back at McClure. "Sorry 'bout that, Hawk. Reckon you haven't made much of a man outta me yet."

He looked from Reb to the two warriors. Neither stirred, but he went to them and toed them to their backs. Both dead—drilled dead center in their chests. He walked toward Reb, and said into the maw of the wagon when he passed it for Bessie and Ned to keep their eyes on the three Comanche out front. If they moved, put another shot into them.

Reaching Reb, he said, "Nothin' to be ashamed of, son. The first time I looked on a man I'd shot caused me to do the same thing. To my way o' thinkin', you're one helluva man right now. I don't count bein' able to kill a man as part of bein' a man. You did what you had to do. That's what counts."

Reb wiped his mouth, nodded, and went to the rear of the wagon to check the horses, neither of which had received a scratch during the shoot-out. McClure went back to the front of the wagon to check the three warriors there.

He stood a moment staring at the three Comanche. None stirred, but he continued to watch. Too many times he'd seen men killed by those they assumed to be dead. After a few minutes, he palmed his Colt and walked to them.

The first warrior he approached lay dead, a hole in the center of his chest. The second lay on his stomach, one hand folded under him clutching his rifle. Not turning his back to the second one, Hawk walked to the third, rolled him over with his boot toe, and marked him off as dead. That extra hole in his head above his right eye gave proof he would not be a further threat. McClure had again stepped toward the wagon to see how Bessie and Ned fared when the second warrior's hand twitched.

He thumbed off a shot into the warrior's back, causing his body to jerk as though hit with a hammer. Then, even though hit hard, the Comanche rolled to his back, brought his beat-up old rifle to his shoulder, but never got off the shot. McClure put another slug into his chest. That one too would give no more trouble. He collected their weapons, then climbed to the boot. "All's quiet now, folks. Come on out. Let's get this mess cleared off the trail."

Not taking his eyes off the dead Comanche, Ned

asked, "Ain't we gonna bury them, Mr. Hawk? They wuz jest doin' what they been taught all their lives."

McClure stared at him a moment, proud that he could be concerned about those who'd only moments before tried to take their property—even their lives. He shook his head. "Don't want to take the chance, Uncle. If they have friends within the sound of our shots, we gonna be in for more of this right soon. Help me drag 'em off the trail, then clean and load your rifles. Want 'em ready if we need 'em."

They dragged the dead Indians a couple of hundred yards off the trail, and again headed west. McClure used every bit of talent he had as a scout the rest of the afternoon. He used all the things Ben Baty had taught him as a boy, and all he'd used while working with the Army. He rode circles around the wagon, cut across the trail into the chaparral, read the ground every step of the way, and looked for broken twigs on the oaks, or crushed scrub. He found no indication the Comanche they'd faced had more warriors in the area.

7

SLOUCHED AGAINST THE bole of one of the gigantic live oaks in front of the Alamo, Jedediah Powers studied the Squires when they led their horses from the livery. He frowned, thinking they were going somewhere in town. They had only bedrolls, saddle guns, and one canteen each.

He thought to see where they went, changed his mind, then, just in case they were fools enough to head west with what they had on their horses, he went to the back of the livery. He saddled his horse, hung four canteens from the saddle horn, checked his gear, tied equipment to his packhorse, and rode from the stable. In less than fifteen minutes he watched them ride west away from the sun, and San Antonio.

He'd prepared for this soon after he got into town. He had provisions, ammunition, and plenty of water. Every merchant, cowboy, or bull whacker he talked to had told him if he headed west to take plenty of water, and shells for his rifle and six-gun. They didn't pull any punches when they told him he'd need both.

And the drover with whom he'd had a drink the night before had recommended he get himself a pair of heavy leather chaps and a leather vest. He heeded this advice also.

For a half day, he rode close enough to the Squires to keep them in sight, and he found out why the drover had said to get himself the chaps and vest. He stayed off the trail, riding in the chaparral where there was little chance he'd be seen.

He sweated such that his clothes were soaked before ten o'clock, and about noon he allowed himself a swallow of water. Several times during the morning, the Squires drank from their canteens, long and deeply. Powers grinned. The damned fools would find out what it was like to be thirsty if they kept that up, and judging by the way they'd equipped themselves, he doubted they'd thought to ask where there might be water. If they lucked out, there might be water at Buckhorn Draw, but from there only luck would save them.

Except for an occasional swallow, the next three days Powers used his water only for the horses, and smirked with satisfaction when Yolanda shook her empty canteen and hung it back on her saddle. By nightfall of the third day, he knew, they should reach the draw. He figured to slip up on their camp and see how they fared.

That night, he ghosted through the chaparral, careful to avoid stepping on dried brush, which might make a noise, and against the white alkali soil he found it easy to identify Spanish dagger, the huge yucca, and prickly pear cactus before brushing into them.

The flicker of firelight and a slight smell of smoke warned him long before he blundered into their camp, then the sound of voices. He moved only close enough to hear their words.

The short stumpy one Powers had been told was Bert looked across the fire at Yolanda. "Sister, I told you we wuz gonna need extra canteens. I got mighty dry 'fore we got here."

She cast a look at him that spit daggers. "Bert, I hear any more o' that 'I told you' stuff, I'll take your canteen an' leave you out here with nothin'." She sat back and squirmed down more comfortably against her saddle. " 'Sides that, we found water, didn't we? There'll be water along the way; all we gotta do is go dry awhile.''

"We better make sure we got enough for ourselves 'fore we let them horses drink it all.'' Tom continued sharpening his pocketknife on his shoe sole while he talked. "Reckon I'da let them drink tonight after we got all we needed."

Bert glanced at him. "Tom, you're 'bout the dumbest bastard I ever seen. All we got 'tween us an' a long dry walk's them horses, an' I'm gonna tell you right now they's amany skeleton out here of folks too dumb to water their horses first.''

Powers had heard all he needed to hear. The Squires were in trouble and didn't even know it. Too, he heard no indication there was any family love between them. When the going got really rough, they'd be at each other's throats like a pack of wolves. He chuckled to himself, and wormed his way back toward his camp— about a half mile upstream of the Squires' camp.

Two days later, well ahead of where Powers rode, he saw seven or eight buzzards floating on migrant up-drafts. Soon after, a slight breeze brought to his nostrils the putrid stench of rotting flesh. It wasn't the Squires he smelled—they weren't far enough ahead, nor had they had time, even in the heat, to smell like this if they'd been attacked by Comanche. Another vulture joined those above, and two or three floated in a down-ward spiral toward the carrion they fed on.

Careful to not ride up on those he tracked, he stayed to the brush. Soon, not a hundred yards ahead of him, the vultures tore at something on the ground. He rode close enough to see the remains of the Comanche war-riors. Holding his hands over his nose and mouth, he pushed his horse to a faster gait, and soon brought the Squires again into view.

As soon as they rounded a bend in the trail, he nudged his horse closer, but thought of the Indians, thought they had crossed the wrong man when they tangled with Mc-

Clure, for to his thinking Hawken had to have been the
one who'd written the last chapter in their lives.

About the time Powers came on the dead Comanche,
McClure led his party into Fort Stockton. He stopped
first at the town well and horse trough. "Uncle, you
folks drink, then let the oxen have theirs." He let the
horses drink their fill, took a drink himself, and again
let the horses drink, after they'd blown for a few
minutes.

He looked up into the wagon. Reb sat alongside Bessie, both looking as though every bit of moisture in their
bodies had evaporated. "Y'all climb down, drink, wash
your faces, an' I'll see if there's a room you can sleep
in tonight." He grinned. "A bath wouldn't hurt either
o' you, although it might take a couple bars o' lye soap
to cut through that grime 'fore you ever got to skin."

Reb looked at him a moment. "Hawk, you got a laugh
comin' at our expense, but I'm here to tell you, you
don't look a danged bit better'n we do. Why, I'll bet if
I stand over yonder in front o' that general store, downwind of you, I'll smell stale sweat, grime, an' tobacco
from your dirty body too."

Hawk let a thin smile crinkle his eyes at the corners.
"Reckon you're right, son. Don't any o' us look fit to
be among polite company." He headed for his horse,
then said over his shoulder. "First, I'm gonna put these
horses in the livery, get 'em some grain if they got any,
then I'm gonna bathe, shave, find somebody to wash my
clothes, an' after all that, I'm gonna see if they got anything in that saloon yonder to cut the dust outta my
throat."

"You reckon I'm old enough, an' man enough, to
have a drink with you, Hawk?"

He looked at Reb a moment. "Son, for danged sure,
you're man enough for that drink, but they just flat don't
let youngsters drink at your age, an' even if they let you
drink, I won't."

Reb giggled. "Just pullin' on your rope, Hawk. Don't want to drink any o' that stuff anyway."

McClure stared at Reb a moment. At times the boy sounded so grown up, and at others he let the little boy in him come out. That giggle had been pure little boy. Hawk would have to remember to not push so much man stuff onto him in the days ahead.

Feeling like a human again, after his shave, bath, and change to clean clothes, McClure stood at the bar and sipped his drink. He'd come to the saloon more to ferret out the best trail to take from here, see if there was much Indian trouble, and what he should expect with the water situation. He'd not stood there long when a man, obviously a cattleman by his dress, shouldered to the bar at his side. "Seen ya ride in, stranger. Figure on settlin' round here?"

McClure glanced at him, then back to his drink. "No, I'm thinkin' to ride right on to those mountains in the Colorado country, see if I can start a horse ranch up that way. Hear tell there're a lot o' wild mustangs up yonder."

The man nodded, and held out his hand. "I'm Park Miller, ramrod for the D-Bar-D." He grinned. "I wuz headed that way myself when I found a job. Never got no farther."

McClure had only told Miller his name when a big, bearded, dirty man elbowed his way between him and Miller. "Gonna take up the whole damned bar? Make room for a man what's a real man." He spread his elbows to take up two more spaces.

McClure glanced along the polished surface. There was plenty of room for the dirty man to stand without pushing himself between him and Miller. Anger boiled within Hawk, barely under the surface. Blood rushed to cloud his thinking. He pushed his feelings aside and picked up the drink the man had shoved him away from. "Mister, why don't you move down here and let me talk to Mr. Miller there on the other side o' you?"

The dirty man raked McClure with a glance. "Don't

nobody tell Nat Carlson where to stand. You lookin' for trouble?''

McClure studied him a moment, shook his head, and said, ''Not lookin' for it, Carlson, but looks like I found it. What's your beef?''

''You. A stranger come in here lookin' to take whatever jobs're here. I wuz gonna see could I hire on with the D-Bar-D, then you come pushin' yore way in.''

The anger pushed its way up behind McClure's eyes, then clouded his brain. ''Gonna tell you somethin'. I'm not lookin' for a job—an' I didn't push my way in. Now, why don't you go out to the hog pen where you belong, an' sober up. Then if you want trouble—come lookin' for me.''

''Don't need to come lookin' fer you. Done found you, an' I still want trouble.''

McClure noticed the tied-down hog-leg at Carlson's thigh, and didn't wait to see if he had gun trouble. He brought his right fist up from beside his leg and connected with the dirty man's chin. A split opened below Carlson's lower lip, his teeth stuck through the cut. McClure followed through with a left to the gut, then swung his right to Carlson's cheek. Blood poured from that cut.

McClure moved in, not giving the filthy one time to set his feet. He swung a right to the heart. Carlson sucked for breath, took a wild swing, and caught McClure on the shoulder, staggering him.

Carlson bored in, swinging with both hands. McClure caught a left and a right to the face, knocked Carlson's arms aside, and brought a right up from the knees. It caught Carlson on the point of the chin. He went down, but not out. He grabbed for his six-shooter. McClure stepped in and swung his foot at Carlson's head. This time the filthy lout went out like a lantern in a strong gust of wind.

McClure bent and picked up Carlson's six-shooter. He opened the loading gate, spilled the loads into his hand, then walked to the bar and handed the bartender the gun. ''Better keep this till we see if he wants more trouble.''

The barkeep nodded. "He'll want more. He wouldn't have fought you with his fists if you'd of give 'im a chance. He usually takes care of his trouble with this handgun. You better leave, mister. He's fast, and mean."

McClure squinted at the man across the bar. "Mister, I came in here right peaceable, wanted a drink an' a little conversation. I've not had either—but I figure to before I leave. Give 'im back his six-shooter if you want to, an' I'll see to it he won't bother you, ever again."

The bartender studied McClure a moment. "If I thought you could beat 'im, I'd do just that. Sure would take care of a lot o' my troubles." He poured Hawk a drink. "On the house."

McClure picked up his drink, nodded his thanks, and turned his back to the bar. His eyes locked on the man he'd dropped. The lout stirred, opened his eyes, stared vacantly at the ceiling, then rolled groggily to his knees. When he gained his feet, he swung his head from side to side, then his eyes focused on McClure. His hand swept for his holster. When it came up empty, he looked down at his thigh. "Where's m'damned six-shooter?"

McClure stared at him through slitted eyelids. "I gave it to the bartender when you proved too dumb to handle it." He took a swallow of his drink. "Tell you what, you can walk through that door an' forget what happened in here, an' I'll forget it—or I'll tell the bartender to give your handgun back to you an' we'll find out how dumb you really are."

Carlson flexed his shoulders, opened and closed his fists a couple of times, and spit a stream of tobacco juice on the floor. "Want my gun—want it now."

Over his shoulder, McClure told the bartender to give it to him, then to Carlson he said, "Walk to the bar, load your handgun keeping your back to me, drop it in your holster, then turn to face me. You make one move I can mistake for meaning to shoot me before I say so, an' I'll shoot you deader'n a church-house mouse."

Carlson, even though beaten and bruised, tried to

swagger to the bar. There, he held his hand out and the bartender handed him his side gun. McClure watched his every move in the mirror behind the bar.

Carlson slowly punched shells into the cylinder, dropped the six-shooter into his holster, and turned to face McClure. He stretched lips over snaggly, tobacco-stained teeth, spit a stream of tobacco juice on the floor, and said, "Now we gonna see who's the biggest an' baddest man aroun' here."

His gut churning, his mouth dry as a lake bed in August, McClure felt his anger cool. He didn't want to kill—or be killed. He didn't even know what this was about. He thought to give it one more try to stop this short of a shooting. "Carlson, I don't know you, don't want to kill you. You can keep that gun in its holster, an' walk outta here. I wasn't lookin' for a job, an' I don't figure Mr. Miller would have given you one if he had one to offer. Now, why don't you let it drop?"

Carlson grinned, again showing his rotten teeth. "Scared, huh? Figgered you for no guts from the start. Go ahead, pull that six-shooter."

McClure shook his head. "Nope. You insist on a shootin', you better get after it."

Carlson's hand swept down and up. His gun almost level, a round black hole punched through his shirt pocket. Knocked backward, he tried again to bring his six-shooter to bear on McClure—another hole, a twin to the first one, punched into his other pocket. He stumbled backward, frantically pulling the trigger. Bullets sprayed into the ceiling, then a dead silence, except for the sound of his revolver hammer falling on spent shells.

Through the pall of gunsmoke, McClure watched Carlson catch his balance, stagger forward, then fall on his face. Hawk snorted from the back of his nose, trying to clear it of the acrid smell of cordite. Then he walked to Carlson's side, kicked the handgun from his fingers, and stepped back. Not until then did the crowd begin to move toward the tables they'd vacated to get out of the line of fire—and each of them talked at the top of his voice. McClure only then realized he still held his unfinished drink in his left hand. The batwing doors burst inward.

A man every bit as large and dirty as Carlson erupted into the room. "What the hell's goin' on? What wuz the shootin' about?" He glanced at Carlson's body. "That Carlson—that my partner?"

At a glance, McClure didn't like this man any better'n he had Carlson—but this man wore a badge, and McClure had killed his partner. Hawk placed his glass on the bar. "Better fill this," he said, and turned to face the lawman. "Yeah, Marshal, that's Carlson, an' I shot 'im. He brought it to me, an' there isn't a man in here who'll tell you anything but what he had his gun outta its holster 'fore I ever made a move for mine."

The marshal glanced around the room, then looked at Park Miller. "How 'bout it, Miller? Don't b'lieve anybody in this town could've beat Carlson in a fair an' square gunfight. You gonna tell me this man did it?"

Miller stared at the marshal a long moment. "Marshal Ridges, I'm tellin' you it was as fair a fight as I ever seen. Too, you gonna find out this man here beat hell outta Carlson then begged 'im to leave it at that, but your partner wouldn't have it that way. He pushed this gunfight far as he could—an' lost."

Ridges swept the room with a look. "Anybody in here see it different?" When no one spoke up, he looked at McClure. "Reckon you better come over to my office. Don't know yet whether I'm gonna hold you."

McClure reached for his drink, took a swallow, and stared at Ridges. If he went to the marshal's office, there might be a wanted poster there. He had no doubt but what posters had been sent out from Shreve's Landing, and had preceded him here. He was damned if he'd go to any jail this marshal had charge of. "Ridges, first place, I'm not goin' anywhere with you. These men in here told you how it was, an' I'm tellin' you it happened just the way Mr. Miller said. If you're arrestin' me, say so."

Ridges squinted at him with a puzzled frown. "Ain't I seen you somewhere 'fore?"

McClure went quiet inside. If the marshal thought he'd seen him, it had to be from a picture, or description on a poster, and going to Ridges's office would put him in the right place for the lawman to put it all together. "You might've seen me somewhere. Don't know where you've been, but I've prob'ly been there. I get around pretty much."

The marshal nodded. "Yeah, reckon that might be it, but you better come on over to the office with me. We'll talk 'bout it."

McClure's right hand hung at his side, his fingers brushing the handle of his Colt. "Like I said, Ridges, I'm not goin' anywhere with you. That man lying yonder was your partner. Don't figure I'll get any kind o' fair treatment at your hands, so reckon I'll stay here, have a couple of drinks, then be on my way."

The lawman stared at him a moment. "You resistin' arrest?"

McClure shrugged. "Call it what you want—then go get yourself a whole bunch o' deputies 'fore you come back to take me in. I'm not gonna be easy to take." He held his glass in his left hand, brought it to his lips, and took a swallow of his drink. "I've not done anything unlawful, here or anywhere else, so be damned sure of your reason for comin' for me."

Ridges stared through hate-filled eyes; their whites had turned red. His glance swept the room. "Every man in here raise your right hand, gonna deputize all o' you, then I want this man took to my jail." Not a man raised his hand, but to a man, each of them turned his back to the lawman. His face got redder by the second, and veins stood out in his forehead. "Damn you, I said for you to raise your hand." Still not a man moved. Ridges stared at their backs a long moment, then spun and headed for the door. "I'll be back." He pushed through the batwing doors.

McClure pulled his Colt, dumped the spent cartridges

from it, reloaded, and looked at Miller, who'd edged his way to his side. "Was I you, McClure, I'd make tracks outta here. They's some in this room what'll side with Ridges when he comes back, an' a few more around town who will."

Although he didn't feel like it, Hawk smiled. "Mr. Miller, my mama always told me to heed good advice. I reckon you just gave me some of the best I'm gonna get, so I'll be moseyin' along. Thanks for the conversation." He tipped his hat, went out the back door to the livery, collected his horse, slung some provisions on his packhorse, and rode to the back stairs of the hotel. He had to see Bessie, and tell her to head for Fort Davis when they left, and that he'd meet them along the trail.

Taking as little time as he could, he told Bessie to make sure they got plenty of provisions, and to stock up on water, and bullets.

Back at his horse, he'd barely settled into the saddle and gathered the lead rope on his packhorse when a mob burst out the back door of the saloon. He spurred his gelding into the chaparral before they could get their guns into action. A few shots, making a slapping sound when they hit the huge prickly pear cactus close to him, were the only sounds he heard, along with a few shouts before he put enough space between him and the mob to drop them from sight.

He wended his way through the brush, dodging the thorny, prickly bushes. His hearing attuned for any noise behind. After the first shouts, shots, and curses, the only thing he heard was birdsong, and the occasional lowing of a lonely cow.

He'd told his "family" to get a good night's sleep, that he'd meet them somewhere along the trail to Fort Davis, and added they probably wouldn't catch up with him until late the next day.

He set his course in a general southwesterly direction, staying as close to the trail as he deemed safe. Twice in the next couple of hours he heard lone horsemen approaching along the road. He kneed his gelding farther into the brush, held his hand over its nose, and waited until they rode on.

Then, about sundown, a rider passed headed toward Fort Davis, running his horse at a pace that would kill it if he didn't slow down. He figured that rider carried news about him, of his resisting arrest—and probably that he had a wanted notice out on him. For the first time since leaving Alabama he felt like an outlaw.

So far, he'd dodged going into a few of the towns along the way, especially those in Mississippi, but that was because of the carpetbagger law in those towns. Now, in far west Texas he'd set himself up to be hunted, but would have done the same thing again.

If that marshal back yonder in Stockton had his way, McClure knew he'd hang. Yeah, Ridges's desire for vengeance would abort any chance that justice would be shown him.

He rode deeper into the chaparral, came across a deep-cut arroyo, and followed it hoping to find a sump with enough water for his horse and enough left for coffee. He found what he wanted.

The brackish water made a passable pot of coffee, and the two horses didn't seem to mind it as long as it was wet. McClure opted for a couple of swallows from his canteen.

With dark settling in, he sat by his small, smokeless fire and sipped his second cup of coffee. A rustle in the brush broke the stillness. He put down his cup, pulled his Colt, and slipped behind a large yucca, glad he'd not given in to the comforting act of staring into his fire but had let his eyes penetrate the dark area beyond the few flickering flames.

"Hello the camp."

"Ride in slow-like, hands clear of your sides." At McClure's words, a rider who looked like he'd been in the brush for a year walked his horse into the meager light. The man wore a bushy gray beard, his clothes were stiff from days of sweat, and alkali dust had formed a crusty cementlike coating where the sweat and dust got together in the creases of his face. McClure judged him to be on the shady side of fifty.

"Stranger, I just want to share a cup o' yore coffee, an' talk a bit. Ain't talked to nobody in a long time."

McClure studied the man a moment. He felt no threat from him, so he said, "Step down an' rest your saddle." He slipped his .44 back in the holster, but left the thong off the hammer. Only then did he move from behind the yucca. The old man studied McClure a moment, smiled, and said, "You got no trouble outta me, stranger. I figger we got the same reasons for bein' out here alone."

"Yeah, an' what would those reasons be, stranger?" Hawk kept his hand close to his Colt.

"Tell you. A man what ain't on the run would be back yonder at Fort Stockton havin' hisself a drink, an' maybe even have a woman 'fore the night wuz through." He held out his hand. "Name's Rolf Mixus." He held out his right hand for a handshake—but he wore his holster on the left. McClure extended his left hand.

"Oooowee, you are the careful one, ain't ya?" Mixus grinned and clasped Hawk's hand with his left. That gesture relaxed McClure's caution a hair.

"Hear it pays to be a little careful. Set an' pour yourself a cup o' that mud."

Mixus took a cup from his bedroll, squatted by the fire, and poured it full of Hawk's coffee. He cocked an eye at McClure. "Been trailin' you ever since you left Stockton. Seen them men back yonder follow you 'bout long enough to catch a few thorns in their town clothes then turn back. What you do to rile 'em up so much?"

McClure wondered whether to tell Mixus what happened in town, then decided to. If the man wasn't what he seemed, the truth might cause him to reveal his feelings in a facial expression, or nervous movement of his hands.

He looked hard at the old man. "Tell you why I'm on the run, Mixus. I had a slight argument with the marshal's partner, beat 'im in a fistfight, then had to shoot 'im. He wouldn't have it any other way."

Mixus gave a jerky nod, then squinted at McClure. "You shot Carlson, eh? Damned good riddance I'd say. Had it comin' a long time." He took a swallow of his coffee, blew a gust of air through his mouth, and smacked his lips. "Whew-ee, that's good—hotter'n hell too." He put his cup aside while he packed his pipe, then pinned McClure with a questioning look. "Carlson wuz said to be mighty fast, although I never seen none o' his graveyards. You must be better'n most with that side gun you're packin'."

McClure took his last sentence as a question. He shook his head. "Don't know. I might be fairly good. I never gave it any thought. Know one thing though, I never have pulled it till the man I faced started his draw. Carlson had his revolver out of his holster before I drew. It was self-defense all the way, an' there were a bunch of witnesses."

The old man eyed him a moment. "Gonna tell you somethin', boy. You let Carlson get his gun out 'fore you started yore draw, an' you beat 'im, you can figger yoreself as bein' right good."

Mixus shook his head. "Pshaw now, young'un, as for self-defense, it don't make no difference in that town. If'n you're sliced from the same cow patty as Ridges, it don't make no nevermind whether it's self-defense or no. If you ain't of the kind o' cow dung as he is—you're guilty."

McClure nodded. "Way I figured it. I ran."

The old outlaw drained his cup, and went to the sump for another pot of water. Hawk took that to mean he wasn't through talking, so he got fresh coffee grounds from his packsaddle.

Mixus again sat, then cast a devilish-looking squint at McClure. "You're new to this runnin'-from-the-law game, ain't yu?"

McClure nodded. "Fairly new at it, old-timer."

Mixus put fire to his pipe. "Figgered as much. Now I'm gonna give yu a few lessons in what to do, an' what not to do, that is if'n you gonna keep yore neck outta a noose.''

McClure smiled inwardly, knowing he would get this lesson in outlawery whether he wanted it or not. Besides, he liked the old outlaw.

Mixus went on to tell him to never build a fire where there might be Indians or the law close-by; to always keep a good supply of jerky with him; to trust no one; to carry weapons that used the same size shells; to always sit with his back to a wall when in a town; and to never go into a strange place without taking the thong off the hammer of his Colt. He talked for an hour, talked until Hawk grinned across the fire at him, and said, ''You keep teachin' me those things, we'll never get a wink of sleep tonight, an' I have to meet three friends of mine along the Fort Davis trail tomorrow.''

Mixus grinned. ''Reckon I did get carried away a little, son, but I like you, don't want to see you head out on your new perfession 'thout knowin' what to do. 'Sides, I knowed all along you wuz gonna meet them two darkies, an' that there young boy you rode into Fort Stockton with. But let me tell you, son, don't you go into Fort Davis with 'em. Meet 'em on the other side when they leave.''

McClure nodded. ''Figured on it, old-timer.''

Mixus stood. ''You gonna let me share yore camp tonight, or you want me to ride on?''

McClure chuckled. ''Reckon if you're not too stove up, you can reach your horse an' get your bedroll—or I'm not above helpin' an old man, an' I'll get it for you.''

''Why, goldanged you, you young whippersnapper, I'll outride, outshoot, an' . . . an' . . .''

McClure laughed until tears came to his eyes. ''Aw, com'on, old-timer. I just wanted to see if you had a sense o' humor. Grab your bedroll.''

The next morning, while saddling their horses, McClure noticed Mixus's glances at him framed in a questioning scowl. ''Okay, what's troublin' you?''

The old outlaw gave him a halfhearted scowl. "Well, reckon I wuz waitin' fer you to give me a invite to ride along with you."

Hawk grinned. "Okay. How'd you like to ride with me far as this side o' Fort Davis?" Although he'd only met Mixus the night before, McClure decided he'd like company out in the brush where he would spend most of the coming weeks—at least until well clear of the area Ridges had friends.

"All right, now I'm gonna give you some more advice about bein' a good outlaw."

McClure figured whatever he said, he was going to get the advice anyway. "Let's hear it, old-timer."

Mixus toed the stirrup before answering. "Jest gonna say, 'fore you go ridin' out into the trail to meet yore friends, reckon I'd hang behind an' scout out if'n anybody left town soon after 'em. Don't you never get the idee that marshal back yonder's a tenderfoot. He ain't give up findin' you yet."

McClure nodded. "Good idea. Reckon I'll drift on back yonder, an' take a look-see."

When Hawk kneed his gelding toward the outskirts of Fort Stockton, Rolf Mixus rode at his side.

REBECCA AND HER two companions ate at the small cafe down the street from the hotel before daylight the next morning, then she and Bessie climbed to the wagon seat while Ned led the team out of town. Rebecca slanted Bessie a worried look. "You reckon Hawk's gonna be all right, Auntie? The way they were shootin' at 'im yesterday, he might be lying out yonder somewhere, needin' us to doctor 'im."

Bessie shook her head and, with words more confident than she felt, said, "Now, don't you worry yo pretty head 'bout that man, little missy. I seen all along he could take care o' himself." She smiled and patted Rebecca on the shoulder. "Why, Lordy mercy, chile, ain't he done took care o' us right along with his own self? Naw now, we don't need worry none 'bout him."

Rebecca sighed—as much as the tight binding about her breasts would let her. "Don't know, Auntie, reckon I'm more fond of him than I oughtta be. All he has to do is walk into the camp and I feel safe, as though I was home with Papa lookin' after me."

Bessie grinned. "Tell you somethin', yo papa was a lot o' man, stack up with any, but Mr. Hawk's special.

I ain't never seen a man, white or black, who could walk in his boots."

Rebecca sighed again. "Hope you're right." She shook her head. "Nope, I know you're right, but I'm still worried 'bout 'im." Abruptly she giggled. "You reckon I'm beginning to shape up to be the kind of man Hawk figures to make me?"

Bessie chuckled. "Lordy day, missy, I shore do hope not. Why, it'd be a outright crime to make a boy outta a woman pretty as you. 'Sides you got a lot o' hearts to break yet. You ain't never gonna be a man."

Almost under her breath, Rebecca whispered, "Don't want to break any man's heart, just want Hawk to be proud of me."

Bessie put her skinny arm around Rebecca's shoulders. "Don't you go to thinkin' 'bout Mr. Hawk like that, chile. Yes'm, he's a lot o' man, but we got a lot of miles to put behind us 'fore you come outta yore cocoon and show everbody what a pretty lady you are."

"Oh, Auntie, I'm only thinkin' 'bout him like I would a big brother. Don't worry about how I'm feelin'." She stared at the chaparral on both sides of the trail. "Wonder where he is, an' when he's gonna join up with us again. Feel sortta lost not knowin' if, an' when, he's gonna show up."

A few miles back of the wagon, McClure had the same feelings as Rebecca. Already, he missed the boy, and Bessie, and Ned—but Reb most of all. He and Mixus sat their horses with brush sheltering them from the road.

They'd watched the wagon move along the dusty, rutted trail, and as it passed Mixus said out of the corner of his mouth, "We'll know soon how the marshal figgers you gonna play yore hand. He might have three, four, or maybe only one man watch the wagon. Know danged well I wasn't the only one what seen you ride in with that Studebaker." He took out his pipe, sucked on the empty bowl a moment, then put it back and pulled a plug of tobacco from his vest pocket. He offered Mc-

Clure a chew, and when he declined, Mixus bit off a hunk, settled it in his cheek, and said, "You might not get to join up with yore friends till we get past Fort Davis—less'n o' course we take care of the men trailin' the wagon."

Hawk thought on that a moment, then shook his head. "Figure we let 'em go ahead an' track the wagon. When I don't show up, they'll take word back to Ridges that I took off into the chaparral, maybe even caught some o' that lead they threw around out yonder yesterday afternoon. Figure that might get 'im off my tail."

The old man stared between his horse's ears a few long seconds, then nodded. "Figger you're right. I could ride ahead an' let yore folks know you're all right, but them what's trailin the wagon would see my tracks an' maybe mistake 'em fer yores." He chomped down hard on his chew, then shook his head. "Nope, reckon we jest better let them in the wagon worry 'bout you some. Better'n gettin' you hung."

Looking down the trail toward Fort Stockton, Mc-Clure squinted against the bright sun. "Yeah, reckon you're right. We'll—" He chopped his words off, and held up his hand for silence. Two riders rounded the trail, obviously not just taking a ride to Davis. They leaned over the shoulders of their horses, studied the ground, looked ahead, then bent their heads again to search the trail.

"Figgered as much," Mixus growled, "them men're lookin' fer yore tracks."

The two outlaws, one old, one young, sat their saddles for perhaps thirty minutes after the riders from town disappeared around another curve, then Mixus motioned McClure to follow.

He led them deeper into the brush, and then paralleled the trail. "Don't dare stay too close to the road, them're Ridges men we seen, an' like I thought, they're lookin' fer you. They might turn back, see us, then we'd have a shoot-out on our hands." He shook his head. "Ain't no need to take a chance." He smiled. "Tell you right now, youngster, I ain't stayed alive this long by takin' chances I didn't have to." He changed course a bit, then explained. "Know where they's a water hole up ahead. Horses need water—if'n we're the only ones what got that there hole in mind."

"What you mean, if we're the only ones?"

Mixus gave him a look of disgust. "Why, dang it, they's Comanche ridin' this here brush same as we are. Don't figger they'll wantta share water with us—they're downright cantankerous 'bout doin' such."

"What'll we do if there are Indians at the hole?"

Mixus looked at him squinty-eyed. "Reckon if we get lucky, we'll eeliminate 'em. But, pshaw, that means we gotta sneak up on 'em 'thout them seein' us first—that there takes some real doin'."

McClure's gut tightened enough to make his ribs hurt. Damn, couldn't he do anything without it resulting in trouble? Seemed like every time he ran, he ran *to* trouble rather than away from it. Maybe the answer was to stay put and fight like hell where he was. He looked at his new friend. "Looks like you're dealin' the cards. Lead on."

Another quarter of a mile into the brush and Mixus motioned McClure to rein in. Then, in a whisper, he said, "Gonna sneak up on that hole. See if we got it to ourselves."

"I better go with you in case you run into trouble."

Mixus shook his head. "I been doin' this a long time, know what I'm doin'. 'Sides, two of us'll be easier to see."

McClure knew the old man played it safe, and worried that he wasn't considered a good enough woodsman to do his part. He shrugged mentally. They'd have to spend a lot of time in such situations before the cagey old outlaw would trust him as good enough to slip up on an Indian. He'd have to prove himself.

Mixus disappeared into the brush as silently as a wisp of smoke. McClure wondered if he was that good. As much hunting as he'd done, and as much time in the woods as he'd spent, he thought he was. He waited a good forty-five minutes before his new friend slipped alongside. "Got three warriors alongside that there hole. We can wait till they drink, an' leave, or go in an' take 'em out."

He pushed his weathered and timeworn hat from his forehead. "Then agin, them Comanche might decide to camp right alongside that hole, and our horses'd go thirsty. My thinkin' is we oughtta take 'em out."

"Could you see what kind o' weapons they had?"

Mixus nodded. "Two with bows and arrows, the other'un had a old rifle of some sort."

McClure thought on that a minute. "Reckon we'll be just as dead if we get caught out here afoot—gotta take care of our horses."

Mixus studied him a moment. "Gonna tell you, youngster, don't take a bow an' arrow as bein' in our favor. Them Injuns can shoot and nock an arrow fast as we can lever the action on our long guns. Only thing them arrers come up short on is distance."

McClure nodded, and tied his horse's reins to a mesquite. "Let's go."

After about fifty feet, slipping from a prickly pear to a yucca, and around another mesquite to hunker behind a large Spanish dagger, Mixus glanced at Hawk with an appreciative expression. McClure knew from the look he'd passed the old man's test of what a man should know about slipping upon Indians.

They'd gone only a couple hundred yards more when Mixus signaled they should crawl the rest of the way. McClure stretched out, his Winchester cradled in the crook of his elbows, and inched his way along beside Mixus.

With the three Comanche in sight, the terrifying whirr of rattles on the other side of Mixus drew McClure's attention, but only with his ears. His eyes never left the three warriors.

Mixus rolled toward McClure, clubbing at the snake

with his rifle butt, shattering any thought of further silence.

The Comanche dropped to their knees—nocking arrows. Everything looked to move real slow-like in McClure's eyes. His rifle swung from the crook of his arms to rest against his shoulder. He fired. One Indian fell to the side. He swung his rifle a hair, and fired about the same time an arrow hit his shoulder. Hawk's shot missed. Mixus still clubbed at the rattler.

Through the most excruciating pain he'd ever felt, McClure jacked another shell into the chamber. Mixus joined the fight. His long gun roared in McClure's ear and a second Comanche, knocked from his knees, fell backward. The remaining Comanche's old rifle belched smoke out its bore. His shot missed, but two bullets hit him at the same time. McClure saw the two black holes punch into his chest before he fell.

The two outlaws didn't move. Each studied the three Indians—two on their backs, the other lying prone. None of them moved.

"Young'un, keep yore rifle on 'em. I'll go see have they shook hands with the Great Spirit." Without a glance at McClure, he stood, walked to the Comanche lying on his stomach, toed him over, and jumped to the side. Then the warrior took a second swipe at his legs with a large knife—looked like a Bowie to Hawk, who triggered off another shot into the Indian's chest.

Mixus went to the other two and found them both dead. He glanced over his shoulder at McClure. "Reckon we won the right to drink at this here hole." His eyes widened, then slitted. "See you done caught a arrer, young'un. Don't try to pull it out. I'll take care of it." He gathered the Comanche weapons, then went to McClure.

"That snake hit you, old-timer?"

"Naw, he missed. I didn't, but he shore messed up gettin' any closer to the Comanch." He squatted at McClure's side. "Sit up, I gotta see where the point o' that there arrer is." Then with Hawk sitting, he studied the arrow, grunted, and said, "If'n they didn't poison that arrer, we'll git it outta you an' you'll be all right—sore as hell, but all right." He studied the arrow a moment longer. "Shore wisht I had some whiskey, but ain't, so reckon we better git on with it."

He took the shaft in both hands. "Suck in yore gut, young'un. This here's gonna hurt, then the next thing's gonna hurt worse. Gotta break this off, then push the arrer head through an' pull it outta yore hide." Still talking, he snapped the shaft.

McClure tried to stifle the moan, but it came from his lips anyway. "That's all right, McClure, ain't never knowed a white man who didn't make some sort o' noise. You gonna do a whole lot worse when I push it through."

Hawk gritted his teeth. Damned if he would be put in the same group as those who made noise. Mixus pushed. McClure felt the head break the skin farther along his shoulder, then the old outlaw pulled it through. All the devils in hell must have danced on the remainder of the shaft—but McClure choked off any suggestion of a moan. If he'd made any noise at all, he feared it would have been a scream.

Mixus walked to a cactus of some sort, broke one of the spines and smeared the gooey, sticky stuff oozing from the broken spine onto each side of the wound. He finished dressing it, then looked McClure in the eye. "Young'un, you're jest one big ball o' guts. Never seen a man nowhere who didn't squall like a danged Comanch on the warpath when the arrer wuz pushed through."

Feeling wrung out, and knowing he must be pale as a ghost, McClure glanced at the sump. "We gonna camp here tonight? Sure could use a cup o' coffee."

Mixus shook his head. "Nope. We gonna gather them Indian ponies, water them an' our'n, then get the hell a long way from this here hole. They might be more o' them red devils around, an' they mighta heard the commotion we made.'' He stood. ''Gonna go get our horses.''

McClure lay there, closing his eyes tight against the waves of nausea and darkness trying to wash over him. Every time he opened his eyes, he searched the surrounding brush for sign of more Indians. And, even as hot as the weather was, he'd have swapped a good saddle to smell woodsmoke, and the aroma of a good cup of coffee.

Mixus led the horses to the sump, let them drink their fill, blow, and drink again, then he helped McClure to the saddle and they headed toward Fort Davis.

Jedediah Powers lay on his stomach only a few feet out of the ring of the Squires' firelight. Two days before, he'd watched them drink the last of their water, and they'd emptied their canteens without giving the horses a swallow. He wondered how long the two men would allow Yolanda to bully them into bowing to her inept leadership—and why.

He cocked his head to hear what they were saying. Bert turned his look from the fire to his sister. ''Gonna say it like it is, sister, you done made a helluva job o' gettin' us anywhere. If we ever find water agin, an' if them horses is still alive, they gonna drink first—they gonna drink first if'n I gotta shoot your sorry butt. You got that, sister?''

Hollow-eyed, she turned her head to look at him. Thin-lipped, and sunken-cheeked, she smiled a smile that would make a rattler back off. ''They's somethin' you don't know, Bert. All that property, an' money we done got since our Southern heroes lost the war? Well, every damned bit of it's in my name. You don't get back there with me, you won't have a cent more'n you had before the war. Know what that means? It means you gonna go back to bein' white trash.''

Bert clenched his fists, opened them, then clenched them again. He nodded. ''Yep. Figger I know what it means. Figger you never thought to share any with me an' Tom. Figger all along you an' that carpetbagger sheriff were gonna keep it all.''

Tom shifted his gaze from one to the other of them. ''Aw, Bert, she never figgered to do nothin' like that, did you, Yolanda?''

To Powers's thinking, she obviously thought it over, and knew she was in deeper than she'd ever get out of alone. With a forced smile, she looked at the two of them. ''Course not. You boys're gonna share it all with me. We just gotta kill McClure first.''

Bert shook his head. ''Don't b'lieve 'er, Tom. She needs us for right now, an' like she's always done, she's gonna use us long's she figgers we gonna be of some use to her—then she's gonna shed us like a snake sheds its skin.'' He shook his empty canteen for at least the tenth time since Powers had been watching, dropped it at his side, and stood. ''Come daylight, if I ain't here, don't look fer me. I'll make it on my own. I like this country.''

Powers inched away from them, grinning. He was camped less than a mile from them, and his camp lay not two hundred yards from a good water hole. He figured if the country didn't kill them, they'd kill each other. He wouldn't give a plugged nickle for Bert being alive come morning.

But Bert was smarter than most would give him credit for. As soon as he'd said he liked this country, he realized he'd spoken the truth. He didn't want the money and property Yolanda had engineered the taking of. To keep peace in the family, he'd gone along with her planning, kowtowed to her every wish and demand, but all the time wishing to be free of her and his no-good brothers. Now, maybe when it was too late, he made up his mind to get out while the getting was good—if Yolanda hadn't already set in motion the death of the three of them to die out here in this rattlesnake-and-cactus-infested, dry country.

He picked up a small round rock and put it in his mouth. It would cause the saliva to flow and make his

thirst more endurable. He reached for his bedroll, spread
it, and crawled between the blankets. He'd found that
even though it was hotter than a blast furnace during the
day, the nights got right-down cold. He didn't go to
sleep, but waited.

Finally, Tom crawled between his blankets, followed
by his sister. His eyes closed to slits, Bert feigned sleep,
but watched them until each breathed slowly, deeply,
regularly. He lay there another half hour or so, then
slipped from his blankets and, his eyes never leaving
them, rolled his blankets, picked up the one saddlebag
in which he knew Yolanda kept most of their money,
and slipped quietly from camp. He hefted the saddlebag,
and grinned. The two of them could have everything
back in Alabama. The money in this bag would keep
him going until he found work. He knew nothing about
the way people handled cattle out here, but back home
he'd worked a few cows all his life. He was willing to
learn the Western way of doing things.

He left the ring of firelight on the side where he'd
picketed the horses. While he saddled his own, the bit
tinkled, metal on metal. He stopped, held his breath,
staring at the two still figures. Yolanda moaned, turned
on her side, pulled her blankets up tighter around her
shoulders, and settled back, again breathing deeply. He
finished saddling, picked up his empty canteen, and led
his horse away from the camp. He'd wait awhile before
riding.

Rebecca and the two darkies made camp that night
alongside the road. Despite the darkness, she cast looks
back down the trail, hoping to see Hawk emerge from
the murky light.

Bessie apparently saw every time she did it, because
after several times, she put her arms around Rebecca's
shouders, then said, ''Done told you, missy, he's all
right. They might be some o' those men from that town
back yonder trailin' us to see does he join up with us.
Mr. Hawk's too smart fo that. He'll most likely wait'll

we leave Foat Davis, then we gonna see 'im ride right up to us like he ain't never been gone.''

Rebecca twisted in her auntie's arms and hugged her. "Oh, I hope you're right. I know it's selfish, but he's all we have standing between us an' all sorts of danger. With men like him we should have won the war."

Bessie shook her head. "No, ma'am, we had lots o' good men, black an' white, fightin' for us, we jest didn't have nothin' to fight with."

Rebecca knew that was true, but she drew on her faith in Hawk to convince herself he could accomplish anything. They'd already eaten, so she went about helping Bessie clean up. Then, the dishes clean, they spread their blankets, Rebecca and Bessie in the wagon and Ned on the ground outside. According to McClure's teaching, each of them placed a handgun and rifle within easy reach.

Sleep wouldn't come. Rebecca stared at the white canvas overhead, wishing for it, wishing to hear Hawk's voice whispering into the darkness of the wagon. Then she heard a whisper—but it wasn't Hawk's. "Little mister, don't get scared, but I'm a friend o' McClure's. Met 'im out yonder in the brush. He's doin' fine, but ain't gonna take the chance o' them from Stockton findin' 'im. He'll join up with you the other side o' Fort Davis." The whisper stopped a moment, then continued, "Little feller, if'n you know where McClure keeps his whiskey, you might get a bottle for me. Gonna take it back to 'im."

She lay there, seeing only a dark shadow hanging over the tailgate, and smelling the weeks-old sweat and dirt of the man. Petrified with fear, stomach muscles tight against her ribs, neck muscles pulled tight into her shoulders, she wondered why she should trust anyone but Hawk. Her hand slipped under the blanket at her side. Her fingers closed around the six-shooter's handle. She put a finger through the trigger guard—and waited. The longer the man whispered, the less scared she felt—but why weren't Bessie and Ned awake and listening to this too?

Then the man said, "Know you don't have no reason to trust me, but here's my handgun. Hold it on me, but get me that whiskey. McClure needs it, he done caught a Comanche arrer out yonder, an' a good stiff drink'll make 'im a whole lot better, not to mention I can pour some o' it on where the arrer went in an' come out." The dark form leaning into the wagon hesitated. "Shouldn'ta told you 'bout him catchin' that arrer—he told me not to, said you'd worry, but don't. He's gonna be all right, jest sore for a while."

"Hawk's hurt?" Her whisper was loud enough to cause Bessie to stir. Rebecca crawled from between her blankets. "I'm goin' to 'im."

"No, now, little feller, you ain't. You bein' with us'd git all o' us killed. You jest stay here an' make like nothin' ever happened. They's two men a-trailin' this wagon, figger they gonna stay with it at least far's Fort Davis. You gotta make like nothin' happened, make like you don't suspect them o' trailin' y'all." Then his whisper became more urgent. "You gotta do it, little feller— for McClure."

Rebecca thought a moment. Nobody she knew would go to this trouble for a bottle of whiskey unless it was like her visitor said. She nodded, even though the man couldn't see her. "All right, keep your gun. I'll get the bottle." She shifted her own revolver to her left hand, rolled to her side, groped under some bags, and pulled a bottle from under them. She handed the bottle to Mixus. "Tell Hawk we miss 'im, an' we'll see 'im outta Davis. Take good care of him."

"You can bet your life on it, little feller. I done met up with a man I'd like to ride the trail with. Ain't seed one yet I figgered wuz good as me in the chaparral till I met him." Then the man, whose voice sounded like a man much older than Hawk, straightened and faded into the darkness.

Rebecca stared at the place she'd last seen him, wish-

ing he'd at least left a hole in the black night, so she'd
have that to comfort her, tell her Hawk was still out
there, tell her he'd met a friend. Somehow she thought
she'd like the old man—if he'd take a bath. She giggled
into the night. Bessie stirred, mumbled something, and
settled back into a deep sleep.

Rebecca's thoughts went to the two old darkies she
loved like her own parents. They were aging rapidly.
The hardships of this trip were telling on them, and
she'd been thoughtless enough to drag them away from
country they'd known all their lives. They never com-
plained, always made light of the worst happenings.
Then, despite the germ of self-recrimination forming in
her thoughts, she realized that nothing she could have
said, or done, would have convinced them to let her
leave alone. She wanted to turn on her side and hug her
auntie, but stopped herself. She'd only disturb the frail
old lady's sleep. She'd tell them about her midnight visitor come daylight.

Mixus walked from the wagon as silently as a puff of
wind. Often during his months and years of running he'd
wished for a family, but knew he wished for the impos-
sible with the way he had to live.

He liked the lad in the wagon. The manly courage
he'd shown, the hesitation to go along with his request
for the bottle, hesitation to trust him—then, abruptly
making the decision to act in McClure's best interests.
Yep. The kid was cut from the same bolt of cloth as his
newfound friend.

He chuckled to himself. Going through a life-or-death
fight with a man at your side sure as hell bridged a lot
of time in making a friend. He chuckled again. Maybe
every time he thought he'd made a friend he ought to
hunt up a passel of Comanche to make the cheese more
binding. He chuckled again. Yeah, that'd be a good test.

Through the darkness, as though broad daylight surrounded him, he homed in on where he and McClure
had spread their blankets. Before he walked into the

small clearing, the ratcheting sound of a revolver being cocked broke the stillness. "It's all right, McClure. It's me." Then from the deeper dark, the young outlaw's form emerged.

"How'd it go, old-timer?"

Even though McClure couldn't see him, Mixus nodded. "Went right well, son. That boy o' yore's is one fine little feller. Knowed he wuz scared when I wakened 'im, but he kept it down such that he figgered he could handle it. I knowed he held a revolver on me the whole time, although I didn't make out like I knowed he had one. Fact is, I like that there boy."

He glanced at the bottle and held it out to Hawk. "This here's yore whiskey, so reckon it'd be imperlite fer me to open it."

McClure grinned. "You open it, Mixus. Figure it's been a while since you last had a drink." A dead silence greeted Hawk's words. "What's the matter, old-timer? Don't you want a drink?"

"Shore as hell do, but I ain't used to drinkin' 'fore breakfast."

McClure laughed. "Well, there's another way you can look at it. Why don't you figure it's after supper—a long time after, but not 'fore breakfast."

"Well now, dag nab it, you got 'nuff sense fer us both. Never woulda thought o' it that a way." With that he pulled the cork, tilted the bottle, and took a long, hearty drink.

Mixus's Adam's apple bobbed several times before he lowered the jug. McClure shook his head. "Damn. Thought I was gonna have to let these arrow holes putrefy 'fore they got any o' that whiskey poured into 'em."

"Naw now, I wuz bein' re-e-eal careful to leave a little to take care o' them." He handed McClure the bottle. After taking a drink, and before knocking the cork back in, Hawk held it out to the old outlaw.

Mixus chuckled. "Naw, 'fraid I might not leave 'nuff for medicine. We'll wait'll daylight 'fore I put any on them holes. Wantta see you sweat when the burn hits ya. Let's get some sleep.''

The next morning, after the old man dressed Mc-Clure's wound, they squatted by a small, smokeless fire. The two outlaws drank coffee. Hawk slanted Mixus a questioning look. "You ever get lonesome out here, always running? You ever just flat want to sit by a fire an' talk to people?''

Mixus shook his head. "Never wanted much to talk to *people,* but they's a many a time I wanted to talk to my saddle pard. Never met a ranny I wanted to partner up with till I met up with you.'' Silence hung in the air a long moment, then Mixus continued, "Course you already got folks with you, so reckon you ain't gonna join up with a old outlaw.''

McClure studied a wisp of smoke from the small fire. He wondered whether he should say anything to Bessie about adopting another outlaw into the family, wondered how Reb would take it, figured Ned wouldn't give a damn. The smoke he watched, caught by a vagrant breeze, disappeared. He shifted his eyes to look at Mixus. "Don't know how those people I'm already part-nered with will feel 'bout it—fact is, don't know how you'd feel 'bout bein' with a bunch 'o people like I'm travelin with—but if you think you could tolerate that many of us, I'll talk to them 'bout it.''

Mixus's grin took in his entire face. "Why, gol darn it, reckon if'n I got tired o' too much talk, an' seein' too many people all at onc't, I could ride out into the chaparral for an hour or two an' let the aloneness settle back into me." He nodded. "Yep, you talk to 'em.''

All that day, and the next, McClure shadowed the two riders from Fort Stockton, then, about four o'clock, watched them draw rein and talk awhile. McClure would have given a prized saddle to hear what they said. But after the confab, they reined their horses toward Davis, and rode as though they had a definite goal in mind. Hawk looked at the old man. "Bet you a dollar they got tired o' trailin' the wagon an' decided to ride right up to it an' ask 'bout me.''

Mixus squinted after the fast-moving riders. ''Ain't gonna take that there bet, young'un. What you figger to do?''

McClure frowned, looked down the trail, then back to the old man. ''First off, we're gonna ride in the roadway like we owned it. Then when we get close to where we figure the wagon's gonna be we'll ease off into the brush so as to get right close to it.'' He grinned. ''I got an idea those two men from town're gonna have a little surprise. That boy, an' those two darkies, are right salty. They don't back down for anyone.''

Mixus returned his grin. ''Yeah, bet you're right, but we gonna be close enough, if them two gits the upper hand, we gonna sit in on the game.'' He laughed. ''Hell, young'un, we got a full house to their pair o' deuces.''

The sound of hooves pounded the trail behind. Rebecca tossed Ned his Winchester. ''Keep it aimed at whoever that is ridin' hell-bent for us.'' She looked at Bessie. ''You an' I'll stay put in the wagon. You stay outta sight in the back, but be where you can hold your rifle on 'em. I'll keep mine to hand till Uncle stops the team. I'll sit here on the seat.''

The two riders came on them from behind, then split, one taking the left side of the Studebaker, and the other the right. Rebecca motioned for Bessie to keep her gun on the one to the left.

Rebecca let her Winchester lay across her knees, but trained on the one she'd taken as her responsibility. Her stomach felt like a bucket of worms crawled in it, her mouth felt like she could spit cotton, and her breath came in short gasps, but she sucked in a deep breath, tried to relax, and said, ''You men got somethin' in mind? You don't, an' if you got no business with us— ride on.''

The slim man Rebecca had taken as hers to watch kept his eyes on her rifle. ''You ain't got a reason to hold a gun on me. Put it away. I got some questions I wantta ask ya.''

"Save your questions, mister, an' I'll do the same with my answers. Ride on."

The slim man grinned, showing two rows of snaggly, tobacco-stained teeth. "Ain't ridin' nowhere, sonny. Look behind you. My partner's sittin' right there, an' I figger he'll git off a shot 'fore you can swing that there gun to him.''

She shook her head. "No need for me to look behind. No need for me to swing my gun. My auntie's got a Winchester .44 lookin' right down his gullet.''

"Yes, suh, an' I shore am itchin' to pull this trigguh an' make what wuz two o' you into one."

The slim man's head jerked to the side, trying to see into the dark maw of the wagon when Ned spoke up from between the oxen. He stood between the two lead oxen, his rifle resting across the rump of the closest ox. His rifle also pointed at the one under Reb's gun. "Gonna tell you this jest onc't. You ride around to the side yore partner's on so's we can all see you."

Through a sickly grin, Slim said, "Aw, we wuzn't gonna hurt you. Jest wantta find out where that man is who rode into town with you."

"Mister, you better ride around the team like my uncle up front said, an' I mean right damn now." Rebecca tightened her finger on the trigger, and the slim man obviously saw the slight movement. He kneed his horse to do as ordered.

Bessie's rifle erupted into a sharp crack, and Slim looked wide-eyed toward his partner. Rebecca twisted on the seat and stared at the broad-shouldered, big-nosed man only now sliding off the side of his horse. Bessie's voice came from the bowels of the Studebaker. "Lordy, little missy, he wuz slidin' his thumb off'n the hammer o' that gun. I couldn't wait, had to shoot 'im.''

Rebecca stared at the one remaining rider, hoping he'd not noticed Bessie's slip in calling her "missy." She raised her Winchester to her shoulder. "Now I'm gonna answer your question. The man who rode into town with us came onto our wagon outside o' town. He had his noonin' with us, then rode into town at our side. We never learned his name—an' didn't ask. Figured from what I hear 'bout you folks out here in the West, it's downright impolite to ask a man's name.''

The slim man looked from Reb to his partner lying half-under his horse. ''The marshal's gonna be right upset 'bout y'all killin' one o' his deputies. Figure you folks gonna be the ones he's chasin' next.''

Bessie's voice rumbled from deep in the wagon. ''Mistuh, you get that white trash throwed crost his horse an' git outta here.'' The sound of another shell being jacked into the chamber of her rifle cut into her words. ''Gonna tell you somethin' else, you come back with a whole bunch o' the same breed as you, an' ain't none o' you gonna ride back to that there town. Now, git.''

''No. Hold it right there,'' Rebecca cut in. ''You drop your gunbelt, then real careful-like, lower your rifle to the ground.'' Without turning her head, she told Ned to gather the guns of both men.

When the old darky deposited the firearms in the back of the wagon, Rebecca stared hard at the slim deputy. ''Now, mister lawman, now you can get goin' like my auntie told you.''

When the deputy rounded the trail to the rear, Rebecca sucked in a tremulous breath, gently lowered the hammer of her rifle, and looked at the two old darkies. ''Reckon we just bought ourselves a pack more trouble. That man's gonna bring back more'n we can handle. Now we're all outlaws, right alongside Hawk. Now's when I wish to goodness he was here with us.''

McClure's deep voice sounded from the brush. ''Well, young fellow, don't see why you need me around. Y'all did yourself mighty proud without me.''

Every inch of her wanted to jump from the wagon seat, run to him, throw herself into his arms, and cover his face with kisses. She held back at the last moment.

What would Hawk think of a young boy hugging and kissing him? Instead, she drawled, "Had to, Hawk, figured you an' that old reprobate I gave the whiskey to were lying out yonder in the chaparral in the shade of a big prickly pear guzzlin' the contents o' that jug."

She had her eyes glued to the spot from which his voice came, then he pushed through to the side of the trail where she could see him—and at his side walked the scruffiest, dirtiest man she'd ever seen. "Where'd you find that old bag o' bones, Hawk?"

"Why gol dang it, you young whippersnapper, I can see yore folks didn't tan your fat little bottom often enough to teach you respect for old folks."

Past her face, which felt on fire, a laugh bubbled between Rebecca's lips, a laugh from deep in her chest. Then, mocking him, she said, "Why gol dang it, if you could see yourself, so dirty I don't know what you look like under all that alkali dust, an' your beard hangin' to your waist, prob'ly hasn't been trimmed since you were my age. All I can see is a bag o' bones."

Mixus chuckled and dug McClure in the ribs with his elbow. "Told you I liked that young'un. Got spunk he has." While he talked, he eased the hammer down on his Winchester, as did McClure.

Reb watched the careful way they handled their rifles. "See y'all were ready to lend us a hand."

McClure let a slight smile break the corners of his mouth. He shook his head. "Nope, figured y'all could take care of it all by your lonesome. Fact is, I told Mixus here you were a right salty bunch." He glanced at the old outlaw. "Was I wrong, old-timer? That whole bunch'd do to ride the river with."

Mixus nodded. " 'Fore we make ourselves known to each other, we better do some plannin'. This neck o' the woods is gonna be plumb overflowin' with lawmen 'fore you can say scat."

McClure stood there in the middle of the road, frowning. He walked down the trail a few yards and kicked dust back in the flattened places made by the wagon's iron tires, then he walked back to them, pinned each with a look, and said, "Got a idea." He looked at Mixus. "You know this country right well—been dodgin' the law hereabouts for years—you know of any place we could pull this wagon to an' hide out for a spell?"

The old man grinned through the forest of a beard. "Why I hope to smile, young'un. I even got me a cabin out yonder in a ravine. Built it myself, up high on the shoulder of a deep arroyo so flash floods don't bother me none—an' best of all, ain't no danged lawman even goes in that part o' the country." He stared hard at Mc-Clure. "Don'tcha wantta know why I ain't never been bothered by the law?"

McClure nodded. "Reckon you gonna tell me whether I wantta know or not."

"Well, gosh ding it. I shouldn't oughtta tell you if you ain't no more interested than that, but yeah, I'm gonna tell you." He chomped down on his chew, spit at a horny toad sitting in the road looking at him, then cocked an eye at McClure. "It's Comanche—lots o' them devils hang around them parts."

McClure raised an eyebrow. "An' they don't bother you?"

Mixus chuckled. "Nope. They figger I'm crazy as a loon. The first day I run in there with 'bout fifteen o' them red devils chasin' me, I wuz outta shells for my rifle so I stopped sudden-like, laughed like a downright idiot, waved my hands in the air—an' ran at them. They hightailed it outta that arroyo like a scalded cat. Ain't never come back."

McClure let a slow grin break the sweat-caked alkali dust around his mouth and eyes. "Yeah, I've heard they won't bother a crazy man." Then, tongue in cheek, he added, "Course they're not all that wrong 'bout the state of your mind."

Mixus glared at him a moment, then smiled. "You're tryin' to get my goat agin, ain'tcha young'un?" He shook his head. "Ain't gonna work. Done made up my mind that boy yonder needs some proper teachin', an'

I'm the one to do it.'' He scratched his head. ''Now, you wuz sayin' somethin' 'bout a idee you done come up with?''

McClure nodded. ''It'll work if we can get this wagon off the road an' through the chaparral without leavin' a trail. First, I figure we can cover the tracks here in the trail right easy, but gettin' through the brush without leavin' sign is gonna be a little harder.''

The old man apparently studied McClure's idea a moment, then nodded. ''I kin lead the wagon through without breakin' limbs an' such. You foller behind an' dust up them wheel tracks such as nobody kin see we been thataway. None o' that bunch'll foller us far into the brush no-way. Scared they are, too dadblasted lily-livered to foller us even if they knowed where we wuz goin'.''

McClure walked to the side of the road, pulled his bowie knife, cut a small brush from a scrub oak, went to the rear of the wagon, and began to brush at the tracks. He looked over his shoulder. ''All right, let's get at it. Not gonna get far with y'all standin' there watchin' me.''

He and Mixus tied their horses to the tailgate. The old outlaw went to the head of the team and took over Ned's job, telling Ned to get in the wagon. McClure stayed behind the wagon brushing tracks while the Studebaker wended its way through the brush.

9

AFTER ABOUT A half mile, McClure called a halt for a few minutes' rest. Reb made as if to climb from the seat, but McClure halted him. "Stay in the wagon, all o' you, don't want no more tracks for them to find than we can help." He looked behind to see if he'd covered their tracks well enough that they'd be hard to find. Maybe if it took the posse till dark to find where they'd left the trail, even a slight breeze during the night would finish the job for him.

They worked their way into the hostile, prickly, thorny land, until McClure wondered if Mixus would ever get them to the right arroyo. His every stitch of clothing dripped sweat. Although it was deep into summer, almost fall, heat parched the desert.

The old outlaw had led them across the ends of several deep cuts in the land, then about sundown they came to the edge of a deeper slash than any McClure had seen.

With the Studebaker sitting on the rim of the ravine, the old outlaw pointed to a shelf alongside the cut. "Right there, under that cutbank an' round the curve a bit, is my cabin, but we gotta head for the end o' this here slope 'fore we can turn back in to the bottom o' the arroyo. They's ways to get to the bottom fer a hoss, but with a wagon we gotta go round. Take maybe 'nother four hours. We'll make a dry camp tonight, then in the mornin' we'll head for home. Oughtta git there 'fore time for our noonin'."

Hands over his kidneys, McClure leaned back and groaned, trying to rid his cramped muscles of the ache the constant bending and sweeping had induced. He looked behind. "Damn if I don't b'lieve it'd been easier to stand an' fight." He frowned and looked at Mixus. "Reckon it'd be a good idea for me to backtrack an' see if they picked up our trail."

Before Hawk finished talking, Mixus worked his head from side to side. "Naw, young'un, you'd only leave fresh sign for 'em to foller. Even if you had moccasins, that'd be a bad idee. Them Spanish dagger'll stick through most anything—'specially that Indian footwear. Might cripple ya."

Less than an hour later, they sat by a small fire, eating and drinking coffee. Hawk wondered when to broach the subject of Mixus joining them, and going on west. Finally, he decided the family might as well know what he had on his mind. He tossed the dregs from his coffee cup and glanced at each of them. "Reckon y'all will all have a say in this, so think on it awhile. What I'm gonna say is Mr. Mixus here wants to join up with us, go on west with us. I'm of the same feelin'. Tell you right now, he's wanted by the law—don't know why, but he is."

Bessie sat forward. "Him bein' a wanted man ain't nothin' this bunch should oughtta look down they nose about. Reckon right now every one o' us is wanted."

Reb spoke up. "What's the law want you for, Mr. Mixus?"

The old man stared between his boot toes a moment, then looked at him. "Tell you true, boy, I never figgered I done much wrong. Stole three horses right outta a corral. Didn't set nobody afoot out in the desert, or Indian country, didn't hurt nobody by doin' it, 'cept the man what owned 'em wuz right ornery 'bout it. Wanted me hung right where they caught me, but the ranger with 'em wouldn't hear of it. He took me into Fort Stockton an' locked me up. I broke out, an' been runnin' ever since.'' He took a swallow of his coffee, and again looked at Reb. ''That there wuz nigh onto twenty year ago. Thought many a time of givin' myself up, doin' my time, an' gettin' out a free man, but never did, on account of Stockton's marshals ain't been the kind who would've let me alone—so here I be.''

McClure squinted at the old man. ''Twenty years? Hell, man, they've probably forgotten 'bout you an' those horses many moons ago. You ever try just walkin' into a town to see if anyone recognized you?''

Mixus shook his head. ''Ain't never had the guts to do it, in case they knowed me an' put me in the hoozegow.''

Ned, seldom the one who expressed an opinion, surprised them. ''Mr. Hawk, bein's you done asked, reckon I got a vote in this here confab. Gonna tell you right now, I'm a-sayin' Mr. Rolf can trail along with us fer as he's of a mind to.''

Bessie sat back and looked at each of them. ''My man's done said it fer me.'' She twisted to look at Reb. ''How you feel 'bout it young'un?''

Rebecca grinned like she figured any young boy would, glanced around the fire at them, and then in a deep drawl, said, ''Reckon we done got us a whole gang o' oulaws.'' She giggled. ''When we gonna rob our first bank?''

McClure tousled the boy's hair. ''You little devil, you haven't grown to be that much of a man yet.'' He shrugged. ''Reckon, Mr. Mixus, you've joined young Mr. Brennan's gang.'' Then, tongue in cheek, he said, ''We gonna have to think awhile 'fore we get into any real outlawin'.''

Still giggling, Reb looked at him. ''Aw, Hawk, you know I was only makin' a joke.'' The boy sobered. ''But despite the joke, I believe every man that marshal back there in Stockton can deputize is gonna be lookin' for us. We gonna have to be mighty careful.''

Mixus pointed to the rim of the arroyo. ''Got no worries on that account, son. We can hole up down yonder in my cabin for a couple o' weeks, leave here, go around Fort Davis, an' head for Marfa. Don't figger nobody's gonna hear 'bout us there. Fact is, don't reckon nobody down yonder ever heard o' Rolf Mixus 'cept'n one man, an' he's my friend. Man by the name o' Trace Gundy.''

McClure frowned. ''Gundy? When I scouted for the Army, seems like I heard 'bout a young hellion by that name. The whole New Mexico Territory was lookin' for him, called 'im the Apache Blanco, laid every crime within five hundred miles at his doorstep.''

Mixus nodded. ''Same man, only Governor Wallace pardoned 'im. Now he's got a big ranch down yonder in that country.'' He chuckled. ''Way he come by that there ranch is 'nother story I'll tell you sometime. Figger if we don't go into Marfa, we'll go by his ranch, tell 'im what happened, an' he'll see to it we ain't bothered till we get clear of Texas.''

McClure thought on the old outlaw's words a few moments, swallowed the rest of his coffee, then cleared his throat. ''We're gonna need to stock up on supplies soon, so we're gonna have to go into some town along the way—don't see how we can avoid it.'' He shrugged. ''Reckon we'll worry 'bout that when the time comes.'' He stood. ''Let's get some sleep. Like to get to Mixus's cabin time for our noonin' tomorrow.''

The next morning about eleven o'clock, Mixus pointed up the side of the ravine to a collection of rocks, half-rotted boards, and brush, all looking as though they had been carelessly thrown in a pile, and announced proudly, ''Yonder's my cabin. Don't look like much, but it keeps the rain an' cold off'n a man.''

McClure glanced at his ''family,'' thinking he'd see disappointment in all of them, but he saw only carefully guarded looks. He grinned at the old man. ''Reckon I've slept in worse, an' the way these nights're coolin' down we're gonna be right proud to have a place inside.''

"That's the way I seed it, young feller. We men can sleep on the ground, an' Miss Bessie can have my bunk."

Down the shelf about fifty feet a pole corral held six horses. McClure looked questioningly at Mixus.

"Naw now, I didn't steal them ponies. Come by 'em a leetle bit harder'n that. Had to shoot a Comanche off'n each one o' 'em 'fore they'd give 'em up."

McClure only shook his head, and said, "I reckon."

They stayed at Mixus's shack several days, long enough to rest, wash clothes—and themselves. Water seeped from a crack in the rocky wall of the ravine only a few feet from the shelter's door, and made cooking and cleaning much easier than having to tote it a mile or more from the nearest stream.

Although with dirt floors, and dark inside, Rebecca found it remarkably clean; free of rats, tarantulas, and insects. She and Bessie slept in the shack, to Mixus's disgust. He said the way he figgered it the boy just flat would never become a man bein' mommycoddled by Bessie.

The day they left the old man's hideout, he picked the three best horses of those in the corral and turned the others loose, saying he figured they'd need pack-horses if they decided to buy provisions. Their layover at Mixus's cabin had allowed time for McClure's wound to heal.

Not daring to go back to the trail, Mixus led them through chaparral at times thick enough that they had to hack down cactus with bowie knives. Several times, Hawk thought to suggest getting rid of the wagon and using packhorses only, but he quickly abandoned the idea. Everything the boy and the old darkies owned sat in the wagon, and Bessie needed a place to sleep. And he figured as frail as the boy seemed to be, he needed the protection of the wagon also. He wouldn't be the cause of putting more hardship on them.

Some days they made as much as ten or twelve miles, but most they covered about seven. McClure frequently went to the water barrels and tapped on their sides. The old man apparently noticed his concern. "Don't worry 'bout water, young'un. Reckon I know ever' danged water hole 'twixt here an' the Rio Grande." He squinted at the sky, and flicked a thumb at the horizon, already heavy with black clouds. " 'Sides that, we gonna have a purty good gully washer 'fore sundown. Better get up the side o' one o' these here hills, find some rocks, an' make us a camp to keep dry."

He picked up a branch from a scrub oak. "Better gather as much dry wood's we can find so's to have a fire for our noonin'." Reb was the first to begin gathering any burnable twigs and dried tender.

Mixus reined to the side of McClure's horse. "Don't want to excite the old folks, or the boy neither, but keep yore rifle handy. We're deep into Comanchero country, an' they don't give one leetle damn 'bout nothing but what they can steal. Course they don't leave nothin' but dead bodies behind. If they wuz any young women amongst us, they'd take 'em an' sell 'em down Mexico way."

"From what I heard 'bout Gundy, he cleaned all of that trash outta his country."

Mixus nodded. "He did. They ain't a one o' them in his right mind who'd git within fifty miles o' the Apache Blanco, but we ain't close 'nuff yet to figger on that." When finished talking, he jacked a shell into the chamber of his Winchester. McClure followed suit and, knowing the other three heard the Winchesters' actions, listened for them to jack a shell into the chamber of their weapons. Almost simultaneously he heard the three follow suit.

McClure led them to a jumble of tumbled rocks with space enough among them for the wagon, livestock, and a place to spread a tarp over a cluster of rocks to afford shelter—if the wind held off enough to let the canvas stay in place. He noticed that while he busied himself with things to do in the camp, Mixus stood to the outside, his rifle held at the ready.

He walked over and stood by the old outlaw. "You lookin' for trouble right soon?"

Mixus looked at him sidewise, squinted one eye almost closed, and nodded. "Why I should smile, young feller. In this country a man's gotta always figger on havin' to shoot 'fore he says howdy. Now, you do like you seen me do, keep a shell in the magazine."

"Already have, old-timer." He cocked an eye toward the lowering clouds. "Damn, if it isn't one thing, it's another." He helped anchor the tarp to the tops of three boulders with three more large rocks holding the canvas down. He checked to be sure they could all get under it, then picked up a shovel and trenched around the uphill side to take the runoff around the shelter.

While shoveling, he told Reb, Ned, and Bessie to keep their Winchesters dry and at their sides. They would have room to sit but not lie down. Mixus watched with an approving eye.

The rain was preceded by strong gusts of wind, wind that threatened to rip the canvas from under its anchoring rocks; it pounded, shook, and flapped the tarp—but it stayed where they'd put it.

Then the rain came, not in a steady downpour, but in sheets. They huddled together, all guarding the pile of wood they'd gathered. McClure's trench did the job he'd hoped for. It channeled the runoff around the place in which they sat. Even with that, wind gusts blew rain under the tarp, soaking their backs.

Reb shivered from the cold, wet shirt clinging to his back. McClure held out his hand to comfort the boy, then drew it back fast. What was the matter with him? Was he going soft? Hell, if caring about a youngster was an indication he was too soft to make it in this hard land—then dammit he'd give up on making it. He sat back and lighted his pipe. Just the same, he'd wait to hold court on himself until he was once again in feminine company: then he'd have something to play his feeling against. Until then he figured to keep some distance between himself and the boy.

The storm subsided as quickly as it came upon them. The rain decreased to a steady downpour, then to light rain, then drizzle. That was when Hawk looked from under their shelter to see a bright patch of blue sky on the horizon. He sucked in a breath of the clean, washed air, relishing the smell and taste of it.

He crawled out, wiped the moisture from his rifle, bent to collect some rocks for a fireplace—and felt a tug on his chaps, followed by the sharp crack of a rifle shot.

He threw himself to the side away from the shelter, rolled, and landed on his stomach. Another bullet whined off a boulder at his side, and another plowed through his shirt, burning his shoulder. Mixus joined the fray, then the rifles of Reb, Ned, and Bessie began to talk.

Four riders, Comancheros by his guess—dirty, greasy, and mean-looking—spurred their horses into the middle of camp. Mixus's first shot knocked the lead rider from his saddle. McClure rolled to his back and shot straight up into one of the horsemen. His bullet went in at the man's crotch, and came out somewhere in his back by McClure's reckoning. The bandit fell from his horse.

McClure rolled again, went to his stomach, and saw a third rider knocked backward from his horse. Reb knelt in front of the shelter and coolly had fired into the man. The fourth leaned from his horse and scooped the boy onto his pony, in front of him.

McClure pulled his finger from the trigger guard as though from the fangs of a rattlesnake. His heart sat in his throat, his guts churned. He yelled, "Hold your fire!" But all guns had gone silent before his yell. A shot at the Comanchero might hit the boy.

McClure ran for his horse, bridled it, and, bareback, kicked the gelding into an all-out run. To ride through the chaparral like this invited crippling the horse—but that was Reb the outlaw had taken.

Hawk pushed fear to the back of his mind, allowing only cold reasoning. The rain had muddied the ground. There would be tracks. He reined the gelding to a walk, then hoofbeats came from behind. Mixus pulled his horse alongside. "Danged fool, you gonna cripple that there horse."

McClure looked at the ground. There was no doubt he could follow the Comanchero. "Mixus, take my horse back to camp. Y'all stay there. If I'm not back by tomorrow night, head for Gundy's ranch. I'll catch you there."

"Hawk, let me go after 'im. I'm better at this than you."

McClure shook his head. "No, old man, you're not. Besides, I got something special in store for that bastard when I catch 'im, an' if he's harmed Reb in any way he's gonna wish the Apache had 'im."

Mixus stared into McClure's eyes a moment, then nodded. "You go after 'im, young feller, an' 'less I'm readin' you wrong, I'd hate to be that Comanchero when you catch up to 'im."

Hawk handed the reins to the old outlaw, checked his cartridge belt to make certain it was full, took the handful of cartridges Mixus held out to him, and set out afoot.

He figured the bandit would ride hard until feeling safe, then he'd slow the horse for the same reason Hawk himself had slowed his big black gelding.

McClure followed the muddy tracks for a couple of hours, then ran out of the rainfall area, but the hoofprints in the alkali dust were about as easy to follow.

Anger settled in his brain as a cold frozen core of hatred, and determination to make the Comanchero pay. It left his senses honed to razor sharpness. His worry now was that the bandit, knowing he'd left at least two good riflemen behind, would ride on into the night.

That thought made him pay more attention to direction than to tracks. As much as the spiney growth allowed, the breed held to a southwesterly course. McClure tested the wind blowing from the southwest, not expecting yet to smell woodsmoke, but making sure the wind blew from the right direction so he could smell it should the outlaw make camp.

By dusk dark, the Comanchero had not altered his course. McClure was certain he could hold the direction during the dark hours. When the moonless night folded about him, he slipped quietly from yucca to towering prickly pear, around the dangerous Spanish dagger, and on past ocotillo branches loaded with thorns.

With autumn now upon the land, the nights had shortened, but the wind being from where it was kept the night comfortably warm. By eleven o'clock, McClure had walked in darkness at least four hours, and each minute of those hours he prayed he'd not erred in his judgment as to whether the bandit would hold to a south-westerly course.

He walked silently on, pushing hunger out of his thinking. His only thought now was Reb. The boy had shown uncommon coolness in the face of fire. Hawk hoped that coolness would prevail during the ride with the bandit.

Another half hour and McClure's hunger sharpened. He stopped. Why had he suddenly become aware of his stomach? What was it that triggered the thought of food? The smell of food hadn't done it—smoke perhaps? Again the faint smell invaded his senses. He sniffed, smelled smoke, then grinned into the night—smoke. The greasy bastard felt safe enough to build a fire.

McClure conquered the urge to run toward where he knew the fire must be. A shadow would have made more noise than his movements through the brush. Although his boots were not made for this kind of work, he placed them softly to the earth, feeling for sticks, or dry yucca trunks, and pushing them aside with the sole of his boots, before again moving ahead.

After about fifteen minutes of slow, nerve-rending progress, he saw the flicker of a small fire through the chaparral. He stopped; his eyes searched. He looked for any kind of movement, wanting to know where the outlaw sat, and where Reb was in relation to the bandit.

He spotted the Comanchero—lean, and with a scraggly beard—leaning against his saddle, a bottle of something in his right hand.

Reb sat with his hands and feet securely trussed, with pigging string by McClure's estimate. The bandit lifted the bottle and drank deeply; his Adam's apple bobbed three times by Hawk's count. He swallowed, belched, wiped his mouth on his filthy, dust-crusted shirtsleeve, and looked at the boy. "*Muchacho,* I sell you across the river, in *Mejico.* Some over there like boys—don't like girls. You make me *mucho dinero,* more than a girl maybe."

McClure waited for Reb's response, wanting to know if the boy was as cool as he'd appeared back in camp. He wasn't disappointed.

Reb raked the bandit with a look of pure disgust. He sneered. "You filthy trash, there're two men back there, both of whom use a gun better'n any of you who attacked us. You won't see the sun rise in the morning." The boy's eyes shifted for only a split second, widened, and recognition flared in them when they homed in on McClure. Reb quickly moved his look back, and pinned the Comanchero with a look which she wished could kill, hoping the bandit had not seen his expression change when he saw Hawk. "Fact is, Droppings from a Coyote, you won't even see this fire flicker more'n a second or two longer." Then Reb's look centered on McClure. "Kill 'im now."

The bandit followed her look, saw McClure standing slightly to the side and to the back of his shoulder. He dropped the bottle, grabbed for his revolver, and simultaneously acquired a hole in his ragged shirt, about an inch above his belt buckle.

His hand had made it to his holstered gun, when a new hole punctured his shirt within an inch of where the other bullet hit.

McClure stepped toward him, kicked his gun from his hand, and turned the Colt's muzzle toward the greasy one's legs. He blew the kneecaps from each.

"You slime, you think those gut shots were an accident, think again. Gonna leave you out here to die slowly, then the coyotes can gnaw on your bones."

The outlaw stared at him a moment, his flat, black eyes showing no fear, no pain. "*Señor,* why you do not keel me now? I don't hurt you no more. Keel me."

McClure shook his head, turned toward Reb, pulled his bowie knife, and cut the ties around the boy's ankles and wrists. "Get his rifle an' revolver. Outlaws usually ride good horses, an' carry even better weapons."

Rebecca, hands free, felt the urge to throw her arms about Hawk's neck and smother him with kisses. She squelched the thought as soon as it entered her head. Instead, she did as McClure suggested, then gathered the reins of the bandit's horse and led him to Hawk. She looked at him a moment. "Figured you'd be along soon. Knew if you could read sign as well as you wiped it out after we left the trail, it wouldn't take you long."

His grin, showed both relief and pride in her. "Son, you've got a lot more faith in me than I felt after dark set in. All I had to go on then was gut feel." He walked to the bandit, went through his pockets, took what little money he had, all in Mexican currency, stripped his gunbelt from him, then looked at the horse. As he'd said, it was a magnificent animal.

Reb watched, and when it looked like Hawk thought to ride back to camp, he said, "Why don't we drag 'im out in the brush and spend the night here?"

McClure shook his head. "Would most anywhere else, but those shots mighta been heard by some we don't want to meet up with. Figure to get away from here 'fore we make camp. 'Sides, we got no provisions, and I sure as hell don't want to eat anything that filth yonder has touched. No, we better head for our own camp." He held the stirrup for Reb to put his foot in it. "Glad this horse'll carry double, or I'd have another long walk." With the boy firmly in the saddle, he mounted behind him.

Rebecca sighed mentally. If he'd held her in front of

him, in front of the saddle, as the outlaw had done, he might have felt curves where a boy wouldn't have any. The bandit hadn't had time to notice.

On the ride back, McClure held a grip on the cantle; to put his arm around the boy's waist might have upset his equilibrium—then the horse stumbled. Without thinking, Hawk's arm slipped around the boy well above his belt, and his hand clutched Reb's chest.

Hawk's eyes widened. Now his hand snapped back as though from a hot poker. Hell, no wonder he couldn't put ropy muscle on the boy—*the he wasn't a he, he was a she*. Why had they kept it from him? Did they not trust him? Hadn't he proved to them he was a gentleman, a friend, a man who would not take advantage of either a man or a woman? He mulled that over on the way back to camp, then shrugged. The girl, maybe a couple of years older than he'd thought—she must be at least fourteen—must be shy of her blooming womanhood. Or maybe she wanted to prove herself capable of doing a man's work and was fearful he'd lighten up on her if he knew the truth. He'd have to take care not to change the way he'd been treating her. Let her keep her secret as long as she thought necessary.

When Hawk's hand had touched her breast, Rebecca had gasped, as a sensation she'd never known warmed her body. Even though his hand had been there only a second before he quickly released her, it had revealed to her something about herself—a man could affect her feelings in a way nothing else could. Could any man do this to her emotions—or only Hawk?

Too, she hoped it *hadn't* revealed anything to Hawk. Was his hand on her breast long enough for him to actually feel that her body belonged to a girl? Mentally she shook her head. She didn't think so. As flat as she hoped she'd tied herself down, she didn't think anyone could have noticed. She took comfort in that thought on the way back to camp.

They rode into camp with the sky beginning to show a thin edge of light under the clouds to the east; the rain

had moved off in that direction. Bessie had coffee made
and breakfast about done. Sitting on the ground close to
the fire, Mixus sipped his coffee and squinted one eye
toward them when they rode into the circle of firelight.
"Figgered it wuz you—slow-walkin' hoss, y'all didn't
hail the camp, acted like a bunch o' pilgrims."

"Aw hell, old man, you're just jealous I didn't let
you go after the boy." McClure glanced at the fire.
"That bacon sure smells good fryin' like that. Smelled
it now for a half mile, an' that coffee's even better—if
you haven't drank it all. Useless bein' like you are,
reckon you mighta done just that."

Mixus unfolded himself, stood, and held out his hand.
"Shore glad to see yu back safe, an' with the lad. Worried a mite you wuzn't good 'nuff at sneakin' up on
folks, you bein' a tenderfoot an' all."

"Mr. Mixus, Hawk just simply walked into that Comancheros camp and was standing less than six feet from
him when I told the greasy filth he was gonna die right
sudden. Hawk put two bullets in 'im, then wasted two
more by shootin' off his kneecaps. You gotta talk to 'im
'bout wastin' ammunition like that."

Hawk made a swipe toward Reb's hair. She ducked,
giggling like a schoolgirl. "Missed me that time."

McClure wondered at how quick Mixus fit into the
family—the joshing, the willingness of each to shoulder
more than his or her load, the caring for the welfare of
all. Yep, they had themselves another partner—only
he'd have to be right careful not to let on to Mixus that
anything, especially Reb, was different.

And the boy was one of a kind, although with more
guts than was good for him. It might get the lad hurt
sometime when a little fear would serve him better.

Bessie told them breakfast was ready, and while they
sat eating, McClure asked the old man how far it was
to Gundy's ranch. "Been thinkin' on that, young feller.
Reckon we kin git there in 'bout four, maybe five days
if'n we don't have any more o' these here gosh danged
fracases."

Hawk nodded. "Reckon we might's well put a spur in our get-along then. Soon's we finish eatin', we'll get goin'."

Yolanda awoke, rolled her tongue around in her dry mouth, groaned, and sat up. Her eyes raked the camp, her first thought that Bert had stepped out in the brush to relieve himself. Then she noticed that his bedding, saddle—all his gear was missing. "Bert! Bert, where the hell are you?"

At her cracked, shrill scream, Tom pushed the blankets down and looked sleepy-eyed at her. "What's wrong, sister?" He looked around, and he obviously missed his brother too. "Where's Bert?"

"Gone, you damned fool. You don't see 'im, do you? An' he ain't answered my call." Her eyes widened. The saddlebags. She made a dive for where she'd put them, moved one aside, scratched frantically around in the dirt, and looked at Tom. "You bother these here saddle-bags?"

He shook his head. "Ain't touched 'em. You done told us never to dig round in 'em, so I left 'em alone."

She felt as if she'd been kicked in the stomach, then grabbed the one saddlebag still sitting there, dipped her hand to the bottom of it, raked it around, and came up with a small package of bills. A quick count of the money Bert left to her and Tom showed only one hundred eighty dollars. As though it would help, she sat on her blankets and cursed for a solid minute without repeating herself.

She glanced at Tom. "You an' me, brother, got only a few dollars to finish this here job we took on—but I'm sayin' right now, first we gonna see if we can find that worthless bastardly brother o' ours. Then after I blow 'is damned brains out, we gonna continue lookin' for McClure."

"You mean we gonna go lookin' for the both of 'em, an' we ain't got much money to live on?"

She pinned him with a look she saved for people she

hated, and those she thought too stupid to give an answer to. She nodded. "Gonna make it as plain for you as I can. Maybe it'll sink into that thick skull o' yores. We gonna find Bert, if we can. Then we gonna continue lookin' for McClure." She shrugged. "We give outta money, we'll find somebody along the trail what looks like they might have some. We'll take whatever they got an' ride on."

"But, Yolanda, them people gonna go right to the law. We ain't gonna be able to travel nowhere without folk'll be lookin' for us. They might hang us—or put us in one o' these West Texas jails to rot."

She stared at him a long moment. "You're even dumber'n I thought. You think we gonna leave 'em alive to go runnin' to the law?"

"We gonna kill people what ain't done nothin' to us?"

She shook her head. "Now, you try real hard to figger this out: We don't leave 'em alive, means they're dead. They're dead, an' we just took their money, seems to me we're the ones who killed 'em. You got that figgered?"

Tom looked at her, fear widening his eyes, and he shook his head. "Sister, you gonna get us in a heap o' trouble." His shoulders slumped. "Don't know as how I can kill a man what ain't never done me no harm."

She dug in the saddlebag, pulled out her Colt .25 revolver, and pointed it at his head. "You better start thinkin' how you can do it, or I'll be the only one of us left to do it. You figgered out what I'm tellin' you?" Tom stared at her, horror twisting his face. He nodded, dumbly. "Reckon we'll do it yore way, sister. Don't look like they's any other way." His face brightened. "Course we could go home."

She cocked her revolver. "Wrong answer, little brother. We ain't goin' home till we done what we come out here to do. Now stand up an' get our gear on these horses. We'll see if anybody in that scrubby little town ahead of us has seen McClure or Bert."

The next evening, about an hour before sunset, leading their horses, dragging their feet from sheer exhaustion, thirst, and hunger, Yolanda and Tom stopped at the town's well. They drank before taking their more dead than alive horses to the trough.

She looked the town over, saw the hotel sign hanging at the front of a two-story, sun-bleached, gray building. Knowing what their finances were, she was tempted to ride out of town a ways and make camp, but the thought of a bath, and putting on clean clothes, swung her to deciding on the hotel.

Maybe after making herself presentable she could go to the law and see if either of the men she looked for had been seen in town. But first the bath, then a good meal, then she'd hunt up the law. Hell, they could always find somebody with enough money to replenish their small funds. She'd already settled her mind about robbing people.

After supper, knowing she looked good enough to turn any man's head, Yolanda walked into Marshal Ridges's office.

As soon as he looked up from the wanted notices he'd been studying, Bridges dropped his feet off the spur-scarred, and cigarette-burned desk. He wondered what a woman of class like the one he looked at could want with the law. He hurriedly stood. "Help you, ma'am?"

"Why yes, sir. My brother an' me been travelin for weeks now, hopin' to catch up with our other brother, an' the man who killed two of my brothers. The brother I'm huntin' now is Bert Squires, an' the man what killed my brothers is Hawken McClure. Wondered if they been through this town."

Ridges looked as though he didn't want to answer, then shrugged. "Yes'm, seen 'em both, but they ain't here now. Yore brother, short stocky man? Well, he rode out without sayin' much to anybody. Don't know where he mighta gone." He pushed his hat back, puckered his lips, and let fly a stream of tobacco juice at a spittoon over by the wall.

"Now, that man McClure's a different story. He shot an' killed one o' my deputies. We been lookin' fer 'im fer quite a spell now. Fact is, I got at least twenty men searching the countryside fer 'im." He shook his head. "Ain't found hide ner hair of 'im since he run into the chaparral, but we gonna find 'im, an' beggin' yore pardon, ma'am—you ain't gonna be gettin' even for him killin' yore brothers, 'cause we gonna hang 'im with a brand new rope."

She had no trouble putting on a disappointed expression. She wanted McClure to die at her hands. Hawk wasn't the kind of man who'd wait for a posse to catch up with him. She figured he was long gone by now. She forced a slight smile. "Know how you must feel, Marshal, but if I don't find 'im, he'll find me. As for my brother, reckon we'll just keep lookin' for 'im. Thanks for your help, sir."

She left. Then she smiled to herself while crossing the boardwalk. Hang 'im with a new rope, that might be better than what she planned for him. She'd like to watch the trapdoor drop from under him.

Four days later, when Mixus's told McClure they should reach Gundy's ranch by the next nooning, the old man asked, "You notice anythin' the last day or so?"

McClure let a slight smile break the corners of his mouth. "You mean the riders who've been shadowin' us?"

"Well gosh ding it, course that's what I mean. Didn't figger a danged tenderfoot would see 'em." He chomped down on his chew, worked it to between his lower cheek and teeth, then spit, hitting a horny toad dead center on its back. The toad looked at him in disgust and skittered under some brush. "Notice anythin' else?"

Hawk nodded. "Yep. There's one o' 'em ridin' off that ridge over yonder, comin' toward us. Reckon he wants to welcome us?"

"Don't bet yore saddle on it, young'un. He's gonna find out if'n we're friendly. This is a right salty bunch, another'un's the Sandoval outfit further south. Keep yore hands clear o' your side gun or you might draw lead.''

McClure crossed his hands on the pommel, while Mixus drew his horse behind the wagon.

The rider, a rail-thin cowboy, and clean as though he hadn't been away from water more than an hour, pulled in about ten feet from the rear ox and swept the two darkies with a glance, then studied McClure a moment. "Where you headed, stranger?"

"Figured to see if Mr. Gundy might let us rest up a couple o' days at his outfit."

Before he could answer, Mixus rode from behind the wagon, right into the face of a drawn six-shooter. The old man grinned. "Damn, Crockett, you gettin' sloppy. Ain't been long ago you'd of knowed I wuz there. Gotta say, though, you ain't slowed down on that draw o' yore's."

The rider gave Mixus a sour look, then turned to Mc-Clure. "Stranger, I wuz 'bout ready to tell you you'd be welcome, but seein' the company you keep, don't know whether the boss'll let you stay or not."

"Well gosh ding it, Crockett, shake hands with Hawk McClure. We done partnered up since I last seen you."

Crockett first shook Mixus's hand and pounded him on the back, then he took Hawk's extended hand. When McClure had introduced Bessie, Ned, and Reb, Crockett looked at them with a sweeping glance. "Looks like you folks been doin' some hard travelin'. Sure, ride on in. I'm 'bout ready to head for the barn myself. I'll ride with you."

They camped that night still four or five hours away from ranch headquarters. Mixus and Crockett caught up on what had happened since the last time they's seen each other while the others listened. Early the next day they headed for the ranch.

10

WHEN THE RANCH buildings came in site, McClure twisted in the saddle and looked at Crockett. "Man, I thought we were heading for a ranch—that's a whole town down yonder."

Crockett nodded. "It is that, but it's still a ranch. It's got everythin' a town's got 'cept women for a lonely cowboy. We gotta go into Marfa for that sort o' thing." He gave Bessie an apologetic look.

"Lordy days, Mistuh Crockett, don't mind me. I knows what's on a man's mind most o' the time." She gave Ned a hard look. "That there worthless man o' mine ain't no different. He makes like it don't makes no difference, but he uses his *husban'* rights ever chance he gits."

Ned chuckled. "Yes, suh, an' if I didn't, she'd be right there usin' her *wife* rights. Them womenfolks're a real problem to a man." He cast an apologetic look toward Rebecca. "Aw now, little miss—uh, mister, we got no right to be talkin' this way 'fore you."

Even though she felt the heat in her face, Rebecca chuckled. "That's all right, Ned. If I'm gonna be much of a man, an' *understand how a man thinks,* reckon I

gotta listen an' learn much as I can. I got no other way
of learnin'.''

''You danged shore better not try to learn no other
way, like from tryin' things at yore age, little mister, or
I'll tan yore chubby little bottom.'' Bessie's look didn't
brook any argument. She turned her anger to the men.
''That there boy's gonna grow up to be a Southern gentleman. He ain't gonna grow up to be no carousin', saloon drinkin', gunfightin' nobody in this here country.''

Rebecca chuckled to herself. Bessie was laying it on
kind of heavy; there was no chance a young lady could
aspire to any of it, even if she was of a mind to. But,
to her amazement, she realized she had fallen in love
with these Western lands. The men were of a kind any
woman would like—they were real men.

She glanced at Hawk. That man would stack up with
any, and stand head and shoulders above most. She
swung her long black hair over her shoulders, wishing
the tall Alabamian could see the woman she was under
the dirt and grime, and the masquerade she'd taken to
herself. As soon as she swung her hair over her shoulders, she decided she'd better start piling it on top of
her head and putting her hat on over it; she was beginning to look too much like a girl.

Inwardly, she shrugged. One of these days she'd walk
out in front of him in the one dress she'd saved, and let
him see her as she really was. She wanted to be able to
see his eyes when he looked at her, see if he thought
she was pretty, although she wouldn't admit to herself
that whether he thought her pretty would make any difference.

Then she thought back to when the horse stumbled
and he'd grabbed her. She sighed. He'd apparently not
noticed a thing. He still treated her like a boy.

She turned her attention to the ranch. She'd never expected to see what several hundred years ago would
have been called a small kingdom. She would not have
been surprised to see knights in chain-mail armor ride
from the gate, lance butts sitting against stirrups, broad

swords hanging at sides. She looked at Crockett. "It's magnificent, Mr. Crockett. Don't know as how a scruffy bunch like us will be welcomed down there."

Crockett chuckled. "Son, stick around awhile. You'll notice when the men ride in at the end of a hard day, they're a mite more scruffy than you've prob'ly ever been."

He pushed his hat to the back of his head. "This here's a workin' ranch. Ain't a man on it ain't a top hand, the boss included. If Trace wuz here—he's the boss, owns all this here—you'd see a real man of this here land. If he wuz here, you'd see he's the same kind o' man all o' us are. He don't look at how a man's dressed, he looks at the man." He grinned. "They's one thing he holds as law around here: You work for him, you stay clean as the water supply'll let you."

With his words, Rebecca wanted to crawl off somewhere and hide. She, all of her family, were as filthy as anyone she'd ever seen. "Mr. Crockett, reckon if there's water down there, we can show you we clean up pretty well. Fact is, that's one o' our rules too. Hawk just flat won't allow us to go dirty."

She let a smile crinkle the corners of her lips. "Fact is, 'fore we let that old reprobate join us, the one there under all that dust, the one you seem to know from somewhere, we stripped 'im down an scrubbed 'bout two years' dirt off him so we could see who we were lettin' join up with us."

Mixus spit, sputtered, and stammered a moment before he could get a word out. "Wh-why, you gol danged young whippersnapper, I thought I wuz the one gonna have to strip you down an' give you a good scrubbin'. Always runnin' off to be by yoreself 'fore you even take a sponge bath. Jest flat ain't normal."

After venting his phony anger, he grinned, and looked at Crockett. "Tell you, though, that there lad's as good a man as you could want in a gunfight, or as a trail partner."

Crockett neck-reined his horse toward the buldings.

"C'mon, let's go meet Gundy's *segundo*. The boss ain't here; he's up yonder in that Montana country. Jest married a mighty purty lady up yonder. They been stayin' at her ranch, gettin' it back in shape 'fore comin' home. They'll be comin' soon though. I don't figger Trace's gonna spend much time up yonder when it turns cold."

McClure shifted his look from the ranch headquarters back to Crockett. "His *segundo* must be a mighty good man to leave in charge o' all this."

Crockett nodded. "He is, an' even better he's Blanco's brother-in-law from his first wife." Then the lean cowboy told them about the Comancheros killing Dee, and Gundy heading out to kill them all—Apache fashion. "He done it too. Killed the last one up yonder on Joy Waldrop's ranch. That's how he come to meet her. She's now Miz Gundy."

Crockett led them down the hill, and when they passed through the huge gate, McClure shook his head. "Man, I'd sure hate to try to take this place with several companies of crack troops. Why, hell, this is a regular fortress."

Crockett nodded. "Needed such a place 'fore Blanco ran the Comancheros to other parts." He grinned. "An' when I say Blanco done it, I mean just that. He done it all by his self. Fact is, all you gotta do is mention Blanco around them Comancheros and they turn tail an' run like a scalded cat."

After Crockett's words, McClure began to form a mental picture of Gundy: ten feet tall, shoulders wide as Texas, muscles splitting his shirt, and waving firearms around with both hands and feet.

Crockett reined in at the hitching rack out a ways from the heavy, hand-carved front door. "C'mon in, meet Pablo. He's prob'ly in there workin' on the books. Hates it but does it 'cause Blanco says so."

Before they could enter the house, a tall, lean vaquero stepped outside. McClure studied him a moment. Gundy's first wife must have been a beauty if she took after her brother. This young Spaniard was not only handsome, but moved with the grace of one of those big mountain cats. Crockett introduced them, and Pablo stood aside and waved them toward the door. "Enter. *Mi casa es su casa.*"

Hawk smiled. "You're mighty gracious, sir, but I don't reckon you want anyone in your home as filthy as we are, despite your sayin' your house is our house."

"*De nada.* 'Tis nothing, my friend, come in. We'll worry about baths and all that after you have had a drink, and have eaten."

Crockett explained that they wanted to rest up a few days before heading toward Colorado. Pablo, or Paul Kelly as Crockett called him, frowned. "As you can see, we have plenty of room here, or if you think you'd be more comfortable in the guest house, the choice is yours, but whichever you choose, you'll have your meals here, and you can stay as long as you like."

McClure shook his head. "Mr. Kelly, we don't want to take advantage o' your hospitality before you know some things 'bout us." He waved his hand toward his party. "There's not a one o' those folks you're lookin' at who's not wanted by the law someplace or other. Let me tell you about us before you invite us in."

Paul raised his eyebrows, smiled, and insisted they come in. "We'll talk about you folks once you're comfortable." He looked at Reb. "I'll bet the lad there, bad outlaw that he is, could use a glass of lemonade, and we have coffee, whiskey, wine—almost anything you could want for you grown-ups. You name it."

Sitting in the room, furnished with massive furniture of Mexican style, McClure took a swallow of his drink—whiskey—and told Kelly the entire story begining with himself. Finished, he sat back and looked at Paul. "There you have it, sir, and although wanted by the law from here to Alabama, there's not a one of us who, in my opinion, can't be trusted to act as true gentlemen—an' the lady, of course, except maybe that old reprobate sittin' yonder behind all that beard."

"Well gosh ding it, you young whippersnapper . . ."

They laughed, while Mixus, realizing he'd again taken Hawk's bait, grinned foolishly.

With an amused smile, Kelly nodded. "Yep, reckon there I have it." He'd taken to talking Texan like his brother-in-law. "Don't reckon Crockett told you that Blanco broke me outta a Mexican jail, or that my brother-in-law was the notorious Apache Blanco, wanted by every law officer and army unit in the New Mexico Territory, or that when given a fair chance he has proven to be a fine, law-abiding citizen." He shook his head. "McClure, if those of us in Texas looked down our noses at those who might have broken the law at some time or other, without exception we'd be the epitome of hypocrisy. Drink up and I'll pour us another."

Bessie, Ned, and Reb chose to stay in the guest house, and despite Kelly's objections, Mixus and McClure stayed in the bunkhouse. Rebecca wished to stay in the guest house for obvious reasons—she could be a woman when there was no one to see her but the two darkies. Too, she was self-conscious about the too-large overalls she wore, the only thing she had to wear other than the one dress she'd saved to wear on her "coming out," as she thought of the time she'd begin being a woman again.

Thinking of that time, and the clothes she now had to wear, her thoughts turned to McClure. She'd never seen anyone but him who could put on clean jeans and a faded denim shirt and still appear elegant. Most men in evening dress couldn't approach the quality that shone through whatever Hawk wore. She envied him, wished she could appear a woman again, but she dared not, even here among friends. They might let it slip, and she and her family still had a lot of country to cross where the Comanchero ruled supreme.

Their second day at the A-B Connected, McClure said he would take a couple of packhorses to Marfa and stock up on supplies. Reb wanted to go, but he vetoed the idea. "That's rough country, son, the terrain and the people. An' from what Paul tells me, they have a fair but hard-nosed marshal there. If he recognizes me, an' wants to lock me up, I'll have to run." He reached a hand toward her shoulder, and hurriedly drew it back. "Don't want to have to watch anything but my own hind end. Mixus wants to go, so reckon I'll take 'im along. He can watch my back."

Two days later, Hawk and the old outlaw sat their horses on the outskirts of Marfa. McClure eyed Mixus. "Know what, old-timer? You look danged near human with your beard trimmed, an' clothes you only wore a couple o' days. Reckon we look passable, so let's see what the town has to offer.

Their first stop was the livery, where they left their horses; then they headed for the closest saloon. McClure wanted to go see the town marshal, but squelched the thought. Kelly had told him the man was a square shooter, believed in a man defending himself, but Hawk wasn't ready to jeopardize Bessie, Ned, or most of all, Reb.

He didn't kid himself about his worth to the safety of the three. They were good folks, and had enough guts to fill a washtub, but they'd not been in the fight or die situations he had.

When they pushed through the batwing doors, Mixus slipped to the side. He said it was to let his eyes adjust to the darkness within. McClure eyed him, a grin twisting his lips. "Old-timer, seems to me you sort o' enjoy playin' outlaw. Hell, there's probably not four men in this part o' Texas who knew you back when you stole those horses. An' after twenty years not a damned one of them would stand a chance of puttin' what you were with what you are. You've changed, Rolf, just as we've all changed. C'mon, let's belly up to the bar an' have a drink."

Mixus gave him a shamefaced grin, and headed for the long polished surface. Regret washed over McClure. He'd taken some of the old man's fun, perhaps some of his pride, from him even though he'd meant only to josh him a bit. He resolved to be more careful of the old outlaw's feelings in the future.

They knocked back a couple of drinks, and were holding their glasses out for a refill when a voice sounded behind McClure. "Don't get excited an' reach for your pistol, McClure. I'm lookin' fer nothing but peace."

Hawk turned his back to the bar. His every move was slow, deliberate. If the voice belonged to the man he thought of, there was no way he could get a gun in action fast enough—if the man had a revolver already clear of its holster. The voice and the man matched up. Bert Squires stood there, his hands wide of his holster.

"Seen ya come in here. Want you to know somethin', McClure, I done split from my sister an' brother. Reckon I listened to Yolanda's hate an' poison-filled ideas long's I could. She used Tom an' me, jest like she did the twins—got 'em killed. Now she figgers to do the same with me an' Tom. Like them Southern Baptist preachers would say, I seen the light. I cut out soon's I seen a way to do it."

McClure studied Bert for a long moment, decided if Squires wanted him dead, he'd had the chance while he turned toward him. "All right, Squires, buy you a drink an' let's sit down over yonder against the wall an' talk."

He told the bartender to fill a glass for the stubby Alabamian, nodded toward a table, and while going to it, said, "She's not gonna forgive me for shootin' the twins." He stopped in the middle of the floor and pinned Squires with a hard look. "How 'bout you?"

Bert continued to the table, sat, and rolled a cigarette. "Hawk, she don't want you dead on account o' the twins. She's usin' that for a excuse. You musta done somethin' to her, somethin' bad, 'cause she hates you right down deep in her gut. Ain't never seen nobody hate so much."

McClure knew instantly why she hated him, if it wasn't the killing she held against him. He remembered laughing at her pitiful effort to draw him into her web. He thought to tell Bert about it, then changed his mind.

It would only embarrass the man. He looked across the rim of his glass at Squires. "I'm askin' again, you holdin' the twins' death against me?"

Bert stared into his drink. "Reckon I oughtta, but I know they brought it to you—give you no choice. Course I know too that Yolanda pushed 'em into that gunfight thinkin' the three of 'em could take you easy. Prob'ly figured you'd take on the twins first, an' leave her a clear shot at you."

He knocked back his drink and signaled the bartender for three more. "Reckon if I had to blame somebody, it'd be my sister. I taken a good look at her out yonder in the chaparral. She almost got all o' us killed with her hard-headed hate. We run outta water. She wouldn't listen to nobody 'bout provisions, water, shells for our guns, takin' care o' the horses—nothin'. But Tom'll stay with her. She's got 'im buffaloed." Their drinks came. Bert paid, then looked at McClure. "Naw, Hawk, don't reckon I blame you for the twins. A man's gotta protect his self."

"Where're Tom and Yolanda now?"

"Reckon if they ain't killed their hosses, they oughtta be in Fort Stockton. Me? I reckon if they's a ranch round here where they don't mind learnin' a man to cowboy, I'll sign on with 'em."

McClure felt relieved, and in with that feeling was amusement. He hid a grin. "You got any kind o' idea what the life of a cowboy's like? Bert, it might be the hardest work you ever did, or even heard about."

"Ain't never been afraid of work, McClure. I like this country an' the people out here. Figger to change my name an' start over, start clean, leave what's behind me in the past."

For the first time, Mixus put in his two bits' worth. "Son, gotta tell yu, that deecision's the best you'll ever make. Wisht I'da done the same thing several years ago. Waited till I run onto yore friend here to make the choice. Shore am glad."

McClure leaned back in his chair, smiled at them, and

said, "Reckon all these decisions deserve a little celebration. Let's have one more drink, then Mixus an' I gotta get outta here an' buy some provisions. But first, you got any idea where your sister an' brother'll head for when they leave Fort Stockton?"

Bert looked at him, his face twisted in sadness. He shook his head. "Don't make no difference, McClure, the way Yolanda is, they gonna hunt till they find you." His sad expression deepened, his lips twisted as though in pain. "Then I reckon she's gonna git Tom killed too."

McClure shook his head. "Bert, I promise you, I'm gonna do my best to keep that from happening." He glanced at Mixus. "Come on, old-timer, we got a bunch o' supplies to buy." He stood, stared at Bert Squires, and said, "Good luck, Bert. You've taken the right fork in the trail, stick with it. You gonna find some mighty nice people along the trail you've chosen."

On the way to the general store, McClure glanced at mixus. "Rolf, I feel like I just got a Christmas present. I didn't want to have to kill that man, an' even better, it's good to know he's sucked it up and is gonna do somethin' that's best for him and all around him."

Mixus stared at him, one eye about half-closed. "Young'un, you didn't seem worried 'bout whether you could beat him to the draw. Why? Are you that fast?"

McClure shook his head. "Don't know, old-timer. Only know I'm still here, an' I been in a lot o' tough spots." He shrugged. "Gonna tell you somethin' though. I don't worry 'bout it, 'cause if I did I'd be like a few cowards I've met along the way. They died a little every day; I figure on doin' it only once."

Mixus grinned. "One way to look at it, boy. That's the way I always figgered it."

They bought provisions, stepped from the store, and almost bumped into a man wearing a star. McClure, his arms full of packages, and two empty gunnysacks slung over his shoulder, stepped back and asked the marshal to pardon him. The marshal stared at him a moment.

"Howdy, McClure, been expectin' ya. Why don't you stash them supplies on yore packhosses and come on over to the office. Wantta talk to you." He looked at Mixus, a slight twinkle in his eyes. "You come on over too, Mixus."

Caught with no way of fighting—or running, McClure said, "My packhorses are at the livery. You gonna walk down there with us to make sure we come back? 'Sides that, you know my name, seems only fair I know yours."

"Ben Darcy, town marshal." He shook his head. "Nope, ain't goin' to the livery with you. You tell me you're comin' back, I'll wait there for you. Don't see no need to walk farther'n I have to."

McClure thought it odd the marshal would trust him, then put it down to the fact the lawman knew this part of the country and he didn't. Darcy probably figured he could catch him if he ran. But Mixus knew how to evade a posse in the brush, and he'd let him call the shots. Maybe he should run.

He decided to meet the grim-faced, leathery marshal. He nodded. "See you in a few minutes. Wantta load these things on my packsaddle so's they won't spill all over the trail."

About thirty minutes passed before he and Mixus sat across the scarred, cigarette-burned desk from Darcy. What you want to talk 'bout, Marshal?"

The lawman stared at him a moment. "Wantta talk 'bout you, McClure." He shifted his eyes to Mixus. "An' you, Mixus." He shook his head, and a twinkle again showed behind his eyes. "Uhh-uh, a couple o' real badmen." He held his gaze on the old outlaw. "They wanted you for horse stealin' in Stockton a few years back. The statute of limitations run out on that charge years ago. So if you wantta go, get lost."

"Ain't goin' nowhere. McClure's my partner. Ain't leavin' 'im."

"Figured as much." Then Darcy pinned McClure with a hard look. "You now, McClure, are a different

story. I heered 'bout you from a ranger friend o' mine.''
He explained he'd spent several years in the Rangers,
and still had a good rapport with them—they exchanged
information. ''Bill McMillan over yonder in Shreve's
Landin' wrote 'bout ever' Texian he still knew all 'bout
you. Far's I'm concerned, I ain't got nothin' agin you—
from over there. But, I also heered you shot Marshal
Ridges's partner over in Fort Stockton. Tell me 'bout
how it happened.''

McClure's gut tightened. He felt sick to his stomach.
He'd shot a lawman's friend. He figured there was no
way he could talk his way out of this. Right or wrong,
they'd hold him for trial. He shrugged mentally. What
the hell, he'd tell it like it was. Never breaking his gaze
with Darcy's, he told him what happened.

His face hard as a piece of granite, the marshal asked
him about the hardcases on the wagon with whom he
traveled.

''Darcy, gonna tell it like it is. The hardcases to whom
you refer are a thirteen-year-old boy and two old darkies
who've been takin' care of the boy since he was a baby.
The old woman shot a man Ridges sent to find me,
'cause he tried to pull a gun on the boy. All three o'
them were only doin' what I'd taught 'em to do—protect
themselves. Too, they had no way o' knowin' those men
had been deputized by Ridges. Fact is, I don't know they
were actin' for the law. Ridges maybe, but I figure he
isn't much lawman.''

Darcy sat back and packed his pipe. McClure and
Mixus followed suit, lighted their pipes, and through a
great cloud of smoke stared at the marshal, who sat staring at the ceiling, brows puckered. Finally he brought
his eyes back to them. ''Gonna tell y'all what's a fact.
Like I said, I was a ranger several years. Out in the field
we kind of had to interpret the law like we seen it. On
most occasions we had to deal out justice based on what
we'd seen, or heard.

''That man, Blanco, you're stayin' on his ranch, he
was the most wanted man in the New Mexico Territory.

I knew it, an' let im have free rein to set himself up in ranchin'. Tried to get 'im to join the Rangers, but he turned me down; wanted to get married.

"Turned out he's one o' Texas's most respected citizens." He nodded. "Most dangerous one too, but at the same time the most respected. He takes right sudden offense if anybody messes with his family or what's his."

He gave McClure a straight-on look. "Figger you for the same kind o' man, and I'll tell you straight, you ain't gonna have no trouble outta the Rangers in Texas, but be damned careful 'bout the marshals. Some o' these towns hire a lawman 'cause he's good with a gun without lookin' to see what kind o' man he is. Too, some o' the small town marshals are men who've just sort o' moved in an' taken over the office." For the first time, he gave them an all-out grin. "Now, let's have a cup o' that there mud over yonder—or, I'll let y'all buy me a drink over at the saloon."

McClure let out the breath he'd been holding. "Marshal Darcy, I'll even buy you two drinks. C'mon, let's go."

In the saloon, they went to a table and signaled for a round of drinks—whiskey. McClure glanced at the next table and saw Bert Squires. He waved him over. "C'mon, Squires, got a man I want you to meet."

He introduced Squires to the marshal and said, "Darcy, this man isn't any part of a cowboy, but knows cows and horses. He wants to learn cowboyin'. Reckon you could recommend a ranch willin' to take on a pure-dee tenderfoot?"

The marshal studied Squires a moment, then nodded. "Figger old Ranch Senegal over yonder on the R-Bar-S would take 'im on. He's a rough, tough old man, son, but one helluva man to work for." He smiled. "Tell you the secret to gettin' next to 'im. 'Fore you ride in to see 'im, take a bath if it's gotta be water from your canteen. He don't allow nothin' but clean on his place. Tell you

too, he sorta took Blanco under 'is wing, feels like
Blanco's settin' in for the sons he lost."

Bert smiled. "Reckon I better buy myself another
canteen to be sure I get re-e-eal clean."

They had a couple of drinks with the marshal and
Squires, got themselves a room, cleaned up, and went to
a saloon with women—women who took customers they
liked to a room on the second floor. McClure wanted,
needed, to answer a question about himself that had been
gnawing at his guts almost from the time he discovered
Reb was a girl—even if she was too young for him now,
she'd grow up one of these days.

They went in, got themselves a table, and waited until
one of the girls came over. Hawk and Mixus ordered
drinks. The girl looked kind of pretty, although a bit
skinny for Hawk's taste, and tired, worn out, and he
guessed her to be not more than sixteen or maybe eigh-
teen years old. He wondered what had brought her to
work in a place like this. He glanced at Mixus, and saw
the old man looking with hunger at the girl. He nodded
and told her to get herself a drink.

Before she brought them their round, McClure noticed
a rather plump, blond girl across the room. She wasn't
busy with anyone, so he told the skinny girl to get the
plump one a drink also.

Then, in response to some signal Hawk missed, the
blonde walked across the room smiling. She sat and
looked at Hawk like he was a dish of ice cream.
"Ummm, you gonna have every girl in here mad at me
for takin' the best lookin' man in Texas before they had
a chance."

McClure smiled. "Don't know 'bout that, but just tell
'em I asked for you. That'll be the truth."

After a few drinks, the girls took them to their rooms.
Hawk's girl had no more than slipped her skimpy dress
down over her full, round, pink-tipped breasts when he
felt himself respond. She excited him, and that very fact
made him wonder if he was willing to wait for Reb to
grow up, wait to see what kind of woman she was under

all the dirt she'd accumulated out in the brush. He backed off. He'd never bought a woman's favors in his life.

He looked at her lush figure, wanting, hurting with all the hunger that had built in him over the months. He stepped back and shook his head. He wasn't going to start paying for a woman's favors now.

He'd found what he wanted to know. Yeah, he wanted a woman, but not this woman. The woman he wanted didn't have a face yet . . . or maybe Reb had that face. He'd wait and see.

He explained to the blonde there was nothing wrong with her, that it was him, that he didn't have time for an all-night stand, that it would take at least all night to do the job right. His explanation apparently mollified the girl. He paid her and left, hurting even worse now that he'd seen a woman for the first time in months.

He went downstairs, and waited over an hour for Mixus to come down. They had a couple more drinks and went to their room. McClure figured to head for the AB Connected come daylight.

Two days later they rode into the ranch yard.

Rebecca watched them ride in, stop their horses alongside the wagon and unload the provisions into the wagon bed, then take their horses to the stable. She wondered if Hawk had done the things she'd heard all men did when they went to town. Had he gotten drunk, raised hell, bedded a woman, or all three? Her unanswered questions left her irritable, with a twinge of jealousy.

Why should she be jealous? Why should it make a difference to her if he bedded every woman in Texas? Unconsciously her hand crept to her breast, remembering the momentary feel of his hand. Warmth flooded her body. Too, why had he stopped touching her shoulder? She'd never said anything to stop him—and she had to admit to herself she missed that simple little intimacy.

Hawk and Mixus came from the barn. She angled toward them to cut them off and tell them Gundy and his wife had arrived the day before. "She's a pretty woman, Hawk, an' Mr. Gundy's almost as good-lookin' as you. An' although slim, he looks like he could fight a bear and win. Figure you're gonna like 'im. There's nothin' 'bout 'im to make one think that all this ranch being his impresses him a bit."

Hawk grinned down at her. "Hey, boy, sounds like you've picked yourself a new hero, one you want to grow up to be like."

She frowned, then shook her head. "No, Hawk, I still figure to grow up to be the kind o' man you're tryin' to make outta me." She again shook her head. "But I gotta tell you right now, I don't feel like I'm makin' much progress toward becomin' a man."

She giggled deep in her chest, inside of her tightly bound breasts. Nope, she hadn't seen a thing when she was bathed and ready for bed at night that led her to believe she'd ever be a man. "C'mon up to the big house, and I'll introduce you to our hosts."

McClure liked Gundy from the first. And his wife was a charming woman, who took Reb under her wing instantly. She pulled her toward the kitchen. "C'mon, Reb, let's see what's for supper." As soon as they were well away from the men, Joy swung to face her. "What'd they shorten to Reb, Rebecca? Doesn't Hawk know you're a woman?"

Rebecca gasped, blushed. "Wh-why what do you mean, Miz Gundy?" Then she felt all the air had gone out of her balloon. She gave Joy Gundy a straight-on look, and shook her head. "No. I don't think he suspects. I hope not, until I feel safe from men with no scruples, or lack of morality. He might let it out of the bag, then if I was insulted in any way he'd fight them, and might get hurt." She shook her head. "I don't think I could stand that."

Joy stared at her a moment. "You poor dear, and I believe you don't realize you're in love with the man."

"In love? Why, you must be out of your mind. I've never thought of him as anything but our protector, a man who seems to know what to do regardless what happens, a man I like to see sittin' by the fire at night, an' just by bein' there makin' me feel better.''

Joy nodded, smiled. ''Sounds an awful lot like the way a woman in love would describe her man. That's a lot the same way I feel about Trace.'' She wrapped Rebecca in her arms. ''Now, don't you worry your pretty head. Your secret's safe with me.''

Rebecca was happy to get off the subject of how she felt about Hawk. She herself wasn't sure what her feelings were. She'd have to think about Joy's assessment first.

Joy stood back and studied her a moment, then nodded. ''Yes, I do believe that under those ill-fitting clothes, and that big floppy hat, there's a very pretty woman—a very pretty *grown* woman, a woman just bursting with the desire to let her man know what she is. A woman itching to see what kind of look is in his eyes when he looks at her. When do you plan to let him know 'bout you?''

''Not until we're outta Apache, Comanche, an' Comanchero country. Not till I figure we're among friends, permanent friends, where we settle down to build our ranch. Travelin' like we are, any kind of men could see me, an' bring trouble to us on the trail. Like I said before, I don't want Hawk having to face anything like that.'' She nodded. ''Yeah, I know here in the West there are but few men who'd molest a woman.'' She shrugged. ''Reckon I just flat don't want to take a chance.''

Joy shrugged. ''Play it your own way. Like I said, your secret's safe with me.'' She smiled. ''Darned if I see how any but a blind man could figure you for a boy.'' She chuckled. ''I'd give a painted pony to be hidin' behind the curtains, or somewhere, when you *show* him you're a girl.'' She blushed. ''By show him, I mean by the way you're dressed—no other way.''

Her last words brought a warmth to Rebecca's cheeks.

"You can bet it'll be by the way I'm dressed long before anything else takes place."

Joy turned toward the huge living room. "Let's go fix the men a drink before they die of thirst."

Hawk sat in one of the large chairs next to Blanco; Pablo sat facing them. They each had a drink in their hands. "Oops, we were just comin' to fix you men a drink. You beat us to it." Joy hardly took her eyes off of Trace while she talked. Rebecca made a mental note not to look at Hawk that way until she made up her mind about her feelings for him—and showed him she was not what she appeared to be.

"Pablo was tellin' us he might like to join us until we get into New Mexico Territory. Says he'd like to go out there to see 'is folks. Now that Trace is back, he'll take over runnin' the ranch." McClure took a swallow of his drink. "Reckon I feel like he's doin' it to be sure we're safe. Don't want to drag 'im away from Trace until they have a chance to discuss how things've been goin' with each of them."

Trace grinned. "Hawk, I can tell you how they're goin'. Pablo pro'bly has the books in better shape than I ever keep them. He's most likely makin' money, an' to top it all, I figger he's 'bout to get mighty antsy with nothin' happenin'. He needs some action, an' figgers stickin' with you folks'll give it to 'im."

McClure had no doubt but what Paul would get his fill of action if he went with them. With Reb and the two darkies along, he wished there could be a certainty of *no* action, but the country they had to cross would not allow such a feeling.

11

THEY WERE FOUR days west of the A-B Connected when McClure's fears were realized. Seven men rode toward them, all hardcases by their appearance, tied down six-shooters on their thighs, and all carrying rifles across the saddle in front of them.

Hawk thanked every deity he knew for Pablo, and the two men Paul insisted on bringing with him: Emilio Sanchez and Fernando Hernandez. He glanced at the wagon, and the terrain around it. None of the three were in sight. He felt as though his hair curled at the base of his neck. Where had they gone when he needed them?

The man in the lead pulled rein when within about fifty feet of the wagon. "You Hawken McClure?" The rifles of all seven had him bore-sighted. His guts turned over and threatened to tie themselves in knots. His mouth dried up. He couldn't have collected enough saliva to wet his lips.

He nodded. "I'm Hawken McClure. What you want?"

The man who'd apparently elected himself as spokes-man for the seven grinned. "Reckon we want you, mis-ter badman. Marshal Bridges sent us to find you. Said not to bring yu back. Said if we could find a tree big 'nuff, to hang yu out here.'' He glanced around. ''Reckon they ain't any trees big 'nuff, but we can use the wagon tongue. Stand it straight up an' it'll prob'ly make yore feet clear the ground by 'bout two feet.'' He nodded. ''Yep. That'll get the job done.'' He looked at the man closest to him. ''You got a new rope hangin' from yore saddle. We'll use it.''

Although dripping with fearful sweat, McClure tried not to show it. He played for time. Where the hell had Pablo and his two men gone? He stared at the man in charge. ''Gonna remind y'all, Ridges has no authority out here. We're outta his jurisdiction.''

The man laughed, showing brown snaggly teeth through the tobacco-stained mustache covering his mouth. ''Now, ain't them pretty words, authority, jurisdi . . . whatever the hell you said.'' He turned to his men. ''Shake out that there rope, men. Don't wanta waste no more time out here. I'm ready fer a drink.''

From the chaparral the other side of the wagon a voice spoke up. ''Ah but, *señors,* I would not be in such a hurry, we 'ave seex new Winchesters trained on your gut. Looks like we 'ave what you Americanos call a Mexican Standoff. *Sí?* You shoot McClure, we shoot all of you. You'll never have a chance to see heem dance at the end of that rope.'' Pablo's voice hardened, and lost any semblance of an accent. ''Now turn those horses around and ride straight back down the trail. You even think about coming back at us through the brush, an' we'll shorten the population of Fort Stockton.'' A chuckle came from the bushes. ''Reckon the decent citizens of that town might give us a medal for getting rid o' you.''

The seven stared at the heavy brush. They obviously couldn't see anyone, and didn't like the odds. All they could do was spray the brush with bullets, hoping for a lucky shot, and one wouldn't be enough.

The leader of the illegal posse glanced at his men, and nodded down the backtrail. ''Let's go.'' When they kneed their horses to leave, the leader said over his shoulder, "Watch yore backtrail. We gonna be there somewhere."

The sound of a single shot from the chaparral cut the air. The leader, knocked back in his saddle, slid off to the side, making a dull thump when he hit the ground. Again using the Mexican accent, Pablo said, "Tsch, tsch. My Englaise must not be ver' good. Thought I said it good enough you'd onerstan'. Don't come back."

McClure's eyes never left the remaining six, until a bend in the trail hid them. He twisted to look behind him. "Why'd you shoot that man, Pablo? They were riding away like you told them."

Paul chuckled. "Reckon I wanted to 'splain it to 'em a little better. Think maybe they understand better now what I was tellin' 'em." He stepped from the brush, Emilio and Fernando beside him. "What I intended to do was take out their leader. Maybe they'll think real hard before they come after us again." He shrugged. "Shoulda emptied all their saddles—then no worries." His smile didn't soften his words.

McClure stared at the slim, handsome vaquero, and shook his head. "You do have a way of explainin' things, amigo. Remind me not to ever cross you." He tucked it away in his mind to remember that Blanco's brother-in-law was made of the same kind of stuff as Blanco himself.

They had traveled in country more given to short grass plains, with only occasional clumps of cactus and scrub trees. Now only rolling hills stretched before them, broken by an occasional butte or great jumbles of rock. Pablo stretched his hand in front of him. "You see there the kind of country we're gonna be putting behind us for many days yet, then we come to the mountains, bigger and more rugged mountains than back there at Blanco's ranch." He smiled. "For now, these plains are our best friend."

McClure frowned a question. Pablo nodded. "*Sí*, it will be very difficult for Ridges's men to sneak up on us with little or no cover. But I'm tellin' you right now, Hawk, we're gonna see those six men again—maybe not tonight, maybe not tomorrow, but we're gonna see 'em again. We'll be ready.''

McClure unconsciously ran fingers down the smooth stock of his Winchester. "We'll keep scouts out. I'll take the rear, you, or one of your men, go ahead of us.''

A cold, long-blowing wind passed across the grass, playing its song on the blades, forming ripples across the top of the grass like waters on a lake. Hawk smelled the sun cooked into the dried stems, and the dust of the land itself.

Eyes slitted to see across the land, he felt he'd come home. The vast distances, with finally the deep blue sky swallowing the land's edge, made a man feel no more than a grain of sand in the limitless panorama.

Far off, several miles by his estimate, a tumble of boulders broke the roll of land. He pictured himself sitting on those rocks and looking at the wagon and its party. They would look as no more than a speck in the vastness of it all.

Then it occurred to him: If he was one of Ridges's men, those rocks would be a good place for an ambush—but only if the wagon and its party thought the boulders to be a good place to camp and made an unwary approach. He pondered the distance a moment and decided the men on horseback could easily circle them and make it to the boulders long before the slow-moving wagon. He reined his horse about and headed for the wagon.

When he reached his party, he asked Emilio where Pablo rode. The vaquero pointed to a speck far ahead of them. McClure headed for him.

He reined his horse alongside of Paul's and pointed to the mound of boulders. "Those rocks'll make a good windbreak for camp. What you think?''

Paul nodded. "Yeah, if someone isn't there ahead of us.''

Still squinting at the distant boulders, McClure said,

"Figure to scout 'em out. See if maybe Ridges's bunch has the same idea. I'll go in after dark."

Pablo grinned. "Now see there, you wantin' to hog all the fun for yourself. I think two scouts'll be better."

McClure frowned. "Yeah, Pablo, but if somethin' should happen to both o' us, that'd leave the darkies an' Reb without two fightin' men."

Paul laughed, a deep-chested sound. "McClure, you've never seen fighting men till you see those two vaqueros of mine go into action." He shook his head. "No. I think you and I are the ones for the job. Your people will be all right." Then, as if on signal, they turned their horses toward the wagon.

The sun, a great red ball, slipped toward the horizon. Ned led the oxen on, but now much closer to the boulders. Paul and McClure stayed with the big Studebaker. The red ball seemed to move faster with the horizon to measure its path by. Half of it disappeared—then the only thing left to remind one of its warm presence in the sky were shades of gold, lavender, rose, turquoise, and purples. McClure glanced at Pablo and nodded toward the rocks.

They split, each going a different direction. McClure circled to the left, wanting to approach the boulders from that direction. After about half an hour, the black, blurred shapes of the rocks rose out of the grass a couple of hundred yards ahead. He ground-reined the big black gelding. Blacky would stand there until he came for him.

On the ride in, his nerves tightened with each step of his horse. Now, afoot, his neck muscles tightened, his scalp tingled, and the well-known mouth dryness made him hunger for a drink of cold water. He dropped to his stomach, cradling his Winchester in the crooks of his elbows, and inched himself along, pulling his body ahead with his elbows.

After a half hour or so, he stopped to rest, then frowned. He and Paul had not discussed what to do when they got there. He figured they both thought to go in shooting. He pondered that idea a moment, then grinned into the night. He had a better idea—if he could get there ahead of Pablo.

Rested, he again inched ahead. His elbows first got sore, then pained like someone peeled the hide off them. He'd known the feeling many times while scouting for the Army. His elbows *did* have the skin scraped from them, and were probably bleeding. He pushed the pain to the back of his head. A bullet would hurt one helluva lot more.

The closer he got, the tighter strung were his nerves, and the harder he sweated. He expected to hear gunfire at any moment, and hoped he wouldn't.

He had to beat Pablo to the rocks—but suppose they were empty? Well, if no one sat there ahead of them, there would be no fight. Pablo would be sorely disappointed—but McClure would not. He continued pulling himself ahead, then without realizing he'd gotten close enough, he felt his knuckles scrape one of the boulders. He relaxed his arms, and stretched full length behind the rock he'd touched. If his rifle had scraped that hard surface, it would have made a sound, and a sound now could make him dead. He lay there a few moments, getting his nerves settled down, catching his breath, and figuring what to do next.

He slowly pulled his knees under him, then stood. He thought there would be spaces between each of the huge rocks—and there were. He squeezed between the one he'd touched and the one next to it. Another boulder reared up in front of him, and he slipped to it and leaned his tired body against its bulk.

Voices. At least two of them talking at once—and he was here ahead of Pablo. He inched around the boulder, careful not to scrape his jeans against it, thus make a noise foreign to the natural night sounds.

When he figured he'd gone far enough to keep from exposing his body, he moved his head around the boulder's rounded, wind-and sand-smoothed surface until he looked at men sitting around what he thought might be a buffalo chip fire, only large enough to boil the pot of coffee sitting on its coals. He wondered, hoped, that all six of Ridges's riders sat there. He counted them—and accounted for only five. He would have bet his hair stood on end. Where was the sixth man? He again searched the darkness surounding the small fire. A splash of water against rock on the far side of the fire brought a careful, slow sigh, as he again forced himself to relax a bit. The sixth had gone into the rocks to relieve himself. The five sat around the fire drinking coffee as though they had the rest of the night to get their work done.

During a break in their conversation, the sixth man walked to them, poured himself a cup of coffee, and sat. One of them said, "Randy, walk off a little from these rocks an' see can you hear the rattle o' that there wagon. Once we hear it, we can get set up to take it."

"Aw hell, Brigo, ain't no hurry. They got a long way to go yet. 'Sides that, we can hear 'em plain from in here." At that moment, McClure poked his rifle barrel around the boulder.

"Move an' you're dead."

All stiffened—except one. His right hand swept for his revolver. And never made it. McClure's bullet blew half of his head away. "Any more o' you wantta try?" The five remaining riders sat as though chiseled from stone. "Now, one at a time, stand with your back toward me, shuck your hardware, then lie facedown." Not breaking his gaze from them, he called, "You there yet, Pablo?"

"Yeah, sittin' here enjoyin' the show, Hawk. Get on with what you're doin'."

One at a time, they each shucked their guns and spread-eagled on the ground. McClure stepped from behind the boulder. "Come on out, Pablo. We got their teeth pulled."

Paul walked into the open place between the stones, frowning. "Why the hell didn't you just start shootin'? We'da been shed o' them by now."

His tight nerves relaxed, McClure grinned. "Came up with a better idea while crawlin' up on this place."

"Yeah, what's better'n a dead damned illegal law-man?"

A grin threatening to reach his ears, Hawk said, "Why hell, Pablo, reckon an illegal lawman out here in the middle o' nowhere, without weapons, horses, water, or provisions, is a lot better'n havin' 'em smellin' up our campsite." He pushed his hat to the back of his head with his thumb, then looked at Paul. "Course we gonna have to keep 'em tied up till we set out in the mornin'."

Paul stared at him a moment, then shook his head. "Hawk, you spent too much time talkin' to Blanco back at the ranch. Only he could think of such an inhuman thing to do to a man." He shrugged. "Course we do what you want, an' they're good as coyote bait. They'll be dead, a long terrible death, in four, maybe five days." He nodded. "Good idea."

"Gather their weapons, Pablo, then tie them. We'll set a watch for the rest of the night." He pointed his rifle at the sky and fired three evenly spaced shots, the signal they'd decided on before leaving the wagon, for Ned to lead the Studebaker on toward the rocks.

With the posse tied, McClure walked to the fire, took his neckerchief in hand, picked up the coffeepot, then shook his head. He had no cup, and sure as hell wouldn't drink after one of that scruffy bunch.

Paul glanced at him. "Drink outta the pot, then give me a swallow. It'll be a while 'fore the wagon gets here."

They sat there, taking sips of the hot liquid, passing the pot back and forth, until the rattle of trace chains and the soft voice of Ned broke the silence. McClure stood and tossed a few more buffalo chips on the fire. "Might's well have it ready for Bessie to cook supper. Know they're gonna be as hungry as me when they get here." He shivered. The night had cooled off considerably since he and Pablo left the wagon.

He'd again made as if to sit, when he thought of his horse. "Gonna collect the horses. Yours out the side o' these rocks you come from?" Paul nodded.

When McClure led the horses into the jumble of boulders, Reb and Bessie were only then climbing from the wagon seat. Reb glanced at the five trussed-up men. "Didn't hear but one shot. Must not o' had any trouble with 'em."

Hawk shook his head. "None. They invited me to their fire for a cup o' coffee, then they did a strange thing, they sprawled on their bellies and said for me to tie them so's they wouldn't get up during the night an' wander around in their sleep."

Reb cast him a sour look. "Hawken McClure, can't you ever give me a straight answer? I kept listenin' for gunfire, and when only the one shot came, I had Ned stop the wagon and wait, then we heard your signal. Thought you were gonna shoot 'em."

Pablo grinned at them. "No, *muchacho,* the tall gentleman from the South took some lessons from Blanco." Then he told them what McClure had decided to do.

Reb stared at their protector a moment. "Hawk, you can't do that. It's inhuman."

His face hardened. "Gonna do it my way, son. What they had planned for us wasn't very human either." He busied himself gathering the posse's weapons, saddles, and trail gear, and placed them in the back of the wagon, along with what provisions the men had. He again looked at Reb, and grinned. "We keep collectin' horses and stuff, I figure I won't have to collect many o' those wild mustangs to start a ranch." He glanced at the back of the wagon, then back to Reb. "Son, while Ned's leadin' the oxen tomorrow, I want you to clean and load every weapon we got in the wagon—an' put 'em where they can be at hand for all in the wagon."

"You expectin' more trouble, Hawk?"

He nodded. "Always figure on it, then we'll be ready."

Pablo pulled his revolver, emptied the shells from it, and proceeded to clean the six-shooter. Mixus looked on with approval.

• • • •

Jedediah Powers left Fort Stockton about thirty minutes after Yolanda and Tom Squires. He'd smiled to himself when they stomped angrily from the marshal's office the night before. They apparently had received no news about either McClure or Bert. Too, the woman had learned a little—but not much. Before going to the hotel, she'd bought a couple more canteens, but had done nothing special for the horses. The poor, gaunt animals should have been fed grain to help them last the long distances ahead of them.

Bert's leaving them had not surprised Powers. But he had been surprised it took him so long to cut out on his own after the way his sister treated him. He'd been watching from the brush when Bert took the money from Yolanda's saddlebags, and had to smother a chuckle when he pictured what it would do to the viper and Tom. When he'd seen the stumpy brother shove part of the roll of money back into her bags, he'd nodded in satisfaction. The boy had a heart.

He thought to stay another night in Stockton, then decided against it. There might be trails branching off from the main one, and he didn't want to chance taking the wrong fork and losing them. If they figured to ambush McClure, Old Jedediah would sort of even the odds. He patted the stock of his Winchester when the thought struck him.

He followed at a safe distance so as not to be seen. When the trail forked to head for Marfa, the Squires stayed on the main road toward El Paso. Powers would have bet his saddle McClure had gone to Marfa. He shrugged. Hawken McClure might go by Marfa, but he'd bet money he'd eventually get to El Paso, and he'd need someone to cover his back when the two parties came together. This would put the Squires ahead of his fellow Alabamian again.

Powers had heard the chaparral would give way to grasslands, so he took it in stride when the brush began to thin and long stretches of short grass waved in front of him. He stopped in the middle of the trail and peered ahead. His problem now? How to stay out of sight of those he tracked? Well hell, it was a free country. He could ride anywhere he wished, and to top it off, the two people he tracked didn't know him. But he used care to keep his distance behind them just the same.

Three nights he camped within sight of their small fire. He grunted; someone must have told them about buffalo chips. He himself had bought a couple of tow-sacks in Stockton, and had been collecting chips along the way, filling the sacks as he went.

The fourth day, early, a group of horsemen appeared far to the north. They seemed to ride so as to cut the trail of the two he followed. Stories of Comancheros were told in every town, and around every campfire. Powers worried that in his head awhile. He could hang back and, if the riders were Comancheros, let them have their way with the Squires, but then that would leave him alone, and they could take him easily. He dug his heels into his horse. There were five riders in the approaching group.

He caught the Squires with the riders still about a half mile from them. He tipped his hat. "You folks mind me an' my rifle joinin' up with you—till them five horsemen make known what they figger to do?"

Yolanda scrubbed him down with a scornful, lip-curled look. "Ain't no cause to worry. We got nothin' nobody'd want. What's the matter, you scared?"

Powers felt blood rush to his face. He pushed anger down and looked at her. "Ma'am, if them riders're Comancheros, you got somethin' they want. *You.* They can sell a woman looks like you for a bunch o' dollars across the border. 'Fore I ride on, we best find out what they figger on doin'."

Yolanda's face blanched a few shades, but she was still her poisonous self. "Stay long enough to find out, then ride on. We don't need no company."

Jed shrugged. "Don't figger I'd like bein' in yore company, ma'am. I ain't doin' this for you; it might save my hind end as well. Now, stop your hosses and stand behind 'em, your rifles layed across the saddle pointed at 'em when they ride up.''

Without further words, Powers pulled his rifle from the scabbard, swung a leg over the pommel, slipped to the ground, and did as he'd instructed them to do. Even though not hospitable, they followed his instructions. He swallowed twice trying to rid himself of the knot in his throat, and tried to will his nerves to loosen.

The five reined in, and sat there looking at Powers and the Squires. ''You ain' ver' friendly. Why you hold them guns on us? We ain' gonna hurt ya.''

Powers spit a stream of tobacco juice across his saddle, and tightened his finger on the trigger. ''Know damned well you ain't gonna hurt us. You friendly, pull them horses round, put them big Mexican rowels to 'em, an' get the hell gone—long gone.'' He spit again. ''You got other ideas, go on, play yore hand.''

They were making as though to rein their horses around the three, when one of them halfway hidden by the others swung his hand toward his thigh. Jed squeezed the trigger. The rider fell, knocked back over the cantle—then all hell broke loose.

Jed levered another shell into the chamber, fired, and did it again. Yolanda's and Tom's weapons were spitting lead at the bandits without a break in the sharp crack of rifle fire. A sickening thud almost in his ear caused Jed's horse to stagger, pull himself up, rear—then fall, leaving Powers out in the open. A tug at his pants leg and one on his shirtsleeves caused him to cringe. He jacked another shell into the chamber—but the bandits all lay on the ground.

Yolanda stepped toward the closest Comanchero. ''Hold it there, woman.'' Powers's words stopped her in her tracks.

She opened her mouth, sputtered a couple of times, then said, ''You talk like that to me? Who the hell do you think you are?''

He cast her a disdainful look, then methodically triggered another shot into each of the bandits. He slanted

her a look. "Reckon I'm the man what jest kept you
from gettin' yore damned dumb head blowed off." He
walked to the Comanchero's horses, gathered up the
reins, pulled his gear off his own horse, stowed it on his
packhorse, and looked at the two Squires. "Know you
ain't gonna thank me for savin' yore worthless hides,
don't want none, an' I ain't ridin' nowhere close to
you—but I'm tellin' you right now: I'm takin' all their
hosses, guns, an' trail gear. Ain't leavin' none of it behind. It's stuff you an' that nagged-to-death brother o'
yores could use.

He pulled his horse around so as to mount from the
side away from them. "Now you folks mount up an'
get the hell outta here. Don't trust either o' you at my
back. Know you'd as soon shoot an' rob me as spit."

The look Yolanda gave him said it all. She'd figured
to take the Comanchero gear and horses for herself, and
when he'd mentioned they might rob him, her eyes
opened wide, then closed to slits to hide her thoughts.
He grinned to himself, then said, "Know the thought
never entered yore head to do the decent thing, like
buryin' them men, but we ain't gonna take the time. First
I don't trust either of you at my back with a shovel, an'
second, there might be more trouble to catch up to us.
Now ride out."

12

PABLO LED MCCLURE'S party ever westward toward El Paso. He and Hawk agreed to rest up in that town before heading for Alejandro Kelly's, Pablo's father's ranch, the Circle A-K. They'd had no trouble on the way, except for the time they'd circled wide of where vultures floated overhead. McClure thought it might be a dead animal they fed on until Emilio scouted it and reported that the bones of five men lay out there. The only way he'd come up with the number were the five skulls he found. The rest of the bones were scattered such that no one could have made a count.

They rode into El Paso about sundown, and McClure immediately found a hotel for the two darkies and Reb. When he walked from the hotel, Ned sidled up to him. "Mistuh Hawk, why for you always get me an' Bessie a room, an' don't get nothin' for yoreself?"

Hawk didn't want to hurt the old man's pride, but how was he to tell him he'd watched him stumble while leading the oxen, even though when offered relief he declined? Pride, pure damned pride, that's what it was. He shuffled his feet a couple of times, then looked straight-on at the old man. "Tell you why, Ned. Reb wants to be treated like a man. He's a tough little bird, but I noticed how tired he's been gettin' out yonder.'' He shrugged. "Too, you an' Bessie bein' married can share a room, an' Reb can take the other. Be a waste to have Bessie sleep in a paid-for room all alone.''

Ned scratched his head and smiled. "Reckon you right, suh. Hadn't never thought 'bout it that way.''

They were no sooner settled in their rooms, when Hawk left and Ned took his belongings to the other room, and moved Rebecca's things in with Bessie. Then he asked the clerk to provide two tubs of hot water for baths.

Rebecca locked the door and undressed. Took the wrappings from about her chest and massaged the itchy flesh until she again felt comfortable. "Auntie, I'm 'bout ready to be a girl again. Don't know if I can stand this much longer.''

Bessie cast her a jaundiced look. "Young lady, it ain't that you're gittin' tired o' bein' bound up like a roped an' tied calf. I done seen the way you beginnin' to look at Mistuh Hawk. You evuh let him see that look an' the cat'll be outta the bag.'' She'd been brushing out Rebecca's hair, long now, long enough to give her a definite female look. "' 'Sides that, we ain't where we goin' yet, an' you ain't gonna be temptin' no man with that there figguh o' yores till we git there.'' She chuckled. "Course from the way you been lookin' at Mistuh Hawk I reckon he's the one you gonna try to tempt.''

Rebecca looked over her shoulder at her auntie. "Oh fiddle, I don't know how I feel about him. Know he's right handsome. Know he's been a perfect gentleman. Know he takes care of us before thinking about himself. And I know one thing for sure, I've never seen any other man come close to bein' the man he is. Another thing is, I've never seen one I figured I could spend the rest of my life with and not tire of him. I'll have to think about Hawk bein' with me forever 'fore I make up my mind.''

Bessie stood back, the brush held in the air, ready to

make another swipe at Rebecca's hair. She shook her head. "If them words ain't words of a young woman in love, don't know as I ever heard any."

"Well, Auntie, think what you will, I'm not ready to admit to such—yet." She knew the "yet" had come out awful late. A dead giveaway. But she had to wait and see how Hawk took it—her being a woman and all.

At the livery on the outskirts of town, McClure and Pablo finished taking care of the animals. Paul looked questioningly at Hawk, looked away, then gave him the same look again. "Okay, spit it out, Pablo. What you got on your mind?"

Pablo gave McClure a sheepish look. "Aw hell, reckon I was just wonderin' why Bessie treats Reb like a *little* boy. Hell, that kid's old enough to shift for himself. Far's that goes, he acts almost like he expects Bessie to treat him special."

McClure thumbed his hat to the back of his head. "Tell you what, amigo, I worried 'bout that myself for a while, then I figured bein' raised like he was," he nodded, "you know, the son of well-to-do parents, he's used to that an', well, sort of expects it. But I'll tell you right now, that boy doesn't take a backseat to anyone when it comes to work, or standin' fast when trouble comes along." He nodded. "He'll do to ride the river with any day."

Pablo only shrugged, then asked, "You gonna get a room, or sleep in the hayloft?"

"Figured to go to the barbershop in the mornin', get the works: shave, haircut, an' bath. Think I'll settle for the hayloft tonight." He stepped toward the big, wide doors. "You reckon they'll let us in a saloon lookin' an' smellin' the way we do?"

Pablo chuckled. "Let's find out. But we better not make it one of the better places."

They had walked only a block when they came even with a place that looked like it would take them. Range riders, vaqueros, bullwhackers streamed in and out of the place. None of them looked as if they'd seen a wash-tub in some time. McClure nodded to the batwings. "Looks like we found the right place."

They stood at the bar, knocked back two quick drinks, and were sipping on the third when a slap on the back caused McClure to turn. The man standing at his shoulder looked familiar, but he couldn't tell for sure; tall, lean, and by any standard as dirty and unshaven as him, the man seemed friendly, so McClure kept his hand free of his side gun.

"Don't you remember me, McClure?" The stranger shook his head. "Naw, don't reckon you would, we met for only a few minutes. The reason I'm here, you told me 'bout all the free land out here, said to come on out, they wuz room for ever'body. So I sold my ferry an' come on out."

"Jed-Jedediah Powers? Well, I'll be damned. You did it." Hawk laughed. "Wonder how many times you cussed me while crossin' that dry country."

Looking smug, Jed smiled at him. "Not onc't did I cuss you. Fact is I been too busy tryin' to take care o' some o' yore business." His smile widened to a grin. "I been in gunfights, fistfights, ever' sort o' thing, tryin' to git out here alive. Man, I been havin' fun. If I'd a knowed the West wuz like this, I'da been here long ago."

McClure motioned to the bartender. "Give me a bottle o' the best whiskey you got." He looked at Jed, motioned to Pablo and introduced them, then said, "Let's find a table an' you tell me what's happened to you, an' what business of mine you been takin' care of."

Jed led them to the back of the dark room, found a table where they could see most of those who came and went, and when they were seated, began to bring McClure up to date. When Jed was finished, he squinted against the dark and said, "Them Squires folks what been trackin' you? Well, they're right here in El Paso."

Hawk took a swallow of his drink, shivered when the raw whiskey hit his throat, then nodded. "Figured they'd get ahead o' me. I'm travelin' with a wagon now, an' I'm here to tell you that's slow travelin'. How you come to know it's them?''

"From what you told me they looked like. I seen 'em in one o' them towns back behind us, and been trailin' 'em ever since." He grinned. "Fact is, I sneaked up on their camp several times an' listened in on what they wuz sayin'." Powers stared into the bottom of his glass a moment, took a swallow, then said, "Friend, that woman purely hates yore guts, an' it don't seem like killin' her brothers has much to do with it. Glad she ain't set on shootin' me."

He knocked back the rest of his drink, then said, "Knowed you wuz travelin' with a wagon. That ex–Texas Ranger over yonder at Shreve's Landin' told me."

McClure poured them each another glassful, put the bottle down, and looked up at three men who'd walked to their table. They were each of mixed blood, judging by their features and coloring, and as an outside guess, McClure would have said they were Comancheros. "You got business with us?"

The short, paunchy one standing to the side shook his head. "Not with you, *señor,* but we got business with the one you just met at the bar." They all twisted to look at Powers.

When their attention settled on Jed, McClure edged closer to the table, slipped his Colt from its holster, and held it out of sight under the table. By their looks, the three meant trouble. The same breed who'd answered Hawk moved his hand closer to his holster. "We seen ya turn them hosses into the livery. Where'd ya git 'em?"

Powers leaned back, apparently to look straight into their faces. "Don't reckon it's any o' yore damned business, but I'll tell you anyway. They wuz five filthy-lookin' bastards like y'all out east o' here what figgered to take some o' what wuz our'n. I didn't see it that way. When the smoke cleared, they didn't need no horses."

Without waiting to see how they took his words, he pulled his six-shooter and leveled it at them.

McClure brought his handgun above the edge of the table when Jed drew his. They made a motion for their weapons, but McClure's one word, "Don't," froze their hands before they could carry out their intent.

Pablo sat relaxed against the back of his chair. He chuckled. "You Alabama boys gonna live a long time out here, sudden as you are with those revolvers." He sat straight and stared at the three. "You ever hear of the Apache Blanco?" Then, not waiting for an answer, he said, "Well, he's my brother-in-law, an' those gentlemen's friend. He'd be sorely disappointed to hear there's still a few o' you who figure to carry on the tradition an' work of the Comanchero. Now I'm gonna relieve you of the extra weight you're carryin' at your side."

He stood, reminding McClure of a mountain cat with the graceful way he moved. He walked to the back of each, pulled their handguns from holsters, placed them on the table in front of McClure, and then told them to unbuckle their gunbelts. That done, he said, "Now *vamanos*."

They backed toward the door and, while moving toward it, continued to stare at Powers. The batwings swung closed behind them, and before the doors could swing the second time, Pablo grabbed McClure's bottle, motioned him to take the Comancheros' weapons and gunbelts, and headed for the back door. "We haven't seen the last of them, *señors*. And this place we chose to drink in is full of men like them. They'd kill us for what's left in this bottle."

Reaching the back door, Pablo pushed it open, waved McClure and Jed through, then followed, closing the door tightly behind. "Was thinkin' o' gettin' a hotel room now 'stead of tomorrow, but changed my mind. Now we oughtta stay in the stable with Powers and watch the horses he inherited back yonder on the trail."

They went in the back door of the livery, McClure

first. Four men stood in the runway between the stalls. An arm lifted and brought something down on the head of one of the four standing close together. Instinctively, Hawk pushed his companions to the side and drew without being aware of it. His gun leaped to his hand. He fired, then dived for the floor.

Bullets knocked dirt and horse droppings to his face and shoulders. Everything now unfolded real slow. Guns at his side and in front of him sent out a steady roar. One of the three took a couple of steps backward and fell. McClure fired at one of the two left standing. In the smoke-filled enclosure the man twisted, grabbed his shoulder, and fell. McClure's left leg went numb. He pulled his trigger back for another shot—but the smoke pall, hanging in a cloudlike curtain about two feet above the floor, showed four bodies stretched in grotesque shapes in front of him.

He squirmed around a little to look at Jed and Pablo. "Either o' you take lead?"

"I'm all right," Pablo answered, and Jed echoed Paul's response, then asked, "How 'bout you?"

McClure climbed to his feet and looked at his leg to see where the bullet hit. "Don't know. The bottom o' my leg's numb." He bent for a closer look, then chuckled. "I'm all right too. Bullet knocked my boot heel off." He walked toward the four men on the stable floor. Pablo had been right. The three men they'd shot were the same three from the saloon. His handgun still in his hands, Hawk toed them to their backs. Two dead, and the other drawing his last breath. "Didn't take 'em long to get more six-shooters."

He looked at the man he'd seen clubbed in his head. The hostler groaned and rolled to his side. "What the hell they hit me fur? I ain't done nothin' to 'em."

"Lie still, old-timer. Reckon we're the cause o' you gettin' hit. They were gonna take the horses one of us put in your keepin'. We came through the back door in time to see them hit you." The words barely out of McClure's mouth, a pounding came on the door, and a man bellowed, "What the hell's goin' on in there? Y'all through shootin'?"

Hawk limped to the door, giving in to his heel-less boot. "Yeah, no more shootin', 'less o' course you're of a mind to start it up again. Three men tried to steal some horses from the hostler. They don't need horses anymore." He stood to the side and pushed on one of the big double doors. "Come on in."

A slim, weather-beaten man stepped into the stable and looked toward the men on the floor. "Who shot 'em?"

Hawk shrugged, figuring the badge on the man's chest gave him the right to ask questions. He pinned the marshal with a hard stare. "Damned if I know. Bullets were flyin' everywhere—but they didn't get the horses." He pointed toward the hostler. He can tell you what led up to it."

A few minutes later, the marshal told them he had no charges against them, told the liveryman to get the bodies taken care of, then studied McClure. "I seen you somewhere before?"

Hawk went quiet inside. His nerves tightened, and his scalp pulled tight against his skull. "Don't know. I been around. What makes you think you've seen me?"

The lawman continued to look hard at him. "Reckoned for a minute there I'd seen ya on one o' my wanted posters." He shook his head. "But hell, I got a stack o' them things a foot high on my desk." He grinned. "Reckon any one o' us would fit several of them notices."

Putting on his most innocent look, McClure returned his smile, his guts tied up in knots. "Figure you're right, Marshal. The lawman over in Fort Stockton thought I was one o' those men he looked for till we talked awhile, an' although reluctant to do so, he let me go." His smile widened to a grin. "Fact is, when I left, he sent me on my way with a warm good-bye." He glanced at Powers, who raised his eyes to the heavens and screwed his mouth around in a look of total disbelief.

The marshal stayed behind to make sure the hostler took care of things, while McClure led them toward the hotel. Powers clapped Hawk on the shoulders. "Man, you the biggest liar I reckon I ever seed. I ain't never heered o' such—sent you on yore way with a warm good-bye?"

Straight-faced, McClure looked at him. "Didn't lie. Fact is, don't reckon I ever had anybody bid me farewell in a hotter, or stronger, way."

Pablo cut in. "We better get the hell outta this town before he goes through those notices again. He seemed like a good enough man, an' I reckon he'd give you a fair chance to tell your side of it, but I don't see any need to push your luck. Besides that, if we had to wait for a judge to show up, we'd lose a lot o' time."

Jed scratched his head. "Reckon if we don't do nothin' but get outta town it'd be good nuff. His marshal business only goes to the edge o' town."

Pablo shook his head. "Can't leave right away. You're both gonna need to buy yourselves a sheepskin. It gets cold as a well-digger's butt in the Klondike, where you're goin'. The darkies and Reb gonna need to buy more clothes too." He glanced at the livery stable, frowned, then nodded. "You two go to the general mercantile store an' buy what you need—then get outta town. I'll go to the hotel and tell our folks what's happened, for them to get warm clothes, an' you'll meet us on the trail to Las Cruces." He raked McClure with a look that said it all. "Reckon even though the water's gonna be right cold this time o' year, you better slant off toward the river—the Rio Grande is right over yonder, an' scrub some o' that grime offa you."

McClure slanted a look at Powers. "No need for you to suffer the way I'm gonna. Stay in town. I'll see y'all tomorrow."

By the time he left the store, the marshal had left the livery. Hawk collected his horses, including those Jed had taken from the bandits, and set out toward the river outside of town.

Not yet back to the trail, he came onto a tumble of boulders. A soft voice came from between the rocks: "McClure, easy now, cross your hands on the pommel and sit light. I got a Winchester .44 aimed dead center at ya."

Hawk thought to put spurs to his horse. Blacky could outrun any horse he'd seen—but he couldn't outrun a rifle bullet. He did as the man told him to. "All right, what you want?"

A chuckle came to him. "Don't mean you no harm. Jest wanted to make sure you wasn't in position to shoot me." He stepped from the boulders, a tall, slim man, appearing to be from one of the old Spanish families, well dressed in the Mexican vaquero style, but the big iron hanging from his side looked like it had had plenty of use, and could speak in either Mexican or American. "Name's Roberto Silvera, Texas Ranger."

Aw hell. McClure choked back saying the words aloud. "You a Ranger, an' you know my name, how you figure arrestin' me ain't doin' me harm?"

Silvera laughed. "Jest wanted you to know you hadn't cleared the edge o' town 'fore the marshal found the poster he thought he'd seen, an' gonna tell ya, the edge o' town wouldn'ta made any difference to him." A short silence followed. "Reckon I changed his mind, showed 'im a letter I got from Bill McMillan. Mac musta writ ever'body he ever knowed 'bout you. You made a helluva friend, *amigo*."

He turned to walk away, then turned back. "You'll be crossin' into the New Mexico Territory real soon. I'm gonna write some friends o' mine over there to leave you alone."

He chuckled. "Not that you'd have any trouble travelin' with the son of Alejandro Kelly. You mighta not knowed it, but Pablo Kelly's family is well thought of out here. You ain't headed for trouble this time." He tipped his hat. "Jest thought you'd like to know where you stand."

McClure stepped forward to shake the ranger's hand,

but Silvera had gone into the jumble of rocks for his horse. He rode out the other side and held up his hand in farewell. His hand still held out for a handshake, Hawk stared at the ranger's back and said, "Well, I'll be damned."

The next afternoon, about ten miles up the trail toward Las Cruces, McClure sat alongside the road. Although he almost froze, he'd taken a bath, shaved, and put on clean clothes. He'd almost given up seeing the Studebaker when, in the distance, the oxen appeared over the crest of a hill. He stood.

He had missed the two darkies and Reb in the short while he'd been apart from them. He scratched his head and grinned to himself. No doubt about them becoming family, and no doubt about him waiting four or five years for Reb to grow up. He'd see how he felt about her then.

He wondered at that. He'd not since before the war let himself get too close to people. He'd lost too many men during the war who's friendship he'd grown to cherish, and he'd vowed to himself not to let it happen again—but he had.

Mixus, Jed, and Paul rode at the head of the wagon, herding the small cavvy of horses they'd collected along the way. Reb led the oxen, and Ned and Bessie sat in the seat. McClure thought he'd never seen a more beautiful sight. He hailed them, and as soon as they were in hearing distance, he told them what had happened. Then he looked at Pablo. "He also inferred you come from a well-to-do and highly-thought-of family. What're you doin' punchin' cows for Gundy?"

Paul frowned. "Gonna tell ya, *señor*, Blanco's offered to make me partners, offered me the whole ranch." He shook his head. "But I don't want what he earned the hard way. He bled red blood for every inch o' that ranch. No way I'd take any of it." A slight smile crooked his lips. " 'Sides that, my folks own perhaps the largest ranch in the New Mexico Territory. Someday I'll have enough headaches running it, soon's Papa figures he's had enough. We're gonna head for it soon's we get this wagon movin' again.''

McClure studied the dry countryside a moment. "We gonna follow the Rio Grande most o' the way?"

"No, we're gonna lose the Rio at Las Cruces. It angles up toward Albuquerque. We gonna slant back east a ways and pick up the Pecos so's we'll have water most o' the way—probably have a few Apache too, but if I get a chance to talk before the shootin' starts, I'll tell 'em we're friends of the Apache Blanco. It might work, but bein' friends with him or anybody else most times won't make any difference. We'll be ready to shoot.''

Pablo reined his horse toward the northwest, stopped, then went to the wagon and checked each water barrel. "All full to the brim." He looked at Bessie. "Y'all get all the provisions we gonna need for at least a month, an' maybe the clothes you gonna need?"

"Yes, suh, we ready to take the trip."

Paul pushed his hat to the back of his head. "Think we better head for the Pecos right now. Las Cruces would only add miles to our trip, an' we have everything we need, so we'll cut straight for the next water. Reason I came by way of El Paso was to try to get out of the usual range of the Comanche and Comancheros. Now all we got to worry 'bout is Apache.'' He led them almost due east.

Two weeks to the day later, they rode to the banks of the Pecos at Pope's Crossing. Except for a fifty-yard-wide easy slant down to the water, banks four or five feet high bordered the stream. Pablo studied the roiling waters a moment. "Looks like there's been considerable rain upstream. Gonna ride across an' check the depth—an' see if quicksand mighta drifted in here. That sand is a killer and can change with every rain.''

Sitting his horse next to Pablo, McClure shook his head. "No. You're not takin' that ride. It's my job to do." He looked at Mixus and Jed. "Shake out your ropes, tie 'em together, I'll tie the end around me. Gonna ride one o' the Comanchero horses. Don't want to lose Blacky in that water.''

Pablo looked at him a moment. "Hawk, I've crossed this stream maybe a dozen times, better let me do it.''

McClure only shook his head, slipped the noose around his chest, changed horses, and rode into the water. The pony, skittish, danced on nervous feet, but it set out under McClure's firm grip on the reins.

At once, the fast-moving current threatened to sweep the horse off its feet, but under Hawk's firm, skilled hand, it stayed on course, its hooves still finding bottom against which to dig for the far bank. The pony would come up on the opposite bank about a hundred yards downstream from where they started.

The cold water caused McClure to catch his breath. Then, the horse fighting to keep contact with the bottom, Hawk slipped the rope from around his chest and pulled it over the pony's head figuring he would hold on to the saddle horn if the ones on the bank had to drag them back the way from which they'd come. He'd be damned if he would sacrifice the valiant horse to his tomfoolery.

Less than halfway across the mustang lost his footing and began to swim. McClure let him swim a short distance, hoping to quickly find bottom again. But no luck. He knew then the wagon would never make it across. They'd have to wait for the swollen waters to recede. He signaled Pablo to drag him back.

The rope tightened around the pony's neck, and McClure reined him toward the bank they'd left only minutes before—but now the horse found only water to dig its hooves into.

Hawk felt it the moment it happened and grabbed for the pony's neck. The horse's legs, swept from under it, caused it to roll over onto its side.

The frightened horse flailed, fought to regain its feet, and hold its head high out of the water at the same time. Trying to save the horse, McClure thought to take the rope off its neck and see if the pony might gain footing farther downstream. He grabbed for the noose around the mustang's strong neck—but couldn't reach far enough to take it over the pony's head. He slipped back and grabbed the saddle horn. Then the rope tightened even more, and the force of the water swung them like a pendulum toward the bank from which they'd left only a few minutes before, but now farther downstream, the length of three ropes, about a hundred and fifty feet.

As he hung desperately to the horse, something scraped McClure's side, then scraped again. The mustang struggled to its feet in shallow water by the bank, and stepped gingerly to dry land. The pony stood trembling with fear while Hawk, half-drowned, choked and spit muddy water from his mouth, still clinging desperately to the saddle horn. Sheepishly, he felt for the ground with his feet, then stood, and softly patted the pony's neck. He wondered which of them were more afraid. His trembles were as violent as the horse's.

He still clung to the saddle horn when Reb, followed by the entire party, ran to him. "Hawk—Hawk McClure, don't you ever try another damned fool stunt like that again." Reb's voice came to him almost like an angry adult's.

He slowly swept them with a tired look. "Gonna tell y'all right now, don't worry 'bout me tryin' that again. Reckon I was scared spitless. Only thing I had in my mouth was muddy water. Couldn't hardly pucker my lips to spit it out."

He swung his head to look at his one hand still holding to the saddle horn, slowly uncurled his fingers, and said, "Found out one thing, we sure as hell not gonna try to cross that river till the water goes down a mite—a whole big mite. Horses wouldn't make it, wagon wouldn't make it, an' for a fact I won't try it. Let's make camp."

Yolanda sat across the table from Tom in a small cafe close to the hotel. Their supper, served a half hour before, had grown cold while she accused Tom of everything under the sun, but most of all she railed at him for not knowing McClure had been within their grasp right here in El Paso. "I told you to check ever'thing in this town—the livery, the hotel, the stores—ever'thing. That wagon with the boy an' them two darkies wuz right under yore nose, an' you did nothin' about findin' where they left McClure."

Tom stared at her a moment. "Sister, there wuz a shootin' down yonder at the livery. Didn't nobody want to talk 'bout nothin' else. I ain't had a chance to find 'im. Maybe the marshal knows his whereabouts. When I finish this cold supper, I'll ask 'im."

She sat back, picked at her potato, then pinned him with a look. "You ain't goin' to see the marshal without me. You ain't done nothin' right so far, so I'll ask 'im the questions."

Tom shrugged, a sullen hangdog look marring his face. He thought of the twins, then his mind switched to Bert. Where was the only brother he had left? He looked down at the plate of cold, greasy food. Bert had been smart, he'd gotten out from under the biting, vicious tongue of Yolanda, but where had he gone? He didn't know anything about this land, but he did know horses. Had he hired on with one of the ranches? Abruptly Tom became aware that Yolanda had changed the subject.

She dipped her hand into her reticule. "We got only a hundred ten dollars left." She lowered her voice. "We gonna have to find somebody with money who's leavin' town, follow them, and take what they got."

"Then you figger to kill 'em, is that it, sister?"

"We don't, an' we'll have every law-dog in the country on our tails. You got a better idea?"

He nodded slowly. "Yep. I figger if we both got us a job, work like hell for 'bout six months, we might end up with enough to get us back home."

Her eyes took on a muddy, hot, yellow look. "We ain't done what we come out here to do. We gonna find McClure, kill 'im, an' take whatever money he got for them horses we wuz gonna buy—if he ain't done spent it all. Then we're goin' home. Not till then." She sat back and looked primly down her nose at him. "Besides, I ain't gonna work for nobody ever again. We got property back yonder in Alabama, an' it ain't fittin' for landed folks to work."

He stared into his plate a long time, only because he was doubtful of giving her the answer he had on the end of his tongue. Then anger clouded his thinking—to hell with her, he'd start saying what was on his mind. He pulled his look from his plate. "Yolanda, them people back yonder got what they had because they worked for it, an' they kept on workin' after they got it. Reckon we gonna have to do the same if we figger to keep it. 'Sides that, I ain't gonna kill nobody less'n they give me a reason to. To my thinkin', Bert wuz mighty smart to cut out, get away from all this."

She leaned forward, a cold, wintry look in her eyes. "You try takin' off, brother, an' the mornin'll come when you don't wake up to see the sun. You got it?"

He shrank down in his chair. "Never figgered to leave you, Yolanda. Jest thinkin' how good it'd be to get home."

She threw her fork onto her plate and stood. "Let's go see the marshal. He'll know where McClure is. He might even have 'im in that jail o' his."

A few minutes later, they stood across the desk from the lawman. "McClure, you say?" He nodded. "Yeah, I seen 'im. He an' three other men shot some Comancheros down at the livery this afternoon." He scratched his head. "Figured then I'd seen 'im before— or his picture. Turned out it was his picture, but he's long gone by now, headed for Las Cruces, somebody said. What you lookin' for him for?"

Yolanda sucked in a deep breath, then said, "He killed two of our brothers. We figger to get even."

The marshal gave her a straight-on look. "Ma'am, the way I've had McClure described to me, yore brothers musta give 'im a reason, an' even then he probably gave 'em a better'n even break on the draw." He'd been toying with a pencil; now he tossed it to the desk and said,

"Somethin' else, ma'am, you'd best do yore gettin' even
outta my jurisdiction. Fact is, jurisdiction be damned,
I'll come after you an' yore brother right up to the New
Mexican border."

Tom hadn't said a word while standing in front of the
marshal's desk, but the more his sister and the marshal
spoke, the smarter he realized his brother Bert was. If
he had a half a chance, he'd do like Bert had done. He
would run.

He didn't want to—wouldn't—shoot his sister, but
unless he could find a good time to gather his things,
he'd have to face her. He had not a doubt she would kill
him as soon as spit.

Yolanda stared at the marshal a long moment, her
eyes as cold as a snow-laden mountainside. She whirled
and, hard heels clicking went out the door. Outside, she
faced Tom. "You heard 'im. We ain't got a friend anywhere in this godforsaken country. But we don't have
to kill McClure in Texas. It ain't but a few miles to New
Mexico." Her look made Tom think of a cottonmouth
moccasin he'd once seen on the banks of the Chickasaw
Bogue. He shivered, more determined than ever to find
a time to leave.

That night on the banks of the Pecos, Pablo looked
across the fire at Hawk. "Tell us about your home, what
you left behind to come out here to my country."

McClure shrugged. "It wasn't anything I built. My
great grandfather took his family to that wooded country, cleared land, and raised thoroughbred horses, cattle,
and some cotton. He and his family lived in a log cabin
till my grandpa took over. He was the one who built the
antebellum home I was raised in.

"Two stories, it had four Doric-style columns in front,
a wide veranda on both the ground and second floors.
The veranda wrapped all the way around the house to
take advantage of the shade at different times of the day,
or different seasons. It was a large white house, but no,
it wasn't just a house, it was a home—warm, friendly,

housing a family who laughed, had parties, many guests, and much music.'' His voice trailed off. ''I miss it.''

''You had slaves?''

McClure nodded. ''A few of them stayed with me after the war, until I sent them up to Ben Baty, who hired them. They were never mistreated.'' He stood, filled the coffee cups all around the fire, then sat again. ''Hell, man, even if one only thought of them as property—expensive property—a man in his right mind doesn't mistreat property unless he's a damned fool.''

Paul turned his gaze on Reb. ''Tell us about your place, son.''

Reb's mouth twisted as though with bitter memories. Her eyes flooded, but she held the tears in check. ''My home was much like Hawk's. When Auntie, Uncle, and I left, I torched every building on the place. There's nothing left of what once was.''

With a saddend look, replaced by a grin, Pablo swept Jed and Mixus with a knowing look. ''Don't have to ask you two rapscallions what you left. You, Mixus, left a posse on your hind end, and you, Jedediah, a ferry soon to be replaced by a bridge.''

Jed shifted his chew to the other cheek and peered at Paul. ''You gonna tell us 'bout yore home?''

Pablo frowned into the fire a moment, then smiled. ''Nope, not gonna tell you anything, gonna let you see it and judge it for yourself . . .'' He broke off what he was going to say and cocked his head. ''Horses comin'. Douse the fire.''

McClure was way ahead of him. He grabbed the coffeepot and threw it on the embers.

13

THE COFFEE DROWNING the fire acted as a signal. The hoofbeats stopped, then a voice came from out of the darkness. "Why for you put you fire out, *señor*? We friends."

In a whisper, Pablo said, "Don't anybody answer. They'll shoot at your voice if they aren't friendly. If they charge us, wait'll you see a dark shape against the sky, shoot, an' change your position."

Silence shrouded them for several long, drawn-out moments. Then a wild yell came, and horses charged the campsite. Rifle fire, low to the ground, split the darkness. A shadow loomed above McClure and he fired into it. A thud as though the slap a side of beef and the shadow slipped to the ground almost at his shoulder. He pulled his bowie, sliced where he thought the man throat would be, felt the blade drag across soft flesh, rolled, and fired at another dark shape. Not until then was he aware the other members of his party were also shooting.

The charge ran through the camp, firing wildly, whirled, came back, whirled, and rode out the other side. By then, McClure had estimated their number to be about six. The hoofbeats stopped out from camp a ways,

then a guttural voice, in Spanish, ordered them farther
out.

"Don't anybody light a fire, an' stay where you are.
They may be back. Don't know how many there were,
or if we hurt 'em much." McClure wanted to check the
two men he knew he'd put lead into, but minding his
own words, he stayed put. But he had to find out how
his own party fared. "When I call your name, if you're
all right, an' by that I mean you haven't taken a hit, just
answer, 'Okay.' " Then in a low voice he called each
of their names—Reb's first. He got an affirmative answer from each and sighed a silent prayer of thanks.

Out about a hundred yards there was a flicker of light,
which then brightened such that McClure figured they'd
lighted a torch. It looked as though they intended to set
fire to the wagon. He drew a bead below the flame,
squeezed off a shot, and watched the torch arc to the
ground—the man holding it fell beside the flame. "They
light another one, fire at the man holding it," he yelled.

He'd no sooner spoken than another torch flamed. It
sounded as though everyone in his party fired at once.
He grinned. That man would probably leak molasses in
January. He strained to see if another torch might be
lighted. No torch, but the sound of several horses riding
away. When they could hear them no longer, Hawk
lighted a lantern. "Gonna see how much harm we did
'em. Y'all stay on the ground where you are in case they
left a sniper behind."

He went to where he'd used his bowie knife on the
first man he'd shot. The man lay on his back, staring
through sightless eyes at the sky. He went to the other
one. That man still lived, but wouldn't for very long. He
walked the entire area and found three more men—two
dead and another shot through the leg and shoulder. He
took the weapons from that man first then stripped the
others of their weapons and money belts.

He dumped the firearms into the back of the wagon.
Bessie grumbled. "Mistuh Hawk, you keep on puttin'
all them guns in the wagon, like you done the whole

trip, ain't gonna be no room left for me an' the boy to sleep in there.''

"All right, Auntie." He held the lantern so she could see his face and let a smile crinkle his lips. "Next time I'm gonna let you go take 'em off them, then I'm gonna watch real close to see what you do with 'em." He looked at Pablo. "Figured at first we had Apache trouble, but I heard somewhere the Apache don't like to fight at night. This's your home territory, is that right?''

Paul nodded. "They will if they have to, but these were Mexican bandits. They thought to have easy victims.'' He grinned. "Just goes to show you how wrong a man can be.''

For the most part, they lay where they'd gone to ground, for what Hawk estimated as over an hour. He held his party at their positions for another thirty minutes, then walked among them. "All right, I think it's safe to move about. Bessie, get Reb and Uncle in the wagon with you an' stay there till daylight. The rest of us'll take turns standin' watch tonight. First I'm gonna see what that wounded man out there has to say.''

He stood over the man a moment or two, then took him by the leg and dragged him to the wagon. He checked him over and found only the two wounds he'd seen before. He stared at the man who'd only minutes before been intent on killing those in his party. His eyes wide with fear, the bandit returned his gaze.

McClure pulled his gunbelt from his waist. The Mexican's eyes squinted, then widened even more than before. "No, *señor*, you can't do this. I weel ride away and do you no harm.'' Hawk slipped his thumb from the hammer. His shot took the bandit between the eyes.

Behind his left shoulder, he heard Paul's voice: "Tsch, tsch, *señor*, you did for a fact stay around Blanco too much.''

His face feeling stiff as weathered leather, McClure twisted to look at his friend. "Pablo, we let 'im go, he might be back someday. We take care of 'im, doctor 'im, he might cut our throats while we sleep." He shrugged. "This way, there's just one more *Mejicano bandido* for the buzzards. Get some sleep."

Hawk took first watch, figuring if another attack came, it would be within the hour. The attack did not come, and after another hour, McClure wakened Mixus and turned in to his blankets.

The next morning they prepared breakfast and ate while most of them cast glances at the bodies lying about, not yet beginning to smell.

Breakfast finished, and camp cleaned up, Hawk walked to his horse and threw the hull across his back. Jed stood at his side. "Hell, McClure, we cain't jest ride off an' leave these men. We gotta bury 'em. Ain't human to leave 'em for the coyotes."

Hawk stood a moment staring at Powers. "Gonna tell you right now, I'm not tryin' to be human. They were intent on killin' all of us. You want 'em buried, get after it. You can probably catch us by sundown tomorrow—if the Apache doesn't get you." He looked over his shoulder at the rest of them. "Saddle up, pack up, we're leavin' 'fore those corpses begin to smell." To a man, they gave him a long, wondering gaze, then went about doing as he'd said.

Riding away from the gruesome sight, McClure asked Paul what he reckoned the bandits were after. Paul pointed at Reb's golden stallion. "He's reason enough, but they wanted all our horses. Then, when we'd walked our feet into the ground, so tired we could go no farther, they'd have killed us and taken what we were able to carry from the wagon." He smiled. "That's why I had us hobble the horses, why we must do it each night. A man out here without a horse is as good as dead."

They wended their way along the Pecos for five days. Wiry tufts of short grass stretched as far as the eye could see, broken only by the dark line of trees along the river. The weather now bitterly cold, all in the party huddled in sheepskins.

Pablo and Hawk rode well ahead of the wagon. Pablo stretched his hands toward the west. "We'll turn straight west about noon. I kept us on this route because of water, an' when we take a westerly course, we'll have about two dry camps before we come onto the Rio Hondo.'' He grinned. ''And about two days from there you'll be guests of my folks. Their rancho sits right up against the Capitan Mountains. From now to the Capitans, we gotta keep a sharp lookout. We're right in the middle of Mescalero Apache country.''

McClure studied on Kelly's words awhile before he asked, ''You figure we'll come on large parties?'' He shook his head. ''Reckon what I'm askin' is, you think we can handle those we run across?''

Pablo nodded. ''If we see any at all, they'll most likely be huntin' parties. Don't think they'll give us any trouble, but want to be ready in case.'' They rode for another half hour, then Kelly said, ''This weather, especially this time o' year, won't stay this cold. It'll be this way a couple o' days then most likely warm up for a few days.'' He shook his head. ''You folks sure picked a helluva time of year to come out here. Wherever you decide to settle, you're gonna be faced with buildin' a cabin during the coldest months.''

McClure shrugged. ''Gotta make do. If we have to, we'll dig into the side of one of these hills till spring.''

Another hour passed, then Pablo drew rein. ''Gonna head west from here. You ride back to the wagon and have them fill the water barrels. When y'all reach that old lightning-struck cottonwood up ahead, have 'em turn off from the river an' head toward the mountains.''

Hawk squinted, searching the distance for mountains. He shook his head. ''Don't see mountains anywhere.''

Kelly pointed. ''See that line of dark purple on the horizon? You'd probably think of it as rain moving in— it's not. Those are the mountains still about fifty miles off. They'll look higher and higher the closer we get.''

''Reckon I got a lot to learn 'bout this country. You gonna ride far 'fore you turn back? I don't like you out there alone, Pablo. Never know what'll happen.''

Kelly laughed. ''I'll be all right. Been ridin' this country all my life. Anyway, I'll get back to you 'fore you make camp.'' McClure nodded and kneed his horse back the way he'd come.

Yolanda led Tom across the border into New Mexico Territory, and stayed on the road leading toward Las Cruces. The trail, well traveled, gave no evidence the wagon had come this way. She gave up trying to find their tracks. Then the thought came that they might have turned off. She watched the sides of the road, hoping to see where the Studebaker might have taken a different route.

Abruptly, she reined in. A wagon had left the trail. She frowned. These wheel tracks were overlaid in places by hoof prints of several horses. She was only certain of one rider with the Studebaker.

She studied the tracks a few moments. Could others have joined up with McClure's party? She nodded to herself—possible, but not likely. Besides, where could he go by heading back toward the east? No. The only reasonable way for him to go had to be Las Cruces. Despite the doubt that caused her stomach to churn, she kicked her horse ahead, and every once in a while she blew hard through her nose then blinked tears from her eyes, trying to rid herself of the dust.

Another half hour and she spotted a luxurious-looking coach ahead. From where she sat her saddle, it looked to be a big Concord—black, gold embossed, pulled by six matched, black stallions—money. Abruptly she felt alive, her head itched with the feeling of exhilaration. Her chest muscles tightened.

Sometimes things worked out for the best. If she'd taken the tracks of the Studebaker as those of McClure's party, she'd have missed this opportunity. The closer she got to the coach, the more certain she was that luck had played into her hands. She looked across her shoulder at Tom. ''We gonna take whatever those in that wagon got to offer—an' I'll bet they have a full load o' money.''

Tom, his face flushed, the corners of his eyes showing a nervous tick, and his cheeks trembling, looked from the coach to Yolanda. "We gonna cover our faces?"

Yolanda stared at him as though he was an idiot. "Little brother, just why in the hell you think we gonna cover our faces? Them in that coach ain't gonna tell nobody 'bout us."

Tom looked from her to his hands crossed on the pommel. He closed his eyes, then looked straight ahead. "Then you figger to kill 'em, sister? Them folks ain't done nothin' to us. Bad enough to take what's theirs without killin' 'em."

Yolanda felt her milky white skin turn warm as angry blood forced itself to her head. "You spineless, gutless worm. You better check the loads in yore six-shooter 'cause you gonna need it right sudden." She spurred her horse alongside the rich-looking vehicle, looked through the curtains, and saw an old man and woman sitting on plush velveteen upholstered seats. She leaned her head to see better and spoke. "Hello, nice day, ain't it?"

At her greeting, the old man gave her a stiff nod. "Yes, a nice day." Then his eyes bulged, for he was looking into the end of the barrel of her .36 Navy Colt. "Now, young lady, what does this mean?"

"What it means, grampaw, is you're gonna give me your money." She glanced at the driver only a little above her head. He pulled on the reins to slow the coach. "Stop them damned horses. Now."

The coach bounced to a stop. "Now, old man, you an' yore wife climb down, an' stand still. Hands in the air." She pointed her pistol at the driver. "You too. Tie them reins to the brake and come down here."

The man helped his wife down just as the driver's feet touched the ground. With the barrel of her revolver. Yolanda waved Tom to the side of the coach. "Get in there an' see what they mighta hid inside." She walked around the pair, felt for a wallet, then a money belt, and found both. She went through the woman's reticule, dumped a few pieces of jewelry to the ground, and took a small roll of bills.

Tom stepped to the ground, shook his head, and said, "Ain't nothin' in there. Let's take what we got an' get outta here."

Yolanda gave him a smile she hoped would freeze hell a mile. "Still ain't got the message, have you?" She turned her attention on the three from the Concord. The driver had no visible weapon. The old man had a pistol of some kind tucked into his belt. She turned her Navy Colt on him first, pulled the trigger, then moved the barrel a fraction to cover the driver, who'd made a move toward his coat, and triggered another shot. Then feeling energy flow from her feet to her head with the heady experience of killing, she turned her gun on the woman, who had opened her mouth to scream but only got out a small squeal. Watching the three of them standing, mouths open, eyes bulging, holding hands over small holes only now beginning to ooze blood through their fingers, she pulled the trigger three more times. She watched them fall to the ground, then pushed the loot she'd collected to the bottom of a saddlebag, mounted, and looked at Tom. "Get on yore horse. Let's get outta here—fast."

She held them to the trail for a couple of miles, then, seeing a pile of boulders up the side of a mountain, she headed for them.

"We'll make camp in them rocks, an' see what we got from those rich bastards."

Tom held back, looking from the boulders to his sister. "It don't bother you none you jest killed three people what never done nothin' to us?"

"Bother me? Nope. Fact is I feel good, like I jest came alive. No, they never done nothin' *to* us, but they sure as hell done somethin' *for* us; they give us travelin' money. Let's git up in them rocks."

In the boulders, without taking time to first make camp, she emptied the saddlebag on the ground, raked the money to the side, and separated the bills—all in

Mexican currency. Her gaze went from one bill to the other. She frowned. How much would this come to in American money? She thought on that a moment. From what she'd heard, pesos were worth far less than good old American greenbacks. It didn't look like they'd gotten much. She made a swipe with her left hand, raked it into a pile, and turned her look on Tom. "Looks like we gotta find somebody else with money. Don't know how much we got here, but figger it don't come to much in our money."

"You sayin' we gonna kill some more people?"

"*We? We* gonna kill somebody else? You ain't done nothin'. All you done is shrink back an' shake with fear." She pinned him with a look she wished could kill. "Tell you somethin', little brother, I found out back yonder on the trail I don't need you. If it wa'n't for causin' folks in these towns to ask questions seein' a woman travelin' alone, I'd shed myself of you right now."

Tom looked at her a long moment. Some fear showed in his eyes, but mostly wonderment that he was only now seeing what his sister really was. "You'd kill me too, Yolanda?"

Her eyes squinted. "Quicker'n spit, little brother, an' don't you never forget it."

They made camp, with Tom doing most of the work. At their supper fire, Yolanda decided they'd backtrack and pick up the trail of the wagon, which she'd now made up her mind was the one belonging to McClure's party. By her thinking, all in that bunch had money on them.

Rebecca had taken it on herself to lead the oxen more and more. Although he was healthy and tough as rawhide, she'd noticed Ned showing his age in many little ways by the fire at night. He was slow to stand when a task confronted him, his hands trembled when tying a rope, he strained more when lifting things, he tired quicker, and he relinquished the bullwhip to her waiting hands without an argument. If anything happened to either Ned or Bessie, it would hurt as much as had the loss of her mother and father.

They were two days west of the old lightning-struck cottonwood. Paul had rejoined them, and as estimated by Paul, the Rio Hondo was in sight, only three or four miles ahead. Until now they'd seen no Apache, but that changed while Rebecca thought of it. Over the rise to her left, seven of the wildest looking men she'd ever seen rode toward them.

Pablo took command. "Keep your rifles to hand, but don't fire unless I say so." He stopped and faced the direction from which the men rode.

When barely within hearing, the leader of the band shouted, "*Hola,* Kelleee. You come home, eh? Many moons you leave us, now you come back. Is good."

Kelly swept his party with a glance. "It's all right. This is Red Sleeves, once a mighty warrior, now a friend to my family." He cupped his hand to his mouth. "*Hola,* Red Sleeves. I come to see *mi padre y mi madre.* What you do out here far from reservation?"

The Mescalero Apache, now close to the travelers, shook his head. "Pablo, eef we eat, we must hunt. The game is moving farther away from my people. Some who hunt stay too close to reservation and the deer, antelope, and buffalo move farther away. My people are hungry."

Paul studied the warrior, whose ribs showed through his once well-muscled chest. "Does not the agent get enough beef?"

Red Sleeves spat to show his disgust. "Agent get few cows, get pay for many, an' put money in his pockets. Mescalero eat few cows too soon, then go hungry."

"Has father stopped giving you cattle?"

"No. Your papa is friend of Apache, but there is not much he can do—so we hunt."

Pablo frowned. How many cattle would it take to swell the women's and children's bellies for a few days? Why did not Washington send out inspectors to see the often crooked Indian agents were fair with the Indians? This outright thievery went on all over the nation: the Sioux, Flatheads, Blackfeet—all the tribes. The answer? The politicians in Washington were as crooked as the agents. They too were skimming the fat off the top.

"Tell you what, great warrior, ride with us till we see some of Papa's cattle. We'll cut out a few head, an' you drive them to your women and children."

Red Sleeves stared between his pony's ears, his face becoming more wrinkled than usual, his eyes sad. He looked up and swept his hand in an arc of the panorama before them. "Once many buffalo roam our land. The Mescalero great hunters, great warriors. Now, Keleee, we must beg to feed our families." He nodded. "We will follow you, and thank you for what you can do. *Su padre* has already done much." He kneed his horse to fall in beside the wagon.

Paul helped them round up twenty head, and only a few hours from Alejandro Kelly's ranch house, Red Sleeves and his men turned the small herd southwest, toward the Mescalero reservation. Before disappearing over the first rise, the old warrior raised his hand in thanks and farewell.

Riding alongside Paul, McClure shook his head. "Giving cattle in those numbers must be hard on your father's bankroll. Admitting those Indians are hungry, why do you do it?"

Kelly looked across his shoulder, his face somber. "Tell you why—first, it's the cheapest way to avoid losing many more cattle along with men, men who have ridden for my family for many years and are like family to us—but most of all, those people are our friends, have been for a long time. My family can't stand seeing them mistreated the way they are." Abruptly his face brightened. "Only two or three hours and we'll see Papa's ranch house. We been ridin' on grass he grazes for two days now."

The prospect of a few days' rest brightened the spirits of all in the party, Rebecca most of all. The thought of a bath and clean clothes, along with food she and Bessie hadn't had to cook, made her feel all bubbly inside. She cast a look at Mixus. "This's gonna be right hard on you, old man. You won't have any excuse for not takin' a bath an' changin' to clean clothes. You notice I been stayin' upwind o' you for several days now."

"Wh-why you young whippersnapper, what you need is fer somebody to tan yore bottom right often, teach you respect fer yore elders." He chomped down on his cud of tobacco, chewed furiously a moment, then spit and nailed a rock at the side of where they road dead center.

McClure chuckled. "Stop badgerin' the poor old fellow, lad. He lived in the brush so long he didn't have to worry 'bout other folks bein' offended." He looked at Mixus, one eyebrow about to hook itself over his eyebrow. "Course, if he doesn't clean up right soon after gettin' there, Jed an' I'll give 'im a good scrubbin'."

"Why gol dang it, reckon I stay jest as clean as you two Alabamians. Y'all jest had more water in that swamp country you come from to bathe in."

They rode along, joshing each other, but giving Mixus the brunt of it because he responded to it so well. When they topped a rise still an hour out from the ranch, a large party, riding like the Apache nation was on their tails, came at them from about a half mile away. They all pulled rifles from scabbards and jacked shells into the chambers.

Grinning from ear to ear, Paul yelled, "Hold it, that's my family." With those words he urged his horse into a dead run heading for them.

Leading the charge, was a petite and very beautiful woman. Even from the distance he sat his horse McClure could see where Pablo got his looks. Riding barely off her horse's flank, was a man with a flaming red thatch of hair, and on the other side a rail-thin vaquero perhaps a little older than the red-haired man.

Hardly slowing her horse, Maria Kelly launched herself from the saddle, grabbed Paul around the neck, and clung to him for dear life while she settled herself behind the cantle. Then Alejandro and the older man dragged Paul's horse to a stop, pulled him from the saddle, and in between hugs from his mother, and pummeling him about the shoulders by his father and the other man, his mother and father smothered him with kisses.

By then the wagon had rolled to where the celebration took place. When they settled down a bit, McClure grinned, and said, "Pablo, if these people're your friends, I'd surely hate to see you meet some enemies. Wonder how you survived that attack."

Red-faced, Paul introduced his mother, father, and the segundo of the ranch, Chico Santana. He explained that Chico had helped raise him, and taught him how to use rifles, revolvers, and knives.

Maria went straight to Rebecca who had led the oxen for the past two or three hours. "You poor little *niño.* They work you like a grown man." She put her arms around Rebecca. Her eyes widened. She opened her mouth to say something. Rebecca cut her off.   "Please, from your look I know you've guessed my secret, but please don't betray me. Only my auntie and Ned know. I'm sure none of the others suspect a thing, but I don't know how much longer I can fool them." She blushed. " 'Nother reason is, I have only one dress and figure to save it for a special time"

Maria stepped back and smiled. "Your secret is safe until you tell me different." Then from where Pablo stood, he waved his hand to encompass the fifty or so riders. "These men are all our family, riders for Papa. Most o' them have been with him longer'n I been in the world."

On being acknowledged, they dismounted and took their turn at beating Pablo's shoulders. He shook his head. "Now you know why I stay away so long. Gotta give my poor beat-up body a chance to heal."

Maria looked at her guests. "Come, we must go home and let you get cleaned up for supper. Chiquita will have food ready when we get there."

On the ride to the ranch, Alex explained how they knew Pablo had headed home with a party of six people he and Blanco had taken a liking to. Blanco had written and given a pretty good estimate when they'd arrive.

When the hacienda came into sight, Rebecca gasped. It was huge, built much like Blanco's ranch house. Alex explained that on entering, it took two steps to get from the outside wall to the inside, the walls were that thick. He went on to say they made their houses like that so the heat of summer and the cold of winter made little difference inside. They seldom required a fire for comfort, but had one most of the time for atmosphere. His eyes twinkling, he glanced at his wife. "Maria likes the romantic way the flickering and dancing of the flames makes her feel." His face reddened. "Yeah, reckon I like to cuddle up some too."

Outside the massive front door, Alex attempted to usher them all into the house, but Mixus and Jed hung back. Jed did the talking. "No, sir, reckon me an' Mixus'll jest bunk in with the rest o' the hands. 'Preciate yore invitin' us though."

Alex insisted, but the two would have it no other way. "Well, come in and have a drink, then you can get on down to the bunkhouse and settle in. I figure to keep your friends here several days."

After drinks, Maria showed Hawk and Rebecca to rooms already made up for them, with a large tub of hot water in the middle of the room. Bessie's and Ned's room adjoined Rebecca's. They too had hot water.

Rebecca opened her valise, and the first thing she took out was the dress she'd saved of all her treasured things, along with shoes, undergarments, and stockings.

Bessie stared at the clothing as it piled up on the bed. "What you doin', missy? You ain't got it in that head o' yore'n to come outta that boy stuff, do you?"

Rebecca faced her auntie. "I'm gonna be the woman I am. If I bring trouble down on us during the rest of the trip, Hawk'll take care of it."

Bessie clapped hands to her skinny hips. "Girl, you

gettin' to thinkin' Mistuh Hawk can take care o' most anything. Little miss, if you think anything of him a'tall, you oughtta know you gonna maybe git 'em into some trouble he cain't git outta—you want that to happen?''

Rebecca, or Becky as she'd been called all her life, was going to tell them to call her by that name when she went in for supper. She continued to unpack.

When they first entered the house, the room they'd walked into made Rebecca even more aware of how grungy their party must look—sweaty, dust-encrusted, and smelly. She'd made her decision then. She would come to supper as herself, a woman, and hope she could look well for them.

The room, large by any standard, was furnished in heavy Mexican-style furniture—leather upholstered chairs, hand-carved tables, marble-topped end tables, with Aztec paintings adorning the walls and with woven Indian rugs on the floor. It was sheer luxury done in the best of southwestern taste. She would not go back into that room looking like a vagabond. Besides, she wanted to see if Hawk's eyes showed any sign of interest if she could once again look as she used to.

Chiquita took Rebecca's dress to iron the wrinkles from it, while she took a bath, content for a while to lie in the warm, soothing water and soak. Then, languidly, sensuously, she laved her body and hair, and when she had rinsed clean, Bessie toweled her hair dry, then brushed it until it shone with bits of sunbeam caught in each strand. It now had grown to almost waist length.

Over her shoulder, she said, ''Bessie, has all that sun and wind hardened me? You think you can still make me look like I used to?''

Her voice soft, Bessie almost crooned her answer. ''Lordy day, little miss, you ain't never gonna look like you once did. In these few months you done become a real woman. I'da nevuh believed it could happen, but you even more pretty now. That there black hair, blue eyes, milky white skin the sun tried its dangdest to ruin, and yoah figguh lookin' like what ever' man hopes he can go to sleep an' dream about, uhh-uhhh." She grinned. "Missy, we done done a terrible thing hidin' all you got, makin' like you wuz a boy. We gonna be hard put to keep ever' man in the New Mexico Territory from ridin' for miles jest to look at you."

Reb picked up the wet wash rag from the floor and tossed it at her auntie. "Hogwash. I didn't ask for all that. Just wantta know—you think Hawk'll think I'm pretty?"

"If he don't, I'm gonna jerk a knot in that pretty hind end o' his'n. Lordy, he'd jest flat have to be blind to not *know* you're the prettiest woman alive. Now let's get you dressed in that there gown you done saved for this very time."

Down the hall, McClure dressed in the one suit he'd allowed room for when packing for the trail. He shrugged into the dove gray swallowtail coat, checked to see if his string tie was neat, then turned to go back to the living room.

He felt good and bad about the way he looked. His suit was wrinkled, his hair needed cutting, but thinking his hosts would allow for his having been on the trail so long, he knew he'd done his best.

Alex handed him a drink as soon as he walked into the room. Pablo stood with a drink in his hand. He had dressed in a black bolero jacket, trousers flared at the bottoms with silver piping up the outside seams, a white shirt and black silk neckerchief. There was no doubt when looking at him, that he was of the Spanish gentry.

They had finished one drink and started on another when McClure realized Alex studied him. He smiled. "What you see that worries you, Alex?"

Paul's father gave a slight shrug. "Your reputation preceded you. Did you know, in the short time you've been in the West, that you're being talked about as a gunfighter? Looking at you, all I can see is a Southern gentleman."

McClure laughed. "Me, a gunfighter? Where in the world did something of that sort get started?"

Pablo cut in. "I could have told him that, Papa. Reckon I haven't helped stop the talk either. He's fast— about as fast as any I've seen with that .44 of his. He hits what he shoots at, an' he doesn't hesitate to pull the trigger when it's called for."

McClure shrugged, then grimaced. "I sure never thought of myself as anything but what I hoped others saw me as: a gentleman. As for weapons, well, I've used them all my life. I stayed in the woods as much as possible while growing up, an' I had a good teacher, a man whose friendship I cherish, Ben Baty. He . . ." He swallowed the rest of his sentence, and rudely stared at the woman coming into the room. Without breaking his gaze, he said, "Pablo, didn't know you had a sister."

Paul didn't answer, obviously as caught up in the woman's beauty as was Hawk. In an aside to his father, he said, "Papa, you didn't tell me we had other guests. Introduce me."

Alex, staring like the other two men, glanced at Pablo. "Didn't know it either. Damned if I know who she is."

Rebecca had stopped only a foot inside the door. She felt her face heat with embarrassment thinking she made a poor showing as a woman. Then, feeling she had to say something, she stammered, "Oh, am I intruding on man talk? I-I felt I had to come out of hiding, so I put on the only dress I now own."

The voice was the same voice-changing boy voice. "Re-Reb? Is that you?" McClure, still staring, squinted, then opened his eyes wide as if to see more that way. "Wh-why danged if you're not a full-blown woman— a full-blown beautiful woman." Inside he wondered that he'd thought she might be only fifteen.

Rebecca giggled. She'd gotten the answer she wanted as to how Hawk perceived her—but she still had no idea how he'd react to the woman she was, beyond just her beauty. But she felt warm all over at the admiration in every male eye in the room. She looked straight into Hawk's eyes. "Yes, my good friend, I'm a full-grown woman. Sorry I kept you thinkin' otherwise for so long," she shrugged, "but I hoped to keep trouble off your shoulders by doing so."

Alex stepped between them, stumbled over his own feet, pulled out a chair for her, and walked over and took her arm. "Please, ma'am, come on in, sit down and let me get you a drink."

She smiled, thinking how long it had been since men had shown her the little courtesies she'd come to expect. And remembering the admiring looks she had once enjoyed, and now seeing the same looks on the faces in the room, she knew the woman in her had returned. She sat and looked up into Alex's face. "Madeira, please. If you have it."

"Of course, *señorita*." He hurriedly walked to the wine closet.

Then McClure did a strange thing to her way of thinking: He sighed, his face reddened, and he mumbled something about her being a woman was a load of worry off his mind. Sometimes he puzzled her. What could he mean? She looked at him. "You're mumbling something, Hawk. Is there anything wrong? Would you like to tell me about it?"

His face turned an even deeper crimson. "No, no, ma'am, don't reckon it's anything I want to discuss right now—maybe someday when I get used to you not bein' a full-grown woamn." He grinned. "But I'm here to tell you, Reb, you were one helluva boy." He scratched his head. "Reckon I gotta give up on makin' you into a man."

She clamped hands to hips just like she'd seen Bessie do all her life. "Hawken McClure, don't you dare start treatin' me different when we get back on the trail. I'm gonna carry my share of the load just like always."

"Yes'm, don't reckon I'd have it any other way."

Alex brought her a glass of wine. She looked into Hawk's eyes, letting a slight smile break the corners of her lips. "You gonna do what you threatened to do if you saw me take a drink?"

Not breaking their gaze, his face sober, he nodded.

"Maybe someday, little one. Reckon I gotta get to know you a lot better—a whole lot better." It was her turn to blush.

Maria came into the room, looked at Rebecca, then at the men. "Ah, I see the butterfly came out of its cocoon, and a beautiful butterfly she is." She went to Rebecca, held her arms wide, and pulled her to her breasts. "As we say in my language, *mi casa es su casa*, welcome." Then she whispered into Rebecca's ear, "That handsome man you've traveled so far with had a look in his eye that bodes nothing but trouble for a young *señorita*."

Rebecca giggled. "Oh, I hope so, *señora*, I surely do."

Maria laughed with her. "And once again, Rebecca, your secret is safe with me."

When they'd gotten over their surprise, they were closer knit. Now they were no longer strangers passing through. Alex would have gotten them all drunk if they had let him, but they settled down to getting to know one another, and became fast friends as the days passed.

Then a couple of days before they were to leave, a messenger brought word that a couple of bandits, a man and a woman, a very pretty woman, were preying on small parties traveling the countryside, and leaving no survivors, except one who'd lived to describe them.

McClure's first thought was of Yolanda and her brother. He had not lost them. His feelings had mellowed. After again being back in this western country, and truly falling in love with it, he could let them have their ill-gotten gains.

He intended to get on with his life. He had a ranch to build, and emotions to sort out where Reb was concerned. How did he feel about her—protective, as a father toward his son, as a teacher, partner? Hell, he didn't know. He had trouble separating the boy he'd grown so fond of, from the beautiful woman he was hesitant to know.

They argued before leaving as to whether, for the rest

of their journey, Rebecca should go back to being a boy, or continue as a woman. Rebecca wanted to stay a woman, saying Hawk could protect her. The rest of the party, except McClure, thought she should return to being Reb, the young boy. McClure hated to see that happen. The deciding factor was that none of them made the decision. The lack of a suitable wardrobe gave the final vote. She had to be a boy.

McClure sidled up to her, his face sober. "Well, ma'am, reckon I won't be checking to see if you've put on any muscle in your shoulders." Then, letting a twinkle come to his eyes, he added, "Sure gonna miss that little intimacy, ma'am."

Not to be outdone, she slanted him a teasing look. "Hawken McClure, reckon anytime you want to you can check my *shoulder* muscles."

Her emphasis on "shoulder" brought hot blood to his face. "Oh, Lordy, hope you don't think I had anything else in mind. Hope you already figured me as a gentleman."

"Of course, Hawk. You know I was only kidding. I couldn't ask for a more perfect gentleman. Now I reckon I better put on my boy clothes so we can get started. Where you takin' us next?"

"Gonna go by way of Taos, then angle up toward Chama. There're rough customers up that way, but I figure to take care of you."

"Never thought you wouldn't, Hawk." She headed for her room to change.

A couple of hours later, with the wagon packed, oxen hitched, and Ned, now fully rested, standing at the head of the team, they said their good-byes.

Pablo stood to the side, toeing a small rock around with his boot. He looked up, and swept them with a glance. "Never thought I'd think as highly of anyone as I do Blanco, but I'm here to tell y'all, you folks, everyone o' you, sit right there in my heart with him. Wish I was goin' on with you, but with Hawk takin' care o' you, along with this sorry old outlaw, and his partner

Jedediah, reckon y'all gonna be all right. You ever get down in the Big Bend country again, stop by and visit.''

McClure hadn't given it a thought until now, but he realized Mixus and Powers *had* partnered up, but still clung to him like cockleburs. He smiled to himself, satisfied with their relationship.

After promising to stay longer with Alex and Maria the next time, Ned popped the whip over the team and they set out.

Still four or five days from Taos, a heavy, gloomy overcast of gray clouds shrouded the land. McClure, worried, searched the landscape for a place to hole up. He dropped back by Mixus and Jed. ''Gonna snow. Don't look for it to be too bad, still a week short o' Thanksgiving, but you never know. Y'all scout out ahead. Find a place alongside a stream where there're trees, maybe a blowdown so we can rig shelter to keep most of it offa us.'' He dropped back by the wagon boot and looked up at Bessie and Reb. ''One of you get back in the wagon and dig out more clothes. The wind's got a bite to it now. Gonna get colder. If it comes on to snow, y'all get in the back outta the weather. Ned can sit, an' I'll lead the team.''

A half hour passed. A few big, wet flakes floated to rest on McClure's sleeves. They didn't melt. The flurries stopped for several minutes, then, almost as though they had been building strength, they started again, heavier. Hawk squinted trying to see through the thickening snowfall, looking for one of the men to return with news they'd found something.

Jed returned first, and with a shake of his head, he said there was nothing except a large buffalo wallow, but it wouldn't give them much shelter.

Another half hour and Mixus materialized out of the curtain of snow closing off the world except for the small area in which they could identify one another and objects close at hand. ''Ain't a goldarned tree nowhere along that there crick, but they's a good cut bank we can get some shelter from.''

McClure eyed the old-timer. "Think you can find it again? Can't see far enough ahead to make out any landmarks."

Mixus chewed his tobacco a couple of times, worked it around in his cheek, spit, and squinted at Hawk. "Gonna tell you somethin', boy: You could blindfold me, an' I could zero in on it. Goldanged right I can find it. Foller me, young'un." He kneed his horse around and set out in a northerly direction.

McClure glanced at the hammock slung beneath the wagon in which they'd tossed every stick, small limb, or buffalo chip they came upon, and hoped the supply would last out the storm. He wasn't worried about himself and the two men—or even Reb—but he felt most concern for Bessie and Ned, whose age told on them more all the time. They didn't have enough meat on their bones to shed off cold.

The snow soon showed it would stick, and build a pretty good cover. A wave of guilt flooded McClure, and worry knotted his stomach. Had he done the darkies and Reb a disservice by bringing them with him? Would they have settled somewhere else if he'd not talked horse ranching in that country west of Durango? They'd get to Colorado in the deep cold of winter, and winter in that country could be brutal—heavy snows, temperatures below zero, and nowhere to live until he could build them a cabin. His guilt deepened. This was a helluva time to think about things that could go wrong. If it took the money he'd gotten from his horses, he'd put them up in a cabin—or somewhere in Durango—until spring thaw, but they were not to Colorado yet—and Taos could match toughness with any town. Unconsciously, he brushed the handle of his Colt with stiff, cold fingers. The snow deepened.

14

MIXUS LED THEM to the banks at the bottom of which a narrow stream, not over three feet wide, flowed. Crusty ice had already formed along the water's edge. "Mixus, Powers, ride the banks, see if there's a place we can get the wagon to the bottom, then take us to the cutbank, old-timer."

Only a few minutes passed before Jed returned. He pointed to his left. "Bank ain't high over there a ways. We can cave the sides in a bit to let the wagon roll down easy-like. Mixus'll have to show us the place he found."

McClure eyed the clouds, a feeling of satisfaction crowding his stomach. The likelihood of a rain flooding the stream was not even a possibility. "Let's get on with it."

Mixus found them before the wagon settled at the bottom of the shallow ravine, and he led them to the cutbank. Hawk looked over his shoulder. "Reb, after I get the wagon parked to block off some of the wind and snowfall, get a fire started. Bessie, you an' Ned stay in the wagon. Pull blankets over you and stay warm. We'll take care of makin' camp and cookin' supper. Don't want either o' you takin' a chill."

Bessie opened her mouth as though to argue. "Don't want any backtalk, auntie, y'all do like I said." He grinned. " 'Bout as good a time as any to find out if Reb can boil water without burnin' it."

Rebecca bristled, but before she could say anything, Bessie cut in. "Mistuh Hawk, I done been teachin' that there young lady how to cook since she wuz old 'nuff to unnerstan' what I wuz talkin' 'bout." She shook her head. "No, suh, she ain't gonna burn that there water. She does an' I'll tan her little bottom."

Hawk smiled to himself. Since seeing Reb in a dress, he knew her bottom would stack up with any he'd seen. Then, embarrassed at the thought, he felt blood rush to his face.

Reb stared at him. Then, as though reading his mind, she said, "Hawken McClure, don't think I wantta know what you were thinkin' right then to cause you to blush like that?"

"No, ma'am, don't reckon you wantta know. Wouldn't tell you if you did."

She stomped her foot. "Like I thought, it musta been one of those things men think that isn't very nice."

Despite his embarrassment, and his red face, Hawk grinned. "Yes'm, reckon I differ with you on that. It *is* very nice."

"Girl," Bessie laughed deep in her chest, "you bettuh quit while you is ahead. Mistuh Hawk's gonna win this one."

They went about setting up to keep the weather off. They pulled back under the overhang of the cutbank as far as possible so as to keep snow and wind off. And then, when it was as comfortable as they could make it, with the fire between them and the wagon, Reb cooked supper. McClure didn't show surprise at how good the food turned out, nor was he surprised at the efficient way Reb went about getting it done. She kept glancing at him, her look asking for a vote of approval. Finally, when the smell of roasted venison, baked bread, and coffee became almost unbearable, he glanced at her.

"Reb, for a boy, I figure you did yourself right proud, that food looks 'bout good enough to eat." Then he laughed and apologized for doubting her.

When they sat to eat, he took out a jug of whiskey and insisted they drink their coffee laced heavily with the strong drink. "Thought you said I wasn't to drink this stuff, Hawk. Thought you said if you caught me doin' it, you'd tan my—" She broke off her sentence. *She* blushed this time.

McClure hurriedly said, "The weather bein' what it is, reckon it's a good enough reason to warm our insides a bit. Now, y'all go ahead, eat, an' Powers and I'll clean up while you folks get bedded down."

When they awakened the next morning, about a foot of snow lay on the flats, and it was still coming down. Jed offered to fix breakfast, but Rebecca pushed him aside. McClure and Mixus climbed the bank to see what traveling might be like that day. After studying the land awhile, and knowing a slight but steady climb would be involved until they reached Taos, Hawk shook his head. "Reckon the oxen would suffer more'n us. What you think about layin' over another day, give the animals, and us, a chance to rest up?"

The old man chomped his chew a moment, squinted across the pristine white expanse, then nodded. "Ain't gonna hurt none, the rest I mean." He chomped a couple more times, spit, and gave McClure a straight-on look. "Anybody needs rest, I'd say it's Ned." He shook his head. "Ain't sayin' he ain't tryin' his dead level best to carry his part o' the load, but, Hawk, he's gettin' *old*— an' it shows more every day. Let me talk to 'im so's he won't think we're mollycoddling 'im. Don't want to hurt 'is pride."

McClure looked at Mixus a moment. He swallowed the lump in his throat. By damn, every member of the party cared for the rest. He loved them all. He swallowed again, then said, "Good idea. Sure don't want that old man to ever figure he's a burden on any of us. He and

Bessie gave up all they mighta had to take care of Reb. We owe him.''

Back at the fire, Rebecca had breakfast ready, and when Hawk told them they'd lay over another day, he thought he detected a sigh of relief from them all.

The snow drifted and banked around the wagon, such that it sheltered them from the wind and cold. They spent the day yarning, drinking coffee, and occasionally Hawk passed his bottle to the men, with Bessie nagging Ned about not drinking too much of the vile stuff.

The next morning McClure noticed the stream to be a little wider, and flowing more swiftly. ''We'll eat, then get outta this ravine. Looks like we got a pretty good thaw settin' in.'' He frowned. ''Don't know as we did the animals much of a favor, 'cause now they're gonna have to drag that wagon through mud.'' He shrugged. ''Reckon it was six in one hand, half a dozen in the other.''

Mixus had his talk with Ned, and the old darkie raised some amount of hell. The fact was, he looked Rolf up and down and said he figured he wasn't but a year or two older than the outlaw. Mixus won: Ned's anger overrode his pride, but he did as Hawk told him.

McClure and Rebecca had taken to walking out beyond the campsite every evening after supper; she, to take the stiffness from her body after sitting all day on the wagon seat, and Hawk, to rid himself of kinks from sitting the saddle. To Hawk's way of thinking, she just wanted the quietude of the walk, because even though she'd led the oxen most of a day, and couldn't have possibly been very stiff, she insisted on it.

He liked it because it gave him a chance to know her better, and his planning for his ranch centered more and more on, at the very least, one adjacent to Reb's.

Even though she could put any woman he knew in the shade where beauty came into play, she took up the chores he'd laid out for her when thinking her a boy, and did them well without a complaint.

When they reached Santa Fe, they talked it over and

all agreed they should take three or four days to get the
wagon in shape for the rest of their journey, and to buy
the provisions they would need for the next few weeks.

The weather held warm for the time of year, and Rebecca fell in love with the old town and its square, with
the Governor's Mansion facing it. The spicy smells of
dried peppers and Mexican dishes cooking kept her
mouth watering most of the time. And the colorful dress
of the vaqueros could have made even Mixus handsome.

At the end of their second day there, she cornered
McClure. "Why don't we settle someplace around here,
Hawk? It's beautiful, the people are friendly, and the
land looks like it'd be good for horses."

He nodded. "You're right except for one thing. All
this land is owned by old Spanish Land Grant families.
These people have been here longer'n most back in the
States have been there. I know of at least two hundred
years of settlement by the Spanish dons." He grinned.
"Don't think they'd take lightly to our tryin' to move
in on 'em."

"Oh, I didn't know." Disappointment cloaked her reply, then she smiled. "Well, I'm sure we'll like that
country out the other side of Animas City."

He chuckled, liking the way she bounced back after
a disappointment.

They stayed another day in Santa Fe, then headed up
the west slopes of the Sangre de Cristo range.

A day out of Taos, they were well into their walk
when McClure felt Reb studying him. "What's the matter, little one, I do something to upset you?"

She shook her head. "Just wondering what you figure
on doin' after you get us located. You gonna ride on
and find yourself another place?"

He looked across his shoulder at her. "Been thinkin'
'bout that. Come to the conclusion, if y'all don't mind,
I'd sortta like to settle right close to you."

"Mind? Why, Hawken McClure, I can't think of a
nicer neighbor." Her eyes twinkled. "Of course you'd
better think twice 'bout that. We'd most likely worry

you to death with questions, an' things needin' a man's attention."

He smiled. "Don't reckon that'll be a problem. Don't figure you're gonna want to ride four or five miles to get me to do somethin' every time you have a small problem."

She surprised him. She took his hand in hers while they walked. "Four or five miles? Land sakes, that's not a neighbor. That's too far away." She didn't release his hand, and he didn't make a move to take it from hers.

"Gonna tell you somethin', girl, we need room to build a ranch. Figured any closer than that and it'd sort o' box you in."

She shook her head. "Nope. Reckon bein' boxed in by a good neighbor would be right nice."

They walked like that, not saying more. McClure breathed of the pine-scented mountain air, looked at the slopes where the pine and spruce appeared black against their rocky sides. Silvery threads of snowmelt streams, often spilling over rocks in rushing falls, threaded the mountain with jewel-like strands sending out faint sounds of water tumbling, chuckling and singing over rocks in its rush to reach some unknown creek at the bottom of the slope.

He breathed deeply again, and glanced at her. "You reckon this is what God had in mind when he thought to create a place called Heaven?"

She cast him a slight smile. "Don't know, big man, but if he has anything better for us I can't wait to get there."

"Don't be in too big a hurry, Reb. I'm kinda likin' the company here. 'Sides that, we have a lot of livin' to get behind us; then, reckon I'd like to go just as we are now."

Her face turned a delightful pink as she obviously became aware they still held hands. She glanced to her side—but made no effort to release her hold on him.

McClure chuckled deep in his throat. "Damn, never gave much thought to holdin' hands with a boy."

She still held tightly to his big, calloused paw, and talking like she'd heard Jed and Mixus talk, she said, "Ain't no boy, but if'n that there'll make you happy, I'll see if'n I can find you one when we get to Taos." She pulled him around, and they headed back to the wagon.

That night, huddled close to her auntie, Rebecca told her she'd held hands with Hawk during most of their walk. Bessie grunted, "You jest make danged sure yore hand's all you let 'im take hold of."

"Auntie, I'm the one took hold of his—never intended to, but it just happened. Don't know why."

Bessie grunted again. "Tell you why, little miss, you been hankerin' aftuh that there man ever since you first seen 'im. Now, you jest go slow, let him make all the moves toward you. You don't, you gonna scare 'im off. They ain't nothin' more scary to a man than a fast-movin' female. Now, you keep quiet, an' think 'bout what I done told you. I'm goin' to sleep." She turned onto her side and soon breathed deeply.

The next afternoon about three o'clock, they rode into a town square much like the one in Santa Fe, but on a smaller scale. McClure's hair tingled at the base of his skull, his shoulder muscles tightened. He'd heard even as far away as El Paso that this was a rough, tough town, that outlaws from all over the West walked the streets without worry about the law, that a day without a gunfight was considered a dull one, that a cowboy, full of stump juice, riding about the square firing his six-shooter, didn't cause anyone to take cover, or even glance toward the noise. He, Jed, and Mixus would have to take turns sleeping in the livery to see that no one took a notion to ride off with Reb's golden stallion, or any of their other horses.

In front of the hotel, he helped Bessie and Reb to the ground, got them rooms, then led the animals to the livery; at the same time he told Powers and Mixus of his plans to watch the horses while they were in town.

They'd all decided Rebecca would continue to appear as a boy.

After his stint of watching the stallion, McClure went to the nearest saloon, knocked back a couple of drinks, and headed for the hotel to clean up. When finished with his bath and shave, he glanced at his holstered Colt, swung the belt around his waist, then on second thought tucked an extra six-shooter behind his belt. He walked out on the boardwalk in time to see a big man, clean-shaven, red-haired, take Reb by the arm and push her.

"Watch where the hell you goin', boy. Squirt like you ain't got no business walkin' amongst men."

Before she could react, McClure had hold of the ruffian's shoulder and swung him to look into his face. But that took all the time before Hawk's right fist connected with the man's jaw. The bully hit the ground, rolled, came to his feet, and brought a right up from his waist. McClure stepped inside the swing and pumped another right to the man's gut, a left to his heart, and another right to his mouth. Blood spurted. The brute spit out a couple of teeth, then charged in swinging with both fists.

McClure took a right and a left to his stomach before he could set himself, then waded in. This was knuckle and skull fighting. He liked it. He'd had a few such bouts when in the Army. They stood toe to toe and slugged it out.

The ruffian stood a couple inches taller than Hawk's six foot, one inch, and outweighed him by at least twenty pounds, but McClure had not spent time swilling cheap whiskey in saloons. The ruffian's belly sank in under the punishing blows McClure threw into him. The big man gave ground, and Hawk followed, unaware that a huge crowd had gathered. A fistfight was not the usual thing. A gunfight would have been a ho-hum thing.

McClure sensed he had the big man on the ropes. He closed in, pumped a right and a left to the gut, then put all he had into a right to the jaw. The bully went down. Hawk swung his boot at the man's head, connected, and the fight ended—for then.

The law, what there was of it, stepped to McClure's side. "What wuz that all about? Didn't see nothin' to cause you to climb his frame."

Not yet feeling anger drain from him, Hawk, stared into the man's eyes, glanced at the badge pinned to his coat, then gave the marshal a hard look. "Figure I felt like a little exercise. Too, I don't cotton to any man bullying a young kid. He pushed and cursed that young'un there, so I took a hand in it."

The marshal glanced at the redheaded man still lying in the street. "Figure Red shoulda whipped ya." He shook his head. "But, mister, when he comes outta it, you better be damned good with that six-shooter you got there. He ain't gonna be fool enough to tangle with you agin; he'll be grabbin' fer a pistol—an' he's right fast."

"You see 'im 'fore he sees me, Marshal, tell 'im to pay for his grave plot. No point in the town goin' to that expense." He turned his back to the lawman and walked to where Reb stood. Her face white, her fists clenched, she stared at the man lying in the street's dust. Hawk took her arm and steered her from the crowd already scattering about the street, with most headed for one of the many saloons.

He looked down at her. "Shoulda warned you not to go out on the street. This's a rough town. Sorry 'bout that."

Color now showed in her cheeks, and her eyes sparked blue flame. "Ooooh, I wish I was a man. I'd have worked him over worse'n you did."

McClure stepped in front and faced her. "Well now, you stand here a moment an' I'll go back an' finish the job—till you tell me to stop."

She grabbed his arm. "Oh, no. Don't you dare, he might hurt you."

Hawk threw back his head and laughed. "Didn't figure on it, little one. Just wanted to see how you'd react."

Reb only shook her head, her mouth a straight, hard line. The sparks in her eyes cooled, then a slow grin broke the firm line of her mouth. She took his arm, then apparently realizing a boy wouldn't hold a man's arm, she dropped her hand from his arm like she'd touched a hot coal. "Let's go eat. All our people should be in that cafe over yonder by now. That's where I was goin' when that animal pushed me."

McClure ate slowly, chewing each mouthful far longer than necessary, his thoughts centered on the man he'd whipped. If he stayed in his hotel room, word would spread that Red Buckstall had him buffaloed; some would say he was afraid to face Buckstall with a gun. This was a large country, but too small for a man to dodge a fight unless he wanted "Coward" tagged to his name.

After supper, he got the darkies and Reb settled in their rooms, sent Powers to the livery to watch the horses, then took Mixus with him. "Goin' to every saloon in town till I find the one Buckstall drinks in, then I want you to cover my back." He eyed the old outlaw. "An' cover my back's all I want. Don't get involved in my fight 'less someone throws down on me from behind. Got it?"

Mixus grinned. "Knowed 'zactly whut you wuz thinkin' while you sat there eatin'. Hell, you could of been chompin' hay an' you wouldn't of knowed it. Yeah, I'll watch yore back. I'd be worried 'bout ya, if I hadn't seen ya handle that Colt. Let's go find that woman-pushin' bastard."

They lucked out. Buckstall stood at the bar in the second watering hole they tried. McClure stopped in hearing range long enough to hear Red telling those around him what he'd do to the man who took a Sunday punch at him out on the street. Hawk walked to the end of the bar, only about ten feet from where the bully stood.

Those gathered around Buckstall obviously saw McClure before he did. Looking as though they wanted to get out of the line of fire without alerting him, they at first inched away, then began an all-out shoving match. Buckstall looked at them, frowned, and glanced to each side. There was only empty space around him for as much as fifteen feet. He glanced behind. No one stood at his back. Then, trying to focus his whiskey-clouded brain, he looked toward the end of the bar.

His eyes focused in on McClure, who stood relaxed, a drink in his left hand, a slight smile crinkling the corners of his eyes. This wasn't how it was supposed to be. The word had gotten around that he, Buckstall, was the bull of the woods around here, one of the fastest gunfighters in New Mexico. That pilgrim down there should be showing fear, should have tried to quietly leave without being noticed, yet there he stood as though he perhaps hadn't heard, or, even worse, thought himself able to face the gunfighter.

"Well, Buckstall, you've made your brag. I whipped you fair out there on the street. I'm willin' to let it drop, or if you insist, I'll whip your butt again, or even better—you can see if you rate the name you've made for yourself shootin' drunk cowboys and old men." His smile broadened. "Frankly, I've asked around an' nobody's been able to tell me where your graveyards are."

Buckstall felt a large knot grow in his throat. A bitter taste pushed past the knot. His gut muscles tightened, threatening to push his last drink up through his mouth. He'd seen this trick pulled before. A man wanting an edge would talk, trying to shake the man he faced. Sweat flowed beneath his arms, down his back, and stood in beads on his forehead. That pilgrim wasn't going to shake *him*. He sneered, and twisted as if to put his back to McClure—then went for his gun.

His revolver cleared leather. He slipped his thumb from the hammer. A wild feeling of exultation swelled his chest. He'd show this greenhorn who was the best gunfighter around. Why, hell, he'd had his handgun almost clear of the holster and the pilgrim hadn't even started his draw.

But something was wrong. His shot went into the floor at his feet. Someone had hit him a sledgehammer blow in his chest the moment he fired. He eared back the hammer again, slipped his thumb—and again splinters and sawdust flew from the floor.

The stranger's gun blossomed at least twice, and twice more someone pushed Buckstall back. The stranger too had missed, but each time he missed someone hit him, Buckstall, in his chest. What the hell was wrong with these people?

His pistol got heavier. He could hardly hold it for another shot. He looked to see if he had the right weapon. Three round, black holes between his shirt pockets showed red edges. Those holes hadn't been there when he put the shirt on after the fight.

His gun weighed a ton, so heavy he no longer could hold it. It slipped from his hand, fell to the floor, and skidded out of reach. He told himself he had to get his pistol back or the stranger would kill him. He fell to the floor, reached for his pistol, but his eyes drooped, tried to go to sleep. Why did he want to sleep during a gunfight? His body flattened to the floor. His face pushed the tobacco-spit-laden sawdust aside with his cheek. He reached for his revolver again. Why couldn't he stretch far enough for his gun?

Tired, he had no energy left. To hell with the gunfight, he had to sleep, then he'd finish the stranger off with another shot. He closed his eyes and went to sleep—forever.

McClure opened the loading gate, shucked five spent shells, and pushed five good ones into the cylinder. He raked the crowd with hard eyes. "Anyone here think Buckstall was a good enough friend to take up his fight?" Even though he said the words, Hawk hoped no one would step forward.

Fear he should have felt earlier pushed its way into his chest, his throat, and only now did he realize he still held his drink in his left hand, and he needed that drink. He couldn't work up enough saliva to moisten his tongue. He knocked the drink back and held the glass for the bartender to refill.

And so legends are made. The story of the new gun-

fighter to the west would race from Canada to Mexico—
about how cool he'd been, holding a drink in one hand
while he disposed of a known man, a man feared for his
gun-swift throughout the New Mexico Territory. Mc-
Clure had heard rumors, campfire talk, and saloon tales
that had sent many a man on the gunfighter's path—and
he wanted none of it—but it would happen regardless
what he wanted. And his troubles weren't over.

He holstered his Colt, raised his head to toss off his
replenished drink—and stared into the eyes of Bob
Bridges and Anse Berglund.

15

MCCLURE CAREFULLY LOWERED his glass while he brushed the walnut handles of his Colt with the fingers of his right hand. "I just got a fresh drink. Find yourselves another watering hole—or pull iron." His words fell between them like chips of flint. He'd come in here to settle one problem, now he had two more—and his temper, already rubbed raw, would allow for no more.

Each of the two would-be holdup artists held his hand clear of the revolver riding on his hip. They stared at McClure a moment, then Bob said, "Another day, gunfighter. You took somethin' o' ours. We figger to get it back, an' then some. We'll wait." They spun toward the heavy wooden doors and left.

Hawk let his breath out. He'd been holding it since telling them to put up or shut up. The two he'd let walk out would never face him in a fair fight. They were the dry-gulch kind. He wished then he'd forced a fight. But beating two of them would have been more than he figured he could handle. He decided for the first time he'd better practice a fast draw.

• • •

Yolanda and Tom Squires sat in her room at the hotel in Santa Fe. She poured the contents of a saddlebag out onto the bed and twisted to look at her brother. "Three holdups. Reckon we got more now than we left home with, little brother. We'll stay here an' rest up a couple o' days, then to Chama, an' from there to Animas City. Figger McClure an' them niggers he's hooked up with'll stay clear of Taos. Hear that's a tough town. Man can get himself killed over there from sayin' good mornin' in the wrong tone of voice."

"Yeah, Yolanda, we got more now than we started with. We got seven dead bodies on our backtrail, an' a whole bunch o' salty lawmen, to say nothin' 'bout that money, an' them necklaces, bracelets, rings an' stuff a-layin' there. We'd be better off to cut our losses, head for home, an' let McClure see if he can make it in this here godforsaken country."

After expressing his opinion, Tom shrank farther into the one chair the room had to offer. He'd seen cold before, but her flat, black eyes took on the sheen of ice. Her face, which many called beautiful, had no beauty in it now. Hard, hard as granite, with tight drawn lines down each side of her mouth, her eyes slitted, jaw muscles knotted, she came real close to what most would call ugly. He'd never noticed before how her soul—dark, cruel, sadistic—shone through the surface thing called beauty.

After several moments, she said, "Little brother, I done told you, we ain't goin' nowhere till Hawken McClure's paid fer what he done to me."

"What'd he do to you, sister? You ain't never said. To my way o' thinkin' he ain't the kind to rape a woman, an' I figger good-lookin' as he is you'da give 'im whatever he wanted."

She shook her head. "Ain't gonna say, neither. You jest shut up 'bout goin' home. I hear any more 'bout it, an' you won't never go nowhere, no more." She picked up her drink of straight whiskey, knocked it back, then poured another. She separated the jewelry from the money laying on the bed, counted the money, then fingered the jewelry. "We see anybody round here what looks like they got anythin' worth takin', we'll break up our rest an' see what they're worth."

Tom's gut churned. How the hell did he get himself into this? He didn't hate Hawk McClure; the fact was, he felt sorry for him. He'd lost his beautiful antebellum home, carriages, out buildings—everything—and now searched for a new place to call home—but Yolanda, not satisfied with that, wanted him killed.

Then it occurred to him Yolanda had no intention of pulling the trigger on Hawk herself. She had *him* pegged to do the job, and from what he'd heard of McClure and guns, he wanted no part of tackling him. And after McClure killed him, Yolanda would pay some small-town coroner a couple of dollars to bury him, then try to find someone else to do the job. Many gunmen out here rode a tightrope between law and the owl-hoot, and would take on killing McClure for very little money—or perhaps what his sister promised with her body. A promise she'd never keep.

He could try to do like Bert did—run. Or he could stay here and die. Either way he figured he'd never see Alabama again. Still cold sober, not having had the first drink, he poured a water glass full, and drank it down as though it *were* water. Get drunk. Stay drunk—that way he'd not give a damn what happened.

McClure had accomplished that which he had come in the saloon to do. Now he would have to think what to do about Bridges and Berglund. Too, he figured Yolanda and Tom Squires still hunted him. He decided whatever they planned for him, there was no way he'd pull the trigger on a woman—but how the hell could he keep her from killing him? He pulled his hat low on his forehead and went out the doors.

One step onto the boardwalk and splinters from the doorjamb stabbed into the muscles of his shoulder, followed instantly by the sharp report of a rifle. McClure

threw himself off the walk into the street's dust, pulled
his .44, rolled, and another bullet kicked dust into his
face. He triggered the Colt twice toward the orange flare
from the rifle muzzle, rolled, and again fired into the
dark maw of the alley across the street. Dead quiet muffled the night, except for running footsteps from the
alley, and another rifle joined the fight from his right
side.

He rolled to his feet and, not thinking to hit anything,
thumbed off a shot in the direction from which the last
shot had come. Again, the rapid pound of footsteps.
Hawk shucked spent shells from his Colt, pushed in new
ones, walked to the saloon front, and leaned weakly
against the wall. His tired body and shaking legs threatened to force him to sink to the boardwalk.

He snorted, tried to clear his nose of the acrid smell
of gunpowder, and only then did he realize he sweated
like a horse run to its limit—and the temperature was
well below freezing.

He shook his head. It hadn't taken those two long to
try and collect his scalp, but it surprised him they'd tried
to get even in the middle of town. A crowd collected
around him.

A hard-bitten old man moved closer to McClure.
Hawk studied him a moment, along with the badge
pinned to his pocket. The lawman looked maybe fifty
years old judging by his stiff, erect bearing and slim, fit-
looking body, but the face topping off the body looked
like it had helped launch the ark. He pinned McClure
with a hard-eyed, straight-on look. "What happened?"

McClure's nerves twanged like a fiddle string, his
throat muscles tightened, and hot blood pushed to his
head. "What the hell's it look like? Two bastards caught
me in a cross fire. They blew it. Now it's my turn."

"What you mean?"

"I mean I'm gonna blow 'em to hell—if I catch 'em.
You got objections?"

The marshal, or sheriff, or whatever the hell he was,
never broke his gaze, never softened. "You better settle

down, son. I'll lock you up faster'n a rabbit can mate.''
His face broke into wrinkles; looked like a dry lake bed.
Hawk reckoned the change of expression passed for a
smile. "Course I could think o' some other reason so's
to save you from gettin' yoreself killed. Them men're
right serious 'bout puttin' you down for good. Don't go
off half-cocked. Now, you gonna tell me what happened?''

McClure sucked in a deep breath, did it again, then
realized the tough, don't-give-an-inch marshal was only
trying to do his job. "Marshal," his badge said, now
that Hawk took time to read it.

Hawk kicked at a crack in the boards, then looked at
the lawman. "Sorry, Marshal. You want me to come
over to your lockup, or will you let me buy you a drink
while I tell my story?''

Again, that dry-lake-bed smile. "Never drink while
on duty, 'less'n o' course it's in the line of duty. This's
in the line o' duty. Let's have a drink.''

McClure hesitated. "First, I'd like to go over to that
alley 'an see if I hit anybody with those two shots. Don't
figure I hit the second shooter; I was firin' blind.''

The marshal nodded and led the way to the alley.
They found spots of blood on the weathered wooden
wall, and drops in the dust beside it. "You winged 'im,
son. If you're goin' after 'em, that might give you the
edge. Might have to face only one.''

McClure nodded. "Don't reckon hurrying's gonna get
the job done any better. Let's get that drink.'' The
crowd, which had followed them to the alley, began to
disperse.

In the saloon, McClure walked to the bar, bought a
bottle, and went to a table against the back wall. When
he sat, he made sure his back faced the wall.

He started his story when Bridges and Berglund
crossed the Mississippi with him and his party, and told
it down to the last detail. When finished, he nodded.
"Yep, I took everything they had. They figured to do

the same to us. You might say I beat 'em to the draw on that one.''

A rumble deep in the marshal's chest signaled his amusement at the story—enough to laugh. McClure shrugged. ''That's all fifty-two cards in the deck, Marshal.''

John Carston—Hawk learned the marshal went by that name. Carston stared at him a moment. ''Son, I outta lock you up right now jest to keep you safe. Them men ain't gonna give you a even break. They gonna do like they jest now done, shoot you from behind, or any other way to get you when you ain't lookin' at 'em.'' He knocked back his drink, and McClure poured another. ''Boy, I'm tellin you right now, you ride mighty careful or you ain't gonna get where you're goin'.

''Figure on it, mar—'' Before he could say what he'd intended, Jed, blood streaming down the side of his face, ran into the saloon, looked toward the bar, then glanced at the tables. McClure raised his voice. ''Back here, Powers.''

Jed walked in long strides to the table. ''Hawk, them two what you took horses from hit me on the head an' stole Reb's stallion.''

Hawk stood, his chair falling to the side. ''Go see the doctor 'bout your head, then tell Reb and the two darkies I'll be back when they see me. Tell 'em to stand fast till then.'' He looked at the marshal. ''Yeah, Marshal, I'll be careful, careful enough to know where I put my shots. See you when I get back.''

He poured himself a drink, knocked it back, and stepped toward the door. Before he took another step, Carston caught him by the arm. ''Gonna tell you, son, when you get back, if'n you bring that stud hoss back with you, you better keep a close watch on 'im even then. They's two others in this town what steal hosses, one a real pale-faced gent, an' his sidekick, a cowboy, only they do it by scaring the hoss's owner with threats of bringin' the law against him, claimin' he stole the hosses they themselves figure to steal.'' Hawk gave him a short, choppy nod and left the saloon.

His only thought was getting the horse back. Before he could head for the livery, he stopped. He'd be a fool to hit the trail with nothing but Blacky, his big black gelding.

He went to his room, collected his rifle and a saddle-bag stuffed with provisions and .44 shells. He rolled his bedroll and took his sheepskin. He stowed his gear on the packhorse, and only then did he let urgency overtake sound thinking.

The tracks of the golden stallion were as familiar as the palm of his hand after seeing them across half the country. Outside the livery he picked up sign of the two. He read the sign as two ridden horses, two packhorses— and Reb's stallion. The tracks cut deep into the soil. They were in a hurry.

McClure glanced at the sun. Still about an hour of daylight. He'd track them until he couldn't see, then he'd pick up their trail come daylight.

He made a dry camp and, feeling hungry, chewed on a strip of jerky, a good supply of which Pablo had insisted he take when he left the ranch. He wished for a fire and a good cup of coffee, but he shrugged that hankering off. The night settled in cold enough to force him to his blankets earlier than usual.

He lay awake staring at the cold, distant stars, breathing the delicate scent of pine and spruce. Reb set store by that stallion—and, he admitted to himself, he set store by Reb. Her beauty had little to do with his feelings. He had difficulty in separating the boy he'd thought to teach the things he needed to become a man, and the grown woman she'd proven to be—and for whom he longed. The fact was, he liked them both. He sighed, turned to his side, and went to sleep.

The next morning, he allowed himself a fire, made coffee, fried bacon, and opened a tin of beans. After eating, he cleaned up the camp, then squatted at the side of the tracks the horses had made and ran his fingers around the deepest part of them to make certain they were dry. He figured to do this until he felt moisture in the bottoms, then he could tell about how far they's ridden before making camp. In that manner he could guess about how far they were ahead of him.

After about three hours' tracking, he noticed the hoofprints to be wet. He put that down to their being in the shade of some large ponderosa pines. When he rode out into a stretch of sunlight, he again tested the prints— they still held moisture. He nodded. They were about three hours ahead of him.

Three hours would be hard to make up. They would ride from can-see to can't-see, and would punish the horses to faster travel while doing so, and they would know he'd follow them to hell if he had to. That brought him up short. If they knew he'd follow them, what better excuse for them to set up a dry-gulch? Too, one of them carried lead. McClure wondered how bad he'd hit the bandit. If he was in a bad way, they might stop to give him a break, and try for an ambush then.

Leading four horses on lead ropes, Bob Bridges pulled his horse off the trail into an aspen thicket. Anse held tight to the saddle horn. His blood-soaked shirt showed signs of fresh blood. Bridges stepped from the saddle and held up his hands to help his partner from the saddle. Berglund turned loose the horn, and fell into the redhead's arms.

Struggling under Anse's weight, Bridges carried him as gently as he could to a clear spot in the trees and stretched him out on the ground. "Hold on, partner, we gonna make it. Figgered to stop here awhile, let you rest up, an' I'll see can I put a fresh dressin' on that there hole in yore side."

"Bob, how bad am I hit? Am I gonna cash in my chips out here a hunnerd miles from nowhere?"

Bridges studied on how to answer, then figured he might as well tell the truth. "Gonna tell you straight, partner, you took a good one, lost a lot o' blood, an' if

I don't get you to a doctor, I figger you done drawed the queen o' spades.''

His face pasty, Anse nodded. Then, his voice wheezy, he said, "Figgered as much. We still 'bout forty miles from Chama. I ain't gonna make it. Take them horses an' git outta here 'fore McClure catches up to us. Leave me—ain't no point in both o' us gittin' killed.''

Bridges shook his head. "Ain't leavin' you. We done rode too many trails together to treat you like that.''

"Well, git me back on my hoss. Tie me in the saddle an' let's get outta here. If I don't make it, make sure the coyotes don't get me. Push some rocks over me.''

"No. I'll bushwhack that bastard. You jest lie there till I can get rid of him.''

His words obviously upset Berglund. His face flushed a deep red, and he moved his hands from side to side frantically, then his voice stronger, he said, "Leave me! Get outta here!''

Bridges stared at his partner a moment. His stomach felt hollow, and a lump swelled in his throat. Standing by his horse, he crossed his hands on his saddle and leaned his head on them. Where did he and Anse go wrong? What led them to this? Only four years since he worked in his father's store, and Anse had left home to work in the cotton gin. They'd started stealing small things like a sack of Bull Durham, or eggs, or chickens, then they'd held up lone travelers—and now this. And worse, he wanted to kill from ambush the man tracking them.

He raised his head and twisted to look at his partner. Anse lay there, not moving, his hands folded on his chest, his eyes unblinking, staring up through the golden aspen leaves at the flawless blue sky. "Anse? Anse, talk to me, boy. You all right?''

Anse didn't talk to him, never would again. The redhead again turned his face to his saddle, and for the first time in years tears streaked down his cheeks.

After several minutes, Bridges straightened, sniffled, squared his shoulders, and took his partner's bedroll from behind his saddle, then took his blanket and wrapped Berglund in it. Then he walked from the trees to find a shallow ravine with rocks close by.

Two hours later, leading the four horses, Bridges rode toward Chama. Every few minutes he cast a look at the empty saddle cinched to the horse closest to him, and his eyes again flooded.

McClure rode with his rifle across the saddle in front of him, aware now that a bullet from the trees, rocks, across a slight swell in the land, might cut him down. Be careful, the marshal had cautioned. His glance again swept the terrain in front and to the sides. If he missed seeing the horse thief when he passed, his only chance of escaping a bullet in the back was if the rifleman missed his first shot—and that wasn't likely.

He rode with muscles tightened against the impact of a bullet—a bullet that would end his dreams of Reb, the ranch, and his future. Every few moments he pulled his eyes from searching all about him to look at the horse tracks. He stopped. The tracks left the trail and entered a copse of aspen not far to his right. He slipped to the off side of his horse, and went to ground. If he was going to take a bullet along the trail, this was the place it would happen. The sharp report of a rifle didn't come.

For a long few moments, he stood at the side of the gelding, then slipped from behind him and dodged into the tangle of trees. Still no shot. From his crouched position, he stood erect. If he hadn't already been shot at, there was no one here to shoot. Had the two pulled off the trail for their nooning?

Carrying his rifle with a shell in the chamber, McClure studied the tracks made by the two horse thieves. He found where they'd stopped in the cluster of aspen, and where something had been dragged from the trees to where a body had been covered with rocks. A chill ran up his spine. Another killing. He wondered which of the two men he'd killed.

He studied the pile of rocks with the crude cross, two

sticks tied with a string of rawhide, and regret flooded his chest that he was the one responsible for the death of yet another man. The regret lasted only a moment. They'd brought it on themselves.

He went back to the trail and soon determined from the depth of the tracks that the horses were being pushed hard toward—where? He pondered that question a short while and decided Chama would be the only place the horse thief could go, unless he cut back south toward Santa Fe.

McClure decided to head for Chama, but he would look for tracks occasionally. With the time lost to bury his partner, he figured the outlaw had lost at least one, maybe two hours. That could only mean that McClure rode mighty close on the heels of the man.

He made camp that night beside a gurgling, rushing stream coming from the mountains behind him. This night he had coffee along with his supper.

The next morning he headed for Chama. Only twenty miles from the town, he figured to make it in time for his nooning. He rode with caution, but thought his man hadn't stopped.

McClure reined in at the livery and arranged for his horse to be grain fed. He unsaddled the gelding and rubbed the horse down, having to push its head aside from a slobbery nuzzle every once in a while. Then he searched the stable and found the golden stallion in the last stall. He was tempted to tell the hostler the horse belonged to someone other than the man who'd brought it in, but figured that would cut no ice with the liveryman. He handed the man his rifle. "Take care of this for me till I come back, maybe in the mornin'."

A slight smile crinkling his leathery face, said, the hostler, "Don't figger this Winchester's gonna eat much, so they won't be no charge fer me takin' care of it fer you."

Hawk nodded. "You take good care of it, an' I'll pay you same as though it had." He asked for a good place to eat and where he could find the hotel.

"Ain't but one o' each." He flicked his thumb toward where McClure had seen a few sun-bleached buildings. "Jest head down the road a piece an' you cain't miss 'em."

Hawk wondered if he should look for the horse thief now, or wait until morning. He decided he better look now; it might save him more days of riding in case the thief got an early start on the morrow. He felt safe in eating and getting a room at the hotel first in that if the man who'd stolen the stallion intended to leave, he'd not have put his horses in the livery.

He cleaned up in his room, then found the cafe and surrounded a steak that hung over the sides of his plate, along with a half dozen eggs and fried potatoes. Feeling like he'd never taken the seventy-mile ride from Taos, and now only noon, and having eaten, he figured a drink would be good. He headed for the town's only saloon.

Crisp, pine-scented air cloaked him. He stopped in the middle of the road to let a lone horseman pass, nodded a greeting, and walked to the boardwalk.

When he pushed through the wooden doors, he stepped to the side, and, after the bright sunlight outside, wanted to let his eyes adjust to the saloon's dim light. He wanted to see all in the room before going to the rough-hewn bar. He stood there a moment, smelling the sour smell of yesterday's whiskey, trying to see through the cloud of tobacco smoke hanging at head level.

Satisfied he could see well enough, he stepped toward the bar, then stopped and studied a man at its end. Red Bridges must have felt that he'd left his troubles behind. He stood there, his back to the room, head lowered, staring into his glass. He looked to Hawk like a man who'd taken a beating and had no fight left in him.

McClure walked to within ten feet of him, flipped the thong off his Colt, and said, "Bridges, you stole a horse in Taos costin' me a hundred-forty-mile ride, round trip. That stallion you stole belongs to a friend of mine. Turn around slow-like, an' I won't have to shoot you without givin' you a chance."

As if by magic, the men who'd been standing close to Bridges melted away to stand against the walls. Before turning, Red flipped the thong off his revolver. "Didn't take you long to get here, McClure. You know you killed my partner in that shoot-out in Taos, don't you?"

McClure nodded. "Saw where you buried 'im. You lookin' to join 'im on his last long ride? I hope not, Bridges. I'm better with a handgun than you; faster— an' more accurate—an' I don't want to have to kill you."

The redheaded horse thief stood there, looking at McClure, his hands close to his holsters. Then he held them farther from his guns, and his face crumpled, tears cut trails down his dust-coated cheeks—then he slapped leather.

McClure, surprised at the tears, stood openmouthed for a split second. That bit of time was all Bridges needed to get his righthand gun clear of the holster. But, his hand a blur, Hawk drew and fired. He pulled off a bit at the last, enough to send his lead into Red's shoulder.

Bridges's six-shoooter dropped to the floor. He put his left hand to the hole only now showing a bit of blood. He pulled his hand away, stared at the gore, then moved his eyes to McClure. "Why for you do that? Know you can hit what you look at. Know I wanted to join my partner."

Hawk shook his head. "Right now you don't give a damn whether you live or die, but each passin' day you gonna want more to live." He nodded. "Figured to give you that chance, but I'm takin' the boy's horse back with me."

Pain now showed in the horse thief's face. He stared at McClure a moment. "Ain't got nothin' 'gainst the boy. Take his hoss an' go."

Men crowded back to the bar. One of them eyed Bridges. "You admittin' to be a hoss thief?" Someone

else said, "Git a rope." Others growled, cursing all
horse thieves.

McClure stepped forward. "We're not havin' a lynch-
in'. The man did me wrong, so I'll be the one decides
what happens to him."

The first man who had spoken shook his head. "You
got it wrong, stranger. In this town we hang hoss
thieves."

Hawk still held his Colt in his right hand. He shook
his head. "No. Gonna get his shoulder taken care of,
then we're ridin' out. Don't try to stop us."

Someone in the crowd said so all could hear, "Don't
push it, Stumpy. You seen that big man draw. You don't
want no part o' him."

While they argued, Hawk took Bridges by the arm
and led him from the saloon.

After seeing the doctor, he took Red to the livery,
collected their horses, and left town amid a crowd standing on the boardwalk, some wanting a hanging, some
talking against. Their indecision gave him time to leave
without gunfire.

Headed back to Taos, Bridges, pale, dejected, gripped
his saddle horn to stay atop his bronc. He looked at
McClure. "Why for you didn't kill me, or let them take
care o' me back yonder in that town? I ain't never
caused you nothin' but grief."

Hawk stared between his horse's ears. "Don't know,
Bridges. Figure I ain't cut out to kill." He nodded.
"Yeah, I've had to shoot a few men now an' again, but
I just flat don't cotton to it."

They rode in silence until they sat by the fire after
supper. They'd already eaten and were drinking coffee.
McClure offered the only words said in hours. "In the
mornin' we split. Gonna send you on your way. Hope
you'll get an honest job an' quit tryin' to be a badman.
You aren't cut out for it." He took a swallow of his
coffee, then pinned the outlaw with a hard look. "Gonna
tell you somethin though', you an' me ever cross trails
again I'm gonna send you to hell faster'n it takes to tell

about it. When you leave me, you leave without guns, or shells. Know you haven't any money, so I'm givin' you a five-dollar gold piece, an' too, I'm leavin you with your bowie knife—that's all."

"Hell, McClure, this here's Jicarilla Apache country. You ain't givin' me no chance."

Hawk stared at him a moment. "Tough. You ride careful, you hear?"

The day after McClure left Chama, Tom followed Yolanda into Chama's livery stable. He'd followed his sister the entire way from Santa Fe, and had thought many times during the trip how easy it'd be to shoot her and rid himself of his troubles, but he just flat didn't want family blood on his hands. She led him to his death, though, and she didn't give a damn.

Again, not far north of Santa Fe, she'd held up another coach, taken money, and killed all within the luxurious vehicle. With a small amount of satisfaction, he felt good that he'd not pulled a gun, taken money, or killed anyone during the four holdups Yolanda had pulled since leaving Las Cruces. But, when push came to shove, when questioned by the law, he knew he'd get blamed by his sister for them all.

She climbed from her horse, tossed the reins to the hostler, took her saddlebags in hand, and headed for the hotel. Tom again followed.

Only a few steps up the road, she twisted to look at him. "In the bar. Get a bottle. Bring it to the room. I need a drink—got 'nuff dust in my throat to choke a maggot."

Without breaking stride, he turned his steps toward the building with the sign that said it was a saloon. Inside, he thought to have a drink all by himself. The peace of not looking at, or hearing, Yolanda plot against others was alone worth the price of the drink.

He stood there when his drink came, knocked it back, and held his glass for another. He drank this one slowly. Then his ears picked up conversation from down the bar.

A slim, stumpy puncher talked. "Man, I shore am glad you held me back yestiddy when I wanted to hang that there hoss thief. The man what shot 'im wuz 'bout the quickest I ever seen gettin' that six-shooter in action. You ever catch his name—the one what wuz so gun quick?"

His drinking partner nodded. "Yeah, the doc said his name was McClure. Somebody said they reckoned he headed for Animas City when he left here. Looked to me like he headed for Taos."

The other puncher said, "Naw, don't figger he went to Taos, even though he'd fit in with the salty bunch what hangs out there. I b'lieve he wuz headed for Animas City."

Tom tossed off the rest of his drink and left. Should he tell his sister what he'd heard? Would it help get this whole thing over with sooner? Would it bring him any closer to heading back to Alabama, or would it bring about his own death sooner? Dead would be better than following Yolanda all over hell, killing and robbing people, although he'd not pulled the trigger on any of them—and to ultimately end up shooting a man who'd done him no harm.

When he opened the door to his room, Yolanda greeted him with "Where the hell you been? I been sittin' here 'bout to choke from the dust, an' I figger you stopped for a drink."

He shook his head. "Nope, didn't stop fer a drink—stopped fer two of 'em." Then, hoping to fend off more of her abuse, he said, "Heard two punchers talkin' 'bout a gunfight they had here only yesterday. Seems yore friend McClure shot a man, then headed for Animas City. We only one day behind 'im."

She snatched the bottle from his hand. "Ain't gonna be long then 'fore I see 'im layin' on the ground, drawed up in a knot from hurtin', an' you, little brother, gonna be the one puts 'im on the ground."

"Yolanda, the short time that man's been west o' the Mississippi he's done made a name for his self with that handgun he totes around." He shuffled his feet, then looked at her straight-on. "Sister, I ain't in the same class as he is with guns."

No pity. No sympathy. Only the flat black sheen to her eyes he'd seen so often of late. "Reckon you better practice like hell 'tween here an' Animas City. Don't wantta pay no one else."

16

MCCLURE WONDERED ALL the way back to Taos why he'd let Bridges go, and wondered why he'd pulled his shot off to the side for a shoulder hit instead of dead center in his chest. When he put the golden stallion in the livery's stall next to his gelding, he had come up with no satisfactory answer. He attributed it to getting soft. Yeah, soft in the head. That kind of softness could get him killed.

He thought to have a bath and shave before going back to the stable to keep watch on Reb's stallion. He could do that at the barbershop, but first he wanted to tell Reb what had happened. He went to her room and knocked. Footsteps sounded, then a soft voice, "Yes, suh, who is it?"

"Me, McClure. Need to tell y'all what's been happening."

He heard a soft scraping of cloth against the door, then the metalic sound of the lock being turned. Bessie pulled the door toward her, then her eyes traveled from his boots to his head, obviously checking to see if he had been harmed in any way, and before she could say anything, Reb pushed her way between them, grabbed

Hawk around the neck, and pulled his face down. She kissed him right square on the mouth.

She stood back, her face flushed, her eyes wide. "Hawk McClure, don't you ever go off by yourself like that again. If someone wants my horse that bad, let 'em have him. Rather lose the stallion than to lose you."

His eyes crinkled at the corners. "Lordy, *son,* reckon I'm gonna leave right now, then come back an' see if you'll give me another greeting like you just gave me." She squirmed a moment while he enjoyed every moment of her embarrassment, then he took her off the hook. "Got your horse back. He's down at the livery, an' 'fore I go down there to watch over him, I'm gonna bathe and shave. How's Jed doin' after that knock on the head?"

She continued to stare at him, her eyes wide, her mouth forming a small O, then she regained her composure. But her face never let go of the healthy rose tint it had taken on since the kiss. "Promise you won't go off on any more danged fool jaunts like you just came back from an' I'll give you a greeting like that every morning."

Bessie had obviously had enough of this nonsense. "Little missy, you let me catch you actin' like a huzzy, an' I'll tan yore chubby little—"

Reb's face flamed even brighter. "Don't say it, Auntie. Think I've had all I can stand for one day." She stepped back and invited McClure to have a chair while he told her about the happenings while he was gone. Then she said, "You asked about Jed. Well, after a throbbin' headache, he's doin' fine. Now tell us how you got the stud back."

Thirty minutes later, McClure walked to the barbershop, still conscious of the feel of lips on his, and the hell of it was—he wanted more.

Clean from the skin out, and smooth faced, he went to the livery. Jed and Ned pounded his back and shook his hand, while Mixus did a jig around him. He had no doubt they were glad to see him. Then he again had to tell of his trip, his gunfight, and letting Bridges go his own way.

Mixus squinted, spit a stream of tobacco juice, and peered at McClure. "Don't figger you gonna be sorry you let that hoss thief go? Danged if I'd a let 'im do nothin' but git buried."

Hawk nodded. "You might be right, old-timer. Reckon I'll wait an' see." His face hardened. "One thing for sure, if he pushes me again, the lead he takes won't be in the shoulder." He stood back and looked at the three. "While I been doin' all the work, y'all been sittin' here on your duff. We gonna leave in the mornin, head for Chama. I want y'all to grease the wagon, tighten wheel bolts, check the harness, an' get us ready to travel."

Mixus squinted out of one eye at Jed and Ned. "Sounds like the big man figgers to set up his ranch and hire us to work fer 'im." He spat another stream of tobacco juice. "Gonna tell ya right now my hands don't fit no plow handles. I'll pull a crosscut saw, use a adze to make logs fit to one another—well, gosh ding it, reckon I'll do most anything 'cept farm."

Jed's quiet voice cut in. "Reckon I can handle anythin' calls for plowin'."

McClure shook his head. "You got it all wrong. What I figure on is for each one o' us to file on a parcel o' land, all adjacent to each other, then . . ."

"That there adjacent word mean we gonna have land smack-dab 'longside o' each other?" Mixus looked hopeful.

Hawk nodded. "That's what it means, you old rapscallion. Way I figure it, we can help each other with whatever comes up, an' if later on any one o' us figures to let his land go, one of us'll buy it from him. Too, we'll have the advantage of usin' that land as one big ranch."

With a look of wonderment, and a grin stretching over his snow-white teeth, Ned said, "Mistuh Hawk, you figgerin' for me an' Bessie to have some o' that land?"

"Yep. We'll all have some, but you gotta know right now, every one o' us who files will have to show improvement on that land if we gonna get to keep it. I don't think that'll be a problem 'cause we can all help each other build our cabins, barns, outbuildins, an' if we work it right, and build in the corners where our property joins, we'll be neighbors and'll start us a small town at the same time."

Jed shook his head and looked at Ned and Mixus. "Men, what you jest heard is why we always been livin' from hand to mouth." He pointed a thumb toward McClure. "Now, that man's done give this a lot o' thought. He ain't never lived poorly, an' won't now. Don't think none o' us'll get along without listenin' to him. I'm, for one, in favor o' doin' 'zactly like he layed it out. Ain't none o' us ever gonna have a better chance in this world to make somethin' of ourselves."

They all agreed to accept McClure's plan, then Mixus frowned. "Ever'body here agrees, but that little lady we all love so much ain't had her say."

Unconsciously, Hawk touched his lips. "Reckon I'll take on explainin' our plans to her." He smiled. "Somehow I don't figure we gonna get an argument outta her on what we've decided."

"Haw! Now that there big man done took on hisself a re-e-ealy hard job." Mixus slapped his knee and laughed deep in his throat. "Seems to me that man's done got a look 'bout him since he found out the little missy wuz a feemale. Seems he's took a more pertective stand, which I'm here to tell you ain't no easy job in itself. Why hell, when he thought she wuz a boy, he wouldn't let nothin' close to her what spelled danger. Now danged if he ain't done got worser."

McClure frowned. "Men, I still got two people out yonder somewhere hell-bent to kill me for some reason, maybe three, if Red Bridges don't head back to Mississipi, or wherever the devil he hails from." His shoulders slumped. "One o' them huntin' me is a woman, an' I'll tell you for a fact I don't know what to do 'bout her. I ain't gonna shoot no woman.''

After leaving McClure, Bridges rode no more than five miles before reining his horse to a stop. He sat there a moment studying the high desert growth, but not seeing it. McClure had killed his partner, the only partner he'd ever had, and here he was riding away, letting the big Southerner get off scot-free. Yeah, the man had given him a break by not killing him in face-to-face gunfight— but there were other ways to kill a man, rather than head-on. He had to try to even the score with the killer of his partner.

Before letting him go, McClure had said he and his party would head for Animas City. He reined his horse toward the west. He'd ride wide of Chama—the people there were set to hang him, but he had to get weapons from somewhere. After thinking about that a few moments, he came up with an idea.

About sundown of the next day, Bridges stopped and made camp in the brush less than a quarter of a mile outside of Chama. He'd wait until after the saloon closed, then break the lock on the back door of the general store, and get guns, ammunition, and provisions. All general merchandise stores carried rifles and handguns.

He made a small fire, and stared into it for hours, all the while letting anger build in him, until his head felt swelled from the blood pushing behind his eyeballs. He took another swallow of coffee, now thick from sitting on coals at the edge of his fire.

He wished for a bottle of whiskey. Maybe there'd be some of that in the store as well. For at least the fiftieth time, he glance at the Big Dipper—about three o'clock on this dark and moonless night. He stood and, leading his horse, headed for town. Less than fifty yards to the back of the store, he ground-reined the horse and stepped toward the building, now showing as only a black hulk in the darkness.

At the back of the mercantile store, he decided to walk

to the front and see if anyone stirred in the small town. Only a few seconds later, he eased his head around the corner, and stared down the dusty trail between the few buildings of the town. The saloon's windows looked like large, dark, staring eyes looking onto the street—closed. Bridges sighed. There were no horses tied to the hitchrails.

He slipped quietly to the back of the store, went to the door, and tested it. Locked. McClure had left him with his bowie knife, so he pulled it from its sheath and slid it between the door and frame.

After working it back and forth for a few minutes, he gave up on able to slip the lock back. He studied the door a few moments. The hinges were on the outside. What fool would build a door like that?

He thought on the problem a moment, then slipped the edge of his knife under a hinge bolt and pried up. It raised about an eighth of an inch. Then, grasping the blade with one hand and the handle with the other, he worked the bolt up, only a bit at a time. Every few seconds, he stopped and wiped sweat from his forehead and face. It dripped into his eyes, blinding him. He squeezed his lids tightly closed to clear his vision, then worked some more.

The smell of dust mixed with that of sweat. He worked faster, then sighed. The bolt dropped free. Two to go. Another fifteen minutes and all three bolts lay on the ground at his side. He stood, pulled the hinges free, and stood holding the door in his widespread hands. He leaned it against the back wall and entered the store.

The close, musty smell of a closed space, mixed with the aroma of tobacco, coffee beans, leather, clothing—and gun oil—came to his nostrils. He grinned into the darkness. If the store carried gun oil, he'd bet there were guns here also.

It was too dark for him to make anything of the dark shapes his eyes strained to see, but he used his hands to identify the things he stood in front of. He touched bales of jeans, rough-cut tobacco, canned goods, sacked flour,

then the smooth stock of a rifle. Temptation flooded him
to strike a lucifer and see what caliber rifle he'd touched.
He pulled the rifle from its wall bracket.

Then he ran his hands along the countertops until he
found glass-enclosed cases. He groped through them and
hefted the handle of a handgun. Next he found boxes of
shells, then he gave in to temptation. He struck a lucifer,
checked the caliber, saw that the handgun and rifle were
.44's, and before he could check the ammunition—*the
front door rattled.*

Someone had tested the door to see if it was locked—
then a voice. "Garner, you in there? I seen a light."
Before Bridges could decide what to do, the sound of
running footsteps headed for the back.

Bridges wasted no time. Clutching the rifle in his left
hand, he shoved the box of cartridges into his coat
pocket, again picked up the revolver, and ran for the
back door.

The rectangle of light showed in front of him. He
jumped through it—and slammed into a man intent on
entering the store. They both sprawled in the dust and
rolled to their feet. A blossom of orange flame spewed
toward Bridges. He swung the handgun at where he
judged his assailant's head to be. A solid crunch ran
tremors up his arm. The man went down. Bridges ran
toward where he'd left his horse, like all the demons of
hell were on his tail. That shot would bring the towns-
people.

He toed the stirrup, swung aboard, and headed east.
It would take at least ten minutes for a posse to grab
their weapons, saddle, and get on his trail. Bridges figured to lead them toward Taos long enough for them to
think that was his destination, then he'd swing north and
eventually west, toward Animas City.

There was no way the man he'd run into when he'd
run out the doorway of the store, could identify him. It
was too dark. So once he'd gotten them off his trail,
he'd be home free. He figured he'd have his chance at
McClure in the Colorado town of Animas City.

. . .

Tom Squires now had no doubt but what he was the one
Yolanda had spiked out to pull the trigger on McClure—
he'd heard it from her own mouth. She didn't give a
damn if he got killed while trying to satisfy her hate and
revenge against Hawk, she'd simply mark him off, and
try to hire someone else to do the job.

The fact was, he was good with a revolver. He was
fast and accurate, but not good enough to outdraw and
outshoot McClure. Too, as good as he was, even if he
could luck out and kill the tall man, he didn't want to.
He didn't want to kill anyone. How then could he keep
himself alive?

If he made even the slightest move to cut out and
leave his sister, she'd shoot him in his sleep, or in the
back while they rode, or perhaps one of dozens of other
ways.

He thought of this while they rode toward Animas
City, and all the while pondered some way to avoid getting killed. He kept coming back to one way to do it—
kill Yolanda. He couldn't do that.

Mechanically, he rode, made camp, ate, then did it all
again while wrestling with the problem, but no solution.

The second night out of Chama, Tom sat at their fire,
drinking coffee laced with a hefty jolt of whiskey, aware
all the time of Yolanda's snake-like stare. Finally, she
broke the silence. "You ain't got the guts to face Hawk
McClure, have you?" Then, not waiting for his reply,
she taunted him even further. "You're scared o' him,
ain't ya? You been braggin' 'bout how good you are
with that Colt, but you ain't got the guts to use it on
nobody. You leave all the shootin' to me when we pull
a holdup."

She grinned, no humor showing behind her evil eyes.
"But you know what, little brother, when, an' if, the
law ever catches up with us, you gonna take the blame
for it, 'cause I'm gonna look at them real sweet-like, an'
tell 'em how scared I wuz to try an' stop you from killin'
them folks. They gonna believe me 'cause these fools

out here in the West don't think of a woman doin' nothin' like we been doin'. You unnerstand, Tom?'' She nodded. ''Yeah, an' if you try to run away from me, I'll find the closest lawman an' set 'im on yore trail for all them crimes.''

He stared at her a long moment, knowing she'd do exactly as she'd said. At that moment he came close to believing he *could* shoot her, and in the next instant, he knew he could never do it. His thoughts were broken by a hail from outside their firelight. ''Hello the camp.''

Yolanda shoved her hand into her reticule where she kept her revolver. ''Come on in, coffee's already brewed.''

Red Bridges rode into the circle of firelight. He squinted at Yolanda a moment. ''Well now. Reckon I never figgered to meet up with you folks agin. You actin' more friendly now than you wuz after them Comanche attacked us.'' He grinned. ''Been thinkin' 'bout you ever since I seen you. You the prettiest woman I reckon I ever looked on.''

Tom looked from Bridges to his sister, amazed at how she could soften her looks at will. He admitted to himself, she now was a really pretty woman—if one didn't bother to look beneath the surface. He turned his look back on Bridges. ''Climb down an' set a spell. You ridin' far?''

Bridges threw his leg over the cantle and, favoring his right arm, slid from his horse. He nodded. ''Figure on makin' Animas City in a couple o' days.''

Yolanda stared at his right shoulder. ''What happened to yore shoulder?''

Bridges's mouth drooped, his eyes widened. ''Some gun-happy saddle tramp back yonder in Chama pulled iron on me simply fer bumpin' 'im. Didn't gimme a chance fer a fair draw.''

Tom's mind flicked to the conversation he'd heard in the saloon. He'd bet his bottom dollar this was the horse thief he'd heard had been shot by McClure. ''You hear the name o' the man what shot you?''

Bridges took the cup of coffee Yolanda held out to him, stared into it a moment, then looked up. "Yeah, seems I heered 'im called McClure." He shook his head. "Don't know how a man could be mean nuff to shoot a man jest fer bumpin' 'im. Course I did cause 'im to spill some o' his drink."

Yolanda's eyes took on that deadly sheen again. "McClure." She nodded. "Shoulda figgered it. He took somethin' o' ours, somethin' I ain't gonna allow 'im to have. We been huntin' im ever since we left Alabama. When we find 'im, I figger to have Tom there face 'im in a head-on gunfight."

Bridges shook his head. "Less'n Tom's mighty good with that six-shooter he's wearin', you can figger on losin' 'im. Don't know as how I coulda beat 'im, even if he give me a chance." He took a swallow of coffee, and shook his head. "Never figgered to take a sneak shot at a man, but if that's the only way I can get even, I might think about it."

Tom marveled at how Yolanda led the man right to where she wanted him. Too, he thought maybe they'd recognized each other as being cut from the same mold. Now Bridges had said the very words Tom knew his sister would pounce on. And she did.

Yolanda put on her sweetest, most defenseless look. "Cain't think it right to shoot a man from behind. Think you oughtta be lookin' at 'im." She shrugged. "But somehow I gotta think it's fair if he's so much better'n you." She stood, picked up the bottle, and laced Bridges's coffee with a jolt. "We goin' the same way, with the same thing in mind, so why don't we ride to-gether—see can we come up with a plan, a sure plan, to get McClure."

Bridges nodded. "Sounds good to me." He grinned. " 'Sides, it'll gimme some company, gimme a chance to get to know you better."

Tom looked from one to the other of them, wondering at the stupidity of men where women were concerned. With a few carefully chosen words, a few studied twists

of her body, and a pretty face, Yolanda had led the redheaded bandit down the primrose path. He could have
found it easy to feel sorry for Bridges if he hadn't
thought the outlaw was of the same mind as his sister.
He stood and poured himself more coffee with a splash
of whiskey. Between here and Animas City, Yolanda
and the bandit would settle on a plan to kill Hawk, and
he, Tom Squires, would have little to say about it.

Rebecca, sat in her room staring at the wall. Bessie said
she'd acted like a hussy, throwing herself into Hawk's
arms and kissing him like she had. Bessie also said that
McClure getting her horse back, and the fact he'd not
gotten a scratch while doing it, was no excuse. She
straightened, and focused her eyes on the window facing
the mountains bathed in sunlight.

She touched her lips. Her kiss had been for having
him back safe, and a way of thanking him for getting
the stallion back, but she'd never dreamed the power of
a kiss. It awakened something in her, gave her the courage to look within herself and study how she really felt
about him.

She admitted to herself that from the very beginning
she'd thought him handsome, and she'd for some reason
thought he could handle any situation in which he found
himself—he just had that air of confidence about him.
Too, when around people he considered friends, he was
always a gentleman, and showed the utmost tenderness
to her and Bessie. All of those things brought her no
closer to the answer she kept avoiding. Since the first
day she'd wanted him to know she was a girl, wanted
him to look at her with approval, both for her beauty
and for the person she was inside.

Each day after he'd joined them, she'd watched the
way he treated Ned and Bessie, and later Rolf Mixus,
then Jedediah Powers, always with courtesy, and when
required, with firmness, and with others he could be
ruthless or friendly as the situation required.

And each day after he'd joined them, she'd found herself wanting more and more for him to see her as a woman, not the woman he'd expect a Southern lady to be—pampered, soft, and more than a little spoiled—but a woman who could walk at the side of her man and help him shoulder the load of whatever problem came their way, and at the same time a woman who could love and be loved, tenderly, and sometimes with strength.

She hadn't known it at the time, but recognized now why she had tried so hard to become the man he "thought she could be." She wanted him to know, eventually, that she had the strength and iron will to walk at his side.

She ran all this through her mind as honestly as she knew how, and when through scubbing her emotions down, she smiled. Yes, she now had no doubt but what she was more than a little in love with Hawken McClure. As much in love as she dared let herself be, because Hawk had never showed he had more than a brotherly, protective affection for her; the same affection he had for Bessie, Ned, Mixus, and Jed. She stood and thought to find Bessie, but before she could move toward the door, a soft tap sounded. "It's me, missy, can I come in?" Bessie's quiet voice asked.

She unlocked the door and held it for her auntie to enter. Bessie took one look at her, shook her head, and folded her to her spare, bony old body. "Bless mah soul, little darlin', looks like you done had a talk with yo'self. It's showin' outta every ounce o' you. You done admitted how you feel 'bout Mistuh Hawk." She stood back, hands on hips, and pinned Rebecca with her hardest, yet tenderest look. "Child, don't you story to me now. I can see yore feelin's shinin' outta yo eyes."

"Oh, Auntie, I won't try to fool you. Yes, I do think I'm in love with Hawk, but he's never said anything to make me think he has any but brotherly feelings for me. Reckon I wouldn't have faced up to it if I hadn't kissed him, at first out of relief he was safe—but then that kiss turned into somethin' else.

"Never knew a kiss could do that to a woman. Bessie, I liked it, but I'm here to tell you right now I'm scared of what I felt, scared I'm not enough woman to handle it."

"Oh, little missy, don't you worry yo pretty head 'bout that. Soon's a girl baby comes squallin' outta her mama's womb she's got born inside her all she needs to know how to handle lovin' a man. An' if her man loves her, she ain't gonna need nothin' else to be a sho 'nuff woman. Now let's you an' me go see what pretty dresses they got in them stores for a pretty lady."

When they stepped from the hotel door, Jed and Mixus were just coming in. They tipped their hats, but Mixus voiced their greetings. "Howdy ma'ams. Hawk an' Ned's down yonder at the livery. Hawk's watchin' the hosses, an' Ned's takin' his self a little nap."

He looked apologetically at Bessie. "He needs to get some rest, ma'am. This trip's been mighty hard on 'im, an' he won't let nobody do more'n him. Why, I'll bet they's a many a man half his age what folded up an' quit 'fore walkin' half as far cross country as Ned has."

Bessie put her hand on his arm. "Bless you for defendin' my man to me, Rolf Mixus, but they ain't no need to. I'm glad you all see he's in need o' rest." She laughed. "Yes suh, I done seen how y'all take on his jobs tryin' to spare 'im, an' him a grumblin' 'bout it all the time." She nodded. "He's gettin' old an' just won't admit it."

Jed looked at the sun and said, "We gonna eat 'fore we spell Hawk with the hosses, then I b'lieve he's got somethin' he wants to talk to y'all 'bout." He grinned sheepishly. "All us men done agreed to it, but decided if'n even one o' you said no, then we'd do somethin' else."

Rebecca stared at Jed, a quizzical frown creasing her forehead. "Jed Powers, don't know what the tarnation you're talkin' 'bout, but you an' Rolf seem to, so we'll wait an' see if Hawk will make some sense outta it." She took Bessie's arm. "Right now we're gonna do some shoppin'. Figure Hawk's gonna wantta leave here soon.''

Jed nodded. ''Yes'm, he said as much not over an hour ago.''

Sitting on a bale of hay in the livery loft, McClure watched Ned snore a few moments, pulled his pipe from his pocket, then put it back. Too much chance on setting fire to the barn. He stood, climbed down the ladder, and went back to the hostler's living quarters. The old man sat at a beat-up desk drinking coffee. ''Smelled your coffee from up in the loft. You got enough to spare me a cup?'' He would have been surprised if the old-timer said no.

At the hostler's nod, Hawk poured himself a cupful, frowned, and looked at the liveryman. ''When you make this?''

The old-timer chomped on his tobacco a moment, frowned, then shook his head. ''Danged if I know. Easter maybe. All I do when it gits a little shallow in the pot is add more water an' grounds. When the grounds git high enough in the pot so's I cain't git no more water in, I dump it an' start a spankin' bran' new pot.'' He shook his head again. ''Don't like to do that though 'cause it takes a few days—maybe weeks—'fore it agin gits any body to it.''

McClure grinned. ''Looks sorta like we could pour this on the desk, take a rollin' pin, smooth it out some, an' use it for saddle leather.''

Never cracking a grin, the old-timer nodded. ''Reckon so. Never thought o' usin' it that a way. Might be a good idee.''

McClure, now feeling safe from setting the livery afire, pulled his pipe out, packed it, and put a lucifer to it. He and the old man sat contentedly, not talking, but enjoying each other's company. After a while Hawk felt the old man's eyes studying him. ''What's the problem, old-timer?''

The hostler shook his head. ''I ain't got no problem,

young'un, but you might have. You say you, them other men, an' that boy you rode in here with come from Mississippi with that stud hoss—you know, the one what got stoled, an' you got 'im back?''

Hawk nodded.

"An' from what you done told me, that wuz the second time someone tried to steal that very same hoss. Well, son, I'm right surprised you ain't had more attempts than that to steal 'im. He's a beauty."

McClure sat forward. "Gonna tell you right now, for anyone to get that horse away from me they better be willin' to walk right down the barrel o' my Colt."

The old man chewed a couple of time real fast, puckered his lips, and sent a stream dead center into a molasses can serving that purpose. "Young'un, they's a couple o' men round here what makes a livin' outta takin' hosses. One'll write up a phony bill o' sale, an' the other'n'll sell 'im." He looked at the Colt McClure wore. "An' they don't mind much havin' to walk down the barrel o' yore six-shooter. They pretty salty gents."

Hawk frowned. "Doesn't the law do anythin' about it?"

"Cain't. By the time the smoke, gunsmoke that is, clears, they got a dead body an' a bill o' sale to show. The marshal cain't do nothin' 'bout it."

McClure nodded. "You know that boy who came in here with us? Well, that horse b'longs to him, an' he's got rock-solid papers to prove it, and I'll be the one who'll stand in the way of him gettin' his horse taken from 'im." He took a swallow of his coffee, grimaced, then said, "Seems like as brazen about their scam as they are, the marshal would see through it—or is he in it with them?"

"No, no, now, young feller, the marshal's a honest man," he shrugged, "but with a dead body to contest what they say, an' them with a paper says the hoss is theirs, he jest flat cain't do nothin' 'bout it."

"Well, one thing they don't know, an' that is the horse don't b'long to me. So the way I figure it is, they try their crooked game with me, an' they'll have a bill o' sale with my name forged on it. The boy'll be able to show the legal papers on it.'' He smiled. ''That is if they can walk down the barrel of my Colt.''

A noise, the scuffling of feet, sounded outside in the runway. Thinking of the horses, McClure stood. ''I'll see what they want.''

He placed his smoking pipe on the desk and went out. Two men walked from stall to stall checking each horse in the stable. They looked toward McClure when he stepped from the office door. ''You the hostler?'' a well-dressed man, pale-skinned, soft looking, about Hawk's age, asked.

''No, he's back yonder in his office. Anythin' I can do for you?''

A tall, lean puncher, looking like he'd come in from a day's work, stepped up beside the pale, well-dressed man. ''Yeah, you can do somethin' fer us—tell us where you got that golden stud hoss.''

McClure's entire body went quiet; his neck muscles tightened. These must be the ones the hostler told him about. He didn't like either of them, and for some reason he figured the pale man as the most dangerous.

Taking them both in with one glance, he said, ''First place, mister, let's get our chips on the table so everybody knows what the stakes are. An' gonna tell you straight out—I don't like either one o' you. Second place, it's none o' your damned business where I got that horse. Third place, you don't like what I just said, I'm here to tell you—I don't give a damn what you like.''

The puncher looked at the pale man. ''Whoooeee, listen to the man. Sounds right salty, don't he?'' He swung his eyes back to McClure. ''Now I'm gonna tell you somethin', mister. We figger to take that hoss, figger we got as much right to him as you. We seen a man take him outta the stable a couple days ago, then seen you leave outta here after 'im, then you come back with the stud. Now you're back with him, I figger we got as much right to him as you. Figure you stole 'im.''

McClure's muscles relaxed; he'd never been more calm. He might as well push these two. "You're a damned liar. And you, you pasty-faced bastard, if you're layin' claim to him, you better have a whole helluva lot better reason than your partner gave me. You're liars and thieves. Don't know how often you pull this scam on people scared of you, but I ain't one o' them. You don't like my words, let's see your next move.''

McClure's words apparently took the two by surprise. They glanced at each other, a worried frown showing between the cowboy's eyes. The pasty-faced man nodded.

The puncher moved to the side, his fingers brushing the walnut handles of his six-shooter. McClure didn't wait, he drew his Colt and thumbed off a shot at the puncher. Then his mind saw everything move real slow. A hole punched through the cowboy's throat. Blood spouted.

McClure moved the muzzle of his gun a fraction of an inch and pulled trigger on the pasty-faced man. The man slammed back against the stall's gate, blood welled from a hole in his right shoulder, then drained in a steady flow. A double-barreled derringer dropped from his hand. Hawk eared the hammer back for another shot. Every emotion he'd ever felt yelled at him to slip his thumb from the hammer, kill the pasty-faced worm— but he couldn't do it. He snorted to rid himself of the smell of cordite; his eyes stung from the cloud of smoke that hung in blanketlike strata in the still air. He let the hammer of his Colt down easy.

"Let 'im stand there long 'nuff, McClure, an' we won't have to get the doctor. He'll be drained dry o' blood in a few minutes.'' The hostler's voice came from in back of his left shoulder. The old man let out a squeaky laugh, slapped his knee, and walked up beside Hawk. "Met yore match this time, you crooked bastard.''

He turned his look to McClure. "Jest hold 'im here

till I get back. Gonna git the marshal." He laughed again. "He shore is gonna be right proud o' you, son. You done took care o' some o' his troubles." He scratched his head, still gazing at Hawk. "Slick as you handled that there Colt, how come I never heered o' you?"

Now feeling the aftermath of having killed a man, Hawk shook his head, feeling empty in the pit of his stomach. "Reckon 'cause I don't want to be heard about. Can't say I'm very proud of killin', even though I've had it to do a few times."

The liveryman headed for the stable doors and said over his shoulder, "Might take me a while to find the marshal. Maybe that coyote'll leak the rest o' his blood out while I'm gone."

McClure watched him leave. The hostler had to push through a throng of curious citizens trying to see into the stable without risking their own skins. McClure wanted to yell at them to get the hell gone, but he held his tongue. He looked at Pasty-Face.

The man stared back. "You going to let me bleed to death?" His voice showed no fear, no emotion.

Hawk shook his head. "Frankly, I don't give a damn one way or the other. One thing for sure though, if the marshal doesn't get here soon, reckon that's exactly what's gonna happen." He walked to where the man's derringer lay, picked it up, shoved it in his pocket, then reloaded his Colt.

17

MCCLURE WALKED OVER and sat on the ground across the runway from Pasty-Face. The man stared at Hawk, nodded, and said, "You *are* gonna let me bleed to death, ain't ya?" He held his hands against the stall and slid down to sit on the ground.

His face feeling stiff as weathered leather, McClure stared back. "Your only chance is if the marshal brings the doctor with 'im—an' that's a slim chance at best. But I figure you're lucky—my bullet saved ruinin' a new rope. Bleedin' to death is easier than hangin'."

McClure kept his eyes on the man, who got even more pasty-faced, then his eyes closed, his head lolled, and he fell to the side.

The hollow place in Hawk's stomach got larger, and even more empty. He'd killed another man. This Western country was hard on men, women, and horses. Back home, the chances he'd have to kill were slimmed down to how much he'd take from the scalawags and carpetbaggers. Out here one didn't have to even know a man to have to shoot him. Running footsteps approached.

The marshal, followed by the hostler and another man McClure thought might be the doctor, pushed through the small crowd at the door. "The hostler told me what happened, McClure, no need to go through that again." The marshal looked over his shoulder at the third man who'd entered. "Check 'im' over, Doc. He may still be in shape to hang."

It took the doctor only a moment to listen for a heart-beat. He shook his head. "Gone, Marshal." He stood and looked at the liveryman. "Fix 'im a box, Jim. We'll put 'im in Boot Hill." He glanced at the body of the cowboy sprawled a few feet away. "Better build two boxes." He turned and left, again pushing his way through the curious crowd.

The marshal searched the horse thieves for weapons, frowned. "Didn't this man in the suit have a weapon?"

McClure nodded. "I got it right here. He dropped it when my slug hit his shoulder." He held the derringer toward the law man.

"Keep it. The way trouble follows you, you gonna need it." He frowned. "McClure? Hawk McClure? Why ain't I never heered o' you? Jim here says he ain't never seen a gun get into action so fast."

Hawk shrugged. "Don't want anyone, anywhere hear-ing about me. I want to live a quiet life and raise good horses. Maybe next time you hear the name it'll be tagged as a horse rancher—not a fast gun."

The marshal studied the two bodies a moment, then looked at McClure. "These are the two men I told you about when you had that stallion stole before." He shrugged and grinned. "Ain't gonna worry 'bout *them* no more." He fingered one of the coins he'd taken from the well-dressed man's pockets. "That gentleman a-layin' there's gonna buy you, me, an' Jim a drink. C'mon, let's go get it."

McClure shook his head. "I gotta refuse, Marshal. It's my turn to watch the horses, an' I sure as hell don't want them stolen on my watch."

Jim looked hopefully at Hawk. "You mind the stable, an' I'll bring you back a drink, a whole bottle if'n the marshal'll pay fer it outta that double eagle he's got in his hand.''

McClure allowed his lips to crinkle at the corners, knowing the old-timer, Jim he'd heard the marshal call him, figured to end up with most of the bottle. "Sounds good to me, Jim. I'll be here after you wet your whistle.''

They left Hawk with the two grisly trophies, and the horses to watch. He walked back to the hostler's office, lighted the partly smoked pipe he'd left on Jim's desk, poured himself a cup of mud, and sat to await the hostler's return.

Yolanda and Bridges rode side by side. Tom brought up the rear leading the packhorses. Every time they stopped for a nooning or made camp, Tom ended up with all the chores, while his sister and the redheaded horse thief huddled together. They didn't let him in on their plan, but there was no question in his mind Yolanda would reap the benefits while he and Bridges would do her dirty work. And the hell of it was, he had not a doubt but what the horse thief thought he and Yolanda would walk away together with it all—whatever *all* turned out to be.

Every day, Yolanda dressed Bridges's wound, showing concern Tom had never seen her show, for anyone. If she chose to put her talents to work, to his mind she could make a mint play-acting on the stage. Bridges swallowed her bait—hook, line, and sinker.

During camp this last night before getting to Animas City, Bridges had lain in his blankets watching Yolanda through slitted eyelids. She was a woman like he'd never dreamed of in his life: a face like an angel, a body any man would kill for, and smart, smart enough to help him plan enough holdups to make them both rich.

But to think in terms of ''both'' didn't jibe with the way he had it planned; he should think in terms of them ''together.'' Hadn't she all but said they would be a team? And if she hadn't said it, the way she smiled, the way she put her hand on his arm when talking, the looks she slanted at him from her soft black eyes, the way she accidentally let a breast brush his arm when they walked together told him he was her man, told him she'd already made her choice.

That dumb brother of hers? Why hell, if their plan worked the way they planned it, McClure would kill him, and the shots all blending as one would put the blame for the tall Southerner's death square on Tom Squires's shoulders. Everyone would think he'd sent at least one of his shots into McClure while dying. He and Yolanda then could fade back into the crowd and leave. They'd have their horses and pack animals ready, and would be miles from Animas City before anyone could begin to put the story together. He took one more look at Yolanda, let his eyes drink in her beauty, then turned on his side and went to sleep.

Yolanda had been aware of Bridges's stealthy looks all during the evening. She felt like her whole body was smiling—inside. The stupid bastard—how could he think she'd have anything to do with the likes of him? Did he really think she'd share herself with any man? Well, maybe with the sheriff back in Marengo County, but with him only as long as it took to firmly get title to all she'd taken from Hawken McClure, and others.

If McClure and that boy had anything worthwhile, she'd take it, but getting him dead was all she hoped for. She savored the taste of his death, embracing it, tasting it, feeling the satisfaction of it until sleep took her in its soft arms.

They now looked on the crooked street of Animas City. This to Yolanda's mind was where it would all end. She'd ride out of here alone, ride out of here with the insult McClure had paid her a forgotten thing. Here she'd wipe the slate clean, and head back to Linden, where she'd be accepted as a lady, one of the gentry.

She looked from the street, lined with saloons, bawdy houses, stores, and gunshops, back to Tom. "Git us a bottle. Bridges an' me're gonna wait in the hotel fer you." She turned away, then spun back to him. "Tellin' you right now: Don't take time to have a drink. Get the bottle and bring it to us."

Tom shuffled his feet a moment stared at the ground, his lids covering his eyes. Then he nodded, and headed for the closest saloon.

In only a few minutes he had the bottle, had checked to see what room Yolanda had set up business in, and was twisting the knob of that door. She looked at him, at the bottle, and said, "For once you thought of someone besides yoreself. Pour us a drink, then I'm gonna tell you how we got it planned for us to take on Mc-Clure."

As they sat sipping their drinks, Yolanda spelled it out for him. She smiled that cold, snake-like smile. "We got it figgered since you think you're the best one o' us with a handgun, you the one what's gonna stand in front of him. We'll be a little behind 'im—on each side. We'll get lead into 'im 'fore he can put any into you. We ain't gonna let you die, little brother."

Tom Squires heard her words, looked into her eyes, and didn't believe a word of it. She figured to get him killed, and he just flat didn't give a damn.

He glanced at Bridges, who had eyes only for his sister. The poor bastard would be lying there in the street's dust along with him, old cowardly Tom Squires, lying there not knowing even then how Yolanda had suckered him into carrying out *her* plan, right down to and including his own death.

While eating breakfast the next morning, McClure told Rebecca still dressed as a boy, and Bessie of his plan for each of them to file on land adjacent to each other, so they could help each other when needed, and thereby have a ranch large enough to handle the livestock they decided to raise.

They agreed with his plan, but puzzled McClure with a secretive glance at each other, along with a sly sort of smile. He wondered what the dickens they had up their sleeves.

Hawk led his party from Taos beneath a lowering sky, with a few wet snowflakes beginning to stick to his hat and shoulders. He glanced at the sky for at least the tenth time since making ready to travel, and as he had each time before, he thought to cancel getting under way until the storm passed. The thermometer hanging outside the livery door showed the temperature to be in the lower twenties—several degrees lower than when he'd looked at it on first entering the stable.

He rode back to the Studebaker. "Reb, it's comin' on to be a right nasty day. We're still not far enough committed that we can't turn around and spend another day or two in Taos."

Reb shook her head. "If you think you can keep us safe, let's keep goin'. The longer we put it off, we're gonna be that much further behind in startin' our cabins."

The load on McClure's shoulders got heavier. Every time, she put all her faith in him being able to take care of them the weight of trust got more to be a burden he hoped he could live up to. He nodded. "Reckon we'll keep goin' till the snow thickens such that we'll have a rough time findin' a good campsite, one that'll protect us from the weather, an' perhaps any rogue Jicarilla Apache. Now y'all get Ned and some o' those blankets out and snuggle down in the wagon bed. Mixus, Jed, and I'll take turns leading the oxen."

He rode to the head of the team, pulled his bandanna from his neck and tied it around his head, then pulled his hat down tight on his head, and drew his neck down into his sheepskin as far as he could get it. Only his eyes showed above the collar.

About midday the snow stopped for about an hour, then got heavier. Only about three inches covered the ground. McClure frowned. He'd not call a stop for their nooning until he found a place which would make a good campsite in the event the snow cover deepened.

He found what he wanted, but by the time they'd finished their coffee the snow had again lightened to sporadic flurries. He looked at Mixus. "What you think, old-timer? You've braved the elements more than any of us. You think we oughtta chance findin' another spot as good as this'n?"

Mixus sliced off a chew, stuck it between his cheek and gum, chewed a couple times to soften it, then settled it more comfortably in his cheek. "McClure, it's gittin' mighty cold, so ain't much chance o' havin' any gully washer come down on us. If'n you reckon them old folks an' the girl kin stand it, I reckon we should oughtta put more trail behind us. Figger 'bout three o'clock we oughtta start lookin' for one o' them arroyo secos, dry arroyos they talk 'bout out here. Find one o' them, an' we'll be able to take good shelter in it."

Hawk nodded. " 'Bout the way I got it figgered. A ravine, if it's deep enough, should knock the wind off, an' shelter us from the snow too." He looked toward the wagon. "We filled the water barrels 'fore we left Taos so that's no problem." He frowned. "Better have Bessie take a bucketful of water out before the water in the barrels freezes solid. Be a little for the horses, an' coffee water for us."

By two o'clock the snow had set in like it figured to stay awhile. By three, there was another few inches on the ground. McClure had been leading the oxen. He hailed Jed. "Take over the oxen. I'm gonna find a place to camp while we still have daylight left to see by." He squinted against the cold flakes. "Can't see a helluva lot even now. Man, I never saw anything like this in Alabama."

Jed chuckled. "Reckon I'll take the snow an' cold anytime, long's they ain't no damned carpetbaggers an' scalawags slinkin' round to take what's our'n."

Hawk toed the stirrup and looked down at Jed. "Tell you what, Jed, nobody, an' I mean no-damn-body's, ever gonna take anything away from me again. Made up my mind to that when I left Marengo County, an' I haven't softened that idea one whit.''

Jed stared at McClure a moment, then, his face sober, he nodded. ''Hawk, the way you look right now, I figger anybody who'd try would've bought themselves one big chunk of hell.'' He grinned. ''Go find us a campsite.''

McClure kneed his horse ahead. He'd ridden only a couple of miles when he found an arroyo, and he lucked out. A small stream trickled down its center, its edges rimmed with surface ice, and a flat shelf bordered the stream's bank. A few cedar lined the bank also, enough to provide shelter over them when cut and woven together.

He rode back to the wagon. ''Y'all think to bring a block and tackle or two when you set out on this trip?''

Ned stuck his head out the front of the tarp covering the wagon stays. ''Yes, suh, I put four of 'em in jest fo' good measure. Why for you wantta know that?''

McClure grinned. ''Hope we don't need 'em, Uncle, but we gonna camp down the bank of a ravine an' we might need 'em to get us back on level ground when this storm lets up.''

He kneed the gelding around, told Mixus to follow him.

A couple of hours later, the four men caved in the sides of the arroyo to provide a ramp for the wagon to roll down into the ravine. Then Hawk rode upstream until he found the cutbank he'd seen before. They cut saplings, leaned them against the bank, then wove stunted juniper into the skeletonlike structure until in under the overhang they had room to all bed down, with the fire reflected off the wall of the ravine. The wagon stood just outside the shelter.

Rebecca stood back to survey the work the men had done. ''You men act like you did somethin' like this every day.'' she shook her head. ''Why, we'll be as snug and comfortable as we would in our own cabin. Wish we had shelter for the animals.''

Hawk smiled. ''Well now, young'un, don't know as

how I'd go that far, but we're surely gonna be a lot better off than out there in that high desert." He scanned the banks along each side of the lean-to. "Men, grab your axes. Find a blowdown, driftwood—anything that'll burn. Bring all you can find up close to the shelter. I figure we're gonna need all the firewood we can get before this blows over." He looked at Reb. "The animals gonna be all right."

Bessie and Reb had already started supper, and the big coffeepot sat on the edges of the coals. "Y'all git on about cuttin' that there firewood. This here coffee'll be right ready to drink by the time you git done."

Later, supper over with, they sat around the fire huddled down in blankets and coats, and gripping coffee cups with both hands for the warmth. Hawk had poured a hefty belt of whiskey into each cup. He took a swallow, frowned, and flicked them with a glance. "Now that we've agreed on the plan for filin' on land, I figure when we get to Animas City, for Mixus an' me to go to the land office, see what's available, then for him an' me to ride out an' take a look. If you trust us to make the decision on the best land for what we want, we'll come back and we can each file on the piece we want."

Reb eyed him with a steady gaze. "Hawk, I hear that country west of Animas City is alive with Ute. I also hear they're not the friendliest Indians around. You think with only two of you out there alone you'll be safe?"

Mixus answered. "Little lady, I thought I wuz 'bout as good a Injun as you could find, then I seen McClure, an' I'm here to tell you he's as good as any I ever seen." He shook his head. "Naw now, don't you worry none 'bout us. We gonna be all right."

She sighed, her gaze still holding on Hawk. "Well, all right, but I'm tellin' you: I don't think I could stand it if anything happened to either of you."

She included Mixus in her words, but it was obvious she talked straight to McClure. A surge of warmth invaded his chest. Maybe his hopes of that one kiss being repeated were not just dreams. Maybe after they got their

cabins built, she'd be willing to let him come calling.
She deserved to be courted, and he intended to see she
got nothing less. He swallowed the last of his coffee and,
talking to no one in particular, said, "Reckon I'm gonna
get some sleep. Figure to scout around tomorrow, see
what the trail up ahead looks like. I hear the Jicarilla
don't like to fight at night, so we won't worry about
tonight, but daytime's different story."

Mixus chomped on his cud, spit, and grinned at him.
"Naw now, Hawk, I figger we the only ones dumb 'nuff
to be out here in this weather."

Each morning for three days, McClure scouted the
area. The only tracks he found were of small animals, a
wolf pack, and a herd of wild mustangs.

The morning of the fourth day the sun rose, gleaming
over the pristine snow white landscape. The sparse veg-
etation looked black against the white background.
Hawk stuck his head into the shelter. "Roll outta your
covers, folks. We've got a pretty day to travel in. With
this snow cover we won't make more'n 'bout eight or
ten miles 'fore we make camp again."

While Bessie and Reb fixed breakfast, the men saddled up and hitched the oxen to the wagon. During their
morning meal, Reb asked if Hawk thought they'd get
any work done on their cabins before spring thaw.

McClure frowned. "Reckon the best we can hope for
is a dugout in the side o' one o' those hills. Won't be
much privacy for you womenfolk, but you'll just have
to make do."

Reb clamped hands to hips. "Hawken McClure,
we've been makin' do slam across this country an' you
haven't heard one peep outta us 'bout it. Reckon a few
more months isn't gonna hurt us."

Again, pride in this girl swelled his throat. It was true,
He'd never heard a word of complaint from either Reb
or Bessie. Before he could turn away, Ned sidled up to
him. "Mistuh Hawk, gotta say somethin' to all you men-
folks."

Hawk nodded.

"What I gotta say is, y'all been babyin' me, takin' on mah jobs, givin' me special treatment." He looked at the three of them. "Gotta say I'm downright 'shamed I ain't carryin' my part of the load. Y'all gotta let me do."

Hawk put his arm around the old darky's shoulders. "Uncle, you got no right to feel shame 'bout any 'o that. When we get to our promised land, there'll be more than enough for all of us. We want you rested so we can put the hard work on you."

Ned chuckled. "Know you tellin' me a big fib, Mistuh Hawk, but I'm gonna hold you to it." His gaze dropped. He stared at the ground a few moments. "But I gotta say, I . . . uh . . . well I'm thankin' you foah bein' so good to me. Yessuh, I wuz gettin' mighty tired back down the trail a ways. Thank y'all."

Embarrassed that the old darky had noticed he was being given preferential treatment, McClure cleared his throat and told them to clean up the camp and get ready to travel.

Ten days after McClure got them again headed toward Animas City, Yolanda sat in her hotel room staring at Tom and Bridges. "Where could we have missed McClure? He should've been here long ago."

Tom shook his head. "Don't reckon so, sister. He's travelin' with them folks in that wagon, an' they's been a mighty lot o' bad weather the last two weeks. They'll be here soon."

She swung her flat black eyes to him. "You better hope so, little brother. If he ain't, you gonna get on that horse o' yores an' ride back to Chama, see where he mighta gone from there. An I'm tellin' you right now, you try to keep on ridin' an' I'll catch up with you— make you wish to hell you'd have rode faster, a whole helluva lot faster. You unnerstand?"

Tom stared back into her dead eyes. "Yeah, I unnerstand."

She picked up the bottle from the washstand, shook

it, and put it back on the washstand. ''Go git us 'nother bottle—no, git two. Ain't no point in runnin' to the saloon so often. 'Sides, me an' Bob got things to talk 'bout.''

The only time Tom had to think was when he made these frequent trips to the saloon. He stood, took money from the pile on the bed, and went out the door. He knew she planned for him to die, but his own plan had begun to take shape. She and Bridges wanted the shooting to take place in the middle of town where everyone could see it, and the way she had it planned not a soul in the town could say McClure hadn't died from Tom's gun. Well, Tom figured to catch them in their own trap.

18

TOM HAD ONLY at that moment pushed the door to the saloon open and stepped into the large darkened room when McClure led his party down the main street of Animas City. He stopped the team long enough for Reb and Bessie to step to the ground, while Ned handed down their valises.

A glance at them all and he gave them a smile. "Almost the end of the trail, folks. We'll take the animals to the livery while y'all get a room." A furrow formed between his brows. "Reb, I figure it's time you came outta those boy clothes and again became the beautiful woman you are." Her face turned a rosy pink at his words.

He turned to Mixus. "Reckon you and me better bathe, shave, eat, then visit the land office, an' from there we gonna head out to look at the land. Jed, you keep close watch on the womenfolk. Don't let anything happen to them, figure we'll be back in four or five days."

After taking care of the animals, McClure, Mixus, and Jed walked to the hotel. When they passed the saloon, a knot formed between Hawk's shoulders. Someone

watched them. McClure had no doubt the gaze came
from Yolanda or her brother. He never slowed his pace,
but decided that before anything could take place between the Squires and him, he'd locate a good place for
each in his party to build and get it filed on. Then he'd
meet the Squires.

After they had visited the land office, and ate, Mixus
asked why they didn't stay in town overnight, and get
an early start in the morning. McClure shook his head.
"Nope. I figure the Squires are here. I don't want trouble
until all is taken care of. When we get back, if they don't
find me, I'll find them. Then I'm gonna get them off my
tail for good, one way or the other." Mixus only nodded.

After perusing the maps at the land office, McClure
stabbed his finger at a valley with a stream running down
the middle of it. He turned to the old outlaw. "What
you think, partner, looks like good grass, water, a natural
corral on all but one side for the horses, an' plenty of
timber to build with."

Mixus nodded. "Why, gosh ding it, I wuz jest gonna
pick that valley myself. Yep, reckon we better git out
yonder an' see what we mighta picked."

The land agent shook his head. "You may not want
that location, men. That's deep into Ute country. They
ain't give us any trouble since the Milk River fight, but
you might be askin' for trouble."

McClure pushed his hat to the back of his head,
looked at Mixus, then the agent, and grinned. "Mr.
McGuire, most in our bunch would say we been runnin'
to trouble ever since we left home. Reckon if that land
looks good we're gonna take it." He tilted his hat back
over his eyes, shook hands, and stepped toward the door.
"We'll let you know whether we want it when we get
back."

By the end of the second day after leaving Animas
City, when both of them hunkered by their fire drinking
coffee, Mixus looked at McClure. "Hawk, I got a feelin'
somebody's done took to watchin' us mighty close. Feel
it in my bones."

McClure's face hardened. "Got the same feelin'. We'll eat supper, spread our blankets like we're beddin' down, then douse the fire, then pack our horses, an' move on down the valley about a mile 'fore we really bed down for the night."

Mixus shook his head in obvious wonder. "Gosh ding it, Hawk, you'd of made a outlaw like the West ain't never seen. An' partnered up with me, we mighta become so danged famous ever'body would be talkin' 'bout us."

Hawk chuckled. "Yeah, they'd be talkin' 'bout us—or hangin' us."

Mixus scratched his head. "Didn't think o' that. Reckon we better off goin' straight." He swallowed the last of his coffee. "Better git busy foolin' them what's lookin' at us." With that he stood and spread his blankets, while McClure did the same. Then they dumped the remaining coffee on the fire—and moved camp.

They made better time than Hawk had thought, and by sundown of the next day, they topped out on the trail overlooking the prettiest valley he'd ever seen: grass fetlock deep, a snowmelt stream flowing down the middle, clusters of aspen the length of the elongated bowl, and up the mountainside a few hundred feet a mixture of spruce and pine darkening the mountainsides.

Hawk sat gazing at the site for several minutes, then, his voice soft, he said, "You ever see anything more beautiful than this, Rolf?" Then, only half-joking, he added, "You rather be a famous outlaw, or have this piece of heaven?"

Mixus, his voice reverent, said, "Hawk, ain't nothin' in the world I'd like better'n this." He pointed to the middle of the long valley. "Let's ride down yonder an' see where we'll build."

They camped that night on the slope into the valley, then rode all the next day, made camp, and the afternoon of the following day came on the spot where they wanted to look for homesites. The feeling of being watched stayed with them.

With their blankets already spread, Mixus said quietly, "Take the thong off'n yore side gun, McClure. We got company comin'."

Hawk nodded. "Saw 'em a while back. Don't make any threatening moves unless they do. Let's see what they want." Three well-built warriors rode toward them. They didn't wear war paint.

The tall man riding slightly ahead of the other two held up his hand in the universal sign of peace. "You ride in the land of the Ute. What ride here for?"

McClure studied their weapons and figured between him and Mixus they could win in a shoot-out. The warriors had only old outdated rifles, and no revolvers with which to fire quickly. He decided to tell them the truth, and let the cards fall where they might. "We figure to settle here, bring our womenfolk in an' build lodges, raise horses."

The leader who'd first spoken sat silent for a moment, then he spread his arms and made a sweep to take in the entire valley. "This land all Ute hunting ground. Chief Ourey, head chief of the Ute, say we not fight white man if he come in peace. You not take our hunting grounds, we think you come in peace." His eyes kept seeking out McClure's black gelding, then he twitched his lips toward the horse. Hawk had learned that a twitch of the lips was the manner in which Indians pointed. The Indian continued. "You raise horses like that?"

McClure nodded. "That's what we figure to do."

"You give us some ponies like that one?"

"Great Warrior, it'll take three, maybe four years till foals dropped next year'll be like that one. Then we'll talk 'bout what you want. You leave us alone to raise our horses, we won't bother your hunting parties."

The warrior sat still a few moments, obviously thinking about what Hawk had said, then pinned McClure with a hard look. "We take horse now, no have to wait you to give ponies."

McClure's face hardened. "One thing wrong with that—that black horse, if you haven't noticed, has been cut, can't sire a foal. We figure to bring in a stallion to breed to the mustangs we round up.''

The warrior's face fell, showing disappointment. "We see when you bring in women and horses." He motioned to the other two and they rode from camp.

Mixus let out a pent-up breath. "Whew. I figured we wuz gonna have to start shootin' right sudden.''

"You weren't alone, old-timer. We're mighty lucky we didn't though. If we'd had to shoot any o' them, we'da had the whole Ute nation down on us" He frowned. "Don't know whether we should bring Reb an' Bessie into this valley. Don't know whether we can keep 'em safe, but I know one thing for sure, this visit's changed my plans 'bout the way we'll build our cabins if we do bring 'em in. We gonna have to build a fortress if our small number's gonna be able to cope with a relatively large war party.''

"Yeah, an' we gotta stash in one helluva lot more shells for our guns. Looks like we might need 'em.'' Mixus grinned. "You heered that story 'bout old Chief Ourey, the one where he likes white men an' the way we live, an' when they're in his camp he serves 'em cigars an' wine?''

Hawk nodded. "I heard it. Also heard he sold his people out, gave up a whole bunch of Ute land in return for one thousand dollars a year for life. Hope it's true.'' He swung his gaze about the valley. Where they now made camp, the mountains pinched in toward the middle such that they were no more than a hundred yards from a sheer cliff.

He nodded. If the womenfolk said they were going to come with him despite his warnings, they would build back into the side of the granite escarpment, and that would mean he'd best buy dynamite when he got back to Animas City. With that in mind, he and Mixus picked the site for their ranch buildings close to the bluff, and a little out from the talus buildup at its base. From the site they selected, they'd have a good field of fire, handy water, and protection for the animals.

He and Mixus spent another night at the site of their choosing, then headed back to Animas City, and all the way back he studied some way to get out of shooting Yolanda without getting killed himself. When he rode down the road between the rows of saloons and bawdy houses, he was no closer to a solution.

The day McClure and Mixus left to take a look at the valley, Tom Squires stood at the side of the saloon door and watched them walk past. He should tell his sister he'd seen them, but he wanted to wait and see what they did. Maybe they'd leave again. He considered not telling Yolanda, hoping she'd not find out they were here. Maybe McClure and his party could get gone, get lost before she found out. He thought on that idea a moment, shook his head, and went to the hotel. If he failed to tell her they were in town, he'd only put off the inevitable.

When he told his sister her arch enemy had only moments ago walked down the street, her eyes lost the soft, adoring look she affected for Red Bridges, and took on the black, oily sheen she so often showed the world.

She took one of the bottles from Tom's hand, poured herself a water glass full, and handed the bottle to Bridges.

She studied the amber liquid in her glass, a deep crease between her eyes, then looked up. "We ain't gonna go out there an' wait fer 'im—might mess up that way. I wantta study his moves, find what he does, an' when. Once we know that, I'll decide when to box 'im in."

She knocked back about half her glass of whiskey, shivered, and refilled the glass. "Tom, you do it. I want you to find out where McClure's stayin', find out where he eats, shops—ever'thing 'bout 'im. Figger two days'll give you 'nuff time, then we'll know the best place to pick the fight." She looked at them, her face slack. She was obviously drunk. "Let's have 'nother drink." She reached for the bottle, missed it, and fell to her side on the bed.

Tom stared at her a moment, disgust twisting his mouth. Bridges shook his head. "Poor thing, she's tired, trip's been mighty hard on 'er—all that ridin', stayin' in hotels, eatin' porely most o' the time. Better let 'er sleep."

Tom shifted his eyes from his sister to Bridges. "Yeah, she's had a helluva hard time of it, sittin' a saddle, gettin' to a town, runnin' me off to get 'er a bottle, then sittin' in the hotel an' gittin' soused. Yeah—pore thing." His voice dripped sarcasm. He stood. "I'm gonna git me a drink among good company. You stay here with 'er if you want." He left the room.

By the time Tom Squires had had a few drinks and left the saloon, he had missed seeing McClure and Mixus ride out of town, and it cost him six days of combing the saloons, mercantile store, barbershop—the entire town—and hour after hour of listening to Yolanda curse him for an incompetent, bumbling fool. Then the evening of the sixth day, about to head for the hotel with another couple of bottles, he saw the tall Alabamian and the old man ride past. He sighed. Maybe now his sister would get off his rear end. But with the relief, more grief piled on his shoulders. His stomach churned, knotted, then turned to an empty void. Now, in a couple of days, he'd have to face McClure—and he didn't want to die.

Before going to the hotel, McClure and Mixus stabled their horses, pulled rifles from scabbards, and walked up the boardwalk. They met Reb, Jed, and the darkies coming out the door, headed for the cafe down the street. Reb raked McClure's dusty, bearded face with a studied look. "Y'all tired, dirty, and need a shave, but I figure you need somethin' to eat before you clean up. C'mon."

Hawk looked at the beautiful woman before him, now dressed as she should be—a woman. He grinned. "Damn, pretty lady, I'm glad to see you too."

"Oh, Hawk, I didn't mean it like that. I just thought if you got in your room an' got cleaned up, you might fall into bed and sleep a week. Don't think I could wait that long to know what y'all think of the land you looked at. Let's eat while you tell us 'bout it.''

While eating, McClure layed it out for them, then said, "Don't know as how I wantta take you folks in there with the danger the Ute pose. Don't know whether there's enough of us to fight them off if they attack."

Reb stared into her cup a moment, then looked at Ned and Bessie. "Y'all want to take the chance Hawk can't protect us?"

They nodded, while McClure felt responsibility weigh heavier on his shoulders. Was there nothing this girl wouldn't trust him to take care of?

Reb looked deep into his worried eyes. "Hawk, we're goin' to that valley you and Rolf think is so beautiful. We'll worry 'bout the Indians when we need to.''

Hawk nodded. "Figured you'd say that. All right. We're gonna stay here a few days, load up with everything we think we'll need until late spring. We'll head for the valley the mornin' of the fifth day. I got somethin' personal to take care of 'fore we leave here.''

"You're gonna hunt down the Squires, aren't you?" Her heart showed in the look she gave him; worry and caring pushing all else aside.

"It's my fight, little one. All I want you, Jed, Rolf, Ned, and Bessie to promise me is that you'll stay out of it.'' He pushed his chair back. "Now, I'm gonna clean up and get some sleep.

The next day, McClure stopped in the marshal's office. When he walked in the door, a crusty, grizzled old man wearing a marshal's badge swung his feet off his desk. "Marshal Nolen here. What can I help you with, young feller?''

"Need to tell you somethin', sir, an' tell you at the same time I'll take it outta your town if I can." He then told Nolen about the Squires, what he thought had started the whole thing, and how to his mind there was no way to avoid a showdown. "I said I'd take it outta your town if I could, but, Nolen, I'll not be the one who chooses the place they're gonna wantta fight.''

Nolen stood, poured them each a cup of coffee, and again sat. He frowned. "You sure you cain't git outta this, young'un?"

"No. Not without jeopardizing the others in my party. Like I told you, we came out here to make a home, an' even if the Squires kill me, I want every one of them safe and able to pursue their dream.''

Nolen stood. "I won't bother you, McClure. Be sure to give them an even break an' I'll not have anything to hold you on.''

McClure nodded and left. He wandered about the town until time for supper, then he joined the others in his party. During the meal he told Reb he wanted to talk with her in private.

The last few days, seeing her wearing women's clothing, wanting her like nothing he'd ever wanted before, knowing the kind of woman she was, one of both softness and steel, his love for her had come out shining like a brilliant sunny day. He had to tell her—whether she had any feelings for him or not.

After supper he took her arm and led her away from the others. A puzzled frown creasing her brow, she gave him a straight-on look. "Hawk, if it's that private, come to my room. No one will bother us there.''

He nodded and led her toward the hotel. When in her room, she faced him, looking into his eyes with all the trust in the world. He gripped her shoulders in his big rough hands. "Girl, back in the world we both came from there would be a different way of sayin' what I got to say, a more gentle, polished way of sayin' it, but despite all that, I gotta say it. Know it's gonna come as a surprise to you. Don't want an answer now, want you to think about it awhile.''

She cocked her head to the side, a forced smile etching her lips. "You gonna tell me you're gonna ride on an' leave us?"

"Lord, no. I'm gonna tell you I love you, want to marry you, want to come courtin' soon's we get our cabins built, want to take care of you, protect you the rest of my days. Want you to think 'bout it, an' if you have any feelin's for me at all, maybe you'd think kindly of it.''

Tears threatened to spill over her cheeks; a tremulous smile crinkled the corners of her mouth. She stood back from him. ''Hawken McClure, if you don't take me in your arms and kiss me, I reckon I'll throw all propriety out the window and kiss *you*.''

Hawk stood there a moment, dumbfounded. He couldn't believe her words. ''You mean you're sayin' yes? You mean you gonna let me kiss you like that one kiss I've remembered ever since you gave it to me?''

She shook her head. ''Not like the one kiss that I too remember. I'm askin' for a kiss even better—an' you better produce.'' If she intended to say more, she couldn't have. His mouth clung to hers, satisfying the longing he'd had building in him through many lonely nights.

Knowing Rebecca gave him her love caused him to want to put off the gunfight he knew had to come. He wondered if there wasn't some way to avoid it—and knew there wasn't. He couldn't run, wouldn't run. She'd lose respect for him, as would the only other people whose opinion he cherished—his trail partners.

From the moment he left her room, McClure left the thong off the hammer of his Colt. Every step he took outside the hotel, he first studied the alleys, doorways, rooftops, and shadows. He'd seen Yolanda walking with Bridges, and knew he'd have another gun to face.

He figured if he was lucky, he could beat Tom and the redheaded Bridges, but despite the hours of thought he'd given it, he hadn't settled on how to keep Yolanda from killing him. In his heart he still knew he couldn't shoot a woman. Besides, here in the West, the towns-people would string him up to the nearest tree for doing such.

The next morning, McClure and the rest of his party went to the land agent's office to file on their land. Before filing, Hawk looked at each of his friends, then turned to the agent. "S'pose a couple in this bunch decides to get married, that mean they can have only one filin'?"

The agent looked first at Rebecca, whose face turned a beautiful rose color, then he turned his look on McClure. "Young feller, long's they ain't married when they file, an' long's they improve the land they file on with buildin's, I don't give a damn if ever' one o' you marries each other soon's you leave this office."

Bessie stood back, hands on bony hips. "You done told Mistuh Hawk you gonna marry 'im?"

Rebecca nodded. "Told him if he didn't marry me before we leave Animas City, I'd tell the whole town he'd forced himself on me."

At Bessie's horrified look, Rebecca burst into gales of laughter. She shook her head. "Oh, Auntie, you raised me better'n that. You know I wouldn't do such. Hawk asked me to marry him when he took me off to talk to me in private. Don't know if I actually said I would," she blushed, "but the kiss I gave him shoulda told 'im better'n words."

Bessie and Ned grabbed Rebecca and hugged and kissed her while Jed and Mixus pummeled Hawk's shoulders. Mixus stood back and eyed them all, one eye squinted almost closed. "Gosh ding it, don't know as I can go along with y'all no more. Might jest break up this here fambily we got." He squinted harder. "You see, I sortta had my cap set to marry Reb myself, woulda already asked 'er if I thought she wouldn't make me take a bath ever' single day. *That* ain't good for no man. Doin' such'll give a man the chilblains." He grinned. "Reckon I done made up my mind to let Hawk have 'er. Ain't gonna break up our fambily neither."

Laughing, Hawk grabbed the old outlaw and, to Mixus's intense embarrassment, hugged him.

On the way back to the hotel, Hawk again took up his watchful ways.

• • •

The next morning, as was usual for him this time of day, McClure left the hotel ahead of the others. He liked to stand a few moments and breathe the clean, pure, pine-scented air of this town at the base of the San Juan range, and look toward the Uncompahgre range to his left, where he'd build his and Rebecca's home.

He walked to the middle of the street, petted a stray dog lying in the street's dust, straightened to look down the street—and felt a chill go up his spine. His stomach felt like an empty barrel, his mouth dry enough to spit cotton, his neck muscles pulled down into his shoulders. Tom Squires stood not twenty feet in front of him, feet spread, hands hanging loosely at his sides. McClure flicked a glance at Squires's holster. His handgun rode free—no thong over the hammer.

But only Squires stood there. Where were Yolanda and Bridges? McClure didn't think Tom would face him alone. He resisted the urge to look behind him to see if they stood to his rear or to the side. Too, he wanted to make sure Rebecca, Bessie, Ned, Mixus, and Jed were not in the line of fire if they'd come out of the hotel. But he dared not look.

"You feel you gotta do this, Tom? You could forget it and head back to Alabama."

Squires shook his head. "Figger I'd as soon have you shoot me than Yolanda, Hawk. She's got somethin' stuck in 'er craw 'bout you. Figgers you done 'er wrong in some way, but it's there, an' she's set me up to draw on you."

The hard knot between McClure's shoulders told him Tom didn't face him alone. He knew he would take lead, and his only hope was that he could get both Bridges and Tom Squires before they downed him. "All right, Squires—when you're ready." Then, as in the other gunfights he'd been in, his mind, and eyes, took everything real slow.

Tom's hand swept for his holster. He was fast, maybe too fast. McClure drew without thinking. Squires's gun came level, then swung slightly to his right. Hawk's finger had already started to slip the hammer. He clamped it tight to stop himself from firing. Several shots sounded as one. Hawk stood there wondering why he didn't feel the shock of .44 slugs.

Gunsmoke filled the distance between him and Tom. Squires let his hand drop to his side, his fingers barely keeping their grip on his revolver. His head sank to his chest, and through a tear-choked voice came the words "I tried to hit her shoulder."

McClure twisted to see what he talked about. To one side, Yolanda lay in the dusty street, her hand still in her reticule, smoke coming from a small hole in its bottom. To the other side Bridges lay on his back, blood covering the front of his shirt. Then McClure's eyes took in the gathering crowd. Mixus stood with a smoking six-gun in his hand. To his other side, Rebecca stood, a revolver hanging from her limp fingers; it too had a wisp of smoke curling from its barrel. Only then did McClure realize he'd not fired a shot. He walked to Tom Squires, and gently took the revolver from his limp, flacid grip.

Tom looked from his gun in Hawk's hand to his sister. "Didn't mean to kill 'er, McClure. She wuz gonna shoot you in the back. So wuz Red Bridges. Couldn't let 'em do that. I never wanted to kill no one." His face crumbled. Great sobs choked him. "Now I done killed my sister."

Squires walked as in a trance to Yolanda, stooped at her side, then turned his gaze on McClure. "She's hit two places, Hawk—one in the shoulder where I figgered to put my lead, an' another in the middle of her chest."

"Mr. Squires," a quiet feminine voice said from the side, "the shot that killed her came from my gun. You hit where you meant to. You didn't kill your sister; your shot turned her toward me. My shot killed her." Tom looked at Rebecca, and even through his grief a ray of relief brightened his face.

He lowered his look back to Yolanda. "She was crazy, you know. She done things on this trip I wouldn't

figger any woman would ever do—cold-blooded killin',
holdups . . .'' He buried his face in his hands. ''Lord,
she done things no sane person would ever do.'' It was
then Marshal Nolen walked up.

''See you couldn't get clear o' town for it to happen,
McClure.''

Hawk shook his head. ''No, sir.'' He handed Nolen
his Colt. ''An' I didn't fire a shot. Those two lyin' there
figured to shoot me in the back, and my friends and her
brother wouldn't let that happen.''

Nolen opened the loading gate of McClure's handgun,
checked the cartridges, then sniffed the barrel and mumbled, ''Ain't been fired, for sure.'' He glanced at Mc-
Clure. ''Reckon you folks ain't et yet, so go get some
victuals, then come by the office and give me a report
as to how it all happened. He looked at Tom Squires.
You come down too, young feller. I'll need yore side o'
the story.''

They ate breakfast, then went to Nolen's office and
gave him their report. Rebecca shopped for a special
dress to get married in, one she could still wear for other
occasions, and McClure helped Tom make arrangements
to bury Yolanda. Tom turned over to Nolen the pile of
ill-gotten gains Yolanda had taken during her holdups,
along with the whole sordid story. Nolen didn't charge
Tom with the commission of any crime, and he headed
for Alabama feeling free for the first time in years.

That afternoon McClure sat next to Rebecca in the
small cafe while they all had afternoon coffee. Hawk
sighed, and swept them with a glance. ''Reckon a simple
'thanks' isn't enough. Y'all saved my life this mornin'.
Don't know how to thank anyone for such.''

''Oh, fiddle-dee-dee, Hawken McClure, how many
times comin' cross-country have you saved us from
goodness knows what, an' we didn't bother to thank
you. Now I'm gonna add insult to injury by sentencing
you to a lifetime of takin' care of us.'' Rebecca lowered
her lids over her eyes. ''Course you still have time to
saddle that big black of yours and leave us—but remem-

ber, if you're willin' to take the chance, I'm pretty good with a six-gun. It won't be a shotgun weddin', but I figure that l'il old revolver will do.'' Then she leaned toward Hawk to be kissed.